the frog king

the frog king

a love story

adam davies

Riverhead Books
New York

Riverhead Books
Published by The Berkley Publishing Group
A division of Penguin Putnam Inc.
375 Hudson Street
New York, New York 10014

First Riverhead trade paperback edition: August 2002

Visit our website at www.penguinputnam.com

Library of Congress Cataloging-in-Publication Data

Davies, Adam.
The frog king / Adam Davies.—1st Riverhead trade pbk. ed.
p. cm.
ISBN 1-57322-938-5
1. New York (N.Y.)—Fiction. 2. Authorship—Fiction. 3. Young men—Fiction. I. Title.

PS3604.A953 F76 2002
813'.6—dc21
2002069756

Printed in the United States of America

10 9 8 7 6 5 4 3 2

for Byes

*"I have more memories than if
I were a thousand years old."*

—CHARLES BAUDELAIRE

could be brillig, baby

Probably I would be better off if I didn't date E women. With me it's always been Laurie, Jenni, Candy, Maggie, Debbi, Stacey—all my life, just me and the cheerleading squad. You should find yourself a nice A girl, Keeno always tells me. I can see myself dating a Sasha. There are plenty of girls out there whose names don't even end in vowels—Megan, Beth, Doris, you name it. I bet I've even slept with a few. A friend of mine in college dated a Sam, and he seemed perfectly happy. One thing's for sure: I should know by now that dating an E girl spells trouble. But then again, I have never been the kind of person who learns lessons.

So I shouldn't be that surprised to find myself at a party with a girl named Evie—Evie Goddard. It's a book party at this underground bar, one of those East Village spots where the only indicator that a bar exists is a tiny night-light of a sign next to a stairwell that's like something out of Goya. If there hadn't been a bunch of people mothing by the door I never would have found it. I am not cool enough to know where these stealth hot spots are.

Inside it is a tired-out exhibit of Manhattan's glitterati in their natural habitat. The scenery is familiar, as is the crowd. Gigless models circulate with hors d'oeuvres and the attitude of overqualified assassins. The usual assortment of slick, black-slipped

New York women caress the edges of their martini glasses, trying to achieve the perfect combination of sexual desirability and haughty unattainability. And there are the characteristically coifed and manicured New York men amid all of it, indifferent as gondoliers.

The conversation, too, is familiar. It's like they're all actors trying out for the same part: they all make the same gestures with their Scotches, all display the same phony emphaticness—always a*doring* sweetie the new book or de*testing* dahling the latest reading—while jockeying around the latest ponytailed/goateed/ski-cap-wearing/body-pierced/dressed-all-in-black/vampirically pale/Buddhistically tattooed/flagitiously alcoholic/piously macrobiotic/contemptuously unfashionable-fashionable author du jour who has just published his memoir about his delinquent youth of incest and driftery.

Please, people. *Please.* I'm only here because invitations to these events are the only real perk of my alleged job as peon in the editorial department of a big publishing house and because I am subject to the sweet delusional sorcery of the Manhattan evening, like all these people have been secretly preparing for my triumphant eclosion into their world of gossip columns and expense accounts.

Harry *Dris*coll, they'll say. Where have you been? It's so good to meet you at last. We've had our plutocratic yet benevolent eyes on you for quite some time. You can come with us now.

Right. Want to know what really happens at these affairs? I have a few drinks, start enjoying the feeling of being out with Evie—letting myself buy into the false picture of young happy couple on the scene—when some swollen bigwig takes me by the elbow and tells me to get him a gimlet and make it snappy.

Which is to say: I hate these parties more than life itself.

But I am here because Evie asked me. She appeared this afternoon at my cubicle, arms dangling like fishing lines over my partition, and said, "Little Harry. I know a girl has to work hard to make your A-list, but come on: let's go rouse the rabble at this so-and-so book party. It will be like life in a Dewar's ad: all high fashion and beautiful people and that fancy kind of no-frost ice in the drinks. You will look the extremist edge of avant-garde in your piece of *merde* blazer and *cravate de* Daddy."

Evie always talks like this. She is the most incandescent person I've ever known. I've seen her use less candlepower with other people, but with me she's always like this—an over-educated auctioneer on speed.

I should have stayed home tonight and gotten some work done. I am behind on several projects at the office, including passing to press the five thousandth annual installment of our *Marathoner's Calendar and Logbook*. For the book to go forward in a timely manner it's necessary that both design and copyediting get a clean copy of the manuscript by the deadline, and this year I'm late with it. Again. Last year I was late, too, and so the calendar missed its pub date by a whole month. "How about that?" I said to Andrew Nadler, my gleefully Old Testament boss. "An innovation. The world's first calendar that can't keep track of its own time."

That was a miscalculation. Nadler didn't take it in the playful, ironic spirit I had hoped to convey.

He never does.

Part of the reason why I didn't put the calendar into production on time is that I couldn't bear to edit it. The calendar is, strictly speaking, a book. It's a spiral-bound, semiglossy, handheld number with one essay on joggerly prudence for every month of the year. In July, make sure you don't run barefoot over glass. In January, avoid polar bears. That kind of interesting stuff.

I know, I know: I shouldn't be denigrating it. It's a very flattering first step to promotion for any editorial assistant, and as I'm the very youngest assistant on the floor, I should be grateful for it. There's this guy we all call Slo-Mo who has his Ph.D. from NYU and has been working for this Brahmin editor for eight years and hasn't even handled a cookbook yet. Four years ago, in only my second year at Prestige, I was given the first calendar—way ahead of the usual assistant's schedule. I should have devoted myself to the mundane details and impressed Nadler with my meticulousness. But I just couldn't bring myself to read through those essays—wicking socks and pulmometers and body fat percentage were not why I'd gone into book publishing—and so before I knew it days turned into weeks, weeks into months, and still the manuscript languished in the bottom drawer of my desk.

Last week my friend Keeno asked me why this year's pub date was in jeopardy again. "What's taking so long? Is it that you just don't care, like last year?"

"It isn't that I don't care."

"You having trouble with the edits?"

"It isn't the edits."

"Well what, then? It's going to be late again, isn't it? Aren't you going to be moderately fucked?"

Keeno's wrong, of course. I'm not moderately fucked. I'm immoderately—fantastically—fucked. I'm so fucked I can't even bring myself to talk about the cause of my extravagant fuckage. It's too awful.

I don't even want to think about it.

Any way you look at it, instead of getting blurred at this party

I should be taking certain corrective steps so I can pass the calendar Monday so I might have a prayer of getting it pubbed on
time. But I've never been able to resist Evie, and considering the
general disintegration of our relationship, I began to succumb to
her suasions when she appeared at my cubicle earlier this afternoon.

"You could set a trend," she continued. "The waif look is out,
the overworked, undercompensated, thoroughly juiced, dead-
beat-Brooks-Brothers-hand-me-down WASP look is in. What do
you say? Could be brillig, baby."

But it is not brillig, mainly because I am having difficulty
keeping my vorpal sword ensheathed.

It's the same old problem. Evie says that if there were a machine for transmogrifying souls into language mine would read,
"Pay attention to me and do it by taking your clothes off."

Evie isn't really one to talk. She has quite a history herself.
She is like a mousetrap to men. One poor guy who had been
enjoying the cheese for a few months before he got snapped
couldn't handle it. Evie refers to this guy as Tooth. After the
breakup ("His technique for clitoral massage was like flicking a
lighter that wouldn't light") he sent her an envelope every day
for almost a month with a bloody tooth in it and a note saying,
"This is how much I love you." It turned out that the teeth came
from a laboratory skeleton and the blood from fresh-packed beef.

But still. You see what she can inspire.

Despite her own black-widowhood, Evie has lately become
much more abraded by my habitual romantic malfeasance, and
much more verbal about it. She's always been talkative, but she
never complained or chastised. Lately, though, she's taken to
more energetic criticism. She used to say that sleeping with me—
sleeping *on* me, as is her adorable wont—made her feel like she

was in a lifeboat. These days, her new favorite reprimand goes, it's got a problem with leaking.

She is, you'll see, a woman given to extravagant and punitive metaphor.

But—if I don't say this now I never will—I love her. Am I allowed to say that? Too late. It's out. I said it. There it is. Stone truth: I love her. I've never told her this, but I love her so much that the essence of Evie clings to me the way scents of certain trades penetrate the skin of their tradesmen: fish on fishermen, sawdust on carpenters.

I'm contaminated with her.

So lately I've been trying to comport myself with the dignity and fidelity that has always eluded me. I even have my own sumptuary Little Train That Couldn't chant to help: I think I can't, I think I can't, I think I can't. And it's working. My transgressions these days are mainly verbal. I've kept myself entirely free of extracurriculars—I mean, I have been *vestal*—for the entire last year. (Well, there is one notable exception. True. But there is a very good reason for her. I could explain but I don't want to talk about her—even think about her—while I'm out with Evie. I can't stand it.)

Tonight, however, I'm already getting into trouble. Tonight I've already flirted (snicker-snack!) with the woman in the Machiavellian miniskirt and the bioluminescent makeup; the woman who had a mouth like a broken promise; the ballet dancer who was so nice that it obliterated her personality; the woman I know sits around her apartment with heavily impasto makeup and Nina Simone CDs playing on repeat in case a foreign dignitary or divorced heart surgeon stops by for a cup of sugar and some matrimony; the doleful aphid who, while doing her most artful

Scarlett, told me about her Bad Luck with idle lotharios who have nothing to offer (like myself) and who I know will eventually marry a bumptious banker from Baltimore and settle for a pyrrhic life of sailboats and polo party invitations that read Mr. and Mrs. Not Happy but Relieved Not to Be Alone.

Currently I'm applying myself to this lopsided Jersey girl who's smoking Camels inexpertly and hoping to upgrade to another conversation elsewhere. I've retained her for the moment by telling her that I'm close childhood friends with the author and that I'd be happy to introduce her when there's a moment. When she asks me what I do I almost tell her I'm a writer myself—I almost tell her about the fraction of a manuscript I have quivering in my closet like one of those monkeys from the experiment with the metal mothers—but I can't do it. It's too embarrassing. Inevitably the following transaction ensues:

"So what is your novel about?"

"Um, hard to say."

"So what have you published?"

"Um, nothing."

"Who's your agent?"

"Um, no one."

And so on.

Normally I say I'm a bookie but this time I say I'm a gay window dresser at Barneys so that I can paw at her Miracled boob, faking like there's a crumb there and I'm just helping her out, girlfriend, which at the very moment, of course, Evie returns like a conscience from the bar.

"You weren't going to celebrate your humanity with that little smudge of a woman, by any chance?" Evie asks when the Jersey girl leaves.

"Oh, no. I was considering a tawdry moment on the fire escape, but I decided that no, it was passé. Too too," I say, mistakenly thinking that humor can get me out of this.

"Wow, Harry, you really know how to take a girl out and make her feel like backwash. Is that little ball of silicone Date? A future Date?"

This is what Evie calls the other girls—Date. She says she can't keep track of their names and so she'll just call them Date.

"Oh, Evie. Don't get like this." Despite my avowals she's still not entirely sure I don't have a few Dates up my sleeve.

"Like what?"

"Nothing."

"No, really. Like what? Upset that you're trying to screw your way through all of 212 while I sit around pining for you like some kind of neglected, sexless governess out of a Brontë novel? Like that, you mean?"

Arguing with Evie is like playing chess against Garry Kasparov—every move you make gets you into deeper trouble—but I want her to know that I really didn't mean anything, that it is just the unfortunate residue of a soon-to-be-conquered habit, that she is the only good and beautiful thing that's ever been in my life. I get this tingly surge of recklessness. I'm going to tell her. It isn't exactly the scene I imagined (a Cary Grant/Eva Marie Saint/edge-of-cliff kind of moment) but it's the truth, and now seems like a good time.

"Evie," I say. "I, ah—"

But Evie silences me with a traffic cop gesture. It's hard to tell if she knew what I was going to say or if she's simply had it with me. This inscrutability makes me nervous, because Evie is not a woman who can easily hide what she is feeling. After a mean, ruminant pause she says, "Let's get out of here. These parties make me want to puke."

This is a good indication of how mad she is. Evie lives for parties like this. She once faked a broken ankle to stay an extra twenty minutes at this thing at Mortimer's. And it didn't even have an open bar.

"Is it the endo?" I say, pointing to my stomach.

"No it's not the endo. I just want to leave, O.K.?"

"Sure it's not the endo?" I say, guiltily hoping that is really why she wants to go. "I've got some Percocet here. Two shiny new pills, snatched from your cabinet for just such an emergency. See? Do I look out for my Evie or do I look out for my Evie?"

"Yeah. You're fantastic. You're Doctor Livingstone."

"Just trying to help."

"Help yourself, maybe."

"What?"

"To a little snack, isn't that right?"

"Oh please."

"I can't breathe in this place," she says, her foot tapping out a song of agitation and the three little scars on her forehead beginning to turn white. Maybe it's sick but I love her at moments like this. Sometimes I can't get enough of Evie being angry at me. "Can we go already?"

Outside there is a wall of photographers standing like British Colonial riflemen: three ranks of them, standing, kneeling, and lying down. They are all screaming at me and Evie and their camera flashes make the night air look like it is full of disco balls. "Hey, you two," one of them cries out. "Give us a kiss. Give us something we can use."

Because I know it is the last thing she wants, I give Evie a wild, sailor-returning-from-sea kiss. She bites my tongue, not a willing accomplice, and whispers, "They've mistaken us for somebodies."

vespers

I live illegally. I lucked into an apartment—it seemed like luck at the time—in Alphabet City. Rent-controlled, bedroom with window, and near the Odessa, this Ukrainian diner whose bad-teethed waitresses try to set me up with their daughters and give me sauerkraut-scented hugs that feel like they mean to break my back. These women have a way of saying "Your kielbasa will be up in a minute" that makes you feel like no matter what atrocious things you've done lately, everything is going to be O.K.

But—the famous "but" of Manhattan real estate—the apartment turned out to be a mistake. It's prewar, but not in the quaint way that the New York Times classifieds usually mean. From the street the building leans shruggishly into an alley like it's decided to just give up on the whole thing. It's above a hardware shop and smells of shoe polish and kerosene. You have to flush the toilet by pouring a bucket of water down the basin. At least it's rent-controlled, although there's a famous "but" with that, too: my roommate, Darrell, is also an illegal tenant. He is not a member of the original rent-control family, and if he gets found out he will be evicted. So he has to remain invisible to the rental office, which means that I must give him the rent every month in green dollar bills, that I cannot get mail delivered, and that I must never talk to any of the old-lady neighbors.

This, my mother says, is a metaphor for my life in general since I've moved to this city six years ago: furtive, shady, unlawful. This is just like my mother. She can't stand that I left Connecticut for Sodomic-Gomorrahine New York, or that I work for a corporate conglomerate. She insists I am being corrupted— even when I explain to her the pay scale for editorial assistants— and is always sending me newspaper clippings of healthy-looking twentysomethings heroically retrofitting damaged sewage pipes in Laos or toiling happily on organic yeast farms or something. You're confusing your sons, I want to say to her. You should be mailing this garbage to my big brother. Kurt is the one who served time. Kurt is the one with the heroin problem. Kurt is the one who needs intervention, not me. Can't you leave me alone for a few weeks? Jesus. I never say this to her, though. I don't have the heart.

In defense of the apartment, I have to say that I haven't done a lot to improve it. I'm not especially neat. I've got fruit flies living under my bed and the whole place is orange. Evie was convinced that it would look good ("patrician" was the word she used in the store) and so we sponged on all this orange Crayola paint. Because of the color and the knotty effect of the sponging, when the dirty morning light leaks through the window it's like waking up inside a hemorrhoid.

My roommate Darrell is still out of town, thank God. Darrell's a musician, but he doesn't make music exactly. He makes sound bites for TV: the few seconds of the seeing-stars song when Pinky or Brain gets brained, the slinky music when Rachel gets all dolled up for her big date with Ross, the segment when Kathie

Lee Gifford walks on stage. He's got his own recording equipment—minus earphones—so every night, hundreds of times a night, while I try to read or write or edit, it's *da da dada, ta-dada, DA!*

"Why didn't it occur to you that Darrell's recording would interfere with reading manuscripts before you moved in?" Keeno wanted to know when I told her about it.

I don't know. It's a good question. Why doesn't anything occur to me until after it's way too late?

Another problem with Darrell is that he's given to sudden rage. Take the blue cheese incident. I had saved up money and bought some blue cheese, which I was going to share with Evie on last New Year's Eve. When I got to the fridge it was gone. This is how the discussion went:

ME: Darrell, you didn't by any chance eat by accident that cheese in the fridge, did you?

DARRELL: No.

ME: I was saving it.

DARRELL: I didn't eat any cheese. There was some moldy shit in there. It smelled like fuck. So I threw that out.

ME *(with good-natured jocularity):* Darrell, brace yourself for a shock. Blue cheese *is* mold.

DARRELL: What?

ME: It's supposed to smell that way.

DARRELL: What are you saying?

ME: I'm saying . . . nothing. Forget it. Doesn't matter.

DARRELL *(sensing a potential slight, he leans in so close that I can smell his bouquet of sweat and Vitalis):* Just remember— don't you ever forget—there's never a time when I'm more than three feet away from a knife in this apartment.

Home sweet home.

Half an hour after we leave the party Evie and I are playing a rousing game of Who Cares Less. And I'm losing.

After a fraught scene in front of a cab Evie comes back to my place for the night and, seeing her bending over the bathroom sink in her bra and panties and with her hair smelling of sweat and cigarettes and toothpaste foaming lavalike down her chest and into her navel, I make a move on her. I can't help it. All those viscosities, all those smells. But the silences of the walk back have made me awkward and gentle, and I just sort of start rubbing her shoulder—unerotically, ritualistically, like it's a genie lamp.

"Not now," she says. "Not tonight, Harry. I have an eyelash in my eye. I think."

"You *think* you have an *eyelash* in your *eye*?" I say, wondering if this ranks above or below I Have a Headache.

"And I don't feel well."

"Do you want the cannonball?"

"Not that kind of unwell."

"Well, what is it?"

She rubs a fingertip of green foam from her navel and the valves in my heart squeeze shut. No doubt about it, she is the most beautiful girl I've ever seen.

"You know, sometimes I can barely stand going anywhere with you. It makes me feel so . . . ."

"What?" I say.

"Unratified."

"Un*ratified?*"

"That's what I said."

"Ah."

"Ah."

"Oh God, don't go looking so sad. I can't stand that."

"I'm not sad."

"You sure look sad."

"Well maybe I am."

"O.K. I'll ask. Why are you sad?"

"You know," she says into the mirror while whisking her teeth. "I just can't figure out how you can treat me this way all the time. I don't deserve that kind of treatment. I'm never anything but totally sweet to you. I'm sweeter to you than I've been to anyone in my whole life. I should be on a stamp I'm so sweet to you. And sweet is nothing to sneeze at."

"Who's sneezing?" I say. "No one's sneezing."

"When you masturbated on my carpet and my cats walked on it, I forgave you."

"That was a misfire. Happens to the best of us." (I consider telling her exactly why I'd been relegated to masturbating to girls on MTV in her living room, but think better of it.)

"When you called my boss and told her that I had been in a horrible car accident because you wanted to go to a Yankees—"

"Mets."

"Game, I wore a neck brace nine to five for two weeks and never complained."

"It was a good game, wasn't it?"

"I dress up like Xena, Warrior Princess. I rub lotion on your rashes. I read up on Green Lantern so we can have discussions about power amulets—"

"Rings, Evie. Power *rings*."

"I leave my apeshit cats in the care of my birdbrain neighbor so I can spend asthma-free weekends with you, even though the cats are so enormously pissed off when I pick them up they trash my apartment."

"I thought your cats liked the neighbor."

"My cats *hate* the neighbor, Harry. I told you they like the neighbor but—you know what?—really they hate the neighbor."

"Why would you lie about that?"

"Never mind," she says, the smell of menthol mixing irresistibly with the sweat and smoke in a way that makes my testicles start their slow suction trip up the cord. "Forget it. Forget everything."

Evie paws her foot on the tile and raises her sole to me demonstratively. It is covered in black grit like some kind of pox.

"Jesus," she says. "Ever hear of a mop?"

By now the toothpaste is leaking frothily over her panties and running down her legs. I can't help myself: I reach out to rub it off. But she isn't having any of that.

"Oh no," she says. "Sorry to inconvenience your libido, but I'm afraid the Jiffy Lube is closed."

I slink back into my bedroom. I flick on the light and VIVA LA EVIE sprawls across the wall. The pipes have burst again and the wet plaster and heat make the whole place smell rotten and gingival. I open the window for some air. A few bloated clouds are idling overhead and the moon is hanging around the church spire like a cheap date.

The pipes whine and water splashes cheerfully in the shower:

I've got at least another ten minutes before Evie comes out. Plenty of time for what is rapidly becoming the new ritual, my desolate vespers.

I peel off my clothes and squat genuflectively on the floor and start wringing it out in pleasureless, workmanlike movements. It's a wank only Henry Ford could love, but it does the job. Eventually I get that familiar feeling of efflorescent wetness in my veins and a gun-shy orgasm gurgles stupidly out. As the stringy discharge of bleach and baby powder splatters onto the crumpled pages of a slush manuscript I never sent back, I can't help blurting out the same words I always do when I come: Viva la Evie.

I can't say "I love you," so I say this instead. Don't ask me why.

"Viva la Evie," I say again as I convulse languidly. A shiny opaline cord of semen stretches like a treacherous tightrope between slit and word. I sever it. "Oh viva la viva la viva."

"What did you say?" Evie calls out from the bathroom.

It occurs to me that there is nothing lonelier than masturbating by yourself when the woman you love is naked, drunk, and lathered up in a hot shower five feet away.

"Nothing," I say.

ancient history

It wasn't always like this. In the beginning Evie and I never fought. It was great back then. It was so great it hurts me even to think about it now.

Evie started working at Prestige about the same time I gave up working there. I was already mired in the hopelessness of the job and spent most of my time pretending to read the manuscripts that came across my desk and ducking Nadler. I was sad, too. I was mourning my waffle iron, held hostage by Cassie, my ex, who, it must be said, was only doing it because I wasn't returning her Alanis Morissette CD, which, I must confess, I had destroyed in the toaster. Evie recognized in me the universal emotive male distress signal and took me out to the Blue & Gold for drinks.

We bonded.

That night we had our first real conversation. Feeling dissolved and liquid, and overcome with the thrill of truthfulness, we traded the beautiful, silly trivia of our lives. She told me about how she collects hats. You know, she said, the way some people collect stamps or stuffed animals. That's weird, I said. Why hats?

"Even hats need heroes," she said.

Then, flushed with courage, I told her about my secret inner life of nerdiness.

"I'm reading the dictionary," I confessed.

"That's absurd."

I tried to explain it to her. When I first arrived in New York I didn't have any contacts—no friends, no family, nothing. And then when I began at Prestige I was so busy and so poor that I didn't really have financial recourse to any sort of recreation, so one day I started reading the dictionary and keeping a little book of entries. "I'm only flipping through it right now, but soon I'm going to start going through it methodically, A to Z."

"How extravagantly silly yet utterly winning. What are your favorites so far?"

"Pitchpole," I said. "Muskellunge. Lozenge. Shuttlecock. Ponce, as in Ponce de León. *Ponce.* 'Where are you, Ponce? Time for dinner, Ponce. Ponce! How could you?' Those are for phonetics, mainly. For meaning I like anaclitic. Crapulous. Serpiginous. Dealated. My current favorite is fremitus."

"Ooh. That's a nice one. What's that mean?"

"It's the feeling you get when you place a hand on a part of the body that vibrates during speech, like the throat or chest. And the really cool thing about fremitus is that when doing it you can tell if you're being lied to because you can feel the words and untrue words feel wrong."

"Are you just making this up or what?"

"I'm being one hundred percent serious."

"We'll see about that," she said, putting my hands on her throat. "We'll do a little test."

"It really works better on the chest."

"Do try to control your baser urges if at all possible," she said, wrapping her hands around mine on her neck. I could feel the warm bigeminal surge of her pulse. "Now. I'm going to say a little something and you tell me if it's true."

"Roger."

"Do I love shark movies or do I hate them?"

"That's easy. You love them *and* hate them."

There was a long pause, taut and lovely.

"Please explain that answer, Harry Driscoll."

"Well, you are terrified of them yet fascinated by them. You rent them and then end up regretting that you have to watch them alone."

"I don't have to watch anything alone, for your information. However, you do happen to be disconcertingly right about the movie thing. I adore them. What's better than watching villains and bimbos getting justly chomped?"

"Very little," I conceded. "And yet it is also a little disturbing."

"Exactly."

"You know what I find even more frightening than shark movies, though?"

"What's that?"

"Claymation," I said. "I find claymation terrifying."

"Claymation *is* terrifying!"

Maybe you think it's crazy, but I assure you: it was there. The cryptographies of our hearts were deciphering each other. Our uncrackable codes were lying down in the dirt for one another, giving up all their secrets.

"You know, Evie Goddard, I have to ask you something. You don't plan on jumping houses anytime soon, by any chance? I'm only asking because, well, I have to tell you, you are not entirely unbearable. I don't think I hate you. And I hate everything."

"You're not so detestable yourself, Hairball. No matter what other people say. And no, I don't envision leaving anytime soon. It's very sweet of you to ask, though."

"In that case," I said, raising my Pabst. "Viva la Evie."

"Viva la viva la viva."

Afterward, standing on the sidewalk in front of the Blue & Gold, I wanted to kiss her. There was the usual night turbulence around us and she was lit up in neon and glowing like red candy foil. Her black hair was curling madly in the heat in a gonzo Pre-Raphaelite way I already knew she hated and she smelled of the street—dirty rainwater and hot tar. A cab rolled by, its headlights making the glass in the asphalt glitter.

"What are you looking at?" she said at last.

"You," I said. "Only you."

At the office Evie turned indolence into a winning proposition. I started killing hours by hanging out at her desk, by emailing her fifty times a day, by sharing sex stories. We called these little get-togethers Treehouse Talks because it felt like we were alone in the world while the rest of humanity, the uninitiated—those poor common bipeds—went about their humdrum lives in ignorance of this kind of thrilling togetherness. It was like we were kids in a club to which no one but Evie and I knew the password.

In the Treehouse we would talk about everything—girls who did me wrong, girls I did wrong, boys she was playing with. In those days we would laugh like crazy at each other's exploits— the time Evie let a too-drunk-to-go-home date sleep on the sofa and woke up to find him standing over her, masturbating. Or the time I intercepted a roommate's blind date, pretended to be him, and ended up sleeping with the girl. Evie emailed all her friends about how the roommate found the girl in the kitchen the next day and introduced himself.

In the entire history of the Treehouse Talks only once do I remember anything unpleasant. I had been badgering her about giving me her home number but she had been refusing because she was still dating this Gordie or Mortie or someone. She just wouldn't give me her number. Finally I told her that as the assistant who was training her, I needed to have her home number in case of an editorial emergency. She at last put her number on a stickie and wrote under it, "Okay okay okay already." I told her that she should really spell it "O.K." as that expression comes from an old copyeditor's joke: at the top of a proofed manuscript they would write O.K., an abbreviation for "olle korrect."

"Instead of 'all correct.' Get it?" I said. "A little copyeditorial humor there."

I didn't notice it until I'd already held pedantically forth on the etymology and spelling, but Evie was almost seething. She is a strangely terrible speller and being corrected enrages her. I didn't know it at the time, but she was constantly being almost held back through her elementary years in Mississippi because of her bad spelling, and apparently Cousin Yvonne (pronounced just like that: why-VAH-nee) ridiculed her on a fairly regular basis.

"Don't correct my spelling," she said. "That pisses me off. In ways you don't want to imagine."

Only one other time can I remember her getting angry at me, and it was over her family.

Evie's family background is sketchy. She's southern. Mississippian. She grew up in a small 1:4 town forty-five minutes outside of Biloxi. (This is the way by which small towns in her area are designated, she explained. It describes the ratio of stop signs to bars. One stop sign to four bars is impressive, even in Evie's neighborhood. One of these bars, The Stumblin' Inn, was won by her cousin Yvonne in a game of poker called Pass the Biscuits.) And almost every store was a bait-N-something: the Bait-N-Beer, the Bait-N-Flick, the Bait-N-Pump. In her town there is always an annelid around when you need one.

Evie's biological parents gave her up when she was a few years old. Her earliest memory is of being thrown back and forth ("like a medicine ball," she told me) between two parents equally unwilling to cope with child-rearing. She was adopted by these people named Uncle Booloo, Aunt Margine, and Cousin Yvonne. By unfailing account her family life was blissful. Uncle Booloo has a habit of calling her up and giving her pep talks. "You go get 'em today, baby. There are big books out there that need your help. You're the only Goddard ever to make it to New York City, baby, you got to go give those books the Goddard help they deserve. What, you just waking up? It's six o'clock. No one ever saved a bunch of books sleeping in. Now you go get 'em. You're a Goddard and I love you."

The one person Uncle Booloo doesn't champion is me. In fact I think he hates my guts a little bit. Cousin Yvonne isn't a big fan, either, and I think what probably happened is she relayed some unflattering anecdotes to Uncle Booloo that really should have remained between girls. How do I know this about him? I heard on Evie's message machine the nickname he uses for me:

Draftdodger.

"Where you been all weekend, baby? I called four times but you're never in. You O.K.? You sick, baby? You want me to send you some shrimp? Or maybe you're just out. Where would you be all weekend? You're not out with that draftdodger again, are you, baby? I *told* you about his type, didn't I?"

I'd think this was pretty funny—in the world of names I've been called by fathers, this is pretty tame—if I didn't know how seriously Uncle Booloo feels about military service. He wears his

Navy dress uniform to church and while watching reruns of *Hogan's Heroes*. When drunk he puts scale models of Japanese destroyers in a special tub in front of the sofa and bombs them with empty beer cans. It's easy to imagine him saluting Aunt Margine after sex.

Aunt Margine likes me, but that's not saying a lot. Aunt Margine likes everyone. She is one of the sweetest women I've ever heard tale of. Listen to this:

She is a teacher. One year a student of hers—a girl named Tinley who was already stricken with the sobriquet Two-Ton Tinley—had to have reconstructive surgery to repair a cleft palate. The recovery was long and arduous and poor Tinley had to wear a huge football helmet everywhere. On the playground Aunt Margine saw the other kids teasing her, calling her all the names you'd expect. The next morning Aunt Margine showed up in school wearing a helmet herself. She said that as long as the little girl had to wear the helmet, she'd wear one, too. The following day a student turned up in a helmet also. And then another and another until the whole class was wearing helmets and what was once the cause of so much pain and humiliation and meanness became a beautiful expression of love and solidarity.

That's what the Goddards are like.

That's where Evie gets it.

Evie got mad for the second time during our first snow day off from Prestige. I was over at her place watching *The Best of Fangs* and having some drinks when I made a joke about these characters. I can't even remember exactly what I said—I think it was something like, "How are things in Hazzard County?"—but in a flash she cracked a wooden spoon on my skull. It was one of the most thrilling moments of my history with Evie. Yes, it hurt, and yes, it was ugly, but it also made me congest with happiness because I knew I could say something that could make a big impact on her.

Is that perverted or sweet? I don't know. But what I do know is: what I said mattered.

I mattered.

Two things to watch out for with Evie: spelling and family. That shouldn't be too tough, I thought.

From then on Evie and I were inseparable. I took her everywhere. She was like a fall coat I had bought in the summer and loved so much I had to wear it all the time, on all occasions, even though it was ninety degrees out. I took her to Great Jones Café, to the only spot in the city that serves corn dogs, to the corner of Seventh and A where a cab hit me and where there is now an outline of my body that some confused Samaritan put down because he thought I'd died there.

In the summer I would wet my T-shirts under the faucet and put them in the freezer so we could wear them to bed to stay cool. Then she'd rub lotion on my back in prayerful circles and I'd rub her feet. She would always leave a pair of her panties in my pillowcase to keep me company ("Aromatherapy, Hairball!") when she wasn't there. We'd beat the heat by going to the movies at the Eighth Avenue Theater. I'd bring the Krispy Kremes from across the street and she'd cook up a package of bacon that we would smuggle in while the other moviegoers wondered at the odor of sugar and grease radiating through the theater.

Once, in the park, while watching skating children falling down on the ice, I said, "Oh little Evie, will you be in my life forever please?" and was amazed to discover I meant it.

*   *   *

That September she gave me the best gift I've ever received. It's this cheap, flea-market lamp shade on which she had written backward and in Elmer's glue VIVA LA EVIE so that when you turn it on the words appear on my wall.

"There I am," she said. "Your own brightest Evie. Big as life." I had never been so happy.

Our first kiss went like this. We were flying in a cab up Amsterdam, on the way to play pool with the guy she was dating. I'd only known her two weeks—we'd had our night at the Blue & Gold a few days before; it would be another two months before she made the lamp—but already I could feel the electrons in my arm arcing through the distance between us in the cab.

"I know what you're thinking, little Hairball," she said. "And you can forget it. There's no way I'm going to kiss you."

"Well, don't get your hopes up, either, small Evie," I said. "The last thing these lips are going to do is make contact with yours. Even the idea is sickening."

I put my hand inside her blouse and under her bra and we just stared at each other like players over a chessboard—silently, inscrutably, antagonistically. Then she was on me. It was great. It was like being in the backseat with a horny and confused Shiva, her hands and mouth everywhere. Struggling madly with my belt as we sat at a light with people walking by the window, she said, "Don't get any ideas, little Harry. There's no way I'm servicing you in this cab."

the endo

This became a refrain. Not the line. The act. Fellatio, I was to discover, would be the only mode of sexual activity between us because, as Evie told me the night I first trotted out the condoms, she has a very dire case of endometriosis.

"What's that?" I said.

Holding herself like an armful of flowers, she told me about the endo.

Endometriosis is a condition where the lining of the uterus breaks away and drifts throughout the abdomen. This misplaced tissue—endometrial implants, they call it—usually just sort of attaches to the ovaries and ligaments that support the uterus. But she's got an especially bad case. She's got implants the size of squash balls and they're all over everything. The problem is that because the implants are uterine they think they're supposed to bleed. So they do. Oh man do they bleed. They bleed and bleed and bleed. Every month she suffers agonizing pain as the implants swell with blood and push on the nerves in her spine. The cramping during her periods is so painful that she has to call in sick to work. And even when she's not menstruating she has such incredible pain that intercourse isn't possible.

"So I'm afraid you're going to have to quit brandishing that prophylactic, please," she said.

"No sex?"

"Not that kind, I'm afraid."

As of that night, Evie hadn't had sex in over nine years, since her sophomore year in college, when it was so painful ("Imagine a bear trap on your uterus") that she swore off intercourse for good. When we met she had had sex a grand total of seven times. In her whole life. It's a miracle that she managed to have sex even once. Doctors often misdiagnose endometriosis, but Evie's case was bungled worse than usual. It took twelve years for them to figure out what she had. They thought she was exaggerating, that she had irritable bowel syndrome, or colitis, or pelvic inflammatory disease.

She told them her periods were unbearable. "It's normal for young girls to experience some discomfort during menstruation," they said. "Take aspirin."

She told them she had painful defecation. "Probably an incipient hemorrhoid," they said.

She told them she had searing pain throughout her abdomen. "Are you getting enough fiber?" they wanted to know. "Have you considered bran muffins?"

She told them about the amount of blood and tissue she expelled during one of her first periods (after Aunt Margine found her passed out, facedown on the bathroom tiles, in a puddle of blood and clots). "Is there something you want to tell us, Miss Goddard?" they asked coyly. "Because what you're describing is a miscarriage."

All of the doctors' efforts were like this—hilariously, stupidly wrong.

So from that first adolescent moment when she became aware of sex she associated it with excruciating pain. She spent years, she said, praying that a date would never try to kiss her because she was terrified of what might follow. She spent the four nights of her period sleeplessly balled up and pressed between her mattress and box spring because the pressure was the only thing that relieved the pain. When I'm with her now she curls up with her back to my stomach, and I lace my arms under her knees, bringing them up to her chest, and we spend the night sleeplessly this way, contorted and compressed.

The cannonball, we call it.

And then there's the Rapunzel therapy. Nowadays I have Evie's cycle down pat, and when the first day rolls around—she always has to take two or three days off work—I come by her place and throw pennies at the window. She opens up and I say, "Rapunzel, Rapunzel, let down your extension cord," and then she'll send down this basket tied to two extension cords and I'll put in the basket Rapunzel treats to help her get through the period: everything bagels, lemonade, fortune cookies, *Metropolitan Home*, documentaries on crocodiles (a bite as powerful as a great white's, which is confusing to me: I can't figure out if I am impressed with the crocs or disappointed in the great whites) or dingoes (smarter than you think) or the African honey badger (the only animal in Africa that kills for kicks). Because the flow is so heavy it's necessary for her to double up on protection and so I also send up boxes of Tampax Super Absorbency tampons and Always Alldays FreshWeave Pantiliners with Wings. A lot of the time Duane Reade is out of the Always so I have to get Stayfree Maxis with Cottony Dry Cover and Four Wall Protection.

When Keeno heard about the Rapunzel treats she couldn't

believe it. "Harry Driscoll being nice?" she said. "And you even know the brands? Uh-oh. Glug glug glug."

"What does that mean?" I asked Keeno. "Glug glug glug?"

"This girl's sunk your battleship. Been nice knowing you."

Evie didn't discover the truth about the endo until her second year in New York. She had spent so much of her youth in doctors' offices ("I was in stirrups so much it was like I was Annie fricking Oakley; ride 'em, cowgirl, eh, Hairball?") that she had almost given up. But when she moved to New York and was finally in possession of an insurance plan, she went to a qualified OB-GYN at Beth Israel who gave her an ultrasound and then— immediately seeing a problem—a laparoscopy. The doctor made a quarter-inch incision in her navel and inserted a tube through which she pumped carbon dioxide gas to inflate her abdomen so the organs were clearly visible. Into this incision she put a tiny, snaking telescope with brilliant lights. Then the doctor made another cut in her pubis and inserted a prod that she used like a fire poker to push organs around. After it was over Evie looked at the photos.

"Chocolate chips," she said. "They looked like chocolate chips. I looked at those photos of my insides and everything was covered in chocolate chips. I couldn't tell what was my stomach or my spleen or anything, but it didn't matter. Everywhere you looked they were there. All over everything." It was the first time I'd ever seen her cry. She sat there, hugging her knees. I wrapped my arms around her and we were warm, entangled, concentric, maybe even sort of O.K.

When I met her she had just gone off Lupron, a pseudomenopausal. The mood swings and hot flashes were too much for her and so she switched to the Pill, but intercourse was still out of the question. For almost this whole time—two years—Evie and I didn't have sex. But she still had an appetite. So she did what you might expect: she became an expert in nonvaginal sex. With her agile hands, her mouth, her ass—the unimpaired, pain-free balance of her body—she made herself the best compensatory lover she could.

Do you know what this means? All her life Evie had been conditioned to loathe sex, yet she makes running leaps into the sack with me? It makes me want to cry if I think about it too long.

"I know," she said when I asked her about it. "It's crazy. I've got the Hairball bug. What's a girl to do?"

She also says that I am the only man who ever made her come. I'm not sure I believe it, but yes I'm glad to hear it. The denigration of the romantic past is a necessary step in the romantic present, and Evie sure has had some bad lovers. "He's was so clumsy," she said once about the ex of cigarette-lighter fame. "Flick, flick, *flick*. It's so nice to be with you. You're so . . . deft."

Our inability to fuck is part of Keeno's theory on my infidelities. "You're the worst slider I've ever seen. It's because Evie can't fuck you, isn't it?"

I thought that maybe it was. But that theory was shot down last month. A few months ago Evie goes out and has this procedure. She didn't tell anyone—not me, not Madeleine, not her parents. She checked in to Beth Israel again. The doctor gave her an enema to clear her intestines, did some X rays, electrocardiograms, blood tests. Then they gave her this anesthetic. It was so fast-acting that after the injection Evie remembered they started wheeling her toward the operation room and she said, "Cruise control. Goody. I love this part," and then lost consciousness. It had been maybe fifteen seconds. In the operating room the doctor tilted Evie's head backward so her organs would fall against the chest cavity and she could see Evie's ovaries and fallopian tubes clearly. Then she gassed her up some more and lasered everything in sight, separating her organs with dissolving fabric—like cheesecloth—so things wouldn't stick together again, and stapled her back up.

Et voila.

Sort of.

Endometriosis is what they call a "gluestick disease." Adhesions—an intractable network of scar tissue that binds things together like a crazy explosion of epoxy resin—form when the endometriosis progresses. In Evie's case she has implants and also these adhesions, especially concentrated on her bowels and ureter. One false move with the laser and you could have peritonitis or urine pumping into the abdomen, which can kill the kidneys, among other unpleasantries. Plus surgery increases scar tissue and can actually cause more adhesions, and because adhesions cause organs to be tangled into an unnatural configuration—you can get knotted intestines or "kissing ovaries," where the ovaries are cinched together—you can have severe pain with any kind of movement at all. And Evie's adhesions were so plentiful that during her period it hurt her even to walk or breathe.

So this procedure to remove a certain amount of the tissue actually exposed her to exponentially greater risk. She shouldn't have done it. But she did it because she wanted to have sex with me, because she loved me. And she did it as a surprise. She told me she went to the hospital for appendicitis. Even during her convalescence she said nothing. Then one night when we were in bed together in my place, our skin silver with sweat, it happened.

We were wearing the T-shirts I'd had in the freezer and sucking on ice cubes. It was late and the fruit flies had calmed down. Outside the window the wrong church bells were ringing. I was stroking the long thready muscles of her hips, the little convexities of her face, the thin, wiry eyebrows. A very placid moment. Then suddenly she was rubbing my stomach in that way that is both a question and a plea and pushing her tongue into my mouth. Our lips were salty and our mouths were cold from the ice cubes. Her tongue felt like a cool sea plant waving inside my mouth. She rolled on top of me in one graceful movement and then—as simple and beautiful as a magic trick—I was inside her.

Afterward Evie asked me if I would stop seeing whichever Date I was on at the moment and I told her I would. That's it for me. No more Dates. Consider Date stricken. She's a necessary cut. Debridement. She's excised. Deleted.

Then Evie curled up in my arms like a tired pilgrim and fell asleep. I lay awake, rigid and miserable, blood curdling, knowing that tomorrow I'd feel even worse because I had lied to her again.

mr. please declines again

Today I am Boutros Boutros-Ghali.

My first week on the job I realized that Joey P. Romano, the chief security guard, never looked at the ID you are required to flash upon entering the Prestige building. So I started cutting out pictures from magazines and pasting them over my photo. I have been Macaulay Culkin, Shaq, Connie Chung, Jackie Chan, Eddie Murphy as the Tooth Fairy, Saddam Hussein, Space Ghost, Meat Loaf, Rasputin, Bonnie and Clyde, and all of the Judds. But the UN is doing something in the Balkans again so today it's Boutros Boutros-Ghali.

I hit the street by ten. Early. I cruise down St. Mark's on the gummy and viscous pavement. It is metallically hot out and my clothes are so dirty that my rashes are flaring up. I can't afford to get my clothes dry-cleaned very often and they get rained on, sleeted on, stained with coffee and oil and tears and sweat and cumshot. They absorb grit. They absorb exhaust. They absorb pollution. Then they rub against my skin and give me these blooming red rashes. It looks like dermal strip mining.

On First Avenue Keeno's store is closed. She is what the galleristas refer to as an extreme artist and what the police call a vandal. Her pieces all involve causing people to move out of their way so they are literally forced to view things from a new perspective. "Reloc-art," she calls it.

Her first big project was called "How You Like It Now?" Four
years ago this tweedy magazine that had not deigned to review
her work took on as guest editor the infamous Bertha Whack,
the comedian whose shtick is to throw slime in someone's face/
insult them/physically assail them and then, clutching her beer
belly, sneer, "How you like it now?" Keeno was so incensed by
this guest editorship that she spent four months following dog
owners around parks and streets, collecting their pets' shit, which
she then gathered into a monstrous pile and, early in the morning before the writers trickled into work, deposited via backhoe
at the entrance of the magazine so no one could get in or out.
On the pile she hung a sign that read, HOW YOU LIKE IT NOW?
Everyone had to enter the building that day at the messenger's
window.

They had been reloc-arted.

Her most recent piece is her greatest. She made life-size concrete castings of cars and deposited them via a massive truck at
various locations around the city. She put three VW Beetles in
Columbus Circle, blocking all traffic in one hemisphere. She put
an enormous, finned, pink pimpmobile Caddy in the Carey Lim-
ousine Airport Shuttle parking zone by Grand Central. Com-
muters woke up one morning to find one of the lanes on the
George Washington Bridge blocked by a Plymouth Superbird,
complete with spoiler and elongated nose. Si Newhouse found a
Hyundai Tiburon in front of his office. All around the city—in
underground parking spaces, on corners, in alleys—people were
being forced to move out of their way to accommodate the concrete cars.

After the initial discoveries, the city was pretty speedy about
removing them. But there was a good morning of consternation
as cabs backed up and people flooded the subways.

Keeno called it, "NYC, Stalled."

Before this project, her work had never made her any money, so she opened this boutique, which she continues to manage today. She buys and sells all sorts of art and knickknacks. Wire figures, porcelain wares, woodwork, beads, various herbs and powders—I don't know what they are. The shop is dark and fragrant with incense and oranges. She keeps a turtle named Spencer. There are a lot of Slavs and Greek Orthodox around so she deals a lot in religious figurines. There's a sign hanging in the window that says, WE REPAIR SAINTS AND SINNERS.

But not today. Today she's not there. Probably she left town. When "NYC, Stalled" debuted she didn't take credit for fear of legal reprisal. But everyone in the art community knew who did it, and the police have called her once or twice.

Or maybe she's just sleeping in with Melvin. Melvin is her successful-at-twenty-eight slam-poet boyfriend who doesn't read the newspaper in front of her at the breakfast table and fetches bagels and coffee in the morning. I don't understand how two artists can be so devoid of neuroses. Through some gnosis of happiness known only to the initiated, they have become kind, well-adjusted people who function without mania or vengeful-ness or spite. They are instead playful, thoughtful, frank, giving, solicitous—pick your good adjective. It's sickening.

QUESTION: How do they do it?

ANSWER: They're autonomous, that's part of it. They do what they want and they get paid. No doubt living a life that isn't based on cowardice and deceit helps. And I have to admit I hate them a little bit for it. Sometimes I wish I could just fuck them both.

It's the only thing that would stop me from feeling so inferior.

The box people who live under the scaffolding by Astor Place are already up and spare-changing this morning. My rashes are burning so I walk gingerly, with my arms stiffly akimbo, and teeter metronomically through the congestion of human bodies. Suddenly this little homeless girl jumps out from behind a box, waving at me brightly with her starfish hands outstretched.

"Hey, scarecrow," she says. "You got anything to give?"

"Sorry," I say, trying not to look at her directly.

"Come on. You don't have to be Rockefeller to help a feller."

"Sorry," I say again. "I can't help."

"Come on, Mr. Please. I got no money. Nothing. Zero dollars."

"Don't call me that."

"What?" she says innocently. "Mr. Please?"

"Yes."

"Yes call you Mr. Please?"

"No. Do not call me Mr. Please."

"Mr. Please doesn't want me to call him Mr. Please? What's so wrong with Mr. Please, Mr. Please? Mr. Please, please explain what you don't like about Mr. Please, please."

I really do not want to talk to this girl. I have a hard time talking to kids. I don't know how to behave with them. Do you touch them? Aren't you supposed to ruffle their hair or give them piggyback rides or Werther's Originals or something? But I remember when I was a kid I hated it if someone touched me. Also I have a bad habit of talking to kids in this weird Chinese accent. I don't know why I do it. Maybe it's a bastardized form of goo-goo talk or something. Or nerves. It's not even a regular Chinese accent. It's a stuttering sort of Foghorn-Leghorny Chinese. It's absurd. Plus, talking to kids reminds me of my own childhood, and I can live without that.

"I have nothing to give. Sorry, kid."

"Come on," she says. "It's O.K. You know me."

Alas, I do know her. I know her name is Birdie and that her

brother is dead and she has run away from her mother. I know all this because last winter when I was feeling especially bad about myself and my transgressions I volunteered in the children's hematology/oncology department at Beth Israel. I was the story-hour guy. I would push around this little cart full of children's books and read to the kids in their beds when they were going to sleep. I took it seriously. I always scanned the books before I read them to make sure they didn't have any mention of death in them—you would be surprised how many children's books have death in them—and I almost never showed up at the hospital drunk. I made it a special point.

But it was a tough gig. At any time almost half of the kids there were "comfort care" patients, which was code for "they're terminal so pump them full of morphine and keep them smiling as long as you can." I met Birdie when she came in with her mother and her little brother Max ("Short for Maximum," she told me). They were homeless, the whole familiy, and the mother had a moderate case of schizophrenia. One day, in a fit of paranoia, she attacked Max with the cutter-strip on a box of Saran Wrap and sliced him up pretty bad. When they brought him to the hospital the nurse discovered a lump on his head that turned out to be a very aggressive tumor. It was so aggressive, in fact, that within a month he'd had four surgeries. His shaved head, swollen and covered with the raised seams of sutures, looked like a beaten softball.

The surgeries couldn't stop the tumor, though. It grew so big that it started pressing on the optic nerve and made Max blind. One day the mom holds up this crayon to Max and says, "What color is this, Max?" Of course the kid couldn't see a thing, but he didn't want to let his mom down so he guessed.

"Blue?"

"Noooo," the mom chided. "Try again."

"Green?"

"Noooo. You know what color this is, Max." The mother's breath when she spoke smelled like ammonia.

"Yellow?"

"Concentrate, Max," she said, getting angry. Max looked like he would start crying any second. He was sucking his lower lip in and out like mad.

"Red?"

"Max, you're disappointing Mommy. Mommy wants you to concentrate. You know the word for this color." She was talking in this real eerie, quiet, furious voice. Max was crying now, but you could barely tell. He was trying to hold it in. He was trying to guess the right color. It was the most heartbreaking thing I have ever seen. The kid is *blind*, I wanted to say. Leave him alone. You're torturing him, you nut. Your son is going to die in a matter of weeks so you can stop being crazy for at least that little amount of time, can't you?

But all I managed to say was "Please." Just like that. I kept saying it, sort of in a whisper, hoping she would stop. "Please," I said. "Please please please."

Next month Max died and I quit. It was too much for me and besides, what kid wants to hear *Where the Wild Things Are* read to them in the voice of a Chinese Foghorn Leghorn? No kid, that's who. And the job wasn't helping me appreciably. It was unpaid, of course, so it wasn't helping me that way. But it didn't make me feel much better about myself, either.

It just made me feel worse about everything.

So the day when I'd come in with a book I had bought for Max myself—it was a pop-up book in which I had pasted scratch-'n'-sniff stickers on the pop-ups so he could interact with the book a little—and discovered that his bed was empty, the sheets neat and orderly and smelling of death, I quit. I just turned around and walked out without talking to anybody. And I haven't set foot in Beth Israel since.

The problem is that now Birdie has this habit of stalking me. She is always asking me to read to her like I did to Max, to listen to this or that story, to give her a quarter. I do my best to avoid her, but it's tough. That winter I would often find her sleeping on the heat vent by the stoop outside my apartment. She finds me doing my clothes at Vendetta Laundretta. I'll be reading magazines at the Astor Place supermegadeluxe bookstore, leaning against the stand, and suddenly she'll be there, pulling on my sleeve. There is an irritating jack-in-the-box quality to these appearances, and once you start talking to her, it's game over. The human barnacle will attach to you for hours unless you drop everything and run away.

"Zero dollars?" I say wistfully. "What would I give to have zero dollars! Zero dollars would be heaven. You know what I've got? I've got negative dollars. Negative thousands and thousands of dollars. If I work for years and years and don't spend a dime I might be able to have zero dollars. Now go on. There's a businessman. I bet he might have some dollars."

I haven't quit walking; Birdie is just keeping up. I turn down the stairs leading to the Astor Place subway, ducking and shouldering my way through the crowd on the stairs, trying to lose her, but it doesn't work. She dodges through people with the agile attitude of one of those bright predatory tropical fish that dart in and out of coral formations.

"You want to play? Pick one. Go on. Any one," she says as she ducks under the turnstile and follows me onto the platform.

"Fine. H," I say wearily. I haven't had any coffee. I haven't showered. I'm wearing clothes that are so dirty I had to put the deodorant on the outside of the shirt, too—I don't deserve this.

"Easy. G and I."

This is Birdie's idea of a game. I give her a letter and she sees how quickly she can name what letters bookend it in the alphabet. I don't know what gratification she gets from this, but she loves it. I can imagine what I look like: a twenty-eight-year-old in filthy clothes, with hair sticking up and rashes all over, being pursued by a prepubescent homeless girl in a HELLO KITTY T-shirt and shorts and bright red elf boots—the only outfit I ever see her in—who is spouting letters at him while—hey, goddammit!—she tries to hold his hand, to which:

"Hey, cut that out."

"Sorry. Give me another. I can take it."

A rat on the tracks scurries away down a drain: the train is coming. Thank God. As the doors open and disgorge a surge of people, I say, "A."

"That's only got one, Mr. Please. Come on. Play for reals." I push into the car and she edges in behind me.

"No. It has two. B and Z," I say. One more person tries and fails to squeeze in behind Birdie as I hear the chimes. "As in buzz off," I say, instantly regretting this little crack. As the doors close I bump her out of the car onto the platform. She stares at me, hurt but unconfused—she must be used to this sort of treatment; she doesn't like it but she isn't surprised—through the glass.

I don't look at her as the 6 pulls away.

In the vesicant heat of the car I can barely breathe. My asthma is acting up and I don't have an inhaler because I lost the last one and can't afford to buy another as my insurance has recently deemed this particular med second class, which means that the co-pay is now forty-six dollars and eighty-nine cents. I can still get air into my lungs—it's not an emergency—but it takes a lot of effort. It's what I imagine it must be like to breathe water. Then the train stalls. We shriek to a halt between Thirty-fourth and Forty-second Streets and the lights go off and people stop swaying.

I hate when this happens. It's dark, there's no movement, everyone is silent. It's one of those moments when you have nothing to think about but yourself.

of cultists and purists

I owe the roach coach guy twenty-four bucks and the line inside Ess-A-Bagel is too long so I have no choice but to go straight up and hope the pantry's coffeepot isn't empty. I flash Boutros Boutros to Joey P. Romano at the security desk and he nods.

"What you working on today, scout?" he says, as always.

"Getting fired," I say, and another day at Prestige Publishers officially begins.

Everyone I hate is waiting for the elevator so I take the stairs. I'm almost to eleven when I hear some noises. It's Paula de Gicqeaux, one of the pom-poms, snotting into her French cuffs, huddled gnomishly in the corner.

Publishing is the survival of the most able to eat and Paula is very well poised to succeed. She fox-hunts and goes to debutante balls and says things like "much chuffed" and "nightmare" and "fuck all" and "bollix." She once sent a bartender home from this fête champêtre she was throwing on her family's island because he was the wrong height—she wanted symmetrical servers. She's also one of the original Cultists—the cult of the phony English accent. Lots of people in publishing think that pretending to be British makes them look smart so even if they're from Brewster or Hoboken or Yonkers they talk like someone out of a Merchant-Ivory movie. I'd like to find them laughable but they are often the ones getting promoted so instead I have to find them loathsome.

Still, Paula's basically a good girl who has the bad luck to work for Cruella De Vil—her boss is almost as bad as Nadler—and my heart, caught unawares, goes out to her.

"Paula," I say. "Hey. Hey." Then I think of the song. "Hey . . . hey, Paula."

"You're just making it worse, Harry."

I almost ask her if she got fired but I don't. That is part of Prestige's mythos: fire no one, promote no one. That way they get to maintain a strong supply of Ivy League can-dos in suspended career animation for years and years. The new grads of NYU and Radcliffe know the legend of Prestige's never firing anyone—a reassurance that they won't be punished for any daredevilry—and they all think *I will be the one to break the mold. Me me me. I can do it.* But of course we all end up like Slo-Mo, the guy who works next to me. Great promise, grad school maybe, years of subservitude, and then suddenly you're thirty-four with a wife and kid and you're still an assistant, filling out your boss's corporate Amex, photocopying reviews, dredging the slush pile. Some people say that you have to jump houses to get promoted, but who's going to hire a thirty-four-year-old who has never even handled a cookbook?

When I signed up for the job, straight out of undergrad, I was looking forward to an imagined underground world of assistants banded together in Dickensian unity by poverty and genius and ambition. I envisioned nights out on the town, trading on our status as future manufacturers of our nation's aesthetics for complimentary drinks at subterranean bars. I fantasized about lunches at Oyster Bar/Royalton/Four Seasons with scurrilous writers and martial agents and brusque yet avuncular editors. I expected intimate and satirically esoteric dialogues between writer and editor, full of allusion and inside jokes—"Oh Bill (Styron/Gass/Safire), you mean Ophelia's *omphalo*skepsis ha ha ha." I daydreamed about literary NYU girls with their little black outfits and rigorous yet lubricious minds full of profanity and wit and sexual largesse for the wunderkinds of American letters.

But when I arrived this world didn't seem to exist. Instead there was an enervating haze of passive aggression, jealousy, and spite. There were too few jobs to go around and almost no promotions and, after all, who wants to be friends with someone who's going to grow up to be a big fat failure just like you?

"O.K.," I say to Paula. "I'm sorry. I just—what did she do this time?"

But I already know what she did. I'm sure it's just one of the usual tricks. The gerontocracy around here has a million of them. Nadler's favorite is to sign up a book without telling me so that when a pom-pom or subrights person or copyeditor comes by my cubicle and says, "Hey Harry, we need a copy of X manuscript," I'll say, "Huh?" Then they'll have the opportunity to say something like, "You know, the *book*. Your *boss*. Just signed *up*. You do work for Andrew, don't you? I mean, that is your *job*, right?"

"You wouldn't understand," Paula says. "You're *pure*."

"What?"

"Just leave me alone."

This girl's been crying so hard her eyes are swollen like a frog's and her mouth is caked in white spittle and still she doesn't want my sympathy. This is pretty representative of how I'm regarded by the pom-poms around here. But I want to help her. I want to tell her that it's O.K., that no matter what happens at the office there is still a world out there of shark movies and skin lotion. I want to tell her that her boss doesn't know every damn thing and that just because you spell an author's name wrong on an invitation doesn't mean that you're stupid and worthless and fair game for public ridicule and belittlement.

"Hey, Paula, easy. I'm on your side. I was just trying—"

"Stay off my side."

"Paula . . . ," I say, reaching out to her shoulder.

"Don't touch me," she says like she's afraid failure might be contagious. "*Purist.*"

I don't need this. I haven't had any coffee, my rashes are spreading, and it's Monday so I know there is already a huge stack of slush manuscripts on my desk. I yank the door to reception and AC washes over me. I inhale as hard as I can and it's like needles on my tongue.

It's the best, least complicated feeling I've had in months.

poof

The pantry is out of coffee so I try to scare up some cold coffee at my cubicle. It's hard to find anything I've got so much shit on my desk. I've got slush manuscripts aplenty, the dictionary I've been reading, matches, old *Metropolitan Homes* that I've stolen from publicity for the purposes of imagining I could live another life one day, Q-Tips, a list of psychological disorders not found or understood in North America (*Koro*; Malaysian; sudden intense anxiety that sexual organs will recede into body and result in death; other symptoms include tremendous feelings of depression and guilt associated with discharge of semen), lozenges, many scented items all of which I hate: Skoal wintergreen chewing tobacco, Old Spice, licorice both red and black, potpourri in a baggie, wintergreen mints, the kind of shampoo this ex of mine used to use that made her hair smell like fennel. (When I feel myself falling asleep I sniff one of these products and am suffused immediately with the odors of things I detest. It's the only way I can keep myself awake sometimes—office smelling salts.) I also have an 800-count box of white birch smoothtex Royal round toothpicks. I have boxes of Pilot V-ball fine and extra-fine blue pens. I have the big, manuscript-size rubber bands. I have a list taped to my monitor that says SEVEN STEPS TO PRESERVING HARRY'S BACHELORHOOD:

1. No weekend phone calls out of state
2. No handmade gifts, no household gifts
3. Weekend sex only; no sex during the week or during office hours
4. No calling from work, no memorizing phone numbers
5. No family functions, no dress-up functions (esp. weddings)
6. No relationships with pets or stuffed animals
7. MOST IMPORTANT: no using the word "love" in any circumstances. Even casual use is prohibited. For example, you may not say, "Boy oh boy do I love hanging out with you." Or, "Don't you just love it when Bruce Banner says, 'Don't make me angry; you wouldn't like me when I'm angry'?" Or, "Do you love squirting windshield wiper fluid as much as I do?" The only time you may use "love" is when its omission would be too obvious. "You want to rent that Audrey Hepburn/Gary Cooper movie tonight? *Whatever-It-Is in the Afternoon?*" In this case you may say "love" as not saying it would call attention to itself. Under no other circumstance is it appropriate to use "love."

I made this list two years ago with Evie's help. This was back when she first arrived at Prestige from FSG and still thought things like this were funny. She helped me tape it to my monitor's screen; it was like a christening.

Now it's on the side facing the wall of my cubicle.

Also on my desk are some old Styrofoam cups, one of which just might have some old coffee in it. I'm on my eighth cup when Horst tries to get my attention. Horst sits at the cubicle next to mine. He's a thick German guy with a shaved head and a constant, unnerving smile. He looks like a homicidal Padding-ton Bear but he's harmless. He's a floater—came on as a glori-fied temp, helping out in contracts, but he's worked a bunch of departments and lately has filled in for an editorial assistant who quit after six years without raise or promotion. Horst has been here for three weeks now. I'm supposed to be training him.

"Harry, do you know if—"

"No *sprechen sie* before noon, O.K., Horst? The Versailles Treaty expressly forbids all Germans to *sprechen sie* before noon. No *sprechen sie* you, no *sprechen sie* me, no *sprechen sie* nada."

This is the way it goes with Horst. He spends his mornings bombinating around the office like a bumblebee on Benzedrine while I can barely put left after right. If I don't get to have coffee in a tranquil, speech-free environment in the morning, it means big trouble for the rest of the day. Horst continues waving some paper at me, I continue ignoring him, and then suddenly some-one jumps on me from behind, scaring me so bad I rip the last of my empty Styrofoam cups into crumbs.

"Jesus Christ, Evie," I say without turning around to see who it is. "Give me an aneurysm."

"Good morning, my little Harry in the box."

I was a little off about Evie's bounce-back time. All Sunday and no call, but now, Monday morning, she's back to her old self. She's quick to get irritated, but she's quicker to forgive. That's what she does: forgives. Keeno calls her Evie Rodham Goddard.

"It's morning all right but you can delete *good*."

"Isn't this one of the signs of the apocalypse?" she says much too pertly. "Seas boil. Dead rise from the grave. Harry Driscoll gets into work before noon."

"Hardy har." My hands are beginning to shake and my head

hurts enough to make me squint. My tongue feels like a desiccated tuber knocking around my mouth. "There's no coffee. Neat. That's just fucking neat."

"Ah, my little baba ganoush. So profane so early in the morning."

"There's no coffee."

"So profane but so *shrewd*."

"This is going to be a problem. This is how international incidents start, isn't it, Horst?"

Horst is waving a note at me but this time it's Evie who cuts him off.

"Ladies and gentlemen, quiet please. Harry Driscoll is now considering how to solve this daunting dilemma. It's going to take strategy. It's going to take planning. It's going to take crackerjack timing. How will he play it? Will he brave the wilds of the sidewalk and walk half a block to the roach coach? Ah no. That would require legal tender. Will he negotiate the dangers of brewing a whole new pot? Probably not—that would require technical know-how regarding kitchen appliances and the arcana of straining hot water through beans. Hmm. Hmm. Or perhaps he will simply extend his mighty arm the perilous three feet to little old Evie and partake of her bounty." From behind her back Evie produces a brown bag.

"You got me breakfast?"

"Ah, *baby*. You don't think I'd let you face slush without your daily lipids and stimulants, do you?"

"You are the best Evie ever made."

"That is true."

"Viva la Evie."

"Viva la viva la viva. Now why don't you tell us why you've come calling so early to our humble little office."

"I've become Amish."

"Come on. Spillez-vous. It's because you're late passing the jogging calendar manuscript to press again, isn't it?"

"Calendar!" I say, remembering. I start riffling through the papers on my desk, searching for the manuscript.

"Late again?" says Horst.

"Last year," Evie explains, "Harry finally gets his chance to edit a book—"

"*Book*. Right. It had twelve puny essays and a bunch of black-and-white photos. Not exactly a book."

"And he blows it. The project was a *sleepwalker*. Manuscript was clean, barely any editing left to do. Pretty much all he had to do was fill out some forms and pass it to copyediting and design. But he sat on it so long that they had to give it a crash pub, and—"

"Crash pub?" Horst says.

"Welcome to your job," I tell him.

"Aren't you supposed to be training him?" Evie says to me.

"Yes," Horst says.

"Anyway, crash pub. A book is like a baby, Horst. It takes about nine months to make it. But there's an exception. Sometimes you can get one out in a few weeks if you have to. It costs loads and everyone hates it, but it can be done. So anyway, they had to crash-pub Harry's calendar last year. It didn't win him a lot of friends in copyediting."

"Or design. Let's not forget how much the design guys hate me. And the pom-poms."

"Pom-poms?" Horst says.

"Publicists, Horst," Evie says patiently. She should have been a kindergarten teacher. "You know, rah-rah? Give me a B, give me an O, give me an O, give me a K. Goooooo BOOK! Get it? Never mind. Harry, what *are* you looking for?"

"You didn't happen to see the calendar manuscript lying around, did you?"

This is the problem I have been trying to forget. The manuscript is gone. Completely disappeared. Poof.

Evie gives me a minute to see if I am kidding. I am not.

"You lost the manuscript?"

"Not lost. Relocated."

"And you can't find it?"

"Not technically, no."

"Aie God, Woodrow! Please tell me it wasn't the original."

"It wasn't the original."

"Was it the original?"

"Yes."

"You mean the only copy of it in-house, right? The author still has it on disk, right?"

"Author's an old-timer. Does everything on an Edgewood manual."

"You mean to tell me that the copy that is lost—"

"Relocated."

"Is the *only* extant copy?"

"*Extant*," I say dreamily. "I love *extant*."

"Harry!"

"Yes?"

"*What are we going to do?*"

"Wrong pronoun."

"What?"

"*We* don't have to do anything. It wasn't your manuscript."

Horst says, "What did the manuscript look like?"

"It's white with black markings. About half an inch tall. Answers to 'Drivel.' "

"When did you first notice it missing?" Evie says.

"What's today? The fifth? So that's one, two, three . . ."

"Three days ago?"

"Weeks."

"It's been missing for three weeks? What are we going to do?"

"Well, right now my plan is to find it."

"Harry."

I'm touched that she is so concerned but it's also a little irritating. I hate it when Evie starts to sound like my mother.

"Oh, it will be fine." I open the Green Lantern lunch box—my briefcase—from my desk and get the flask out and pour some sour mash into the coffee.

"Breakfast of champions," Evie says meanly, and just like that the subject is changed. "Does Nadler know you drink on the job?"

"I don't drink that much."

"Your breath could sterilize a wound."

It's true. I do drink more than the average editorial drone. It's impossible not to. When I first got here, before whatever promise I'd had had been inexplicably broken, there was never a problem. I drank coffee and that was it. But now I drink at the office because going to work feels like a war between genuinely stupid hopefulness and despairing repetition. It's like going up to the same counter every day with the same losing lottery ticket and saying, What? Again? I lose again? When do I get to win already?

"Nadler's too busy Dingling to notice my drinking anyway."

Horst stops waving that note at me to ask, "Dingling?"

"Don't you tell him anything?" Evie asks me. "Laura Dingle, Horst. She's so famous she's a verb."

Evie explains Dingling to Horst:

Ten years ago, when he was still an assistant like us, Nadler went to Hector Campion, our apiarian president, and said that Dingle was an alky. Nadler said that her editing was shoddy and that he was doing all the work on this really important manuscript. He had made a secret copy of the manuscript and copied all Dingle's edits over in his own handwriting, spilled bourbon on the pages, and taken them to Hector, who bought the whole story. Dingle didn't get fired, of course, but everyone believed Nadler and poor Laura Dingle's phone stopped ringing. Bigwig editors stopped enlisting her services. Agents got wind of her alleged problem and sent projects elsewhere.

She quit and suffered the humiliating fate of so many publishing rejects: she took a job teaching prep school in Jersey.

"So there it is, Horst," she says. "The only way to get promoted in editorial. Dingle somebody. Well, either that or find the Next Big Thing in slush."

"The Next Big Thing? No one has ever in the entire history of this publishing house found *any* publishable manuscript in slush, let alone the Next Big Thing."

"Well, now that you've had your morning boozer, what do you say," Evie says, gesturing like a game show hostess to the manuscripts and SASEs piled around my desk.

"Forget it. I'm not doing slush. It's insipid."

"Fine. Sign your own death warrant. See if I care."

a word about slush

Slush is an absurd pantomime of futility that is practiced by almost no other American publisher but Prestige. Every week hundreds of unagented writers—slushies—send in their manuscripts to New York publishers. Most houses just recycle or return them, but at Prestige the assistants have a meeting every Monday where they gather around a huge table in the conference room and push through the Sisyphean piles of slush submissions and reject them via form letter. None of the assistants thinks it's worth the time or vulcanized pizza that's served, but the meetings are required and legend has it that if an assistant finds a slush manuscript that gets published the reward is five thousand dollars and, possibly, a promotion.

I can't help but feel bad for the slushies. They have spent years of their lives writing these books. They're not under contract, they have no agents, no money flowing in from serial rights or movie rights or foreign publications. They have no track record, no resume, no mentors, no supporters, no fans. Probably even their mothers don't like their writing. And yet they sit at home, during their off hours, when the kids aren't screaming, scribbling out what they think is the terrible beauty of their lives. They do it alone, in the basement, late at night. It's the same way that bombs are made. No wonder they're crazy. And worst of all, the poor slushies have nothing to do but send in their life's work to a burnout like me who gives it maybe sixty seconds before rejecting it. ("Dear Slushie, Thank you for your submission. It is clearly a serious and ambitious work, but I'm sorry to say it isn't right for this publishing house. Good luck with this elsewhere.")

There was a time when I would actually read the manuscripts and try to help the slushies, I'd send them handwritten letters with suggestions for changes and entreaties to keep trying. But my altruism has been eroded. Five years of rejecting slush does something to you. It makes a toxic spill of meanness and disappointment in your heart. Besides, the mathematics of failure is absolute: in my five years here nothing from the slush pile has ever been published. You figure a hundred submissions a week, fifty-two weeks a year, times five—that's a lot of futility. Statistically it's harder to get your slush submission published than it is to play any professional sport you can name.

Also, I've had some threats. After receiving my rejection two summers ago, one slushie wrote me a note saying, "Dear Mr. Driscoll, Here are some letters you might be interested in: C4, H5, AR. Recognize it? It's cacodyal. A neat little compound. When it is exposed to oxygen, say when a bottle of it is thrown at a certain desk on the eleventh floor of a certain publisher's offices on a certain corner in midtown Manhattan, it immediately turns into white arsenic, which, as you mayhap perchance to know, has the delightful property of causing death in seconds. Sure you won't reconsider *Possum Death Spree?* PS You looked very sharp in your blue striped shirt today. Do you always get into the office at ten-fifteen?"

So now I just rough up the pages to make it look like they've been read and send them back with the form letter that I fraudulently initial GL, for Green Lantern. Let them track down that guy and throw cacodyal at *him*.

splinter skill

"You'll never get promoted that way," Evie continues, nodding toward the door of the empty office.

This doesn't even deserve a response. It's true there is a vacant office next to Nadler's and that the publisher has been trying to fill it for two months. It's also true that somehow word has gotten out to the assistants that the applicant pool is dry and that maybe this time Prestige will break its own rules and promote from within, but Evie knows better than to try this: if I ever were to be promoted at Prestige, it would have happened in my first three years here, not now that I am the well-known *assistant maudit* of eleven.

But Evie isn't a girl who gives up easily.

"I know you have a very progressive idea of work," she tries again. "But don't you think that sometimes you should do what your job description calls for? Just to keep Nadler on his toes, I mean?"

"Let me show you something," I say, holding up the first slush manuscript that comes to hand. "*A Little Off the Top: Tales of a Homicidal Barber*. And this one. *Great Expectorations: My Life as a Spitter*. And get a load of this subtitle. *A Novel Based on Real Life*. Like anyone needs to listen to *that*."

"They're not all that bad."

"You see this brown mess? The author enclosed two Klondike

bars as a thank-you gift. And this one. You see the blank pages?
Know why they're blank? They're written in lemon juice. And—"

"That one I found last month is, I don't know, kind of O.K."

"The one I rejected? *Love Is a Ladder*? By what's-his-schnozz?"

"Drakkar. Jason Drakkar."

"Drakkar? Ha! What kind of name is that? It's a cologne, for
Christ's sake. And Jason. I hate that name. Every Jason I've ever
known was either retarded or beat me up on the playground.
Most serial killers are named Jason, you know."

"Be nice, Harry. It was pretty good. For slush, I mean."

"Full of clichés, every chapter. That's why I sent it back."

"Clichés?" Horst manages to say.

"Clichés," I say, mockingly. "Clichés, clichés, clichés?"

"Clichés," Evie says patiently. "You know, an expression that
is so overused it becomes . . . useless. You are looking at possibly
the greatest enemy of clichés this publishing house has ever
seen." I can't help indulging in a little preening here as she
explains. "Editors from all different floors give Harry their manuscripts to vet for clichés. He can't manage to get a sleepwalker
published on time, he loses manuscripts, he can barely get into
the office in the a.m., but he can eradicate every trace of cliché
from any manuscript faster than you can say unemployment
check. It's like that thing autistics do with matches. What do you
call it?"

"Splinter skill," I say.

"Yeah. Some people around here say that if it weren't for that
freak skill of Harry's he would've been fired long ago."

"Please," I say. "They have to know my name to fire me. I tell
you that last week Nadler called me Larry?"

"Will you at least do some slush as a personal favor to me?

Life around here would be pretty dull without Hairball. Who else would I have Treehouse Talks with?"

"Two letters, one syllable: no."

"Not even for a repulsively chocolatey Krispy Kreme?" she says, producing a doughnut from behind her back. It's a Krispy Kreme, all right. Cold, but the real thing. Krispy Kreme is on Eighth and Twenty-third. She walked seven blocks—crosstown— out of her way for me.

"Wait a second," I say. "This is too much. What is it?"

"What is what?"

"*It.* Why all this special treatment? What is it you want?"

"I just want you to be as happy a little ear mite as possible."

"And?"

"A feasible alternative to fossil fuels?"

"And?"

"Your promise never to piss in my shower again?"

"*And?*"

"O.K. OKOKOKOKOKOKOK. You got me. I want you to take me to this New Year's masquerade party. Is that so horrible?"

"Aha!"

"Oh come on, little Harry. I'm giving you *months* of notice."

I consult my calendar—I can't find mine, actually; Evie hands me hers—but I don't need to look to know that I can't go. For the past six months I've been working a secret night job, and I have to be there on New Year's.

"Like to but can't."

"Please?"

"Like to but can't."

"Please?"

"Like to but can't."

"Pretty please with Omar Sharif on top?"

"Um . . . Like to but can't."

"Everyone from Doubleday will be there. Everyone from ICM will be there. Madeleine's going. It will be a chance for you to meet her at last. She still doesn't believe you exist."

"That's because I'm a genie."

Madeleine is Evie's best friend. They went to Radcliffe together. I've never met her because she's an associate editor at Holt—"Dare to dream, Harry"—and a year younger than I am and I can't stand to be reminded of my status around here.

"Come on."

"I don't have anything to go as."

"You could go as a healthy, happy, well-adjusted person. No one would recognize you."

"Funny girl."

"There will be all manner of important publishing people there, and let's face it, your career could benefit mightily from making a few contacts."

"Exactly. There will be all those *people* there. You know how I feel about other people."

"You're going to grow into a sad, strange, lonely little man, you know that?"

I place her hand on my throat so she can hear the words vibrating there and say, "I just can't, O.K.?"

"Why? Because you have plans with Date?"

She tries to be offhand about this, but she's pissed, I can tell. The scalene constellation of scars around her left eye are radiant.

I hand Horst the lemon juice manuscript and say, "Horst. Very important. I need a copy of this. O.K.?" When he leaves I say to Evie, "Now look. I'm telling you: there is no Date."

"O.K. Fine then."

"Fine."

"Fine."

"Fine."

"*Fine*," she says. She ruffles some pages busily but can't let it rest. "We never go anywhere. We never do anything. Dating you is like living in a biosphere."

"Church and state," I say.

"*What?*"

"Church and state. I just feel like our friends should be . . . mmm . . . separate but equal."

"That is one of the all-time stupidest things I've ever heard."

"Evie, you're vociferating."

"Would you just—"

"Concentrate on the vibrations entering your ear. I can't go to the party. It's got nothing to do with Date. End of story."

"Fine." Evie gets up and retrieves a manuscript from her desk drawer and shoves it in her purse. "Enjoy your breakfast."

"Where are you going?"

"I'm doing something consonant with my job description. You remember that old gag?"

"Job . . . job . . . I know I've heard that word somewhere before."

"Keep it up, Harry."

"And what urgent job-related meeting do you have to attend right now?"

"I have an appointment with a writer."

"Fine."

"*Fine!*"

I lean back in my chair to survey her—a gesture of passive aggression, I know—and knock over a pile of slush submissions.

"Writer," I say as I bend over to fix them. "Sure. What writer?" But when I get back up she's gone and Horst is standing there, holding the lemon juice manuscript like a platter.

"The photocopier doesn't seem to have a setting for lemon juice. Do you know—"

"Appointment with a writer. What bullshit. Did you see her flying out of here?"

"She looked pretty upset."

"Fifteen seconds, Horst. Thirty tops."

"What do—"

"Shhh! Just watch. Ten, nine, eight . . ." I imagine Evie getting as far as publicity, maybe subrights, possibly *Books in Print* if she's really pissed, and then it'll be volte-face. I know it.

Right on cue there is the sound of heels clicking and Evie appears. I smile more smugly than I mean to but when Evie gets to my desk she blows past it and grabs something from her drawer.

"Forgot my ID," she says.

the gorillas and me

I do not believe in visions. They're the fortune cookies of the intellect. They rank right up there with horoscopes and epiphanies and clichés.

I repeat: do not.

But—I can't believe I'm saying this—one changed my life.

I received the vision one night about two years ago when I was out at a postevent party. I had been at a party for the Westminster dog show with Cassie—owner of toasted Alanis Morissette CD, stealer of waffle iron—and was feeling a little down about all the pampering these dogs were getting. Honestly, there I was, standing amid a carpet of wiener dogs, stashing pigs-in-blankets into my Ziplocs while the dogs lapped up Pellegrino from crystal bowls. It was maddening. The dogs were better groomed than I was and they had nary a rash, let alone armpits in full red bloom. At one point I tried to steal a piece of what looked like steak tartare from the bowl of a Lhasa apso and it bit me.

"That's great," Cassie announced. "My boyfriend, stealer of dog food."

"*Attempted* stealer of dog food. And look. I'm bleeding. You believe that?"

"Boo-hoo," she said. "Poor you."

Cassie was not a terribly sympathetic girl. She had the face of one of Puvis de Chavannes' angels and the heart of a mollusk.

Then we bumped into a guy I knew from college, Mitchell Lowengrab. An insipid conversation ensued involving undergraduate reminiscences during which it seemed like Cassie spent a lot of time giggling and touching Grab's elbow. Then he invited us back to his "pied-à-terre" for an "aperitif" with his "associates." I was about to say no—I reeked of pigs-in-blanket and had no intention of letting him give Cassie the famous Grab—when she fell all over herself accepting.

"Great," he said, leering at Cassie. "We'll see you there." He extended his hand. I had to shake it. "Hey," he said, looking down at a smear of blood on his palm. "You O.K., sport? You get in a fight with a lawn mower?"

"Lawn mower?" Cassie said. "Ha!"

Then he fake-boxed me chummily like the pals we never were and left. When he was gone I said to her, "Enjoying yourself?"

"What is that supposed to mean?"

"*Lawn mower? Ha!* How could you laugh at that? That wasn't funny."

"It was so funny."

"He's a buffoon."

"He doesn't seem like a buffoon."

"Oh, I see."

"What do you see?"

"Don't tell me you actually like that guy? Is that what you're telling me? What's so great about Mitchell Lowengrab?"

"For one thing I bet he has something besides hors d'oeuvres in his pockets."

But things didn't get really bad until we went to the party.

More on that soon.

I come from an affluent (sailboats, cocktail hour, domestics) and hypereducated (Ivy, Ivy, Ivy) family that lived in a pink bubble of exultant solvency. There was money for cello lessons (my brother) and racquet sports (me). There was money for winter vacations in the Virgins and summers in Maine. There was money for a standing Saturday night dinner at the Polo Grill. Everyone I knew drove German cars. We all went to private schools with dress codes and Latin mottoes and mascots like the pelican and the wyvern and the ambassador. Our mothers organized charity fund-raisers and our fathers macerated their disappointment in us with covert dinnertime vodka tonics.

You know the demographic.

In college I decided that not only didn't I want to work in the family law firm, I didn't want to work in any law firm. Not for me the fuscous and furrowed life of tax law. Instead I decided to follow my only velleity and pursue a life in book publishing. Paternal support vanished faster than you can say disinherited, but that was O.K. For the first time in my life I was making a decision that I wanted to make. It was an entirely new pathology for me, and it felt good.

When I got to New York and took the job at Prestige, making $17,500 a year, the pink bubble finally burst. I had eight hundred dollars in savings and needed thirty-five hundred for the deposit on my first apartment, and the pater wasn't taking any requests. Fine, I thought. I can do this. That's the point of being a grown-up, isn't it? Besides, I had a job as an editorial assistant at Prestige, one of the best publishers in New York, working for Andrew Nadler, no less. Not a legend, but a certified big shot. Everyone in the industry knew him. He had lectured at NYU and Columbia. He was a guest on *Booknotes* once. I had good prospects. And I was on salary with overtime for the first time, wasn't I? With thirty overtime hours a week, I would have *some* sort of money, wouldn't I? I mean, I could subsist, right?

Wrong.

The other assistants made it clear when I arrived that you never log your overtime hours. If you work forty-five hours you report thirty-five. If you work sixty hours you report thirty-five. If you work eighty hours you report thirty-five. That's the way the human resources people on thirty-three want it, that's what you do. When Evie arrived and I informed her of this, she said, "Interesting. I have no penis, yet I must fuck myself." She was right.

But wait. There's less.

We don't get to put legitimate business lunches on the company Amex. You can forget about using the office copier or fax for personal reasons. Instead of a Christmas bonus last year the assistants got lapel pins in the shape of the Prestige colophon. "Spirit pins! For our valued assistants," the memo that came with the pins read, which, I have to say, is probably a pretty accurate representation of our value.

I'd laugh if it weren't true.

I'm not saying all this because I feel sorry for myself but because I just didn't feel prepared. I wasn't ready. All those years of schooling (Yes I speak Old English!) and resume-building bullshit (Yes I interned on Capitol Hill!) didn't pertain at all to the life that was waiting for me. I felt misled, the recipient of wrong and useless instruction, ill-equipped. It was like I had been airlifted to an uninhabited desert island with only a piñata and a bundt pan and was told, Well, that should do it. Good luck.

What did I do? I started charging.

I thought, Well, I've got to put the deposit down, right? Nothing wrong with a little cash advance. And I've got to eat. Nothing wrong with putting that on plastic. And it's O.K. to go to a flick. Plastic again. And CDs and gourmet coffee and name-brand detergent aren't really luxuries, are they? It's perfectly reasonable to charge that stuff.

And there were some other purchases, unfortunately. I felt like even though I was pulling in only a few hundred dollars a week I still had to maintain at least the appearance of a life. This applied especially in New York: assume one if you have it not.

I know: *vanitas, vanitas.* But you can't keep slugging around the office in the L. L. Beans your mom bought you when you left for college while your colleagues are sporting smart black urban gear, can you? It's hard to go stalking around the office very impressively while squeaking on the linoleum in your worn-out duck boots while the pom-poms go clicking confidently by in their Sigerson Morrisons, isn't it?

So I kept charging.

As ever, I couldn't learn the first lesson. It was there in the first Visa statement—Pull up, pull up, it said, you're coming in too steep—but I didn't listen. When the third or fourth bill arrived I didn't understand it. I had racked up *how* much? That's ludicrous, I wanted to tell them. I don't have that kind of money. This can't be right.

But the numbers weren't wrong and they weren't going away. I had to make some adjustments. This is how the essentials shook down for me after the fourth month. Food: I had a weekly budget of nineteen dollars, which included potatoes (baked and eaten like apples), pasta with no sauce, bread with no butter, tea with no milk, kielbasa and corn, Pabst Blue Ribbon cans, and croutons. (NOTE: Why are croutons the ideal snack? They're *already* stale.) After a few weeks on the job I discovered the bookroom in the basement, where we keep copies of all of Prestige's new pubs and the more popular backlist. I also discovered that I had a knack for forging Hector's signature, and that by so doing I could order free review copies of most books. I let it be known to the maintenance staff that I was amenable to exchanging such books for certain intelligence regarding the goings-on of other floors. I developed quite a network of informers.

"Hey, Driscoll," a janitor or messenger or mail guy would say to me on the sly at my cubicle. "Meeting just ended on seventeen."

"Understood."

I'd take the elevator to seventeen and scrounge all the half-eaten bagels and fruit left over from the meeting. Later that day my informant would find a copy of the book he wanted sitting on my partition.

Crafty, no? But it only helped with the hunger. It didn't do much for my other problem: shelter. All tolled I've lived in nine apartments. I've never been on a legal lease. At no time have I lived with someone I've known. I've lived in a Hell's Kitchen walk-up whose ceiling collapsed into my bathtub.

And then, of course, there is Darrell, wielder of knives, maker of jingles.

Eighty percent of my salary went to whatever ye olde shitbox I was living in at the moment. That didn't leave a lot of cash for discretionary spending. In the beginning I tried to look past it. I fantasized that I was in a Russian novel. I imagined improvements, promotions, a dollar-green light at the end of the tunnel. But things got complicated with Nadler and the picture of eventual solvency retreated into another galaxy of possibility. After another year it ceased being funny. I started having this dream where I would round up a truckload of rich people and electrocute them anally—like minks—so I could steal their clothes. When I'd see certain people walking around midtown wearing their Kenneth Coles and their Hugo Bosses, I'd think, *Bzzzz bzzzz*.

Clearly something needed to be done.

I would make rolls of quarters, only I'd fill the wrapper with kitty litter and bookend it with real coins in case the teller happened to check. Fifty-cent investment for a $9.50 return. You can guess how long this lasted, and what happened when the teller noticed incriminating clouds of kitty litter emanating from a tear in the ten-dollar roll of alleged quarters.

I saved postage from SASEs that slushies would send in with

their submissions and use them to mail in my minimum pay-ments on all the maxed-out cards.

For a while I'd make twice-weekly visits to the stab labs. It's medically suspect, I know, but it's too good a deal to resist. They need clean blood. I need orange juice and cookies. Symbiosis, right? Eventually I had to quit. I started going too often and passed out one night on the E train and ended up somewhere in Queens with a homeless guy standing over me, demanding, "What is Heinz 58? What is Heinz 58?" while brandishing with malicious intent an empty squeeze bottle of ketchup.

I spent a week last summer egg-breaking. The profit margin was great, but the net was barely useful. I would go to D'Ago-stino's and buy a dozen eggs for $1.19 and then approach club-bers on their way out of Webster Hall or drunks shuffling out of the No-Tell Motel and give them the spiel: Life is hard and real entertainment scarce. You work work work and if you're lucky you can catch a rerun of *Moonlighting* on Bravo. However, I, proudly, would like to offer you an alternative form of amuse-ment. For a dollar, ladies and gentleman, I will now break an egg on my head, right here in front of you. [*Pause to let seriousness of offer sink in.*] For two dollars, you can do it.

A possible twenty-four dollar return on a buck nineteen? It seemed worth it. Problem was drunk people didn't practice much restraint. They got creative with places to break the eggs, and they were often ungentle. What sealed it was this one night when I was making my pitch to a crowd outside Bouche when a voice from the back called out, "Is that you, Harry?" The owner of the voice extruded from the shadows in a red wig and fishnet thigh-highs and bangles aplenty—very un-Cultist—but no doubt about it: it was a very amused Paula de Gicqeaux.

"What is it exactly you are doing, Harry?" And then: "Hey, people, I work with this guy. Isn't that a riot? Editorial assistant by day, omelet by night."

I dimly said something about a daring undercover magazine piece for *Time Out New York*, but they knew better. The next day I overheard Paula and Nadler yucking it up in his office. A month after that I got stuck in the elevator with another pom-pom and she said, snickering into her collar, "How's the article going, Harry? Has it run yet?"

The worst thing I've done, though, has to be selling books. This is a dire no-no in the publishing industry. It's simple and easy. No fuss no muss. It goes like this: Let's say you just pubbed a new Crichton, or Grisham, or whatever, and it's moving thousands of units a day. You go get yourself a review order slip, write 50 in the quantity column, put your address in the ship-to column, make an X in the expedite box, forge Hector's signature at the bottom, and take it to the bookroom. Before you know it you have fifty hardback copies of the latest mover sitting in your kitchen, new and shiny. Then you set your alarm for 6:30 so you can get to the Strand before anyone you know from the office might show up and you sell all of those hardcover beauties retailing for $29.50 at $12.00 a pop. Boom. Now *that* math I can bear to contemplate: six hundred bucks.

The first shovelful toward digging yourself out of your deep hole of debt.

Aside from the inherent ethical questionableness of the act, the reason this is so bad is that it undermines the entire business of book publishing. Every book that the publisher gives away is many books that don't get sold. It's the pass-around problem, and it's especially bad for the big 6 x 9 hardcovers. Someone buys the book and has a friend who wants to read it but—Hey!

What the hell! It cost twenty-five bucks!—they don't see why their friend should have to buy a new one. So it gets passed around. That six hundred dollars for you turns into thousands of lost dollars for the house. Also, if it's a sleeper and not enough copies were printed in the first run, the warehouse can have problems shipping them in time to get them on the shelves while your order, because of that X in the expedite column, gets priority. That means sometimes you're selling your fifty cool copies to the Strand while the guy at the B & N information desk is trying to soothe old ladies shaking canes for the most recent installment of the charming British veterinarian with a store of trite country wisdom and a knack for resurrection.

This is a big deal to publishers. It's the same reason that they pulp surplus copies instead of giving them to schools or prisons or hospitals or whatever. They just can't stand the idea of free books. I tried to joke with Nadler about this once when I first got to Prestige, back when I thought we could be friends. I said something about its being like the Fourth Reich. He told me to get back to work.

Work is freedom.

Is it funny or stupid?

I don't know.

Is it right?

Almost. In the Fourth Reich it really goes like this:

Promotion is freedom. Money is freedom.

I came to this realization at the beginning of my third year, when Evie was about to show up. It came to me that night of the Westminster dog show, at Mitchell Lowengrab's pied-à-terre, while sitting on his toilet, stuffing yeast egg rolls from his buffet into my Ziplocs and hating the ever-living shit out of Cassie.

*   *   *

Cassie had spent most of the night crossing and uncrossing her legs at Mitchell Lowengrab while I tried feebly to regain her attention. What had happened to my date? It was like she had been knocked silly, brained by all that silk and all those shiny surfaces. I made a few attempts to get back in the discussion (the only thing worse than laughing at someone's insipid jokes is not being noticed laughing at someone's insipid jokes) but nothing worked. Lowengrab's crowd was an alien species of upper class. I came from an affluent family, but this was like nothing I'd seen before. They were serious money. No matter how I angled, I couldn't find a point of entry. I felt like I had been dropped among a gang of dangerous, sophisticated gorillas and my only hope of not becoming banana mash smear was to learn their language—convince them that I was one of them, Dian Fossey style.

But I just couldn't. All the words—the same vowels, the same consonants, I kept telling myself—sounded wrong and indecipherable. "Ugga bugga," I wanted to say. "No! No! I meant Bugga bugguga! Seriously, guys: bugga bugguga! Bugga bugguga already!"

Simultaneously reviling them and longing to be accepted by them (a feeling I thought I had left behind in high school), I'd gone to the bathroom to regain my equilibrium. I sat on the toilet and thought: how did Mitchell Lowengrab get all this *stuff*? How did he gain access to the Free Masonic world of the rich and well apartmented? Why does he have so many friends? Five years ago we were the same. I met him on my hall freshman year, in the all-boys dorm. We frequented the same dining hall. We both dated cross-country runners. We were both English majors. He passed his comps. I passed mine with honors, for God's sake.

What happened?

How is it that now he's giving me that high-octane, date-stealing grin and living on the twenty-second floor of a full-service, doorman building on Park fucking Avenue? How is it that his kitchen is full of German knives and bread machines and copper pots? Why does he have that monolithic Bang & Olufsen stereo? And is that a Giacometti standing in the foyer? No, probably it's a fake. Please tell me it's a fake.

Who am I kidding? It's not a fake. This guy has got money ebola: he's bleeding it out of eyeball and asshole.

How can I catch it? Please, please let me catch it.

Cassie was gone; I had to admit that. But the pain I was feeling, I honestly knew, wasn't due to her loss. She was a fundamentally silly girl—she thought pancakes and hotcakes were entirely different foods and refused to eat pancakes under any circumstances; once she almost vomited in Odessa when I told her that they had substituted pancakes for hotcakes—and I didn't enjoy our social time together that much.

So why did I feel like I had just been sucker-punched by certain gorillas?

Because his apartment had Giacomettis and mine had fruit flies. Because I walk forty-six blocks to work every day even if it's raining and he takes a climate-controlled Lincoln. Because he is in his living room cavalierly annexing my girlfriend and I am on his toilet stuffing his egg rolls into my Ziplocs. Because he is winning at the big game that for twenty-five years I refused to believe existed while I am losing losing losing.

Why else?

It was then that I had the vision. Spreading out before me in vivid Technicolor detail was My Life, and I couldn't believe it. I forced myself to say it: I am almost twenty-six years old. (Twenty-six!) I'm in a go-nowhere job with a boss who is constantly out to make me look stupid. Instead of relationships I've had a long string of fatuous Dates and tawdry moments on fire escapes and in bathroom stalls and taxis. All too often I drink myself to sleep while watching *Mannequin*. At least one meal a day is constituted primarily of stolen condiments. I cohabit with fruit flies and a jingle-maker possibly given to violence. The rashes in my armpits get so bad I have to walk like a scarecrow everywhere I go. It's possible my gums are receding. I'm starving yet pudge is beginning to hang over my belt. How does that work? Can someone explain that to me, please? How you can be twenty pounds underweight and still need to buy new pants because the pudge is seeping over your belt like biscuit dough pushing out of its tin?

QUESTION: Where were my twenties going?

ANSWER: Nowhere. It's like they were stillborn. They just never got going. I have almost no memories of them. I feel like my whole life—all almost-twenty-six years—has been in abeyance, like it's been waiting to be told: There you go. Go get it.

But there was nothing to go get.

What did Gawain do before Arthur sent him on noble quests in strange lands? Sharpen his sword? Sit around watching *The View*?

Why am I like this? All of my friends are married and living in real apartments and building careers and working on making the memories that will sustain them in old age. But not me. I'm cruising through my twenties, accumulating nothing, building nothing, accomplishing nothing. Such a waste.

Am I feeling sorry for myself? Maybe I am. But it isn't supposed to be like this. I'm sure of it. Aren't you supposed to improve with age? Isn't that kind of the point? I remember I used to think that when I grew up I would be sort of a less disgusting Lowengrab: killer apartment, lots of friends, respect of my colleagues, legitimate invitations to parties. But I didn't turn into that person.

I turned into banana mash smear.

I am in danger of turning into Slo-Mo.

When I finally slunk out of the bathroom, Mitchell was administering the famous Grab to my former girlfriend and I was drunkenly limping shitboxward, my heart pumping pure jealousy.

After my periscopic look at the world of the solvent and happy, I became mad with desire. I'm not embarrassed to admit it: I wanted *everything*. I wanted a Manhattan chair from the Door Store. I wanted a full set of stoneware dinner plates and bowls and mugs from Fish's Eddy. I wanted tatami rugs from ABC. I wanted a killer blue lowrider sofabed with white trim and fringe along the bottom from Jennifer Convertibles. I wanted a Krups coffeemaker with a timer. I wanted a whole set of those cool copper pots and pans and a Good Grips lemon zester and a garlic roller and a new gas-powered stainless-steel Viking stove. I wanted flowerpots and cookbooks and soft quilted toilet paper and soft towels and white curtains and soft 300-count Egyptian cotton sheets.

And finials: Jesus. Don't even get me started on finials.

You know what, though? It took me almost a whole year to realize this, but: these things weren't what I really wanted. There's a joke at Prestige that *The New Yorker* will publish any story that ends with the word "home." That, I finally had to admit after many long nights of perusing magazines and staring through windows and whispering to silverware, is what I really, really wanted.

I wanted a home.

I attended three different colleges. I've lived in nine different shitboxes over the last five years. Even as a kid I didn't feel like I had a real home. Our house was a knotty little wonderland of pressure and silences. Never had I said to myself, after a hard day's work when I was exhausted and irritated and in need of some comfort, Ah, time to go home. I've always said, Shit, guess I've got to go there sooner or later.

I want a home. Say it to yourself enough and you will understand how powerfully totemic the word is: home, home, home.

And I'm not talking some wacked-out hit-the-lottery/Robin Leach/Xanadu wet dream, either. All I'm talking is a 600-square-foot, well-lighted, hardwood-floored space to which I can retreat. I want to cook my own dinners. I want to be fruit fly–free. I want to sleep without dreams of anally electrocuting innocent people. I want to feel like a person, not banana mash smear on the heels of certain gorillas.

In other words: I want to *begin*, already.

QUESTION: Why did it take me so long to realize what I really wanted?

ANSWER: I hadn't yet met Evie Goddard. I hadn't yet felt what a home could be.

Problem is, by this time I had this epiphany I'd been on a long streak of getting 4s and 5s on my performance reviews at work. ("Harry does not follow directions or demonstrate initiative. He is not punctual. He is not a team player. He does not play well with others. He is often drunk at the office. He cannot locate desk. Etc.") So promotion was out of the question. As was the money necessary for the down payment, which raises another very important

QUESTION: How can I preserve my career and get together

enough money for the down payment so that I may live happily and with dignity in a home with the woman I love?

ANSWER: Judith.

girls girls girls

I don't deny it. It's true: my nights used to be full of women. They were like a terra-cotta army—different features, different figures, assuming different positions, but all virtually indistinguishable.

When I met Evie I was still so used to sliding from one bed to another that it took me a while to quit. Ergo Evie's attitude about Dates. Since I'm being honest about everything, I suppose I should include here a representative sample of some of the Dates and the reason for their heave-hoing.

MELANIE (took fortune cookies seriously)

SALLY (thought *travesty* was an extra bad *tragedy*)

KAREN/SHARON (what was name?)

DEBBIE (didn't understand Green Lantern, said was metaphor for xenophobia; "Invulnerable to everything but yellow? Get it?")

VICKI (only dated her in first place because liked her family; was using her for her parents)

VICKI II (thought VIVA LA EVIE lamp was stupid)

NELLIE (gurgled)

BETSY (shuffled)

VICKI III (baked)

WHITNEY (a psychology Ph.D. candidate who thought I was "shallow, rude, lazy, condescending, antagonistic, petty, predatory, a penis Nazi, an aesthetic snob, a black hole of selfishness, a distraction, a botched experiment in optimism on her part, a perpetual rookie of life, a commercial break, an in-between meal snack that did nothing but spoil the appetite, a sad case of squandered talent and abandoned dreams, a cheat, a liar, a moral subidiot with antisocial/borderline/narcissistic tendencies, a ruined almost-man whose chance at adulthood was obliterated by loneliness and whose soul was thoroughly corrupted by insecurities and paranoia and childhood deficits and obsessions and neuroses and who was stupidly, tragically possessed of exclusively the wrong ideas about the world and his place in it.")

The funny thing is that all of these extracurriculars were about as satisfying as melba toast. And I knew they would be going in. No electrons leapt off my skin when I touched them. I never thought of giving them Rapunzel treats. I never longed to see them at my cubicle. In fact, I rarely even wanted to see them outside of my bedroom. Typically they would just come over to my place and we'd watch a rental.

Film and fuck, that was the routine.

I always hear Keeno's voice in my head asking the same question: if you know it isn't worth it, why all the sliding, Señor Swank?

It's a good question. Because I have the unalterable Mendelian neural hardwiring for infidelity? Because it is an evolutionary imperative to broadcast as much sperm as possible? Because men cannot tolerate the foreclosure of other opportunities and have to prove on a regular basis that they are not subject to it? Because in a city of relentless hardship and poverty, and in a job that daily diminishes me, the ability to seduce a woman is one of the few ways I can achieve? Because my father had his own practice (Gorilla, Gorilla & Gorilla) by the time he was thirty-two, pulled himself up by his bootstraps (whatever those are) and expects me to achieve in the same professional vein (which I haven't), and because the best substitute I can think of is to call up my father, saying, "Yeah, dating a new girl, a lawyer/ballet dancer/advertising exec named Millie/Jeanie/Shelly?" Because if I get involved with a rich woman I can enjoy luxuries like dining out that I otherwise cannot afford? Because love is too impenetrably complicated to figure out? Force of habit? Boredom? Because I am a child? Because New York City is like fucking Sex Disney?

In the case of the above Dates, I just don't know. But with Judith it was simple: accidental opportunism.

Don't laugh, but I teach ballroom dancing. When I was a kid my mother thought I was too frail to play boy sports. (I wasn't. Seriously. I'm not kidding.) So she signed me up at Arthur Murray. While other kids were out playing rowdy contact sports in the mud and rain while adjusting jockstraps and spitting and cracking dirty jokes about female anatomy that they didn't understand,

I was practicing my Cuban motion and my rise and fall and how to say things like "Shall we?" without sounding ridiculous. Eventually my mother let me quit, but when I arrived in New York, fresh out of college, I discovered how lucky I was to have had that experience.

Like most other assistants, I had to work a night job. When my various harebrained schemes to make money failed in their various extravagant ways, I realized I had to get a regular, steady night job. Quite by accident I discovered how rife New York was with ballroom dancing schools. I joined up at Dancesport (six dollars an hour) and taught for six months before I quit to freelance at a spot on the West Side across the street from the old Studio 54 (eighty dollars an hour minus ten dollars floor charge). It wasn't a bad gig. It was the same as teaching ballroom everywhere: you had to suffer in couvade all manner of insulting overtures—you were part dance teacher, part well-mannered gigolo—but at least I was starting to get out of debt.

I began looking through catalogues for finials.

Judith signed up because she wanted to learn fox-trot for a friend's wedding. I didn't think much of it. She is attractive, yes. She has the sleekness of a gazelle and the attitude of an adrenalized pachyderm but with an Achilles heart tucked away somewhere in her Donna Karan blouse. She's the same successful single middle-aged New York career woman I've taught to dance a hundred different times: She wears Manolo Blahniks and makes sure she has the legs for it. Maitre d's at the Four Seasons and Gramercy Tavern bow and scrape. She goes out with the boys and throws back the same martinis, tops their dirty jokes, waves good-bye to the crowd grandly—so devoted, they think; look at her go back to work when it's ten-thirty; so together; how game she is. Then Judith takes a cab uptown, crying decorously because while she was buying drinks and batting meticulously curled eyelashes they were all looking beyond her at the twenty-two-year-old cocktail waitress whose robust boobs were nuzzling the beer bottles on her tray.

Then she tells herself to stop it. She doesn't want those men anyway. They're cretins really. Would she really want one of them as a husband? She would not. What she really wants is a little *attention*. She's devoted her life thus far to her career but she's still got so much to give. Where are the takers? Why are all the men of her rank and age picking mates the way you pick out appetizers from a menu while her plate stares back at her, cold and empty? She has a heartbreaking moment in which she realizes that for all her work, for all her sacrifice, all she's got to show for it is a cushy office and the perfunctory respect of her sickeningly vivacious assistant, who (she is almost certain) gets more attention from the CEO than she does when he comes around to deliver those reports. And why (she reluctantly thinks) is the CEO coming by in person, anyway? Doesn't he have an assistant? And why (here she reddens) is he always dropping said reports at the feet of her cantilevered, camisoled assistant?

Well, let them have each other, she thinks. But who will I have? What about me? I deserve someone, too, don't I? Don't I deserve to be held when I fall asleep? To nudge at funny parts in movies? Someone to bring me juice and lozenges when I'm sick?

Then she feels ashamed of being jealous of something she really doesn't want anyway. But it doesn't help the loneliness. And as she sits there idling on the corner, waiting for the light to change, she'll see couples locked in embraces so ardent that it's hard to tell where one of them ends and the other begins, and she will start crying all over again.

One day she gets a call from her girlfriend who tells her about this ballroom dancing class she's taking. Men in black pants and Cuban heels. Men with rhythm and minty-fresh breath. Men who, for eighty dollars an hour, will waltz and fox-trot and cha-cha with you across the floor while staring meaningfully into your eyes and regaling you with inane yet winning flattery.

Men who are tens of thousands of dollars in debt and sleep with fruit flies and are looking for a way out. Any way out.

In the beginning it was easy. Judith wanted to learn fox-trot and swing so she could get through the wedding. She had a lesson twice a week for three weeks before the ceremony, then signed on for six more months of lessons. She wanted to learn cha-cha and rumba so she could go to Copa and Latin Quarter. One lesson a week with occasional nights out at Swing 46 or Louisiana Bar and Grill or Birdland with dinner and drinks and chit-chat across a candlelit table and a cozy cab ride home—attention.

It was fine. Textbook. And totally sexless. But things got complicated when I found out who she was.

Judith Krugman. Of Krug Books.

Judith, it turned out, is one of the few editors in the business who has her own imprint. That means that instead of Doubleday or Random House on the spine of a book you see her name and her little Krug bottle colophon. I didn't put Krugman and Krug Books together because she introduced herself as Judy and—as I know Evie's friend Madeleine would take great pleasure in aver-ring—because I am not really in the publishing loop the way I should be. Anyway, having your own imprint is a very big deal. There are maybe three or four people in the entire business who have their own imprint. All the decisions at Krug—from who gets signed to what paper stock is used—are exclusively Judith's. It's a lot like running your own principality. She is therefore one of the very most powerful women in publishing and able to pull strings and call in favors and invoke histories in a way that you can't imagine. She started in publishing as the assistant to the guy who invented the paperback industry as we know it; she is best buds with the überagent we call Georgie Porgie because he makes all the editors cry when he screams at them on the phone; she went to Radcliffe with the woman who runs the *New York Times Book Review*. Et cetera et cetera. True, Judith is kind of a schlock-jock—most of her books have titles like *Forbidden Love* and *Saintly Sinner* and *Forgive Me, Mother*—but still, she is a true Brahmin.

And when you're as junior varsity as I am—and as perilously close to getting fired as I am—that's a connection too valuable to pass up.

I discovered her real identity one night out at Louisiana Bar and Grill. We had been lindying to the Flip Fedoras and were sweaty and drunk. Someone at the bar was reading a book titled *When the Husband's Away* and Judith said, "What a miracle."

"What?" I said.

"Someone bought that book. I specifically said the jacket should be glossy and I got matte, but it had already been printed and it's just a midlist book, so it wasn't worth the trouble. But what a stupid mistake. I mean, really, look at that cleavage. It looks like scratch-'n'-sniff. Who wants to buy a book with scratch-'n'-sniff cleavage?"

Then it hit me: Krug on her books, Krugman on her personal checks.

Judith Krugman used to be married to Morton Chenowith,

CEO of Prestige and Hector's only boss. Together Judith and Morton made Prestige a leader in both hard- and softcover publishing, Judith with her blockbusting mass market romance titles and Morton with his shrewd acquisition of literary talent. Prestige became hot because Judith's romance novels produced so much income that they could publish all the award-winners they wanted, which in turn attracted more best-selling authors. The big sellers, of course, were willing to go to Prestige for less because they felt better about themselves in the company of last year's National Book Award winner or the current Poet Laureate, and the literary authors went there because Morton could always offer the biggest advance—a self-perpetuating cycle. Under their guidance Prestige became one of the largest, most profitable publishers in the world. After ten years they divorced, Morton remaining at Prestige and Judith going on to found Krug Books, but they are still very close, a real power semicouple nonpareil.

If Morton is looking to fill that vacant office next to Nadler's, I realized that night at Louisiana Bar and Grill, no doubt he will be consulting Judith.

Finials loomed brightly in my imagination. I saw blond hardwood floors and bay windows and coffeemakers. I saw Evie in clean sheets, reclining like a starlet in a claw-footed bathtub. I saw my name on that plaque:

HARRY DRISCOLL
EDITOR

But I didn't make the decision until later that night. I was walking her to her apartment and, leaning heavily on my shoulder, she asked me what I thought was erotic and I, kidding around, told her when a woman buys a male porno. She marched up to a newsstand guy and said in a theatrical falsetto, "Excuse me, but do you have a copy of *Inches*?" and walked back to me pressing her lips to one of the photos.

"Like this?" she said.

In that moment I had a vivid neural flash: if I want to get out of this life I can either 1) hope that Nadler is eaten by a sewer crocodile and I inherit all of his books, or 2) wait for the publishing fairy to tap me with her promotion wand, or 3) become Harry Gurley Brown.

On the one hand, yes, fine, it's wrong. On the other hand, it's nothing I haven't done before, and this time it could very well save my career and promote my life with Evie. It's just one more teensy little time.

In a way I'm doing it *for* Evie, aren't I?

This is how I made the decision:

I remember the stars knocking around the sky like lottery balls. I remember the heat of the liquor on her breath and the way the loose skin on her turned neck looked like a furled sail. I remember the pressure of the moment in my ears like radio static and the lights from her lobby glowing invitationally. I remember the rain on the awning overhead sounding like meat cooking in a skillet. I thought what Slo-Mo would have done if he had the chance. I thought about Laura Dingle, teaching prep school in Jersey, staring bitterly at Prestige books in the stores, thinking it should be her name in the acknowledgments, not Nadler's.

I thought about banana mash smear and dangerous and sophisticated gorillas.

And what did I do?

I fucked her. Oh yes I did. I fucked her forthwith. I fucked her *vigoroso*. I fucked her into a low orbit, in her doorway, with her keys still dangling in the lock, with her purse still on her shoulder, with her cook in the kitchen making flan listening to "My Favorite Things" on repeat.

Afterward we had flan and stingers (it must have been good brandy; I didn't recognize the name) and then I fucked her again for good measure, in her bedroom this time, pleasurelessly, with a miasmic headache as the stingers wore off. The next morning I was in such a hurry to leave—despite my rationalization I couldn't get the image of Hogarth's *The Rake's Progress* out of my sledgehammered head—that I forgot my boxers behind the potted plant in her bathroom. (I still haven't gotten them back. I miss them. They had a picture of the Muppet character Animal with a caption that read ANIMAL WANT WOMAN.)

I rode home in a cab that morning, early, hurtling from Judith's Upper East Side apartment down Second Avenue to the Village. At that hour it was a dirty ghost-town city and the taxi sped along, hitting all the greens, the buildings blurring past me in the curdled morning fog. It was hard to tell the buildings apart. Bars, delis, diners, shoe repair places, newsstands, they all looked like the same thing. We finally stopped at a corner where a dead pigeon—ugly in life, beautiful in death—was lying on its back, its rigor-mortistically upturned legs like twin question marks. Behind it was a restaurant called Global 33. It reminded me of something Evie had said to me a few months before. "Tell me, what's it like being the sole occupant of Planet Me?"

I didn't have an answer when she asked me, but I had an answer that morning: painful. It was like every bad thing that's happened to me since the age of five happening all over again at the same time.

are you available? or, the bushido of the shitbag

Our routine now is this: Judith calls me up (Harry's Attention Service, open twenty-four/seven) and says, simply, "Are you available?"

Three words: the ready-aim-fire of self-hatred. I have nightmares about *Are you available?* When I'm old and have a weak heart you could probably kill me by sneaking up behind me and saying *Are you available?*

Probably you'd be doing me a favor.

After the Hello and the Are You Available and the Yes we hang up without nicety and I take a cab to her apartment, where I will be reimbursed for travel expenses and fucked summarily.

(CORRECTION: In theory I will be fucked. More on that excruciating state of affairs later.)

Then as I'm lying there in her bed, the postcoital stupefaction receding as self-awareness surfaces painfully, I realize that my arms are curled around Judith in the same manner that they curl around Evie and I am disgusted with myself again. I feel an eviscerating and fraudulent redundancy. I should at least lace my arms around Judith in a different way, shouldn't I? But there are only so many ways to hold a woman after sex, and I can't avoid the overlap. This moment in Judith's bed is bad, but it's worse when I'm in Evie's bed, stroking her back and looking at the way her spine pushing through her skin looks like a garden hose wrapped in pink paper, and I'm suddenly reminded that I was massaging Judith's back the same way eighteen hours ago.

It's a good way to demean three people at once. Very efficient, you'll agree.

In fairness to myself I should say that there are some minute but important differences. Yes, I spoon Judith, but it's different. With Evie I sleep with my mouth in the synclines of a vertebra, my pelvis articulating with hers, our bodies moving through sleep in sinuous togetherness like a pair of sea snakes. Yes, I spoon Judith, too, but my body resists it. My arms encircle her stiffly and with reluctance, the way you might hug a Christmas tree. And in the morning we're always disengaged.

But the guilt is the same, and so is the lesson: you can't think about what you're doing. Ever. Read books, watch rentals, obliterate your awareness with Pabst, daydream about finials, volunteer to read books to terminal kids at hospitals—whatever it takes. Do anything, in other words, to avoid thinking about yourself.

I explained this theory to Keeno once, when we were basking in the hemorrhoidal glow of my apartment. "You know what that is?" Keeno said. "That, my slider friend, is the Bushido of the shitbag."

persistence of poe

You want to know the worst thing about Date? Besides the actual fucking and lying, I mean?

The VIVA LA EVIE lamp.

I'm serious. The lamp makes things very hard on me. It's giving me an ulcer, if you want to know the truth. I mean, here I am carrying on with Date—sometimes I can't stand to say the name Judith—while lying to Evie, a woman who loves me and underwent a dangerous operation just so she could express that love in the best, most primitive way, despite a lifetime of fearing sex. And then I come home to my empty orange bedroom, sometimes with Judith's smell still on my fingers and in my hair, and the words "Viva la Evie" are spread out over my wall.

Sometimes I can't decide if I love that lamp or hate it.

That lamp is like the instantiation of my conscience. Some nights I can't sleep without it on. Others I have to put it in the closet and lock the door. It's like something out of a Poe story. "The Tell-Tale Lamp Shade" or something.

You know the kind of story I'm talking about. The kind where the protagonist is subject to dire physical peril—maybe torture—all the while desperately asking himself, *Am I crazy or just lonely?*

logomachy

The bad thing about my cubicle: it's ten feet from Nadler's office.

The good thing about my cubicle: it's also ten feet from Hector's kitchenette.

Tonight after everyone's gone I sneak the key from under one of Nadler's plants. I don't know why, but Nadler is obsessed with plants. It doesn't seem to fit his personality. A more logical hobby would be kiddie porn (this is just an educated guess here, but you don't want to bet against it, do you?) or tape recorders and secret cameras (so he could get the dirt on everyone and therefore Dingle more effectively) or torture chamber devices (self-explanatory). But no, he collects plants. He's got all sorts: green leafy ones, bright flowery ones, cactusy ones. It's a regular Yosemite in his office.

And he's a sick little plantman, too. He treats those plants better than he does people. He coos to them in this eerie sibilant voice ("Who's my best cactus-wactus? Who's my good guy?"). He sprays their leaves with this chemical and wipes them down with a chamois. Last fall when he went out of town for a week he hired a plant-sitter because he didn't trust me to water them while he was gone. Another time one of the cleaning people moved some of the pots around one night so that they could vacuum behind them and failed to put them back in exactly the same places they had been. Nadler didn't say anything to her—

that's not his style; he's got a J. Edgar Hoover sense of vengeance—but after the woman put them back in the right places and apologized, I heard him on the phone with her boss, telling him that he discovered her snooping through his files one night and that he is missing seventy-something dollars from his desk. I'm not sure what happened to her, but since that day I haven't seen her working on this—or any other—floor.

QUESTION: Is Nadler's affection for flora, however deranged, not some reassuring indication of his ability to value some forms of life?

ANSWER: No. He is just a sick little plantman.

But one of his plants does conceal the key to Hector's kitchenette, and for that I am always, always grateful.

If I were a winner of one of those contests where you are given ninety seconds to stuff your grocery cart with whatever you want, I'd choose all the things that are in this kitchenette. Hector has got everything. He's got all sorts of cereal, including Captain Crunch Crunchberries. He's got crackers, cheeses, Ramen, fruit sometimes, milk, sodas, seltzer, bagels and cream cheese, all manner of teas and various cookies, including but not limited to Vienna Fingers, Hydrox (why not the real stuff?), E.L. Fudge, and Archway ginger snaps. And he has got Fruit Chewy Newtons. Holy shit does he have Fruit Chewy Newtons. He's got the Newton motherlode. He's got all the flavors and he's got many packages of each. I've got to give him credit: the English know how to snack.

Tonight, with a fresh bag of Newtons and a paper cup half-filled with Uncle Booloo's blueberry moonshine that Evie keeps in her desk, I go disport myself in the vacant office, my possible future home if things with Judith work out. Who hasn't done this? I sit in the chair, punch the buttons on the phone even though it's dead, imagine the bookshelves filled with books I've edited.

Kicking back in the chair, I survey the city outside the window. At night Prestige shuts down the air-conditioning, so it's getting hot and the rashes are starting to itch. Suppressing the urge to scratch, I let myself slide into the fantasy of being an editor. I am getting fitted for custom-made suits and am putting big-deal agents from William Morris on hold to take a call from Philip Roth, who is cataplectic with desire to blurb this first-time novelist I've discovered . . .

PHILIP ROTH: Is this Harry Driscoll?

ME: It is.

PHILIP ROTH: This is Philip Roth.

ME *(not at all kiss-assy)*: How do you do.

PHILIP ROTH: You sent me an unsolicited manuscript for blurbing purposes.

ME: Yes I did . . .

PHILIP ROTH: I don't ever do this sort of thing for editors I don't know. I don't have the time. Do I seem like the kind of person who has that sort of time? Do you know where I'd be if I read every manuscript that showed up on my doorstep?

ME: Well, I, ah . . .

PHILIP ROTH: However, Mr. Driscoll, in this instance I have made an exception. [New Writer X] is quite possibly the most important new writer I've read in years. It's a revolutionary novel that will change the way the next generation writes. I wish I had written it. And it's only taken me so long to get back to you because I want to write a blurb that is the equal of this novel and quite frankly, it isn't easy, Mr. Driscoll. *(Pause.)* You are a new editor at Prestige, correct?

ME: Yes. That's right. I've been on the job about two months.

PHILIP ROTH: And already you've found a novel like this? How do you do it, young man?

ME *(with Burt Lancasterish aploms)*: Well, Mr. Roth . . . it's my job. It's what I do.

. . . then the fantasy changes. I am not in a suit. I am not at the desk. I am not on the phone. Instead I am in front of a laptop in an otherwise empty, featureless room that is dark but for the soothing blue submarine glow of the laptop's screen. My fingers are flashing like Japanese knives on the keyboard and all the right words are stretching out in perfect lines in front of me. This is it. I am writing. This is an especially voluptuous fantasy because it is so unlike reality.

Like everybody in publishing—or every young person, at least, every person who hasn't had to endure a Nadler for ten years and therefore had their soul crushed into tiny particles of dying light like the discarded cherry of a cigarette scattering along the highway—I envision being a successful novelist. Sometimes when I'm reading the manuscripts Nadler has signed up I find myself thinking, Damn, I'm better than *this* guy. I can do this.

But of course I never can. I set aside time at night and dutifully sit in front of the computer but nothing happens. I start typing but all the words are wrong. So I stop. No reason in contributing to the shit that is accumulating in shameful piles around the world even as we speak, right? Maybe I'm not a laptop guy. Maybe I'm a longhand guy. Styron writes longhand, right? So I break out the yellow legal pad and go at it. But that doesn't work, either. Perhaps I'm not a pen guy. I might secretly have an old soul—that's it, I must use pencil. So I steal a box of pencils and an electric sharpener and try that. But no. Nothing. In about ten minutes I get lonely and distracted. (Is that an acorn there in the corner? Wow. How did that get in here?)

I figure I must be a café writer. Yes, yes, this sitting-at-home thing is all wrong. I have to go someplace without all this psychic contamination. So I go to No Bar and sit at a table in back, but it's a no go. Then it becomes clear: I am going about this the wrong way. I shouldn't just be diving into a novel. I should hone my skills by starting a journal. Exactly. I should have thought of this all along. So off I go to the Astor Place supermegadeluxe and buy myself a large sketchbook with unlined archival-quality paper and sit down right there in the store with my brand-new Pilot V-Ball, but it doesn't take long for me to see the folly of this strategy: to keep a journal you must write down the things that you do and that have happened to you that day, and as I can't stand to think about either of those things, as in fact it flies in the face of the Bushido of the shitbag, this is just about the stupidest thing I could do.

But this is what I want.

Or is this what I want?

I don't know.

Maybe I'm not supposed to be a writer. Maybe I'm not supposed to be an editor, either. Maybe I am just the kind of person who likes to imagine himself doing these wonderful things but

who lacks the courage and energy to make it happen. Maybe I
am just a common biped. The more I think about it the more it
seems like it. It seems like I always have this image of the ideal
me but it never happens. When I was a freshman in college I
made this list of goals. By the time I graduated I was going to
1) speak two foreign languages; 2) have a premed's knowledge
of the human body; 3) pick up a new sport and play it at the
varsity level; 4) know enough shit about religion and philosophy
to sound enigmatic and spiritual at cocktail parties; and 5) play
concert piano.

How much of this liberal arts wish list did I accomplish by
graduation? I could say "My name is Harry" and "I am too
drunk" in French and Spanish. I could say "endoplasmic retic-
ulum" without cracking up. I picked up croquet. I could spell
Kierkegaard. And I could hammer out a mean rendition of
"When the Saints Go Marching In." But that's all, folks.

Is this a pattern in my life? It doesn't have to be. I'm sure of
it. At least I think I'm sure of it.

Luckily I don't have time to indulge this train of thought. I'm
interrupted by Jordie Wesselesh. I see his reflection in the window behind me. Framed by the limbs of two tall exotic-looking
plants that Nadler has edging his door, Jordie looks like some
prehistoric subterranean predator come up to score some hom-
inids but really he's just up from the seventh floor, where he is
in charge of Prestige's reference section.

The troglocenes on seven usually don't make it very far beyond
their floor, but Jordie's different. He is second in command—a
full editor—in Prestige Reference, and he pretty much *is* the
Prestige New College Dictionary. He is the youngest lexicographer I have ever known (true, he's the only lexicograhper I have
ever known, but still: he's awfully young to be in charge of a

dictionary) and he is always hanging around on eleven. He is buddies with Hector and all the old-timer editors on the floor and is even outwardly respected by Nadler, although I'm sure it kills him. He often has pieces on language in *New York* magazine and shows up now and then in gossip columns. Before he got married he was always being photographed with pouty Siberian models with deep collarbones who attached themselves to him at literary glamoramas like this big-deal celebrity writer spelling bee, which he hosted, and last year's Latin Wheel of Fortune fund-raiser for AIDS research, which he won. ("I'd like to solve the puzzle. *'Nusquam tuta fides,'* or 'Nowhere is fidelity sure.' I believe that's Virgil, Pat.") And he is always very nattily dressed, often with bow ties and sometimes in stylish spectators. He does what he likes and he gets paid for it. He is respected by others and is kind. Now he is married and by all reports it is a happy marriage based on mutual affection and trust. He has about him an air of assurance and dignity and seriousness.

In other words, he is leading the life I want to lead.

I swivel around in the chair and we stare each other down wordlessly. After a long, squinty, gunfightery pause he fires one off:

"Corvée," he says.

"The unpaid labor that a feudal vassal owes his lord," I fire back. He's not going to get me with one like that, one from the early part of the dictionary and that reminds me of life at Prestige. "Nepenthe," I say grandly, thinking ha ha ha, I got you now, Jordie Wesselesh.

This is our game: logomachy. A dispute over words. We play for a dollar a word and the victor always writes the winning word and definition on the dollar. Jordie has a lot of my money, alas.

But I have some of his, too. I am a little ashamed of this, but it is so hard to catch Jordie at any words that sometimes I take some liberties: I make them up. Last week this Don Kinging of mine produced "protemplorate," which I said means "to accomplish meaningful work in spare hours that is made possible by enduring meaningless work." For example, a man works six days a week on the late-night shift at Denny's or buffing floors after hours at the public school or as a part-time bus driver so that he can spend every morning until noon painting or writing poetry or making Reloc-art pieces. During those hours when he is not sleeping or working his money job he is protemplorating. He is engaging in protemploration. (Before Keeno's "NYC, Stalled" she protemplorated a lot; now that she doesn't have to work a regular job to support her art she just works. I *should* be protemplorating.) Jordie protested, of course, but I bluffed it out and he hasn't bothered to check it in the OED, as far as I know.

At least he hasn't asked for his dollar back.

Jordie isn't stumped on nepenthe. "A potion used by the ancients believed to induce forgetfulness or freedom from pain." Damnation. This was one of my best hopes. I came across this one a few months ago and it stuck with me because of what I am doing with Judith. I have always been a drinker but nowadays drinking has taken on this aspect for me: it numbs my interactions with Judith and blurs my memory of it. It isn't pleasure. It's an analgesic and amnesic at once.

"Misoneism," he says.

"Intense hatred or fear of change." I always confuse this one with misology, "hatred or fear of reason or enlightenment." They come right next to each other in Merriam-Webster's. But Jordie nods. Phew. Lucky. "Philoprogeneration," I say.

His face contracts in thought. I might have him here. But then he says, "The act of producing? And approving of what you produce? Liking what you produce?"

I can't tell if he really knew the answer or if he just pieced it together but of course he's right. This one has been in my mind because I have only recently completed the P section of the dictionary but also because it made me think about my parents and the way my father's face fell apart when I told him—after acing the LSAT and being accepted by his own law school by its president, his old friend—that I wasn't going to law school after all. Then or ever. When you have my kind of family history you will never forget a word like that.

"Pretermit," he says. Shit. Shit shit shit. I don't know this one. It's not exotic, that's part of the problem. If a word looks too ordinary in the dictionary I can pass it by. It doesn't seem worth my time. That's why I have to look up "discreet" and "discrete" every time I use them but I know these other words no problem. (Another example: "telesis." This is another Judith-inspired word. It means "attainment of desired ends by application of planned, intelligent human effort." I like to think of my sliding with her as telesis rather than as a despicable betrayal. It doesn't help much but every little self-deception counts.)

"A phase or period directly before the end, the termination?" I guess.

"Negative. 'To leave undone, to neglect.' "

"Blast." I extract a dollar from my pocket and write

PRETERMIT: to leave undone, to neglect

on it and hand it over to Jordie. I smile in comradely good cheer, as if it isn't one of the last eight dollars I have in my pocket until next payday.

"How's things, anyway, Harry? That troublesome manuscript ever turn up?"

"That what? Oh, the marathon calendar thing? Oh yeah. Sure. Of course." How many people know about this? Outside of Evie, Jordie is the closest thing I've got to a friend at Prestige, but I don't remember telling him about the lost manuscript.

"That's good. So . . ."

Jordie looks around uncomfortably. I pick invisible lint off my shirt. This is the way it is with me and all my male friends—if we're not openly competing things get awkward. The first words out of my best friend's mouth when we met each other as room-mates freshman year: "I will run down the hall to the bathroom, brush my teeth, floss, gargle mouthwash, take out my contacts, and wash my face before you are done brushing your teeth. See ya!" Then Toby raced off down the hall. It was the beginning of a fine friendship.

"Testing out the new desk, huh?" Jordie says at last.

"Yeah," I reply, thinking, Say something, idiot. You're not this dull. You're not. "Ha ha." Oh yes. That helped.

"Word is they might actually promote from within, if you can believe that." This *is* hard to believe. I know of one pom-pom who made an almost lateral jump to editorial, but otherwise— with the exception of Nadler and his brilliant Dingling, of course—no one from within Prestige has been promoted to a meaningful editorial position in our own house.

"For real?" I say.

"That's the Cronkite." I almost laugh at this. Because Jordie is so upright, so dignified—oracular—I always forget that he is a student of all language, including subcultures like hip-hop. Whenever he comes out with an expression—like "Cronkite" for "news"—it makes me want to crack up.

"That's nuts," I say. "Any idea who it might be?"

"Not much help on that one, Harry. Could be anyone, I suppose."

"You?" I ask, trying to sound indifferent. If Jordie wanted this position no one else would stand a chance.

"I don't think so. I've been looking into some other things."

I know what he is talking about. Jordie doesn't confide in me about such things. No one does. But people talk to Evie. She has this magical force of extraction. She doesn't even do anything crafty. She just sits there and people spill everything. And Evie, of course, talks to me. Apparently Jordie has been courted by some Internet company that wants to start an on-line literary magazine and he would be one of their featured writers. This is another fantasy of publishing: put in some painful years in the industry, make a name for yourself in certain important quarters, then get the call from another industry—film, TV, Internet— that needs some brain cred, and hit the big bucks. I can't think of anyone more likely to turn into this kind of success than Jordie, and it makes me hate him a little bit.

"That's great, Jordie. Power to the people," I say, schooling the sarcasm out of my voice. "Doing what, exactly?"

Don't say Internet shit. Don't say Internet shit. Don't say Internet shit.

"Something with the Internet, maybe. I don't know. It's just exploratory surgery right now."

"Ah," I say. I am going to cut off all your fingers with garden clippers and feed them to your dogs. "That's cool. That's cool. Well, good luck with that."

"Thanks. What about you? You've been here for a while. You must have thought about something other than Prestige now and then."

Like volunteering for medical experiments in third world countries? Yes. Yes I have.

"Nah. I like it here. I figure I've got a good shot at this office right here."

"Oh. Well sure. Absolutely," he says, with manufactured sincerity. "But—I don't know, Harry—this job just seems like it doesn't make use of your talents, really." I'm all ears. I haven't heard the imputation of talents in a long time. "It always seemed to me that you were better suited for . . ."

"For what?"

"I don't know. Something else, though." For a moment it's hard to tell if this is an insult or not. I've spent all these years at Prestige but it's not the right thing for me? That's not exactly flattery, is it? In fact, in a certain light it looks like I have wasted a lot of time.

"Like what kind of something else?" Maybe I could be your asssitant, Jordie. Even though we're only separated by a few years I still would be a lot happier working for you than Nadler. We could sit around the office together, engaging in lively logomachy, typing it up and sending it out on the Internet as work. We could go to literary parties together. I would stop being mistaken for a waiter because I'd be with Jordie Wesselesh. We would become a force, a tandem. Maybe we could even have matching outfits, like a uniform, something jumpsuity, maybe something with epaulettes and patches on the sleeve.

SOCIALITE ONE: Are we forgetting anyone? Who else should we invite?

SOCIALITE TWO: What about that delightful Internet dictionary person?

SOCIALITE ONE: Oh. You mean the one with Harry some-body. Jordie, I believe. Yes. Jordie Wesselesh. And Harry . . . Driscoll.

SOCIALITE TWO: Precisely. We *must* invite those two. They're so . . .

SOCIALITE ONE: Oscar Wildey? Noël Cowardy? Errol Flynny?

SOCIALITE TWO: Precisely. No party is complete without those two brilliant men. Invite them immediately.

SOCIALITE TWO: Should we invite Tyra or Helena for that Harry person? I know Jordie is married but I understand that Harry is single. Perhaps we should make arrange-ments. Is Linda available?

SOCIALITE ONE: Oh dear no. Harry Driscoll has a long-standing relationship with a young woman named Evie Goddard, an important editor at Prestige. They are one of New York's most divine couples. We simply must see that she can attend, also. [This is an interesting subject. I've often wondered how I would respond if Evie were to be advanced over me. What would I do, for example, if she were to be the one who got promoted to this office? Prob-ably the same thing I would do if anyone except me got this promotion: something involving great indignity and ex-cess.]

SOCIALITE TWO: Our little event is looking brighter all the time, isn't it?

SOCIALITE ONE: The stars certainly are coming out, aren't they?

Also, you really know your words, Jordie. Nadler doesn't even know that. It's hard enough to work for a sick little plantman, but when you don't respect him it makes it even tougher. For example: Nadler's flap copy. I don't know how you can spend over a decade in book publishing and not learn how to knock out a few paragraphs promoting a new book but Nadler cannot do it to save his life. In place of sentences he has picked up a list of publishing clichés that he arranges and rearranges for every book like a toddler playing with letter blocks. Everything is always a "tour de force" or "an important new voice" or "devastating yet beautiful in its scope and range."

Oh, and also "dazzling." This is his favorite. "Dazzling" has appeared on every single piece of flap copy Nadler has written every single year I have worked with him. Probably he'll find a way to work "dazzling" into the flap copy of my marathoner's logbook. If the manuscript ever turns up, that is.

"I don't know, Harry. Something more fast-paced, maybe. Something that makes use of your . . . creativity . . . a little more. Magazines, maybe. I know you can write—I've seen your flap copy. Why not write for the soaps for a year or two? It's not art, but you could get some money, figure out where you really want to go. Did you know I used to work for a travel agency?"

This is so ludicrous I almost laugh out loud.

"No. I didn't."

"Well, I am embarassed to say that I did. When I graduated with a degree in linguistics I sort of panicked. I took a job that my uncle offered me and I did it without enthusiasm for almost two years before I took a chance on working as a lexicographer. But thank God I did."

"Ah. Good point," I say stupidly. "I'll think about that."

"You think I'm being avuncular and simple? Hmm. Maybe I

am. Maybe you don't need my advice. Fair enough. But believe me, Harry, there is nothing worse than doing what you don't want to do, day after day, to little remuneration or applause. It's the death of your soul, Harry."

What can I say to this?

"Oh," Jordie says before he turns to go. "Here's another one for you: overslaugh."

I know this one. It means "to pass over for a promotion."

What the hell is that supposed to mean? Is this Jordie's idea of a joke? Or some stygian pronouncement? Double, double toil and overslaugh? The hell?

After a long moment of consideration I choose to think of it as a big-brotherly barb—evidence of our chumminess. Yes. A verbal noogie. Ha ha. That Jordie. He kills me. What a jester.

protemploration

After my run-in with Jordie I am fired up about writing: I need to make use of my talents. That's right, he said "talents." The common biped doesn't have such talents, does it? I think it does not. O.K. then.

I tidy up my bedroom and sit down in front of my laptop on Darrell's sofa in the common room but I can't get comfortable. I'm not superstitious or New Agey, but this room has all the wrong vibes. I can't work on furniture that habitually has his ass energy all over it.

So I relocate to my room even though it has no chair. I try the bed but the sliding is a problem: my mattress is plastic—it is garbage-picked from the street outside the NYU dorms; I suppose they were piss-proofing it—and the elastic of my fitted sheet is all worn out so either I keep sliding down on the plastic or the bed rolls away from the wall. Then I try the floor, but that's not good. I'm too bony. Pillows don't help, either.

Finally I drag Darrell's chair into my room and drape my sheet over it. This way I am not touching the chair itself and it is in my room, which I feel in some ways battles his contaminant. It seems like this might just work. But then I can't get anything done for other reasons:

—Too hot (get T-shirt from freezer)
—Too thirsty (get water)
—Water too warm (get ice)
—Rashes itch (steal some of Darrell's lotion)
—Laptop makes lap too hot (insulate with copy of cookbook I worked on)
—Book jacket is slick and makes thighs sweaty (insulate with dirty boxers)
—T-shirt from freezer starts getting melty, fear melting onto laptop, which is now making noises like wheezing hair dryer (take off shirt, wrap around head)
—Realize left notes on other side of room (carefully put down laptop, book, boxers assembly, retrieve notes, reconstruct assembly)
—Realize my window blown shut (get up, prop window open, repeat above procedure)
—Realize water now empty and still thirsty (go to kitchen, repeat above procedure)

—Not so sure outlet I have laptop plugged into is the best
(spend ten minutes searching for extension cord, find
one, plug laptop into different outlet)
—Become distracted by mess under bed (how can one create with Fruit Chewy Newton remnants under one's
bed?) and spend fifteen minutes cleaning out
—Become keenly interested in pigeon on fire escape outside window and spend fifteen minutes trying to com-
mune with pigeon
—Realize first paragraph sucks (delete; fail to write new one
because:)
—Realize second paragraph sucks (delete; fail to write new
one because:)
—Realize all other paragraphs suck; who cares about this
guy who sets up these elaborate deceptions to impress
his wife and therefore feels like a fake and therefore risks
his life to prove himself in the boxing ring? You? Me
either. (Delete remaining pages.)

Mercifully the phone rings. Maybe it's Evie. Maybe she wants
to play. Maybe we can climb into the Treehouse together and
forget about everything else.

But it is not Evie. It is the person I least want to hear from.

"Are you available?"

"Oh yes," I say, my heart shriveling.

messages

My calculations are off. It's Wednesday when I first hear from
Evie. A whole day overdue. All day Tuesday she was out of the
office and out of contact but when I roll into work at ten-thirty
my jacket is on my chair, my computer is on, and there is a
message from her on my email.

TO: hdriscoll
FROM: egoddard
RE: Hannibal Nadler

Good morning/afternoon/evening, my little crêpe suzette. I
check in at 8:30 (the time you may remember when assistants
are due at their desks), but alas, no. I check in at 9:30: I weep.
I check at 10 and there was not so much as a trace of Hairball
b.o. from your otherwise fragrant cubicle. There was much
discomfort and gnashing of teeth.

Where o where could my little Harry be? I'm not asking
because I'm not utterly confident that you can take care of
complicated, problem-solving situations like picking the correct
subway to work and crossing busty (whoops; a Freudian slip
there; I of course meant to say "busy") streets alone. I'm asking
because I am once again awed at your inimitable ability to evade

your boss. (Inimitable—how very Cultist of me.) How does a
man who sits ten feet from his boss's office manage to go days
on end without uttering a syllable to him or making even
fleeting eye contact? So fast and wily you are, just like the
mongoose. Still, I thought I'd avail self of the opportunity to
give you a heads-up about Nadler.

N emerged from his office today, inspecting your cubicle
(cleverly prepped with jacket on chair and turned-on PC,
courtesy of yours truly), looking every bit like he had for
breakfast a portion of kidney with a nice Chianti and some fava
beans and saying all manner of unpleasant things re: delinquent
ms. and absence of his faithful famulus. (See, you're not the
only one who can read the dictionary.) I told him that I had
seen you flitting about early this morning on thirty-three, no
doubt at that very moment attending to some extremely crucial
and esoteric business on his behalf but that you also had a very
stricken look, a look in fact of someone bravely struggling
through a dire illness for his boss, a look of someone selflessly
putting his runny nose to grindstone in service of
postpostpostmodern (where are we now, anyway?) American
literature etc. etc. and that possibly—just maybe—after
completing your herculean chores on the executive floor you
might perhaps have gone home or to nurse or ER or
something, drained as you were, no doubt, from so much
overwork. Am I not ever so thoughtful? Am I not a worthy
associate of the mongoose? Am I not Bonnie to your Clyde? Do
I not exude the glamour and excitement of collusion? Was I not
a jewel thief or con man in some other life? Are you not
hopelessly in my thrall and debt? Yes, yes, yes, yes, yes, and yes
I say to you.

Unfortunately then N told me he was heading to the country and that you need to call him on his cell about the manuscript a-sap. And he said it just like that, too: a-*sap*. He is, in all ways, a thoroughly unbearable person, I will admit, who deserves not at all the pleasure of your conversation, but probably you should bear in mind that he is an executive editor and (although it is very tiresome and traditionalist of me to say so) he is also technically your quote unquote boss quote unquote, and in a position to fire and otherwise humiliate and debilitate you and your career. So I guess my point here is that despite whatever time I've bought you today, you might want to consider taking a few moments out of your busy drinking schedule to find that ms. And maybe you should call him avec catarrh on the phone, being that an ounce of ass-kissing is worth a pound of employment, or a brown-nose in time saves nine or something.

I don't know. You're the cliché expert. You tell me.

Anyway, my little bed lichen, while you are burning the mid-afternoon oil you will alas be without the grace and joy of my company as I am constrained by exigencies of job (that's J-O-B) to be away from the office. So today you must play with Horst and maybe compose sonnets about me, or skywrite sweet nothings over Central Park, or paint flattering portraits of me in winsome gowns set against sylvan scenes with anthropomorphic foliage and sun-dappled pools etc. etc. in the Pre-Raphaelite manner I so clearly deserve.

They'll never take us alive,
Bonnie

The red light on my phone is blinking. I enter my code. It's a message from my mom.

"Harry, it's Mother. I saw Meredith Crosswhite at the symphony last night—her husband is the headmaster at the Bancroft-Ash School—and *she* told *me* that *they* are looking for an English teacher and *I* said that my *son*, the big editor at Prestige, might be talked into leaving the city for Connecticut. So Meredith might be calling you soon. It doesn't have to be any big thing, and I know you hate it when I do this, but I hope you'll talk to her. Meredith is an old family friend and it would be embarrassing if you didn't listen to her. O.K.? Love you."

I seventy-six the message. There's another one. It's from Nadler. I hear something about blues, copyeditor, and pub dates—and something alluding to some nonfeasance of unacceptable magnitude—and I seventy-six that one, too. There's another message.

"Harold, it's Andrew again—"

Seventy-six.

"And also—"

Seventy-six.

"And if you don't—"

Seventy-six.

The next one is from Horst.

"Harry, Nadler asked me to—"

Seventy-six.

I write a note to my mom.

TO: asdriscoll@gonet.com
FROM: hdriscoll@prestige.com
RE: mom's headhunter service

Mother,

Thank you for your missive anent career development, but I
must respectfully decline offer of prep school teaching as am
not dead yet. Further, I would appreciate your restraint from
dispensing inane advice on personal or professional matters in
future as am entirely capable of handling such affairs without
baby-sitter or similar. If you feel you absolutely cannot resist
such irritating (and implicitly insulting) egurgitations, please use
the following as a guide:

—I do not want to repair Shaker furniture in New Hampshire.
—I do not want to run an adorable B & B with cats and
croquet.
—I do not want to beekeep or volunteer at the disabled
children's petting zoo or grow hydroponic cabbage in a
neokibbutz colony of envirofriendly geodesic domes in the Gobi.

If after considering the above guidelines you are still unsure
whether I might be interested in some ideas you might have re:
life in general I suggest you reread whatever email you have
written and then press the DELETE button.

Your citified son,
Harold

I examine the note. It's not really what I meant. What I want
is for my mother to realize that I'm not twelve years old. I want
her to understand that the only thing I want is to get my career
back and have a clean, well-lit apartment in which I'd wake up
with Evie every morning.

I delete my message and write a new one:

TO: asdriscoll@gonet.com
FROM: hdriscoll@prestige.com
RE: thanks

Mom,
Thanks. I look forward to her call. Everything here is great, but I'm happy to talk to Meredith. Out of courtesy.

Love you, too,
Harry

I write a note to Evie.

TO: egoddard
FROM: hdriscoll
RE: my distant early warning system

E,
Thanks for your warning, but there's no need to worry. The ability to evade one's boss is what separates man from the animals. And if I should ever run out of hiding places, who knows, maybe I'll just find the thing? (Seriously, I'm on it. It's bound to turn up soon.)

Still, it's nice of you to keep lookout. You are a thing of beauty and a joy forever. I kiss you in a grateful yet prurient fashion:

Mmmm-wah,
H

I hit SEND and the phone rings. My computer chimes in with an email from Jenkins, the author of the calendar. Down the hall Paula is squawking into the phone about a new "spot-on" memoir about to pub. I consider running off to build bridges and administer lifesaving injections in third world countries. I debate trashing the office with a sledgehammer. Probably I could call that slushie to cook up some cacodyal for the whole place. Instead I wait for the phone to stop ringing, seventy-six the message without listening to it, and record a new greeting.

"You've reached Harry Driscoll at Prestige Publishers," I hack into the receiver. "I will be out of the office for the remainder of the week, but if you leave a message I'll return your call as soon as possible. Thank you."

Then as a safeguard I take a pinch of Skoal Wintergreen and pack it against a molar and go to the recycling area and wait. In a minute Paula arrives with an armload of manuscripts that are now in galleys. Perfect.

She dumps the paper and regards me hunched histrionically over the bin.

"Harry," she says, looking at me like I'm a spoonful of arterial plaque. "Are we not feeling well?"

"It's nothing," I croak. "Have work . . . need to do . . . for Nadler . . . Nadler needs . . . must go on . . ."

By now I've got a mouthful of tobacco juice and spit sloshing bitterly around my gums. I give Paula a martyr's look, convulse dramatically, swallow everything in my mouth—the whole wad—and cough up a bright bolus of spit and chew and bile.

pillowfight

Evie lives in an insulting little apartment on Mott and Grand Streets, on the sixth floor of a six-floor walk-up across the airshaft from a sweatshop. Nights I fall asleep with her to the smell of old Asian women perspiring and to the mesmerizing whirring noise of foot-driven sewing machines. On the stoop below her window is a sign that says, NO DODO HERE, PLEASE, put up by her neighbor Elmo, a WWII vet who spends his days chasing dogs away from the doorway, which he considers his responsibility to keep clear of excrement. I tried to tell him once that he'd misspelled it, that "dodo" is a bird, but Evie leapt to his defense and told me to keep my dictionary to myself, please.

Inside, her space is bravely tidy and organized, making the most of her studio. She joyfully subscribes to the minimalist philosophy of interior design: no shelves cluttered with scented candles, no insurrection of knickknacks on her counters, no family photos encroaching from the walls. Her one irregularity is her bed, which is always fitted in such clean, chlorine-bleached sheets that it's like going to sleep in the town swimming pool. And she keeps it smack in the middle of the room.

"Hieratic design," she said when I arranged it for her. "Let's not kid ourselves about what's important here."

I have been outside on the fire escape for twenty minutes now, surveying the scene. For some reason I have a vertiginous feeling of unease, but everything looks the same as always inside her apartment. The sun is just going down and it has cooled off a little bit but it's still hot enough to make my skin feel it's being rubbed with steel wool. The sky is smudgy with bruised clouds and dull stars. The livid pavement below me is quiet and it's getting easier to breathe. The air is becoming night air—cooler, penitent. Still, my asthma is acting up. I take a hit of Albuterol but the inhaler is almost empty and all I get is a throatful of stinging oleic acid.

I'd be worried about getting arrested sitting out here on the fire escape, but no one ever looks up in this neighborhood and besides, I'm always sneaking in and out of Evie's window to leave little surprises for her. She didn't like it at first but she couldn't argue with the logic.

"It's not burglary," I told her. "It's the exact opposite. It's givery."

Tonight I'm bearing a copy of *Shark Attack!* I picked up at Kim's Video on my way over. I'm still trying to muster the right apology for the boob-handling at the book party, and I need to do something to make myself feel less awful about seeing Judith last night, ergo *Shark Attack!* Evie has been wanting to see this movie for months. Since that first conversation we've seen countless movies about animals tearing people to shreds. Together we've seen all the *Mistreated Pets Get Even* movies probably ten times, *When Good Parrots Go Bad*, and the movies where piranhas are mated with tragic consequences to exceedingly aggressive flying fish. The day I found out about failing to clear permission for an author photo and the resulting threat of lawsuit, Evie brought me a copy of Xavier Maniguet's *Jaws of Death* ("WARNING: This Book Contains Disturbing Photographs") with a picture on the jacket of a great white. Evie had drawn a stick-figure man about to get chomped above the caption, "Nadler goes fishing." Our first post-Luther date was staying in with Krispy Kremes and bacon and watching *Croc Rock* over and over. It was New Year's Eve.

Inside the apartment I find Evie asleep at her desk. She is hunched over her desk and her hair—so black it's blue—is spread out over the pages of a manuscript like an oil spill. Her cats blink impassive glycerine eyes at me. I wake her up by rubbing her feet. When she comes to and appraises the situation, she says, "Oh no. I know that look and the answer is no."

"What?" I say innocently.

"You have the look of a man in need of ministrations, and I've got to work."

"But think of the *synergy*."

"Huh?"

"We've got so much in common. You've got viscosities, I've got viscosities . . ."

"Oh no—"

"You smell good, I've got a nose."

"No no no no. And I don't mean that in the usual 'I know what you're thinking and you can forget it' way. I mean it in the 'Really, no way' way."

I sit down next to her.

"You're estrus, I'm isthmus."

"Nuh-uh."

"You know that 'estrus' comes from the Greek word meaning 'gadfly,' that insect that agitates cattle?" I learned this interesting bit of trivia from Jordie in a recent logomachy. I knew it would come in handy sometime. Thank God for that Jordie Wesselesh.

"Really?" she says, wedging a pillow between us.

"Moo!"

"Harry . . ."

"Moo I tell you moo!"

"Noo I tell you noo!"

I edge closer to the bed and start shaking it.

"Ladies and gentlemen, we seem to be experiencing some turbulence," I say, starting to shake the bed more vigorously. "Please return to your seats and fasten your safety belts. I'll try to find a calmer altitude." Then I start shaking the bed violently. "Oh my God! Oh my God! OH MY GOD! We've lost pressure in the cabin! We're going down! Quick, Evie, before it's too late," I yell, thrusting my pelvis at her. "Grab the emergency penis! The emergency penis, woman! It's our only hope!"

"For God's sake, Harry."

"Now's no time to balk, woman! GRAB THE EMERGENCY PENIS! IT'S OUR ONLY HOPE!"

"Do you see what this is? This is me telling you no: no."

"But—"

"Harry, Madeleine made me swear not to have sex with you if you can't keep your hands off other women or do me the simplest favors, like putting aside your misanthropy for one night so I don't look idiotic going to New Year's Eve parties alone and miserable. And I happen to agree with her."

"But I brought you *Shark Attack!* See how nice?"

"Sorry. I swore."

"Promised or swore?"

"What?"

"Promised or swore?"

"Swore."

"Swore by your mother's grave, or maybe just by, I don't know, a lobster?"

"Madeleine made me swear by Daphne du Maurier, Wicca, and the WNBA, O.K.?"

"That sounds pretty final," I concede.

"Very."

Later it starts to rain and we lie there, naked, as cabs creep by beneath the open window, their slowly rotating tires on the wet asphalt sounding like unrolling tape. The weak light of the street-lamp seeps through the glass and makes the interior of the room look washed out and barren—lunar.

"*Man* is it good to be a mammal," I say, rubbing Evie's skin.

"Soooo good."

"Reptiles don't get to enjoy the skin like this. Geckos don't have it this good."

"Nor squids," Evie says.

"Nor tree frogs."

"Nor sea monkeys."

"Nor the GOP."

"Nor the Gingerbread Man."

"Huh?" I say.

"You know, he's a man but instead of skin he's got ginger. Quel bummer."

"You mean Gingerbread Man, as in 'You can't kill me, I'm the Gingerbread Man'?"

"Catch."

"Huh?"

"You can't *catch* me, I'm the Gingerbread Man," Evie says.

"Kill," I say.

"Catch."

"Kill."

"Catch."

"Kill."

"*Catch*."

"Evie, you're gainsaying."

"It's catch, Harry."

"You don't know anything about kids' books, do you? The Gingerbread Man is invulnerable. He gets little kids and no one can kill him."

"Like a delectably sugar-coated boogeyman?" Evie says.

"Precisely."

"You had some kind of twisted childhood, didn't you?"

"I didn't write the story."

"The Gingerbread Man is on the *run* from little kids."

"That's preposterous."

"He's afraid of being eaten."

"*What?*"

"Here's this man, made out of gingerbread—God knows why they made it gingerbread; it's downright disgusting; I don't know anyone in their right mind who likes ginger, but there it is . . . Anyway, in the story everyone wants him so he's on the run."

"Why is he on the run from that?"

"Have you been having this conversation? It's because they're going to eat his head off."

"Sounds like the NC-17 Gingerbread Man to me."

"He dodges all the townspeople only to get caught and eaten by a crafty fox. Trust me on this. It's *catch*."

"You better cut the sass before I feed you some chocolate."

"Oh shut up and rub my feet before you lose me forever." After a few moments of my rubbing her feet she says, "Quick, say something nice about me."

"What?"

"This book I saw said that the fifth step of love is that a person should be able to say something nice about the other person on demand."

"Seriously?"

"Seriously."

"Nice . . . nice . . . nice . . ."

"It shouldn't be this hard."

"I know most people would say personality, or smarts, or something like that, but I've got to go with . . . abbreviations."

"What?"

"You're abbreviated. Evie. E.V. See?"

"This is a compliment?"

"Of the highest order. Abbreviations make everyone's life easier. They're like the BASF of language. And you're phonetic. I mean, poor E. L. Doctorow. He has to use his initials. But you, your name itself is the abbreviation. Glorious, is it not?"

"I would have liked 'beautiful,' " she says, almost to herself. " 'Smart' isn't bad. 'The most wonderful woman I've ever met' would do. But no, I get 'abbreviated.' Why am I not surprised."

"Hey Eves. You know how I'd feel without you? *Evi*scerated."

A long disconnected moment of silence ensues and then, tentatively, as if she were formulating a new mathematical proof that she isn't quite sure about because it hasn't been sufficiently tested:

"Harry, do you love me or what?"

"Say what?"

"Do you love me?"

"I don't understand."

"It's only four syllables: do you love me?"

"You know how I feel about this."

"Do you love me?"

"Love is an absurd and tiresome idea."

"Do you love me?"

"I detest clichés and love is the biggest cliché of them all. Consider the Hallmark store on Forty-sixth."

"Here we go," she says. "Here we go with the Hallmark store on Forty-sixth."

"Know how many cards they've got? Millions."

"Hundreds."

"And they all contain the exact same words—"

"I-love-you," she says along with me.

"Right. You know what those are?"

"Three small words, getting smaller," she recites.

"Right. Love shouldn't even be considered the biggest small word. With should be."

"But you can be *with* anyone. You only *love* one person."

"I love you is the clichéd expression of the moronically unimaginative. It's for greeting cards for people who don't have the originality to say what they really mean. It's the Henry Fordization of emotion."

"It's not the Henry Fordization of emotion," she says tiredly.

"People who say I love you also go around buying Hallmark cards for each other and sending prefab flower arrangements with mini stuffed animals in them and watching *Love Story* together while drinking white zinfandel and eating drugstore bonbons."

"You haven't even seen *Love Story*."

"Mercifully."

"How can you derogate something you haven't even seen?"

"I don't have to see it to know it's sickening. I've seen the jacket. I've heard the theme song. It has Ryan Cry Baby O'Neal in it. All he does is stare at the camera with those dopey golden retriever eyes. I bet it's not even a movie. I bet it's just two hours of PDA on film."

"You've got it all wrong, Harry. *Love Story* is good. It's great. It's beautiful."

I make a gesture with my finger in my mouth.

"God, Harry, you are so . . ."

"Discriminating?"

"Idiotic."

"Watch the language, sister."

"Let me explain some things to you, Harry. *Love Story* is a masterpiece. And love is not the Henry Fordization of emotion. It is normal, Harry. Nor-mal. Normal people love. It's healthy. It makes them happy. You remember happy, don't you?"

"Unless you live in a Rodgers and Hammerstein musical there ain't no such thing as real happy. There's only episodic happy. Like tonight. It's nice being naked, isn't it?"

"It's lovely."

"See?"

"But it isn't all."

"Please don't say it's love."

"It's love."

"You're trying to teach the world to sing in perfect harmony, aren't you? Who are you today? Will the real Evie please step forward."

"Will you quit acting beastly for one tiny second?"

"Will you quit acting childish?"

"What's wrong with children?"

"Uh-oh. Objection. Leading question. Move to have the mention of children stricken from the record."

"We'd have beautiful children, Harry."

"Oh boy. Oh boy oh boy oh boy oh boy."

Evie has always wanted children. Mine, specifically. Last month I snuck in to her apartment from the window, meaning to plant a bottle of wine under her bed so that when I came over for dinner that night I could pull it out like, Surprise surprise, here's a Beaujolais *de Frère Jacques,* what super luck. I had made it inside and was crouched down by the bed when I overheard Evie rummaging around in the closet. She came out with the belly of her shirt all stuffed with dirty laundry. She hobbled around comically for a while, bracing herself against the counter, then said to her cats, "Mommy's pregnant. You're going to have a little sister or brother. A little Harry or Harriet. And won't we all be so happy together?"

Of course I freaked. Of course she freaked when A) she saw a man jump out from under her bed and B) saw me freaking out over something that didn't mean anything anyway. Of course women fantasize about pregnancy, she said. It doesn't mean they want to be pregnant at that moment. And no, I'm not pregnant. How stupid can you be? You're an idiot. Sub-idiot, she said. Way below dolt or moron. God. Did you forget that because of the endo I probably won't be able to have children even under the best circumstances? Did you forget that little bit of tid? Do you know who you're dating? Would you like an introduction?

God.

And what the fuck are you doing under the bed, Pink Panther?

"Beautiful," she says again.

"Right. They'd have your sense of moral uprightness and my inveterate inability to adhere to it. They'd be miserable. They'd be little Raskolnikovs."

"They'd be beautiful and brilliant and kind. They'd be articulate and loving and passionate. They'd write poetry and plays. Other parents would have to get counseling because our kids would give them complexes."

"Could we at least skip the barfing, puking, plutonium-shit stage and go right to the playing-ball stage?"

"I don't see why not," she says, willing to play along for a moment.

"Why not just adopt? There are plenty of seventeen-year-old Filipino girls looking for a loving home."

"You know," she says, the constellation of scars at her eye flushing, "sometimes your levity belies a real inner vacuum of profound loneliness and desperation."

"Well," I say, shrugging. "Nature adores a vacuum."

"Nature *abhors* a vacuum."

"Adores."

"Abhors."

"Adores."

"Abhors."

"Adores, I tell you."

"Nature *abhors* a vacuum, Harry."

"Well, don't you know every little thing."

"I know your problems, bub."

I pull on my boxers and a T-shirt and pour myself some sour mash.

"I disagree with you about children's literature and the axioms of science," I say. "I misplace manuscripts. I am unfastidious."

"You drink too much."

"And you cry eighty-proof tears, toots."

"You're vain."

"Nuh-uh," I say. I start to jump up and down in front of the mirror. "Now be honest with me. Do my cheeks jiggle when I do this?"

"You have pedophilic tendencies. You have wet dreams about Little Debbie."

"Hey! That's not me, that's my subconscious!"

"You flirt with waitresses."

"I do no such thing," I say guiltily.

"Oh my God."

"When have I ever?"

"Last week. Great Jones Café. Waitress with the pigtails who kept rubbing her tits against your shoulder. 'Excuse me, miss, but isn't "cannoli" Italian for "testicles"?' "

"What do I know about Italian?"

"You can't say even the most simple affectionate words. Forget 'I love you.' Try 'girlfriend.' "

"Girlfriend," I say grandly. "See?"

"Now say, 'Evie is my girlfriend.' "

"This is silly," I say from the bathroom. I piss noisily into the toilet with her cat perched on the side of the tub, mesmerized. I don't know why but this cat can't get enough of me pissing.

"You don't introduce me to any of your friends. Or your brother. Or your mother."

"Whoa," I say, entering again and tossing a tube of lotion to Evie. "You'd plain old hate my mother. She's artsy-craftsy. She wants me to move into the country and teach prep school. She wants me to spend my time mending walls and taking roads less traveled and loving my neighbor. She wants me to marry a cookie-baking wife who carpools and wears flannels and teaches pottery to underprivileged inner-city kids."

I sit down on the edge of the bed, drink in hand, with my back to Evie.

"I'd bake cookies," she says meekly.

"If you ever baked cookies, baby, CRACK! Sonic boom and I'm gone. You are emphatically not the cookie-baking type. You are the leggy, satirical, noirish, unsentimental type. I always half-expect to find a gun in your garter."

"I am not La Femme Nikita. I am Evie Goddard. I'm thirty-one years old and lonely. I have about eighty thousand bees in my bonnet and they're all named Harry Driscoll." She shakes the tube of lotion, squirts some flatulently out, and starts rubbing lotion on my arms and neck. She uses the nonscented Curel stuff I like so much.

"That means I love you, you ridiculous little man, and want to marry you and pretend we're normal people. But you don't love me, do you? I mean, not really. Forget your rules on aesthetics for a minute and tell me if you love me."

I want to. I do. And now, I have to admit, would be a good time. But the Strunk & White in my soul won't let me say it. It's too banal. People go around saying "I love you, schnookylumps" and "I love you too, honeybear," and the world isn't an appreciably better place.

"Ah," I say as she's rubbing the lotion. "Ooh. Viva la Evie."

"You are the Harry Houdini of conversation, you know that, don't you?"

"I can't help it. The lotion scrambles the neural message center."

"Neural message center," she says. "You're absurd."

She lifts up my shirt to get my back but stops before she really starts.

"Evie?" I say. "Hey. I'm having a dermal event back there. Little lotion, please? Little help?"

There is a long, bristling moment of silence.

"Harry," she says. "Where'd you get all these bruises?"

"What?"

"You've got bruises on your back. Where'd you get them?"

This is one of Judith's problems. She thinks it's romantic to bludgeon her partner.

"Running with the bulls?" I say.

"Shock the nation. Tell me the truth."

"I don't know, Evie. What can I tell you? I've got a back. It's got bruises. They're not that bad." Evie touches one with a finger and it makes my kidney feel like it's being scrambled. "Ouch!"

"Harry, turn around right now. You see this? Do you know what this is? This is me being very, very serious." The scar is radiant and mottled. I want to reach out and stroke it. "Now. Who is Date? I think I at least deserve to know who she is. Does she know who I am or am I just another Date to her?"

"Evie . . ."

"Harry."

"I prefer 'Hairball.' "

"Harry!"

"Evie, there is no Date."

"Say something believable, please."

"Honest to God, I'm not seeing any other woman."

"You're seeing some kind of S & M woman. Admit it."

"I'm not."

"How do you explain the bruises? The scratches? The limping?"

"I have a proprioceptive deficiency?"

"A *what*?"

"Proprioception is the body's ability to perceive and maintain its natural balance. It's damaged by things like ankle sprains. It interferes with the messages your nerves send your brain or something and you end up falling down a lot. Drinking does the same thing."

"Would you step out from behind your dictionary for one moment, please? In case you haven't noticed I'm trying to have a conversation with you here. You know, a dialogue about events? A dialogue about events concerning us? Maybe this isn't the appropriate time, you think. Maybe it's un*seemly* to you, but seeing as I'm sitting here oozing your sperm while contemplating the marks on your body made by another woman, perhaps you'll indulge me on this. So what do you say? Will you tell me who Date is or shall I just sit here picking up the remnants of my self-respect for the rest of the night?"

"There is no Date."

"Don't treat me like I'm stupid. I hate it when you do that. I know a lie when I hear one, even from a wordster like you."

Although it's a serious transgression—the words coming out of my mouth feel like vomit—I put her hand to my throat so she can feel the vibrations and I say, "Evie, I am telling you there is no Date. We both know I drink enthusiastically. Well, I also drink athletically sometimes. I didn't want you to worry about me, but sometimes my body ends up having some drunken misadventures. Now, it's nothing serious. It's nothing nefarious. It's just . . . bad judgment occasionally."

"There is no Date?"

"No Date."

"You swear?"

"Cross my heart, hope to work in publishing."

aubade

We don't watch *Shark Attack!* We don't have sex again. We utter nary a syllable to each other. She lets me sleep over but refuses to touch me. I try to hold her and discover that it's possible by minute, resolute cellular retreat to resist being held. She's like a tai chi master who doesn't move a muscle but who directs his energy so that he cannot be punched.

In the morning when I wake up Evie has already gone to work. I go to the kitchen for some water and see that she has written out in brightly colored crayons: "WITH is not the biggest small word. GONE is."

hello kitty

There is no one I want to see less right now than Birdie, but there she is.

After the blowup with Evie I couldn't bring myself to go into work, so I'm taking a personal day. I got a bottle from a liquor store on Houston that hasn't got me blacklisted yet and a couple of slices and I'm headed to the East River. The river always makes me think about nothing. And the bottle always makes me feel nothing. Somewhere in between I might find a way to feel better about last night.

There's a long stretch of homeless people lined up along the rows of checkers tables. In the heat with their coats and tattered blankets wrapped around them, they are slumped and listless. They look like whales that have washed fatally ashore for no discernible reason. All except for Birdie, that is, who is curled up on a bench with her head bent over a copy of the *Daily News*, her lips flexing and unflexing like mad, like the activity of inch-worms on time-lapse film, trying to pronounce words I know she's never seen. I'm almost by her when she looks up and sees me.

"Hey," she says. "Put me in the freezer and call me a Popsicle. Slapshot! I said slap*shot!*"

This is the fruit of a bad joke. After I left the hospital and Birdie started following me around the Village and asking me to read to her all the time, I got so sick of it so fast that I started making up expressions and giving them fake and ridiculous meanings. I really didn't mean anything by it, but she seemed to enjoy them so much—being so rah-rah about reading and whatnot—that I kept feeding her new ones, and now she's got an extensive library of nonsensical idioms that delight her, con-fuse listeners, and embarrass me. For example, once when she told me that she had just finished her very first book, cover to cover (in fact, she had even memorized it, the whole thing, front matter to back matter, and she recited it to me, word for word: author bio, ad-card, acknowledgments, copyright page, you name it), and asked if I was really proud of her I said, "Wow. Slapshot."

When she looked at me funny I told her that "slapshot" was an expression of happy surprise, like "great" or "wow."

Last winter when I got locked out of the apartment—I knew better than to wake Darrell up to let me in—and she found me almost passed out on one of the benches in the Astor Place Station and tried to huddle up with me I sputtered, "Bite the window, Birdie!" For weeks after that she went around saying, "Hey, bite the window already, pal, can't you see I'm trying to sleep?" Another time I apparently told her that "Call me egg-breaker" is a polite admission of error or embarrassment. Later I saw her in Vendetta Laundretta watching closed-captioned infomercials with some off-duty waitresses from the Kiev—she loves watching closed-captioned anything because she can hear the words and then read along and try to figure them out that way—when one of the waitresses knocked a Petr I out its black pack and lit up. She let Birdie smoke one and she started hacking and coughed up her gum into a basket of clean aprons. "Hoo-eee. Ha ha. Call me egg-breaker. Sorry about that."

The list goes on, I'm afraid. As I am often drunk when I make up these expressions, I can't always remember what their putative meanings are and we have conversations in which she says these things like, "So then I told him, 'You can put your hat on your ass but it don't make it any smarter,' and he just stood there looking all Ezra Pound about it and I was just like, 'Well, ALCOA can't wait.' You know?" And I just sort of have to nod and smile in what I hope is the right way for what she's said.

I'd feel worse about this if I ever wanted to listen to anything she has to say.

"You again," I say. "Shocker."

"What's in the bag?"

"Go away please."

"It doesn't smell like go away please. Smells like pizza."

"You don't like my food, remember?"

One time last winter Birdie was huddled in the stairwell of my buildling with this white Rasta guy named Jammers. He's a bad guy, a small-change dealer and thug who lives with the box-people under the scaffolding at Astor Place. He preys on the other homeless in the neighborhood—especially children—and is famous among the nurses at Beth Israel for his violence. Lots of kids have come through the ER who have been beaten or poisoned by the bad paregoric he sometimes pushes. Many of the kids show signs of sexual abuse. That night when I startled Jammers and Birdie there in the stairwell she was hunched into him with her hands inside his coat. When he saw me he jumped up and sprinted down the street, fiddling with his belt. Then Birdie stared at me. I mean, she just gave me this *look*. It was hard to tell if she was grateful to be saved from something or angry that I spoiled something.

"Now what?" she said.

I let her come inside and I served her some tomato soup. (Ketchup soup, really: I pour boiling water down Darrell's ketchup bottle when he trashes it and get out all the remaining paste, which I mix with water to make the soup. I do the same thing with his grape jelly to make ice pops. They're not good.) She didn't like it much. She spat it out all over one of Darrell's display cases and when he found her asleep on the sofa the next day—I didn't have the heart to put her back out in the cold with Jammers still on the street—he pressed a knife to my cheek and explained in detail what he could do if something like this happened again. The blade was either very cold or very hot.

For the rest of the winter I tried to avoid Birdie.

"But I'm hungry as a lark," she says.

"I can't help you."

"Just a little bite?" I want to say no but she does look hungry. She is thinner than I have ever seen her and her skin looks sandblasted. She's wearing the same HELLO KITTY T-shirt and the bright red elf boots she's always in. And then she's staring at me with these eyes. I mean, the tractor beams are on *high*.

"All right," I say. And then, when she makes her move, "But no hand-holding!"

For a second her features disassemble—a jigsaw sadness— and I feel bad again. (Guilt: my favorite indoor sport.) But then it's over. She corkscrews in delight.

"Slapshot!"

Half an hour later I've already downed a third of the bourbon, making my stomach feel like it's being punched with a handful of hot needles.

"What you looking at?" she says. I realize I've been watching her eat. On the street she was so dirty and thin that she looked ribby and sickly—exoskeletal. But now that she's sitting cross-legged next to me here on the concrete, a smear of tomato sauce making her face look like the overwrought makeup of a Chinese opera singer and with her hair shining in the red sunlight reflected off the river, she looks totally different. She's lost some of the hardness, some of the brittleness. Normally she is like a human oxymoron: having the physical appearance, the bonesuit, of a child, but also the awful attitude of a beaten-down adult, the dreamless dead fish-eye of an adult inculcated with failure and disappointment and deprivation—a milked, taxidermic look. But now she looks healthy. Her muscles, sweaty and befreckled as if by a dusting of brown sugar, look lean and flexible—amphibian, salient, like she could easily leap from here to the garbage barge if she felt like it. And her skin now looks vibrant and healthy, like the skin of any other little girl you might see around. She is eating the pizza with her mouth wide open. While one hand is holding the slice, the other one is picking at a toe.

She is, in other words, suddenly beautiful.

"You've got a little something," I say, indicating her cheek with my napkin.

"Yeah?" she says, dabbing at it with utterly useless Victorian daintiness. "Got it?"

"Not quite," I say. She dabs a little to the left. The total amount of tomato sauce encrusting her face is now reduced by perhaps 8 percent.

"That do it?"

"Yep," I say. "Looking good."

"Ooh!" she says. "I got a good idea! You can braid my hair."

"I don't know how to braid." I wriggle my fingers to demonstrate their maladroitness but she is already scooting over to sit in front of me, her back against my front, her knees drawn up in a miniature, upright cannonball.

"It's easy." And she demonstrates, looking over her shoulder at me.

"All right, but don't complain if it turns into one big knot."

"I won't complain."

After a few minutes I get into a good rhythm. I separate the hair into three strands and weave them together. It's not so tough. The wind is blowing, the gulls are crying, the water is lapping the barrier. It's nice. Her head is startlingly warm. The only head I've touched in a long time is Evie's—I never stroke the heads of Dates, not even Judith's—and there's a different quality to the heat of Birdie's head. It has a different smell, too, an undifferentiated smell, like it hasn't decided what kind of smell it's going to have until it becomes adult. Kid sweat is this way, too, I have noticed. It doesn't smell any certain way. It rarely smells at all. An adult could have the worst stale-leather-polish sweat smell in the world but as a kid that person wouldn't have had any special odor at all.

What makes you start to stink? Puberty? Hormones? The promise of sex?

"Let's play a game," she says. She is bracing herself with her hands on my knees, and I let her. "I'll ask you a question and you have to tell the truth and then you ask me a question and I have to tell the truth."

"That's it?"

"That's it."

"Some game."

"You're new at it so you go first."

"O.K. Let's see. How many Birdies are there in a quart? Four, eight, or sixteen?"

"Sixteen," she says without even thinking about it. "How old are you?"

Old enough to regret almost everything I've done.

"Twenty-eight. What's your favorite color?"

"Purple. Do you have any pets and if so what kinds and what are their names?"

"That's three questions." Birdie glares at me until I say, "Had one. Mosby. Cat. Aged twenty-four years. Died this year. He lived with my mother. He was a good hunter, slept under the covers with his head on the pillow next to you like a person, and he liked to be held upside down." In fact, he was put to sleep just two months ago. My mother, unbeknownst to Kurt and I, took him into the vet for the injection. She was there with him in the room and held him until he went cold. "You?"

"No pets. Why is your bedroom orange?" she asks through a mouthful of pizza, which brings to mind an interesting

NOTE: Normally the sound of other people chewing makes me want to punch them. Especially my poor mother. This can't say anything good about my personality but all my mother has to do is take one bite of an apple, one crunch of cereal, and I can feel my blood surge and I get this overpowering feeling that I might lash out from across the table. But here I am with Birdie's wood-chipper mouth working twelve inches away from me, and I don't feel like punching anyone. Bizarro.

"An accident. Where did you get that HELLO KITTY T-shirt?"

"My dad gave me that shirt." Birdie pulls out a lighter and a bent and wrinkled cigarette—it looks jointed, like the back of an armadillo—from the elastic of her shorts and fires up. She looks like someone out of Truffaut. "Why do you drink so much?"

"I'm bleaching my intestines. Why do you smoke so much?" This, I suddenly realize, is one of the tough things about hanging around a kid: it makes it very hard to be a hypocrite. I want to reprimand her for smoking but I can't very well do that while I'm gargling a mouthful of bourbon, can I?

"Something to do."

"How do you get the money to buy them? And who buys them for you?" Then it occurs to me: someone like Jammers. There are probably a lot of things about Birdie's life I'd be just as well off without knowing.

"That's cheating. It's my turn to ask questions." She takes a long defiant unblinking drag. She may be a little girl but she's not a kid. "Who would you want to be if you could be anyone in the whole world?"

This is an interesting question. I can think of a lot of people I'd rather be than myself. When I was in college I wanted to be Bob Dylan. Three friends and I went around in dark pants and short-sleeved shirts with ties and goofy hairdos and called ourselves Dylan's Witnesses. After smoking up and listening to *Blonde on Blonde* for about three hours we would stagger from dorm to dorm with our Dylan newsletter and try to convert our pop music peers to Bob. I also wanted to be Jack Tripper, for obvious reasons. One of the Baldwins is married to Chynna Phillips, so that sounds pretty good. But in the world of real prospects I'd have to go with:

"Jordie Wesselesh."

"Who?"

"Jordie Wesselesh. He runs the dictionary at Prestige. He's only a few years older than me. He's got it all. He has a real title, a real salary, a nice midtown apartment with these Persian carpets and finials galore."

"What's a finial?"

"And he knows all these words. I mean: he *knows* them. And he gets paid for knowing them. What a life."

I feel a jealous twitch in my heart as I think about Jordie and his life. I *could* be Jordie. I could. If I had more time I could finish the dictionary and then I wouldn't have to Don King all the time to win at logomachy. I'd be legitimate. We'd be peers. Maybe even like brothers.

"What about you? Who would you most like to be?"

I've finished one whole length of braid. It doesn't look so bad. It has a few errant sprays of hair here and there, but it is recognizably a braid. At this angle, with the sunlight coming off the water, her hair has the color of cornflakes. I pull off a long thread from my cutoffs and tie the braid up.

"You."

I almost spit out my bourbon.

"Me? That's ridiculous."

"No it is not ridiculous."

"It is as ridiculous as a thing could be. No one wants to be me. Even I don't want to be me. Shit, I *especially* don't want to be me."

"You've got a good job. You've got a good apartment even if it is all orange. You get to read all the time. You've got it all."

"I don't even like my job."

"What do you want to do, then?"

I want to write. I want to write. I want to write.

"Lion tamer. I'm great with chairs and whips already and this friend of mine has got these two cats and I can boss them around no problem. I'm a natural."

"Whatever. I'd still want to be you."

"Believe me, sister, you don't want to be me. I'm weak. I lie all the time. I hate everything, including myself. No, don't try to be like me."

"You're not like that. You're *good*, Harry. You read to Max when he was dying. You read to me. You read to other kids who have cancer. You're like a dad or something. To all those kids. Yeah, you're like a dad to all those sick and dying kids."

I finish another braid. It's an improvement. I'm getting the hang of this.

"That wasn't goodness, Birdie, and I sure as fuck—hell— wasn't being dadlike to anyone. That was just something to make me feel less awful back then. And I quit after you left. I couldn't take it. I don't have any guts, Birdie. Nah. You shouldn't try to be me. Be someone like Hillary Clinton or Camille Paglia or Madonna or somebody."

I spit over the edge into the river. Pause. Birdie tries to spit into the river too but she doesn't have the lungs for it and the saliva doesn't make it over the edge. It stretches out in a watery cord and falls across my leg.

"See?" I say. "It doesn't pay to try to be me."

"I'd still want to be you." She wipes the spit off my leg with her HELLO KITTY T-shirt.

"Whatever. Hey, I've got one. Why don't you sleep in the shelter instead of with those boxpeople?" After a second I think: uh-oh. Rewind, please. Rewind rewind rewind. I know Birdie's life is filled with things she'd rather not talk about and this—like Jammers—I'm sure is one of them. But she doesn't seem to mind. She just shrugs and says:

"Shelter sucks. Cots two feet apart. Have to ask for toilet paper every time you need it. Most of the people in there aren't really homeless. They're thieves. They're just waiting to roll on someone easy. Like if a woman comes back to the shelter at night wearing makeup, they know she's got a job, so they roll her. Can't keep what's yours for more than ten minutes at that place. That plus there's all these rules. Have to be gone by nine in the morning, can't come back until seven at night. And who wants to be in at seven at night? Nah, the shelter sucks. Least with the boxers you can do what you want, and most of the time they leave you alone. Most of the time." She clears her throat. "What do you read to that Evie girl?"

"Why do you want to know that?"

"I like being read to. I like reading. You got me hooked."

"You know, you're like a public service message or something."

"Only one way up," she says. "Can't do too much if you're like all the other dumbasses on the street. Most of those dumb fuckers can't fill out an application. Can't read street signs. Can't sign their names. I was born street, you know? But I'm not staying here. My dad lives somewhere in Jersey and I'm going to find him and then we'll be together and everything will be O.K."

I happen to know that Birdie's father is dead. The nurses at the hospital showed me the case file. He was an addict. Like my brother, just unluckier.

"Birdie," I say as gently as I can. "Your father's dead. He died years ago."

"What? You're crazy. My dad lives in Jersey."

"No. Listen to me. He's gone."

"You're talking nuts. What's the matter with you?"

"I'm just trying to help. Seriously. He's gone, Birdie. I'm sorry, but—"

"Shut up shut up shut up! You don't know what you're talking about! My dad is so alive. He lives in Jersey and he's a banker and when I find him I'll be out of here forever and everything will be fine!"

She leaps up and stares me down for a long moment. Her open mouth looks savage and ghastly, like a gouged potato, and her eyes are radiant with hatred. She is triumphant, wild, maenadish in her anger. I should have known better.

She hisses something at me under her breath that I can't make out: "Dumb fucking [something]." Then she's off. She hurdles the barrier and sprints through the street and down the sidewalk, her bright red elf boots blurring in the rising vaporescent heat like a prizefighter's gloves. Before she disappears I can see that her hair is snapping fiercely behind her like the tail of a kite, the braids coming undone.

A moment later I figure out what she called me before she fled: a dumb fucking *Stimpson*. This is the fake word I once drunkenly told her means "supreme asshole."

It also happens to be my middle name. Harold Stimpson Driscoll: that's me.

madame bovary, anyone?

"Pilot calling copilot. We're having some trouble here. Total systems failure. It's been two days and we're not having any fun at all. We need help. Please respond, copilot. [*Sound of static.*] Copilot. Come in, come in. We're losing you . . ."

I hang up and wait a few minutes. It's starting to rain. An old Chinese woman hobbles by the phone booth. She is wearing an umbrella that has a hole cut in the top of it as a neck opening—a raincoat—and carrying a bucket twitching with two live purple eels. I smile at her but don't get anything back. Even from here at the pay phone I can see Elmo on the stoop, lovingly fixing a garbage bag over his NO DODO HERE, PLEASE sign to protect it from the rain. A couple walk by with a dog and Elmo gesticulates madly at them, running them away from his stoop.

I ring again and again there's no answer, but I know she's home. I can see her light on, even from down here on the street, and she's not the kind of girl to leave a light on. She's very careful with electricity these days. She's had some run-ins. What happens is she goes out with Madeleine and comes home from parties drunk and decides that what would really make her happy is some *poisson mee-noo* ("That's catfish to you, Yankee yahoo") and candied yams. So she fires up the stove and puts the water on and then promptly passes out on the floor, spoon in hand. Once she was out so long that all the water boiled away and the pan started melting on the burner, filling the apartment with rancid black smoke. She opened all her windows and flapped some oven mitts over the stove, but the smoke was so bad that she had to evacuate her apartment. Then the firemen showed up. When they approached her door, masks down and axes out, she flung herself at them like a soap opera semistarlet and drunkenly blurted out, near tears and still in her underwear, "Don't chop anything! I'm too poor for you to chop all my stuff! Please!"

Since that first "Don't chop anything!" incident she's had the fire department called on her four times, so she has tried to discipline herself to be careful about electricity. Now her kitchen walls are covered with pages from a fire safety booklet the firemen left her and notes from me that read FRIENDS DON'T LET FRIENDS DRINK AND COOK and IF IT'S AFTER MIDNIGHT STAY AWAY FROM THE STOVE and RED LIGHT ON STOVE MEANS IT'S ON. I stole a Breathalyzer from Beth Israel and tied it to the oven dial with a wire and a note that said BLOW BEFORE YOU BAKE and OVEN WILL NOT START UNLESS BLOOD ALCOHOL REGISTERS BELOW .07. In the bottom of her saucepan I used a permanent-ink marker to draw a picture of a martini glass with a circle around it and an X through it. With the same marker I also wrote on all her oven mitts a reminder saying simply EVIE: NO NO NO.

She has an additional note on her bathroom mirror saying A HAIR DRYER IS NOT A TOY. In her bedroom, on her nightstand, she's got one that says HOT POT DOES NOT TURN SELF OFF. Above every light switch I've put signs that say PEOPLE CHARGE YOU FOR ELECTRICITY and UP MEANS ON, DOWN MEANS OFF. Like me, she is not really capable of indulging in the rock-and-roll lifestyle that allows you to go around leaving lights on willy-nilly.

So I know that if her light is on she must be home. I pull out my last twenty-five cents and call her number again. Evie finally picks up the phone.

"What is it, Harry?" she says wearily. This is the same tone of voice that Ms. Prolski, my long-suffering sixth-grade English teacher, would use whenever I would raise my hand in class. I had a big crush on her. I asked her out to every school dance that year, even once sending her a bouquet of flowers and a handwritten note asking her if she would do me the honor of allowing me to escort her to the Evening in Paris dance. It didn't work but I kept on sending her notes and invitations. At the end of the year she handed all the writings back to me tied up in a big bow and said, "Look what you've done. You've written a whole book. And it's lovely. You're a natural writer, Harry. Now go write one for some other lucky girl."

Even now when I think of her it makes me happy. Ms. Prolski, my first muse, wherever you are: I kiss you in chaste devotion.

Now, nearly two decades later, standing in the street outside Evie's apartment in the enervating heat, I hear the same tone in Evie's voice. It is the sound of a woman who knows what's coming but doesn't have the heart to stop it.

What is it, Harry?

"Why didn't you pick up the phone?"

"I had the answering machine turned down. I didn't hear you. I only heard the beeps."

"Then how did you know it was me?"

"Who else calls three times in a row?"

"Ah. Good point," I say. "Can you come out and play? I've got Evie on the brain. Which is a lot like having water on the brain, only worse because whereas water is pretty much limited to the brain inside your skull, Evie infects the brain that is inside the skull proper and also the—"

"Harry . . ."

"Well, you get the gist." I wait but there's no sound coming from the receiver, although I imagine I can hear the scratching of a pencil on paper. "Hey. Are you listening to me or what?"

"You haven't had me too much on the brain the last couple of days, I've noticed. Why the sudden attack?"

This is not true. I've been thinking of her pretty much nonstop but I've also had to service Judith—further evidence of the need for a doppelgänger.

"You don't believe me? Very well. Let's do a word-association test. You say a word and I'll tell you what it makes me think of, and you'll see how much everything makes me think of you. Fair?"

"Moxie."

"Evie."

"Style."

"Evie."

"Brains."

"Definitely Evie."

"A certain je ne sais quoi."

"Huh?"

"Taste in hats."

"Evie."

"A razor-fine acumen regarding international affairs and domestic issues concerning the body politic and the subplots of popular culture."

"Evie again."

"Killer legs."

"Minnie Driver. Let's be fair."

"Good-bye, Harry."

"Come out and play. It's murdering me in nineteen different ways being out here on this island by myself. I need the cheese, baby. Everything's better with cheese."

"I'm working."

"On what?"

"And I'm trying to have some Grape-Nuts."

"Fuck those misnomers. I'll buy you some more. After all, what is a sugar daddy for if not to buy you more high-fiber breakfast products?" Silent pause. "What are you working on?"

"A manuscript, Harry. A manuscript. You know? It's like a book in nascent form?"

"That sounds awfully dreary. What are you wearing?"

"I don't know," she says, exhausted. "A shirt. Pair of shorts. Socks."

"That is so hot. Give me the whole story. Give it to me straight, doc. I can take it."

"Tennisy shorts."

"Hell yes. Bend over to pick up those balls! What color?"

"Sort of taupe."

"Sort of taupe is the color of passion, you know."

"Long-sleeve shirt with cuffs rolled up."

"Show me those wrists, baby. Show 'em!"

"With a pocket on the sleeve."

"I love pockets. Fill 'em up, I say."

"And buttons."

"Don't you just want to palpate buttons?"

"Pointy collars."

"My first wet dream was about pointy collars."

"Green socks."

"You are a *tempt*ress."

"With those Fraggle Rock guys on them."

"Talk it, baby, talk it!"

"Harry, why are you calling me like this? What are you doing?"

"Well, for one thing I'm now holding the phone with my *left* hand."

"You're a barbarian."

"Bar bar," I say happily. "Please please please come out and play."

"I really am working, Hairball. I don't have time to disport myself with you or men of your ilk."

"I have an ilk?"

"Oh you've got an ilk all right."

"Interesting. Do we have secret handshakes and wear funny little hats with antlers and whatnot?"

"And have jackets embroidered with a little annular crest that says *Semper assholis.*"

"I adore you. You know that, right? Where did you get 'annular'?"

"And I adore you. Now go away."

"Where did you get 'annular'?"

"You really are the most exasperating person I've ever met. I was saving it for a special occasion but I couldn't wait, O.K.? Now go away. Honest, Hairball. I'm working."

"Work schmork. Let's quit, Evie. We'll go on the lam. We'll get us a few Gatling guns and some devoted half-wit henchmen and we'll knock over banks out west. People at Prestige will talk about us for years to come in hushed tones of awe and jealousy. Just like you said: Bonnie and Clyde."

"Is that what I said? I meant the Donner Party."

"What is it that's so important that you can't come out?"

"I told you. I'm working on a manuscript."

"Ditch it."

"It's important to me, O.K.?"

"Well, after all that work I think you deserve a break."

"I've only been working on it for forty-five minutes."

"But a very grueling forty-five minutes, no doubt. Have you taken a break for a bubble bath? Or a cup of tea? Or a G & T?"

"No, but—"

"Then it's high time. You deserve to come play with me."

"Is that what I deserve?"

"Yep."

"What did I do to deserve that?"

A robotic voice cuts into the line telling me I need to deposit more money to continue. "Come on," I say. "I'm sorry about the other night. I spent my last twenty-five cents down here. Come play before I get cut off and embarrass everybody by serenading you at your window."

"Nope."

"Come on," I plead. "We can play Madame Bovary."

"Madame Bovary?" she says, unable to disguise the interest in her voice.

"Why not? We've been good. Absolutely: Madame Bovary."

"How do I know we won't have an incident like that last time at Barneys?"

It's true: I got us into a certain amount of trouble at Barneys last time. I had a few drinks before we went out to play and I ended up in the men's room playing with the laser-eye flushers of the urinals. I discovered I could conduct them. I stood in front of them and waved a pair of mannequin's arms like batons—disassembled for this very purpose—in front of the eye, making the urinals flush in a little symphony. Trouble was I conducted while people were at the urinals, and not all of them appreciated my artistry. Shortly thereafter security arrived, with Evie in tow. "Does he belong to you?" they wanted to know. "Yes," she said. "I'm embarrassed to say he does." As I remember it, the next morning when I woke up hungover and disoriented, I accidentally drank Evie's contact lenses. She had run out of saline and had put them in a glass of water next to the bed—a common remedy for not having the cash for more saline—and I gulped them down. Evie tried to stop me but it was too late. Burp.

"Hey," I plead. "I was drunk, your honor."

"Are you drunk now?"

"Nary a drop."

"And I get to be Emma?"

"Why not? You've been good. Absolutely: you're Emma." This is not a difficult concession for me to make. I don't like being Emma. Dressing up makes me feel sort of Falcon Cresty.

"And you won't humiliate me?"

"When have I ever let you down?"

stop drop and roll

When you're poor New York is a forbidden city. You can't go to movies regularly. You can't afford real dinners or drinks out anywhere nice. You can't really shop. Doors close, doormen frown, psychic salespeople sniff and ignore you. So you have to come up with your own diversions. Here are some of the games and activities Evie and I have devised:

FOOT/RASH THERAPY: Evie will rub therapeutic lotion on my rashes and/or I will wash her feet. Evie is very self-conscious about her feet—it was six months until she even let me touch them and now I'm the only person on earth except Cousin Yvonne who has that privilege. Last year for Christmas I bought Evie a Dr. Scholl's Foot Spa that I customized with flames and a very helpful L and R in the footwell. Often I will wash her feet, put them through the Foot Spa, and then do what I can in the way of a pedicure. This ritual often precedes a

SOUPER À SONNETTE: This is based on the invention of Louis the Sun King. He would have an extravagant dinner prepared, with the finest foods and musicians. The men would appear in their best clothes and the women would arrive wearing perfume, powder, and jewels—that's it. They had a bell they would ring for the servants to bring in the next course, at which point the ladies would temporarily don the silk robes they had on the backs of their chairs. Otherwise the women would dine in exquisite nudity. Evie and I do the same thing. Only we don't have any glamorous guests. And we're usually eating frozen pizza. And it's me who serves the food. And I don't wear my dress clothes because they would exacerbate my rashes and the music is a worn-out tape of Edith Piaf played on Evie's alarm clock and Evie doesn't have on any perfume, only her fruity-smelling Bumble & Bumble hair goop. But still, Evie is naked at the dinner table with me and we have Edith Piaf on and red wine and we feel very European, which is nice.

But probably our favorite thing to do is

MADAME BOVARY: This is essentially a role-playing game. We will go out to all the fancy retailers in the city and try on their clothes. The trick is to invent characters for ourselves to convince the sales staff that we're celebrities or at least children-of so that we get smothered with servility and flattery. We keep score by how much money the clothes we try on are worth (Evie once wore almost $23,000 in dresses in one night).

"That's the stupidest game I've ever heard of," Keeno says. "It's like playing house or playing grown-up or something. Where's the fun in dressing up in new clothes? I swear: ultra-dumbo."

But I ask you: what's more ultradumbo, limping through the workweek feeling beaten down by your job and poverty, devoid of amusements, or spending an occasional evening out engaged in a game that makes you feel like you've got resources, like you might be leading a life of excitement and glamor, like you're someone to be reckoned with, like you really are a somebody?

*   *   *

We go to Bendel's. This is one of Evie's favorites. They have the best hats in the city. There is a silvery flapper dress with silvery skullcap to match that she's been coveting for weeks. Nearby are silvery shoes and purse.

QUESTION: The price of the whole schmeer?

ANSWER: If you have to ask, you can't afford it. You can't even afford to hear it. But for half an hour she can live the illusion.

We mill around. Bendel's is choking with people who we all can't help but resent because it's clear they are legitimate shoppers. The fact that they are waiting in line with plastic in hand demonstrates this, as does the fact that they walk out of the store holding shopping bags. There's a handsome Brooks Brothersy couple (*bzzzz bzzzz*) looking at purses. They are both physically attractive—you can tell they have done it all, from their once-a-week haircuts to their pumiced feet: they are *clean*—but they also emanate this moral goodness. He looks like he spends his days righteously punching tabletops and passionately yelling, "I want the truth!" to evasive and sleazy witnesses while a jury looks on with nodding approval at his sagacity and integrity. She looks clipped and smart and no-nonsense, like a financial correspondent for a TV newsmagazine. She probably wakes up at five A.M. so she can be on the air by nine, when she'll look squarely into the camera and say without any puberty-squeak or hyperventilation, "A bearish call by Morgan Stanley's telecom analyst spooked investors, who led the market down at the opening bell, but we're keeping our eye out for a late-day rally. Back to you, Katie."

But what really hurts is their way with each other. They aren't soulless suits, as one would like to believe. They are holding hands like high-schoolers. They are giggling at a private joke that he feels necessary to dispense with his mouth inside her bob, almost touching her ear. Their togetherness is like a force field, keeping the hostile outside world from entering. It is impregnable, you can tell. It is stonger than photons or antimatter. It is generated out of the symbiotic bioethereal energy of two unique and sympathetic organisms working in harmony. If you look close you can detect a faint light—like the white halation on maps of distant galaxies—around both of them.

It is pure love.

In other words, he doesn't look like the kind of boyfriend who is hiding a filthy Date up his sleeve and she doesn't have the exhausted, paranoid look of someone trying constantly to figure out if she's being lied to.

CORRECTION: I'd like to amend my answer to Birdie when she asked me who I would most want to be if I could be anybody on earth and I said Jordie Wesselesh. I'd like to amalgamate this couple and Jordie into one person so that I could be all of them at the same time, always together. I'd be lumpy but happy, and I would never feel untogether again.

"Ahem," Evie says, nudging me when she sees me staring at this couple. "Eyes on the crisis."

"Sorry, I wasn't staring at that woman. I was just . . . gathering information."

When Evie was on a post-Luther, pre-me date, this alleged writer guy took her out to dinner at Gramercy Tavern and had some palmist come by whom he had hired to say all sorts of the-stars-mean-us-to-be-together things. ("I see you with a dark stranger, a handsome stranger, a stranger who is handsome despite his slightly receding hairline, who in fact has that handsome I-know-I'm-bald-and-I-embrace-it way and who is very nurturing to animals and likes kids and moonlit walks on beaches—an artist, a painter perhaps . . .") Then he took her on a carriage ride around Central Park, which terminated in a romantic stroll to his Fifth Avenue apartment. I agree: this whole date sounds ridiculous to me too, like something from that dating show on TV, but it worked well enough to get Evie back to his place, where he blew everything by sitting on the sofa, cradling his fancy bulbous red wineglass in his hand, and sniffing her.

"What are you doing?" she asked as he sniffed around her hair.

"Gathering information," he said very seriously.

So now this is our joke.

"Gathering information for your novel, I presume?" Evie says to me now.

Uh-oh. Not the novel. Please don't ask how it's going.

"How's it going, anyway?"

It's not going at all.

"Going great. Guns blazing. Showing those keys who's boss."

"What's your work schedule like these days?"

I ignore it all day long until late at night when I take it out, look at it, and put it away again, unmolested.

"Two hours in the evenings."

"Wow. How many pages you up to?"

Eleven, tops.

"Around one-fifty or so."

"And what's going on in it now?"

I have no idea. I don't even know what I'm writing about. Everything changes all the time: the characters, the plot, the setting. I really don't have anything to write about. It started out life as a story about this guy who is married and is always doing these things to impress his wife. He stacks a deck of cards so that he can play solitaire in front of her and she can see him win it, flat-out; he stacks more weight than he could ever lift on the barbell so that she'll see it and think, Wow, he's really hunky etc. etc. His wife eventually catches on, though, and she loses respect for him, which only makes his attempts at impressing her more outlandish. Finally this fraudulence gets to him and he decides that he needs to do something that is genuinely impressive and manly so he enrolls in a boxing school, where he gets beaten to a frothing pulp on a regular basis. I got stuck on describing the physical abuse. Also I had difficulty imagining a married couple.

None of it sounded true.

"Um, it's sort of hard to explain right now. You'll have to wait and see."

"Have you shown any of it to anyone at the office yet?"

In fact, I have shown it to someone. I showed the first chapter to Nadler. I put a fake name on the manuscript and wrote a note that said, "Andrew—found this in slush. It's the first chapter from a novel-in-progress by this young guy who lives here in the city. I know it's rough, but I think there's something really interesting here. He's got some style, I think. And he seems to know a lot about loneliness and grief. I don't know. Maybe I'm wrong, but I thought you might want to take a look anyway. Let me know what you think.—Harry."

The next morning the chapter was back on my desk with a note attached that said, "H—Reject under form letter.—AN." Not even anything about "Promising but no, not right for us" or "I see what you mean about style, but our list is already too full." Just "Reject under form letter."

And that was that: my brush with publishing acclaim.

"No. Haven't shown it to anyone yet. You know how I am about revision."

"Boy do I know. You haven't even let *me* see."

"I just don't want to write one of *those* novels. You know . . ."

"Ah yes. Let's see if I can remember all your criteria for novels you hate." Here she goes. "You hate anything with the word 'chiaroscuro' in it."

"Especially if it's used as a verb. 'She was chiaroscuroed in the flickering light of the candle.' "

"The same goes for women who are described as 'elfin' or 'pixielike.' "

"This isn't Middle Earth, you know."

"You hate anything that uses the word 'member' for penis."

"Doesn't everybody?"

"You hate anything that says hair 'frames a face.' "

"Yeah. Leave it alone already, I say."

"You hate anything with a gerund title."

"I know. Novelists lately are always Asking for something, or Looking for something, or Losing someone. It's maddening."

"The same goes for anything with a 'song' attached to it."

"*Bloodsong, Painsong, Blahblahblahsong.* Hate them all. No singing, please."

"Or anything with 'Artist.' "

"*The Pain Artist. The Bone Artist. The Art Artist.* Save me from Artists."

"You hate novels that begin with a description of what someone is eating, or how their childhood smelled, or what they drive."

"People are always sticking K-Cars or broken-down Dodge Omnis in there to make you feel sorry for them. And I am just about worn out by the smells of clean towels or mother's pies or father's toolbox, aren't you?"

"You hate epiphanies. You hate reversals of fortune. You hate anything written by anyone younger than you are."

"Boy, these are really piling up, aren't they?" I say. "I hate that."

"You stop reading anything immediately if it has even a whiff of a cliché."

"Well, that's just good sense. Why waste your time reading something that is banal and stale and doesn't say anything new to you about anything and—"

"Why can't you cut those books a break? They aren't doing any harm. The authors are doing their best. Why do they all have to measure up to these snobbish criteria you've got? You know, every book is a love letter and—"

"What? Every book is a what?"

"A love letter. Even if it's not a romance book. A book is just taking three hundred pages to say 'I love you.' No one's out there helping these young, anonymous writers along. No one's dangling the big bucks in front of them. These people are out there—yes, even the slushies, Harry—working night jobs as waiters and bartenders and security guards at warehouses, without health insurance or respect from their peers, trying to write these novels because they have to, because they are compelled by love to do it. Even with the slushies who can't spell their own names, you can feel it in their sentences, like you can feel the nervous energy of a first date with someone you really like but don't know how to express it and so you end up saying all the wrong things. They've got it, they're feeling it, and they want us to feel it too. That's something noble. That's something about love. And I just think that maybe you could be a little less scornful of it. You used to write nice little notes under the form rejection letter, you know. I don't know why you stopped doing that. It wouldn't kill you, and it would make the slushies feel very good. What happened to you?"

It's a fair question. And she's right. I did used to write encouraging notes to slushies. Before Evie arrived at Prestige I even had this pen-pal relationship with a woman named Ida Duffendack who wrote editorials for a weekly in Dubuque. She wrote these atrocious children's stories about magic sneakers that would talk to their wearer when unlaced and happy gnomes that did your homework while you were sleeping. I recommended she send her stories to Prestige Juvenile, which she did, and called in a favor to one of the assistants I knew there, asking him to write a nice rejection under real letterhead. She was so grateful she would send me holiday cards she made herself. Sometimes they were the only cards I would receive besides Evie's.

I could do this. I could still write nice rejections. I'd solved the safety issue by initialing GL, so it wouldn't be impossible for me to write something nice in the margin, something sort of close-callish, something to make them feel good about the months and years they'd put into their manuscript but something that would still prevent them from finding out who I am and then inundating me with manuscripts. It would only take a few seconds.

"Like with the Drakkar manuscript? I should have said something nice about that?"

"Exactly. It's not a bad book, Harry."

"It's a bumper sticker, Eves. It's a fortune cookie. It's like a *Cosmo* article about love dragged out to three hundred pages."

"It's more than that, Harry. It's a serious effort at figuring out love, and trying to help people with it. It's a book that means only well."

"It sounds like you've been really thinking about this."

Evie fingers through a row of dresses on the rack. They have a bunch of dresses of different colors together, making them look like a boxful of crayons.

"I've given it a second glance, yes. I'm thinking about passing it around for a read."

"What, to other editors?"

"Yes."

This is nuts.

"This is nuts, Eves."

One of the ways assistants can angle for promotion is to get in good with the bigwig editors. If you can convince them that you've got taste, that you can spot the winner, even if it's only a small project, they start to develop faith in you and they might farm out one of their smaller novels to you. But you have to be careful: if you bring them a manuscript that's garbage, you will be blacklisted and you will not even get to handle a cookbook. This is what happened to Slo-Mo. He brought a bad project to a full editor—a senior editor—and the guy didn't like it. Slo-Mo hasn't had his own book since.

"I wouldn't do it, Eves. Why don't you wait for something from one of your assistant friends at a legit agency."

"I think you're wrong about this book, Harry. Frankly, I'm surprised you didn't show it to Nadler. I know you think it's beneath you to work on a book that might simply be a good seller and could make a lot of people feel better about life. *Quel horreur!* But it wouldn't hurt to do something to get on Nadler's good side right now, you know."

"What do you mean?"

"You know what I mean: thin ice comma you're walking on comma with deadly frigid career-ending waters beneath italics underlined bold exclamation point."

"You know what I have to say about Nadler? 'Jimmy crack corn and he can kiss my ass.' "

"Funny, but I've never heard you say that to Nadler."

"Just wait."

"O.K. It's your funeral, bub."

"If you pass Drakkar around it will be *your* funeral, toots."

"Yours."

"Yours."

"*Yours.*"

"Shut up."

"*You* shut up!"

Just then—right when we're starting to have fun, right when the scars on Evie's forehead start turning red, when her lips start twitching like a butterfly flexing its wings—a saleslady approaches us. Her name tag says RHONDA. She is a mushroomy, fat-fingered woman who has the look of the nun substitute teacher everyone dreads getting, the one who thinks paddling is a good idea.

"Can I help you find something?" she says. She squints at me in a way that says I will brook no foolishness from you, mister.

This isn't going to be easy.

I make a mistake. I go for too much and Sister Rhonda doesn't buy the story of our celebrity: Evie is Consuela Reynes-Cordoba, Spain's first female bullfighter. (I do this because I think matador outfits—those little spangly Napoleon numbers—would look very sexy on women and because I know that Evie cannot fake

a Spanish accent.) In fact, when I tell her about Consuela's bra-
vado *faena* in her most recent bullfight, and how she turned her
back to the bull in contempt, on one knee with chin high, old
Rhonda looks decidedly squinty. Eventually she wafts away to
another more promising customer and Evie says to me, from
inside the changing room, "If you're going to be the assistant to
Consuela Reynes-Cordoba, don't you think you'd better make
yourself presentable?"

"What do you mean?"

"You look like *you're* the one who's been fighting bulls."

"Again: what do you mean, Consuela?"

"Inspect your pocket. You'll find it's bleeding."

Sure enough, my pocket is oozing red. "That's just mara-
schino juice. I stole cherries from the bar tray last night at the
Blue & Gold. Olives, too. See? There's some green in there. And
if you need any lime wedges, I'm your man. Hey. There's a
cherry still in there. Want it?"

There's an old man staring at me. He looks like one of those
daguerreotypes of people being electrocuted—his body crackling
and alive with galvanic energy but frozen into complete immo-
bility. "It's only a cherry," I say, offering it up for him to see.
"It's still good." Then I realize he's not looking at me. He isn't
even hearing me. He's looking beyond me. I turn around and
see what he sees: Evie. She is leaning against the door of the
changing room in the silver dress, with the gloves on, the hat,
the shoes. She is hamming it up, sliding down the doorjamb and
pouting outrageously, but it is working. I hear the old man's bag
fall to the ground.

"Holy shit," I say. "Stop drop and *roll*, Eves. Jesus. You're
giving me a cardiac event over here." Then: "You know what,
Eves, you'd better put those things away before someone gets

hurt." I nod toward the old man, who turns to look at me. We have a moment that seems to say, We are men. I may be an old man and you may be a young man, but we are still men and isn't this a wonderful moment to be a man?

"Does that young lady belong to you?" he says to me.

"Title and all."

He makes an exultant, gustatory noise somewhere deep in his throat that doesn't seem very old-mannish to me. Then he gives me a look that is partly avuncular, partly menacing. "Treat her right, sonny. Take my word."

"I do," I say. "I'm nice."

"Didn't say treat her nice. Said treat her right."

This *senex* routine is charming at first but I don't much feel like getting lectured from an enigmatic, stern old-timer on the finer points of romantic comportment.

"Right," I say, handing him his bag. "That's what I meant to say. Right. Thanks for the tip." I put the bag in his hand and pat him on the shoulder in a send-off kind of way. He totters away, staring appreciatively over his shoulder as he goes.

"Pervert," I say when he's gone.

"He was cute."

"He was staring at you like you were a filet mignon."

"So are you."

"Yes," I say, "but I have the title."

I inch up next to her. She has her usual jungle scent emanating from her, but she also smells of new textiles and glass—the warm, antiseptic smell of new-dress and the cool blue smoothness of glass. She does a little coquettish twirl, and I can see the dress is backless. Even in that quick movement I can see the muscles in her back tense and release, her spine twisting and undulant like a snake being charmed out of its basket. The silver in the dress makes her skin look even whiter than usual—bright but liquid, like the light from milky stars. And her legs, her strong arms in those gloves, her hair spraying out from under the hat in insurgent curls. And her collarbones, her deep collarbones: ouch.

You could put *eggs* in those collarbones.

I take her face in both hands like a grail and kiss her. It feels like my whole body and my beaten soul are compressed into my lips and are trying to tiptoe across and into her body, into her soul.

"Sorry, Mr. Whipple," she says. "Please don't squeeze the Charmin."

"Just one squeeze? No one's looking." I haven't investigated this, in fact—the fat-fingered on-to-us saleslady could be coming with security in tow for all I know—but I do not care.

"Not here. Too many people."

"But it's too much. You're too much."

"I know. Isn't this getup grand? Look at this dress. Is it not perfect? And the purse and the shoes? They are the highest heels I've ever seen."

"Those heels," I agree, "are punching holes in the ozone."

"And the hat. Was he not custom-made for the purpose of delighting my hat-loving soul?"

"He is a wonderful hat. You deserve each other." In fact, I have started a secret fund for this hat. Even though most of the ballroom dancing money, and whatever money I can squirrel away from Judith, goes straight to the apartment fund or to credit cards, for the past three weeks I have been putting aside money for this hat. It costs $450 and I am already about halfway there. I plan on giving it to her for Christmas. I have to be with Judith on New Year's, but I'll be there, hat in hand, on Christmas with Evie.

"Now how about one little squeeze?"

"You'll mess the dress up."

"Then take it off."

She pauses a second to see if I am serious. I am.

"What? Here? You want me to take this dress off?"

"Yes I do."

"I'd have to go in the changing room."

"O.K."

"So, what, you want to stand outside and snake your arm in to grope me up? I'm not sure how I feel about that. If I'm going to be groped I would like the gentleman involved to at least have the decency to be in the same room with me. It's only right."

I shrug. "I could come inside."

"You could come inside?"

"Right."

"With me?"

"Right again."

"And I'm naked?"

"You can leave your hat on."

"And you are . . ."

"Naked, too, if you like."

"That's a lot of nakedness for one changing room."

A little ballet springs to life in her eyes. I know this ballet. I've seen it many times and I know how it ends. It has ended, in the past, with Evie perched on the sink in the bathroom of the Blue & Gold. It has ended with Evie lifting her skirt and sitting on my lap on the downtown 6 late at night when the car is empty. It has ended with me holding Evie up against the wall in the stairway of my apartment under a strip of flypaper the color of stale ear wax that is twitching with struggling raisin-fat flies. This is the ballet that signifies Despite Whatever Disagreements We've Had Lately We Are Once Again Gloriously in the Treehouse Together.

She picks up a blouse from a nearby rack and holds it in front of her face like a scarf and hams it up, doing this shuffly-geisha/hippy-bellydancer routine. It is all so silly. It is also totally arousing. My brain and my pelvis are connected by a coruscating bolt of lightning in the shape of a backbone.

"Mr. Whipple never had to put up with this much," I say. "It isn't fair."

Evie makes a few sultry veronicas, backing her way into the changing room. I follow but she stops me at the door with a fingertip in my sternum: I am to wait until she's ready. The ballet in her eyes accelerates. Through the crack in the door I can see as she shoulders off one strap of the dress—those collarbones: please let me put eggs in them!—and then the other. She does a little shrug and the dress slides down around her ankles, around the silver glittering shoes. Then she closes the door.

"I'll call you when I'm ready," she says.

I am going to make love to Daisy Buchanan right here in the changing room of Bendel's with other people—those poor common bipeds—milling around outside the door. I can barely contain myself. I have an embarrassing loper—an interloper, a porrection, a half-hard-on—pushing through my pants. I'm so excited, so full of roiling sexual urge but also of sheer effervescent joy, that I feel like I want to burst into some wild act of madcappery. I could vault over parking meters, dance on car roofs in the spray of opened hydrants, leap from a parapet while holding on to a banner and evading the hapless soldiers of an unjust king. I could Riverdance I'm so happy.

Am I or am I not a complete sucker for Evie?

I have to try to shake it out. I pace around in front of the door. I rearrange some blouses on the rack in correct order from X-small to X-large. I fold and unfold some gunmetal-colored tank-toppy shirts on a table. Then I hear it:

"Harry," Evie is whispering to me. I can barely make it out from the other side of the door. "Harry."

I ease through the door, backward, making sure no one sees me entering, and close the door behind me. I pause there for a second, squeezing shut my eyes—curtains of white, curtains of black as I flex and relax the lids—to prolong the pleasure. Then I turn and see Evie. She is curled up and rolling around on the floor, knees to her chest, her arms encircling herself, naked, blood leaking from between her legs into a murky brown puddle on the floor at my feet.

"Help me, Harry."

at your service

I am the janitor.

Whenever Evie is hit with the endo I clean everything. This is no small thing for me. I am not domestic. The only other time I recall ever really cleaning the apartment was the first time Evie came over. I remember sweeping (well, I don't own a broom, so: toweling, really) and mopping (wet-toweling) the entire apartment. I tidied up my room and killed as many of the fruit flies as I could. I scrubbed out the toilet (don't ask with what) and since for some reason I thought blue toilet water would be really impressive (and because I didn't have actual blue toilet cleaner) I dumped a packet of Darrell's blueberry Kool-Aid in it. Stylish and seductive, no?

I wanted to be hygienic and organized. I wanted her to see me as the kind of guy who was clean and together, who knew how to handle the small responsibilities of daily life and ergo the larger ones as well—an adult, in other words. During the endo I do even more. I become the janitor. I tidy up the place, true, but I also clean up the wrappers from tampons and pads. I deal with the bathroom. I wash soiled underthings, if necessary. You get the picture.

I am also the bellhop. And the delivery boy. And the laundry guy and the doctor and the counselor. I am everything. I know exactly what to do, from how much Percocet she can have to what movies to get her to how to administer the perfect cannonball. I am the best at all this.

But today's endo attack catches me off guard. Evie is not due for another week. She should not be menstruating yet. I am not prepared for this. The place is not clean. There are no T-shirts cooling in the freezer. There may not even be any Tampax or Always under the sink. I had meant to get more but hadn't gotten around to it yet. I thought I had at least a few days. This is a disaster.

"This is all wrong," I say as I lower her into bed. "What's happening?"

"Not bed," says a tiny voice coming from Evie's mouth. "Bath-room."

We limp to the bathroom together, where I sit her on the toilet. "Now go," she whispers.

I do as she says. Then I implement emergency endo proce-dures: I towel down bedroom, make bed, put T-shirts in freezer, make sure have juice (check: it's Darrell's but oh well, sorry, Darrell), make sure have Evie's favorite endo CD (check: it's Mad-eleine Peyroux, which officially belongs to Darrell, to which I again say, sorry, Darrell), make sure have movie (check: one copy of *Australia's Killer Spiders*), make sure have book to read to her (check: Anita Loos, she'll love it), swat fruit flies (gotcha, you little bastards), move TV/VCR from common room into bedroom (a bold move: Darrell does not know I do this; I normally do this only late at night and then replace it first thing in the morning, making sure it's replaced without disturbing the dust prints around it).

O.K. It looks good.

Then there's a horrible noise from the bathroom—it sounds like chicken fat being ripped through a garbage disposal—and I run down the hall. Every floor in the apartment, including my bedroom, is linoleum and I almost crash into the door I'm run-ning so fast. I fling open the door and Evie is sitting there, slumped on the toilet and half-hanging on to the edge of the sink with her pants around her ankles. Her body convulses and a jet of thick vomit sprays scattershot into the sink.

"Out. Out," she says, gasping.

"No, Eves," I say, getting a facecloth, wetting it, and wiping her mouth. "I got you. I got you." I turn on the faucet and wash down the vomit. Evie has some in her hair and I squat down beside her, holding her up, and wipe her hair with the facecloth. She's very weak. I can feel the exhaustion, the quivering in her muscles. She starts twitching and I feel her stomach spasm, her backbone go snap-tight, and she lets go another violent stream. I'm holding her head up under the jaw and I can feel its velocity in her throat. It's terrifying. I wipe her mouth and hold her head. Her hair is too curly and too short to hold back effectively so I take off my shirt and wrap it around her head. She looks like an ailing pirate.

"This is disgusting," she says. "I'm disgusting. Go away."

"No, Eves," I say again, wiping her forehead. She's boiling. The scars on her forehead are glowing like a soldering iron. "I've got you."

"Puke puke puke. I'm like some . . . kind of fucking . . . nineteenth-century French political cartoon. Where did . . . this come from?" Another convulsion, more egesta. The vomit is becoming thinner, yellowish but watery, like cerebrospinal fluid. I flush the toilet with my free hand and wash the sink out.

"Leave me alone," she says again.

"No, Eves," I say gently. "And if you say that one more time I'm going to make violent use of this facecloth. Now shut up and let me take care of you."

She lets her head drop into my neck, nuzzling like an exhausted foal. I hold her head there between my shoulder and ear, the way you do a phone, and stroke her hair. Her breath is hot and fast and smells of scorched bile.

"Thank you, Hairball," she whispers to me, full of love.

Eventually I carry her to bed. She is in too much pain for *Australia's Killer Spiders* and she doesn't want to be read to, even when I bill Anita Loos as her spiritual grandmother. I dress her in one of the T-shirts from the freezer and wrap her head in the other one. She only wants the cannonball, which I administer. I align my pelvis under hers and lace my hands under her knees and draw them up to her chest. It's stifling in the bedroom. The windows are open but there is no breeze and the traffic from below is alive with horns and squealing tires. An ambulance rips through the intersection, sirens wailing. This happens a lot: within a few blocks of my apartment is a hospital, a fire department, and a police station. I pull Evie in closer into the tightest cannonball I can. Contorted shrimplike this way Evie feels tiny. When she inhales I can feel her chest pushing her knees outward.

"Harry. Talk to me. Tell me something." Her pupils are black pinpoints: the Percocet is kicking in. Another few minutes and the worst of the pain should be gone.

"What do you want to hear?"

"Tell me what's going on in your novel."

She has a jolt of pain. Her body tenses. Through the gaping neck of the T-shirt I can see the small cervical bones push through the skin like a little row of keys tied together. Her fingernails cut into my forearm. Then she relaxes again and the keys in her neck submerge beneath her skin. When she relaxes her grip on my arm it stings from the air in a way that I know means she's dug down through one layer of skin, making small white gibbous gouges.

"It's sort of a boring moment in the book right now. You know, flashbacky, family-treeish sort of stuff. The mother's unhappiness, the father's travail, the brother's addiction blah blah blah. Not much to tell about."

"Tell me about the brother. I like brothers."

This actually is an interesting lie I've told. I've never even considered writing about my brother's heroin problem. I've never written a word about my family, about myself. The only writing I've ever done has been about purely invented worlds. I wonder why it never occurred to me to write about my own family. Bushido of the shitbag, I guess.

But on the endo Evie gets whatever she wants, even stories from an imaginary novel, so I make it up. I substitute stories from my brother's real life that I have never told anyone. If Evie knew these were real stories from my family she would flip. I never talk about my brother or parents. It's too painful. Looking at them I always see images of myself, and I can live without that. But Evie wants material, so I tell her some real-life things about Kurt: how he used to call me up, geeked out, talking about the messages he was receiving from the TV ("a message box for God"); the times he has gotten jumped by strangers while trying to cop in unfamiliar neighborhoods; the time he unwittingly took some heroin cut with scopolamine while sitting on the toilet and ended up walking around the block with his pants down at his ankles, barefoot and shitting until one of his friends saw this and clothed him in a garbage bag; what it was like when he was in jail. But I also tell her the good stuff, like how he and I used to do this crazy shit together, like canoeing this one time during a hurricane when neither one of us knew how to canoe or pulling up backward at the Burger King drive-thru to get free food. (Once the girl at the window wasn't amused and refused to give us free food. In fact, she said she wouldn't give us anything until we turned around and went back through the drive-thru "proper." I told her that my car only went in reverse and to prove it she made me drive off all the way down the street and back. It wasn't easy but it cracked up her manager enough to score us some free chicken tenders.) Or the way we once made up a language all our own, using food terminology. It was really quite an eloquent little language. All concession items were pronouns. All adjectives were Chinese food. All vegetables were verbs. The present tense was the vegetable itself; the past tense was the vegetable preceded by "rotten"; the future tense was the vegetable preceded by "fresh." If a word had no Food Language equivalent—this was the beautiful part—then you could use the corresponding native language's word. For example, "She is going to drive Frank to work because his bus is late again" would be "Cheeseburger fresh avocado Frank to meat loaf pork rinds hamburger bus potato no chopsticks again."

Evie asks for a sampling of the more common Food Language vocabulary, so:

VERBS:
To be: potato (most common vegetable, therefore most
    common verb)
To have: rice (similar logic)
To make love: jalapeño pepper (self-explanatory)
To like: green pepper
To dislike: red pepper
To drive: avocado (from a Burning Sensations song: "The
    girls turn the color of an avocado/when he drives down
    the street in his Eldorado")
To kiss: pea (for the shape the mouth assumes when
    accepting a pea)

NOUNS:
Work: meat loaf
Boyfriend: chocolate

Girlfriend: peanut butter
Father: steak
Mother: little steak
Brother: fried steak
Sister: broiled steak

ADJECTIVES:
Bad: no soy sauce
Good: soy sauce
Great: extra soy sauce
Fat: extra MSG
Skinny: no MSG
Smart: fried rice
Dumb: no fried rice

MISC.:
Because: pork rinds
Good morning: coffee
Good night: milk
Hi: lemonade
Bye: lemons

I surprise myself. Telling these stories about my brother makes me miss him, miss the way we used to be with each other. We were a united front against a dull and empty world, a little like I am with Evie now. And then he picked up the heroin habit. And I moved to New York. And he held up a liquor store with his finger inside his shirt and gave the old-timer clerk a heart attack and got sent to jail and I never visited him. Not once. My brother was in jail and I never once went to see him. Never wrote and never called. Nothing.

QUESTION: Why didn't I visit my brother?

ANSWER: I don't know.

My only brother was cooling in a cell and staring at the wall for an entire year, and I never even wrote him a letter. I guess since we hadn't been talking for a long time when he went to jail, we just sort of . . . well, you know what brothers can do.

And we did it.

But talking about him now makes me want to call him. I have his number. My mother is always sending it to me. He just lives in Connecticut. It would be easy to call him up and say, "Hey, Kurt. Harry. Just thought I'd ring up and say hi. Nothing much going on here. What's new with you?" like we had not spent the last eight years learning to hate each other, like maybe I would just cruise on over to play some Frisbee golf or go through the drive-thru backward and score some free chicken tenders. Maybe we would, too.

"The brother's pretty funny, eh, Eves?" I say to her. But Evie's sleeping. I hadn't realized how long I'd been talking. The sun has dipped to the horizon and the room is filling with smeary light and the walls are expanding and contracting with the sound of Evie breathing.

I get up to clean up the bathroom. When I turn on the light I see it. In the toilet is a cyst. A hot thrust of gorge rises in my throat and I have to swallow it back. The cyst is an angry bloody spheroid of semisolid tissue floating in the thick water. It has a motion all its own. Evie was right: where did this come from? She isn't due for her period for days. She almost never has bleeding like this when she isn't menstruating, and I certainly have never seen a cyst like this except in *Consultant*.

I fill the bucket and pour it down the toilet but the cyst only disappears for a second, then bobs back up. I stab at it with the handle of the toilet scrubber and finally with a flush it disappears in a red-black swirl, a maelstrom made out of human tissue. Then I push toilet paper around the sink with the coiled end of a tube of toothpaste, cleaning the residue of vomit. The room still has that chemical-burn smell of bile—it's otherworldly, like how I imagine a room that has had a poltergeist manifestation must smell—so I spray some Lysol around. Darrell, like a snooping parent back from a vacation, will probably be suspicious of the order and cleanliness in the apartment. He'll start sniffing around and will find that his juice is gone, that his TV has been moved, that his Madeleine Peyroux disc has been played—and then look out for cutlery.

But you know what?

Fuck Darrell.

In fact, I steal some of his liquor. It's just that all of a sudden the sadness hits me. It's not fair about Evie. It's not fair what I'm doing with Judith. It's not fair about my alleged career, the shitty apartments, the constant hunger, the dirty clothes, the rashes, the homeless people out there spare-changing on Avenue A, Birdie's brother. It's all wrong. It's too much. And also I feel sort of shaky—it's hard to tell if my hands are quivering or if I'm just imagining it—and my eyes feel desiccated and hard, like rendered globes of albumin and fat. A drink is exactly it. *Carpe drinkum*, my friends in college used to say. (Where are those guys now? Maybe we could get together or something.)

Then the phone rings. The answering machine has a bad habit of erasing messages and Darrell always thinks I have something to do with his lost calls so I should really pick up the phone and see who it is. But the only person I want to talk to is in my bed so I don't pick it up. Darrell doesn't have an announcement on the machine—just a stretch of staticky silence and then the beep—so it doesn't take long to hear the harrowing voice, the dreaded words.

"Are you available?" it says. "This is very disappointing to me, Harry—"

I dash over to the machine and turn the volume way down so Evie can't hear it. Judith thinks she has some big news on the promotion front. She has been talking to Morton Chenowith and it seems she has something cooking with him on my behalf. She gives me to understand that it might transpire very soon, whatever "it" is. She concludes the message by making noises that approximate the sucking sound of a boot being pulled out of mud but which I know are really the sound of her kissy-kissies.

I should be delighted. This is what I've been waiting for. This is what I've been living this double life for. This is it. The big time. My big chance. But I am not delighted. I feel sick to my soul. Can I do this on a night when the endo is this bad? I delete the message and pour myself another drink. I knock it down but it doesn't make me feel any better.

I drink a third, with identical results.

When I finish what's left in the bottle I go back into my room. The sun has slipped below New Jersey and my room is drained of orange. The weak light of streetlights makes the inside of my room look milked and spectral. Evie is still curled up in the cannonball, on her side, knees to her chest, mouth open, her chest rising and falling, her body in exactly the same position, as if I had never left her.

close call

I can't get back to sleep. Judith's voice and those three words keep resounding in my head. I wonder if the words of the hanging judge resound in the head of the condemned this way.

I spend the rest of the night wide awake and cannonballing Evie. She usually twitches a lot in her sleep but when the endo is bad she can be almost epileptic. Tonight she twitches so much that sometimes she breaks the cannonball and I have to gather up her legs and pull them to her chest again in her sleep without waking her up. Cannonballing makes the rashy skin on my back split open and start itching like mad. It makes me want to get up and rub my back against the doorjamb, but I don't even get up to put on some lotion. I don't want to break the cannonball.

Near four in the morning I have this moment. Evie has a violent spasm and for a second I can feel her pain. I am sure it is just a scintilla of what she experiences, but I feel the endometriosis in a vivid red wave. When she relaxes she feels small and involuted—nautiloid, drifting through the dark ocean of my sheets. Her hot breath is on my fingers. Her body is haloed by the drained light of the streetlamps. The room dilates with this silent shared frequency of pain and I think: I know you, Eves. I know every last vibrating particle of you by name. There is nothing I do not know.

I want to say it. I want to say "I love you, Evie Goddard." I crane my neck until my mouth is so near her ear I can feel the delicate hairs on my lip. But when I move my lips no noise comes out.

alpha malery

The next morning Evie is better. She is up early enough to go back home to change into clean clothes before going into work. I tell her I'll see her there, but I don't make it. It's an accident, but before I know what hits me I've watched Katie Couric, Regis, Rosie, and *The View*. By the time I'm ready to make any decisions it's noon and my brain is enervated by advertising and people who insist you do not go there. It's the exact opposite of terminal velocity: it's terminal inertia.

Story of my life.

That's it for the rest of the day, I decide. Best to wait out the workday and then ransack the office tonight, find the manuscript, edit it, do the pass to press (modifying certain dates on the forms so it looks less late than it is), be done with it, then get the scoop on Morton Chenowith and voila: problems are solved.

I hit Tompkins Square Park and hang out with the homeless guys playing chess with bottlecaps. I don't know why but the homeless around here always look sunburnt in winter and frost-bitten in summer. There's one lady with pink plastic spoons for earrings and clay in her hair who's creaming this guy who last year had a shunt in his head that drained gray liquid. In the distance some Russian kids are throwing rocks at the streetlamp.

Finally they hit it and they all stare, frozen by the beauty of the moment as the glass falls—perfectly intact, round as a crystal bowl—until it shatters into scintillant dust on the sidewalk. It's hot and my rashes are burning from the sweat but it's O.K. This is my neighborhood. I know its rhythms and am almost a part of it.

This amniotic sense of well-being is almost fully intact when a guy in a coonskin hat and pilgrim-style buckle shoes thinks my general staring around is specific to him.

"What is your fucking problem, pendejo?" he says.

If he only knew.

An hour later it's the worst-case scenario. I'm back in the office, about to start searching in earnest for the manuscript, when I make an unpleasant discovery: Nadler is back from the country. It's just me and him, alone, no witnesses.

Nadler brings me into his office and I sit down surrounded by books that aren't books at all but little totems of passive aggression—look what I've done; look what you haven't—and he lets me sweat it out in silence. I try to assume the unflappable mien of certain British war heroes, but it's not working. I itch. My scalp is constricting over my skull. My asshole twitches nervously like a rabbit's nose and it's making me squirm in my seat.

"Harold," Nadler says at last.

"Yes, sir?"

"Is there something wrong with you?"

"What do you mean?"

"Have you been seriously ill?"

"No, sir."

"Are you in serious emotional distress?"

"No, sir."

"Is there any major trouble in your family?"

"No, sir."

"I'm just trying to understand the reason for your performance."

"My performance, sir?"

Nadler sighs. "Maybe you can help me with something."

"Of course."

"Now let's try to work through this methodically and logically."

"O.K."

"You are my assistant. Right? O.K. We'll start there. Square one. You are my assistant. Now what sort of duties do you think that might entail? Would you say returning phone calls?"

"Sir, I—"

"Would you say, mmm, forwarding my messages to me in the country?"

"I can explain—"

"How about turning up in the office during standard working hours?"

"You don't—"

"Would you say passing manuscripts to press in a timely manner?"

"I've been having some difficulty getting in touch with the author to go over edits."

"Jenkins has called me five times in the last four days."

"Oh. Hunh. That's strange. Maybe I've got the wrong number for him. Maybe I should use your Rolodex."

"Harry," Nadler says, his mouth puckering. "I don't give you enough work to fall this far behind. The Jenkins manuscript is a ten-thousand-dollar book. If it pubs late it will cost us tens of thousands of dollars in production costs and we can lose countless orders. That's unacceptable."

I say nothing.

"I find myself constantly wondering how we could have gotten in this position. Let me ask you: when I told you to pass the manuscript, did you think I was kidding?"

"No, sir," I say miserably.

"Do you think someone else should be doing it for you?"

"No, sir."

"Perhaps you think this project is beneath you. Perhaps you think it's not exalted enough for you."

"No, sir. I mean yes, sir. I mean, it's plenty exalted."

"I don't know what else to say, Harold. You've been here six years. This isn't complicated. Horst has been in editorial three weeks and he already knows how to put a book into production."

"I know *how*."

"This conversation is not a good use of my time." There is always a lunglike sheen—purple and grayish and pulpy—to Nadler's skin but now it becomes even more pronounced. It makes me wonder if I am beginning to redden myself. "I'll say it as plainly as I can: pass the manuscript to press."

"Yes, sir."

"I'm going back to the country. I'll be gone next week. I want you to call me when it's done."

"Right away, sir."

Nadler looks at me in a way that makes me feel like a botched chemistry experiment: a little sulfur, a little lithium, a little Harry Driscoll, and—whoopsie daisy—a lethal reaction. I cringe and sniff back tears.

"And Harold," he says, his lips drooping like an obscene or-
chid. "We won't be having this conversation again. Understand?"

ribbit ribbit

After Nadler's gone and I've exhausted the places the manuscript
could be, I notice that Evie's computer is still on and her system
is up. Normally I'd never do this kind of thing, but Evie's note
about "GONE" being the biggest small word has me worried a
little, and so I punch up her email account and do some recon.
There's nothing in her corporate account but I check her personal one (I know the password, ha ha ha) and find a saved chat
conversation with Madeleine. It's dated from last week, when we
had the pillowfight.

MTIERNEY: Why you stay with him is a mystery and an insult
to women everywhere. You should only subject yourself to
treatment like that if the sex is good.

EGODDARD: Harry's a good lover.

MTIERNEY: Message from Evie to Madeleine, dated three
days ago: "Harry fucks like he's playing Operation."

EGODDARD: I think he's just worried about the endo. It's
sweet, in a way. Everything else we do is wonderful.

MTIERNEY: But you never orgasm when you do I-T it.

EGODDARD: No. I cry wolf.

MTIERNEY: You cry wolf! I knew it! I bet you cry all sorts of wolf!

EGODDARD: But only with I-T it. In all other ways he's very attentive.

MTIERNEY: Attentive? ATTENTIVE? O.K. Let me quote from another email. Upon examining the number of messages in your TO HARRY folder to your FROM HARRY folder you said, and I quote: "859 to 227. Not a ratio that sets a girl's heart to pitter-pat, is it?"

EGODDARD: I was mad at him that day. That's all.

MTIERNEY: And with good reason. He got caught pissing off the fire escape at the O. Henry Awards ceremony. He humiliated you. He's always humiliating you.

EGODDARD: He was drunk.

MTIERNEY: INCROYABLE!

EGODDARD: He hates those parties.

MTIERNEY: He hates PEOPLE, Evie.

EGODDARD: Those parties just remind him how far he has to go. They make him feel bad about himself.

MTIERNEY: We've ALL got far to go. We're in publishing.

EGODDARD: He wants to be a writer, you know.

MTIERNEY: And where is said manuscript?

EGODDARD: I know.

MTIERNEY: You know you know you know.

EGODDARD: Why are you always so hard on Harry?

MTIERNEY: He's selfish, he's childish, he's lazy.

EGODDARD: He's not lazy.

MTIERNEY: He should have bedsores and a catheter he's so lazy.

EGODDARD: I tell you how he got the job in first place?

MTIERNEY: Voodoo?

EGODDARD: Listen to this. When he was still in college Harry went to the bookstore and read every new book Prestige published—two a week. He couldn't afford to buy them, so he just read them there in the store, leaning up against the bookshelf, and then he sent the president reader's reports on them. He did this for eight months. Every week, for eight months, the president got extensive reports on our books from this undergrad guy named Harry Driscoll. Finally the president gave in and gave him a job. Harry just wore him down. And you know what, Maddie? Those reports were the best the president had ever seen. They are still used around here to train new assistants how to write good reports.

MTIERNEY: That doesn't make him any less of an idiot.

EGODDARD: You're being too hard on him.

MTIERNEY: Well I am half German. We are a warlike people.

EGODDARD: He's better than you think.

MTIERNEY: Whatever frog-kisser.

EGODDARD: What?

MTIERNEY: You know. Frog. Princess. She kisses. He transforms into hunky prince. A very amusing fairy tale, but it doesn't work like that on Planet Gotham. Too bad though.

EGODDARD: That's ridiculous. It's not frog-kissing with Harry and me.

MTIERNEY: NOT FROG-KISSING???? Sister, PLEASE! I said RIBBIT!

EGODDARD: Noooooo.

MTIERNEY: Item: he has some very slimy habits. Item: you supply him with affection despite this unappealing aspect. Item: you hope he will change. In fact, you even have this operation so you can make love to Harry the Frog. Item: HE NEVER CHANGES. Despite your best efforts and prayers. Ergo: ribbit ribbit.

EGODDARD: Harry is not a frog.

MTIERNEY: Girl, he is the fucking Frog KING, all right?

EGODDARD: Nooooo . . .

MTIERNEY: What does he ever do besides fuck poorly and piss in your shower? Does he ever give you anything? A dress? Flowers? A subway token?

EGODDARD: He gives me words.

MTIERNRY: HE GIVES YOU WHAT?

EGODDARD: Words. For my birthday this year he gave me "callipygian." It's a nice word. It means "of or pertaining to having shapely buttocks."

MTIERNEY: So basically, for your birthday, he told you you have a nice ass. That was it?

EGODDARD: You don't understand. We don't have your kind of salary, Maddie.

MTIERNEY: You think giving you vocab words is sweet?

EGODDARD: I think it is sweet. Yes.

MTIERNEY: THEY ARE A CHEAP WAY TO AVOID SAYING I LOVE YOU!

EGODDARD: Lay off, O.K.?

MTIERNEY: Fine. Let's change the subject. What news of the delicious J.J.?

EGODDARD: Never use delicious for anything but food. It's a disgusting adjective.

MTIERNEY: God, he has you talking like him now.

EGODDARD: Well . . .

MTIERNEY: WHAT NEWS?

EGODDARD: He's not newsworthy yet.

MTIERNEY: He has great buzz, though. Friend of a friend had a moment with him in a stall at Double Happiness and said he was delightfully . . . rough.

EGODDARD: I wouldn't know about that.

MTIERNEY: That's not what I heard.

EGODDARD: Leave it, Madeleine.

MTIERNEY: Open your eyes, Evie. He's not worth all this defense. He's seeing another woman.

EGODDARD: We don't know that.

MTIERNEY: I bet she's a horsey type. Fox hunts, Range Rovers, high tea, mint juleps, missionary sex, plaids everywhere. God.

EGODDARD: I think she might be an S & M person.

MTIERNEY: WHAT?

EGODDARD: Harry always has these bruises in weird places.

MTIERNEY: Do you need another reason to dump him?

EGODDARD: I'm giving him the benefit.

MTIERNEY: You are such a pushover.

EGODDARD: Lay off, Maddie.

MTIERNEY: Okay okay okay. Fine. Don't heed good sisterly advice. Just at least tell me you're not going to see him tonight.

EGODDARD: Don't worry about that. Even if he came crawling through my window I wouldn't see him tonight.

MTIERNEY: You need to start making a stand.

EGODDARD: OKOKOKOKOKOKOKOKOKOKOK already. Standing.

MTIERNEY: I mean it. Swear you won't see him.

EGODDARD: I swear it.

MTIERNEY: Swear on your word as a member of the sister-hood.

EGODDARD: I swear by Wicca, Daphne du Maurier, and the WNBA I won't see him tonight. Satisfied?

advice

After I reread the email eleven times I call Keeno.

"What is she doing telling Madeleine about the words I give her? Madeleine doesn't have that kind of clearance. She shouldn't have this information. And what the hell does she mean 'cry wolf'? What's she talking about? That's not true. She almost always has an orgasm with me. She said so. I can tell. Honest to God. And what the hell is Operation?"

"You don't want to know," Keeno says.

"And who the fuck is J.J.?"

"Well, at least he's not newsworthy yet."

"Oh, yeah. Right. That's true. I've got Evie's girlfriend talking about how delightfully rough this J.J. person is in the stalls at Double Happiness but at least he's not newsworthy yet. True. Good point. Silly of me not to accentuate the positive."

"If you'd stop your bellyaching for one second you'd see you're being a fucking hypocrite right now."

"*What?*"

"In case you've forgotten, you're boning your way to the top. I think that entitles Evie to a prospective."

"Do you know whose friend you are supposed to be?"

"Sorry."

"For whom?"

"It's just like you to use correct English when pissed, you know."

"Oh my God! I just had a thought. What if this guy's the purple penis? What if he's the one with the purple penis?"

"What are you talking about?"

purple penis

Not too long ago—right before Evie's operation—we were lying in bed after having ministered to each other. We were naked and slick as seals. Heat was pouring off the walls in orange waves and the wrong church bells were ringing again. I remember I was stroking her eyelids. I remember how her sweaty hair, matted to her face, was tangled and complex, like the handwriting of children. I remember feeling a little embarrassed as she played with my unhard dick under the covers. It always feels like it's been caught red-handed at something obscurely shameful when she does this, like someone saw it watching daytime TV or reading relationship books.

"You know," Evie said as she stood it up and let it fall down.

"It really is a silly apparatus. It gets so surly and cooperative afterward. Look at it. *Bloop.* Who's in charge here anyway?"

"No question. You are."

"Unhard they look so funny. Like a plucked turkey kind of."

"Nice, lady."

"I know, I know. I should pick better adjectives. Let's see. How about . . . *masterly.*"

"Indomitable," I countered.

"Redoubtable."

"Conquistadorian."

"Sears Towerish."

"Juggernautical."

"Godzillan."

"Now you're cooking with butter," I said. *"Humbabauan."*

"Say what?" Evie asked. "Humbarbaran?"

"Humbabauan. Of or relating to Humbaba? You know: Gilgamesh? 'I am Gilgamesh, king of Uruk, builder of walls and slayer of Humbaba whose name means Hugeness.' You know? That legendary monster? That mythical beast? Never mind. I think you were about to compliment me."

"I can't think of any other expressions for"—here Evie made a gasping, eye-popping face—*"huge."* I am of two minds about this sarcasm. Clearly we were playing around, but a part of me wonders if that sarcasm (*"huuuuge"*) was a part of the game or if it was at my expense.

Hmmm.

This is what it means to have a penis: undying doubt.

"Then perhaps we should denigrate all other penises," I said.

"Very well. All other penises are tiny."

"Wilting."

"Pinkyish."

"Tom Thumbish even."

"Travel-sized."

"Uvular."

"One thing I'm glad about," she said. "It isn't a purple penis. I can't abide those distasteful sickly eggplant-purple penises."

"What?"

"The purple penis. I do not like it."

"What do you mean 'purple penis'?"

"I mean an anatomical unit that is at once a penis and also purple."

"You've never experienced a purple penis."

"O.K."

"That's simply absurd."

"If you say so, Harry."

"There's no such thing as a purple penis."

"There are many purple penises, for your information."

"Many?"

"Well, *you* know . . ."

advice con't.

"What do you think?" I say to Keeno.

"I think you're acting like a fucknut."

"No way."

"Harry, go to her. Say, 'Evie, I'm sorry. Evie, I love you.' O.K.?"

"Fucking purple penis! Who's got a purple penis?"

"Did she mention in the chat with Madeleine anything about a purple penis?"

" *'There are many purple penises, for your information.'* "

"You know one of the real problems with being dishonest all the time? You think everyone else is, too. Lies abuse their victims but they corrupt their speakers."

"You're sounding like that fucking Drakkar slush manuscript again."

"Maybe you should read that—"

"Will you cut that out, please? Jesus. If I wanted stupid advice I would have called my mother."

There's a long, static-filled pause.

"Remind me again why you were reading her email. Can you explain that?"

telesis

I decide to go to Sis's Place and ablute myself with Pabst. The mansuscript will just have to wait. Fuck the fallout. If my friends can't help me at least I can surround myself with mindlessly agreeable drunks. I'm about to leave when I see a package addressed to me on Horst's chair. He must have signed for the messenger while I was out. I open it and find inside my ANIMAL WANT WOMAN boxers. On top of the boxers is a note in Judith's eighth-grade bubble handwriting that says

I believe these are yours? They made a lovely remembrance. Which reminds us: if you do not pleasure us tomorrow night we will send a mail bomb to one professor a day until you comply.

                                        Signed, the Unaboxer.

I effect a change of plans. I pick up the phone and dial Judith's number.

"Hello?"

I hate myself for this. Evie was better this morning, true, but I feel like I should be with her every day between now and when her period is over in case she needs an emergency cannonball or unusual Rapunzel treats. I know that is what I should do. I know I should just tell Judith sorry that I can't subserve tonight. But my judgment is clouded by a purple haze.

"Hello?" Judith says again.

"Hi," I say, trying to sound happy to hear her voice.

You'd think sex with Judith would be feral and cruel, full of clutching and tussling. But it is mechanical and banal. Only by a resolute tacit agreement do we overlook the absurd pantomimic meaninglessness of the act. I don't know why she wants to maintain such a relationship—perhaps my performance is more convincing that I give it credit for—but it seems to me that our carnal movements are all listless and animatronic. It's like we're sex robots instead of people.

And there's something else, too. With Evie I have never—honest: *never*—had any erectile reluctance. Every time we have frolicked I have enjoyed instantaneous, aggressive, vacuum-packed erections. With Judith I often have trouble even mustering a twitch of a hard-on. Last week I lost it while trying to gain entry. I was fine during the preliminary stages, but when Judith's face was thrust deeply into a pillow, her back lordotically arched in cooperative expectation, my hands clutching her veiny ass as I tried to find my way, it happened.

"Sorry," I said. "Pilot error. And we seem to be having some technical difficulties back here."

It didn't seem to bother her. We took a break and had some of her Mountain Blush (for her: with grenadine and cherries added; for me: with two jiggers of vodka furtively added when she wasn't looking). Then she inserted her index finger forthrightly into my anus—alas, to no avail. Finally I had to make the metaphorical literal and I dropped to my knees to perform what she likes to term "worshiping the high priestess."

Half an hour after the phone call I'm in Judith's Upper East Side apartment surrounded by quietude and luxuriant order. No fruit flies, no sweatshop, no vindictive roommate. There's a collection of apples and oranges in a bowl which are so colorful and vibrant that they look like a bunch of flowers. I wash my face in the bathroom and press it deeply into a fragrant, pristine towel. The rest of her apartment is furnished like the interior of Barbara Eden's bottle in *I Dream of Jeannie*: a supremacy of pink and velvety cushions and hanging beads and candles. It's tawdry, I know, but I can't help feeling a stab of jealousy.

She owns, after all.

"Here you are," Judith says, putting the bowl of steaming soup in front of me. "For strength."

"Thanks," I say. "So what is this party exactly that Morton Chenowith is throwing?"

She explains: Morton Chenowith is having a big-deal party this coming weekend. It has come to Judith's attention that it's true that Prestige is having trouble finding the right editor to fill the vacant office—Prestige wants someone young and au courant— and she is willing to lobby on my behalf. She thinks that if I were to go to this party with her endorsement and make a good impression, the job would almost certainly be mine.

Problem is, of course, that the party is on the night of Evie's period, when I need to be there. The image of the purple penis flashes before me but even that—even the painful graphic image of Evie's prospective—does not make me hurt enough to leave her alone with the endo.

I cannot do it. I will not do it. I may get chewed out by Nadler five thousand more times and get fired but I cannot leave Evie alone on the endo.

"I don't know, Judith. I mean, it sounds great. It sounds wonderful. And it means a lot to me that you would think of me like this. But . . . I . . . um . . . uh . . ."

QUESTION: You are a very accomplished liar. Why are you having trouble coming up with an excuse for why you cannot go to this party?

ANSWER: I do not know. Because deep down I really want to go? That doesn't sound right, does it? Because you're sick of lying? That doesn't sound especially plausible either, does it? Then why? Hmm. Soulwise, this bears some looking into.

"I can only help you so much, Harry. You have to put yourself out there too. It would be good for you to meet Morty under these circumstances."

"I know. I know. It's just that . . ." I resort to the old standby. "My mother's coming to visit this weekend, Judith. I just can't make it."

Judith gives me a long, evaluative look, trying to figure out if this is the truth. I know she must be stunned. This is the big chance I have been waiting for and she knows it. But I have obviously chosen the right strategy: she is susceptible to all things maternal.

"O.K., Harry. Guess we'll just have to think of something else some other time."

"I really am sorry. If I could make it I would. You know that. I would love to make it."

"Oh," she says with a lubricious grin while rubbing a fingertip down my wrist. "I bet you can *make* it."

That's the kind of terrible line I have to endure all the time. I think she lives her life according to plots she lifts from the romance novels she edits. She wants to meet me out in bars and pick me up, pretending we've never met. She asks me to wear a rose in my lapel and wait for her on shadowy corners. Once I had to sing to her wearing starchy Edwardian garb and holding parasol while piloting a rowboat in Central Park.

She wanted to be serenaded in a boat. And she got it.

Judith undresses me and I gamely essay a fuck. It should be a simple fuck—guileless and precatory, uncomplicated and aerobic. It should be a snap. With Evie I am sometimes freaked out because I can sense her hips asking mine a question I don't know the answer to. Judith's body isn't capable of that kind of communication, and even if her body were to start talking, I wouldn't be listening. In other words: I should be able to do this no sweat. Problem is I can't. As we start to entangle I feel myself beginning to detumesce. I attempt to put it in as fast as I can without looking unnatural but that doesn't help. In fact it has a decidedly unhelpful effect. There's no stopping it now.

Tim-*berrrrrrrrrrrrrrrrrr*.

There is no way I am worshiping the high priestess tonight. No way. I am through with that. I refuse. There's only one thing for it:

Faking it.

This I do. In the spirit of excruciating honesty I have to tell you that this isn't entirely new. I resort to this a lot. I can't count the times lately I have produced a luxuriant shudder while crossing my eyes and making burbling noises all so I can stop thrusting away with a penis that I know is about to start flapping around like a flag of surrender. (Once I had a conversation about this with

KEENO: That is dumbest thing I have ever heard.

ME: Thank you. Thank you very much.

KEENO: Are you convincing at least? Does she know?

ME: I don't think so. I don't think she knows.

KEENO: Yeah, you must be pretty good at faking it, with all that experience you've got.

ME: What do you mean?

KEENO: I mean, with all those women you've been with. You must have picked up something from them in the way of faking skills.

ME: Har har. Very funny. What a friend you are.

KEENO: I don't think you really want to have a conversation about what constitutes friendship, do you?

ME: [*Silence.*]

KEENO: Figured as much.)

As the blood rushes out of my penis I start in on the routine. With two fistfuls of Judith's hamstrings and standing above her, I hunch and spasm in simulated orgasm while making these hacking kraken noises, all the while thinking, Viva la Evie, Viva la Evie.

"Phew," I say after a few seconds of posturing. "Wow. That was huge. I think I just came a third world country. It's like Yemen just came out of my penis."

Judith's face is invisible to me beneath her interlaced ankles but I hear her mumble, "What did you say?"

"Huge," I repeat. "Burkina Faso. Papua New Guinea. United Arab Emirates. Wowser. Sorry it was so quick, but you can be very arousing, you know."

"No, Harry. I heard you say someone's name."

Uh-oh. Dire strategic error. The reflex to utter "Viva la Evie" is so embedded in my subconscious that in my attempt to be convincing I have actually said it. Judith has made it very clear on many occasions that if I were involved with anyone else things would be summarily over.

"What did you say?" I pull out, fully flaccid, and Judith reassembles. "Towel?" I suggest helpfully.

"What did you just say, Harry?"

"Say?"

"I heard you say someone's name. You said someone's name. You better not be fucking around on me, Harry boy, because I can be a real bitch when angry."

"Oh," I say. "O.K. You got me. Look, I don't know how to explain this—"

"Well, you'd better try," Judith says, candent with suspicion. Her face has the orangy complexion seen in colorized movies.

Think, Harry, *think*.

Then: aha!

"It's embarrassing. I did say someone's name. I've got this obsession—boy this is embarrassing—but do you know the actress Viva? Popular in the sixties? In all those Warhol movies? One of Avedon's favorite subjects? And well, it just happens that you look a lot like her—I mean, she looks a lot like *you*, ha ha ha—and sometimes during . . . when we . . . you know . . . I just sort of start thinking that you're Viva. It's nothing. Just a turn-on, you know? I never meant to say it out loud. If you didn't look so much like her it never would have happened. I'm sorry."

"I'm a brunette, Harry."

"Yes, but the *cheek*bones," I say, trying not to sound desperate. "It's the cheekbones that matter. You have very similar features."

"You really think I look like Viva?" She cranes her neck to regard herself in the vanity. The craquelure of her day-old makeup is clearly visible even in the dim lighting. She looks haggard, eroded by disappointment, but also excessively cosmeticized and falsely upbeat. She looks, it occurs to me, like a lifer stewardess.

"Not exactly," I say. "You've got a better ass."

"You can be such a nice boy. Flattery will get you everywhere."

Too close. Jesus.

We recline in bed together and I have to hold her. With Evie at times like these I have this oxymoronic feeling: I'm drained yet filled with something, exhausted yet vitalized. But with Judith

I just feel disgusted. The best thing I can say about these post-coital moments with Judith is that I feel like I have just accomplished a necessary chore. It is the same feeling I used to get in high school when I finally changed the oil in my car.

Judith falls asleep almost immediately in a fuck-drunk collapse but I can't. I feel clotted and wrong. I know this is probably the last best chance I've got to save my career, but it's not fair that it comes on the weekend when Evie is having her period, when she needs the cannonball—maybe more, even. I lie in bed, scare-crowed with self-loathing while Judith sleeps limply alongside with a string of gluey saliva stretching from the pillow to her mouth. She can sleep that way because her soul isn't rotting away with guilt.

"You know the way most people's cells are made up of ninety percent water?" Keeno said to me once. "Well, yours are ninety percent guilt."

It's true.

Bushido of the shitbag, I think. Not much longer now. Just don't think about it and soon enough it will all be over.

I get up for some air and go out onto Judith's balcony. I can see out across Central Park. In the pearly darkness the tops of the trees look soft and doughy. There is no turbulence in this neighborhood even at this hour. The night is deep and unpro-testing.

Squatting naked on the balcony, my back up against the cold glass door, with a glaze of Judith's viscosities still on my dick and my face, I dial the numbers on Judith's cordless phone and wait for Evie's message to come on. I do this a lot after sex with

Judith when I can't get to sleep. I'm not sure why I do this so often—it exposes me to risk; if Judith knew about Evie it would ruin everything—but every time the machine picks up and I hear her voice it all seems worth it, there is a velvety humming in my ears and a rush of vasocongestion in my head and stomach. Evie's voice can have this effect.

"This is Evie Goddard in Prestige's editorial department. I'm not available to take your call but if you leave your name and number I'll call you back as soon as possible."

I press the phone close to my mouth. I can smell my own breath in my nose—it has Judith's scent on it. I want to tell Evie the truth about everything. I want to tell her that soon I'll have enough money together to get a new place, that soon I'll have a new job, that soon everything will be perfect and that this tawdriness with Judith is almost over. I want to tell her that I'm sorry for missing her this weekend.

Sorry for everything.

Sorry for being me.

Instead I hang up and dial again.

"This is Evie Goddard . . ."

And again.

"This is Evie Goddard . . ."

And again.

But this time someone picks up. "Evie Goddard's office."

"Hello?" I say.

"Hello?" says a female voice I've never heard before.

"Who's this?"

"Who's *this*?" it says. "Harry?"

"No. Not Harry. This is, uh."

Then I panic and try to hang up, but I confuse the buttons

and end up pressing a bunch of wrong, beeping ones. "Fuck,
fuck!" I can't help saying before I find the OFF button.

I stare out over the park. Lights from the apartments on Central Park West wink at me in the darkness like they know something I don't. I'm trying to figure out who the hell could be at
Evie's desk at one A.M. when the phone in my hand rings. I
juggle it—it almost goes over the railing—and it rings a second
time before I'm able to pick up.

"Hello?" I say. But the line is dead.

weekend

Judith wants it and in light of my refusal to go to Morton Chenowith's party I know I need to please her so I stay the whole
weekend. This is difficult as what she wants to do is to stay in
the apartment all day and night getting this ugly brown vermi-
form Chinese food delivered and making sweet passionate love.
I do not like Chinese food and the PSI in my genitals never
makes it to an even useful level so I spend a lot of time worshiping the high priestess and explaining my flaccidity away.

One thing I do not do is risk calling Evie's machine again. I
know she will be pissed but I figure it is better to sacrifice this
weekend than the next weekend when the endo hits.

As for missing the party and salvaging my career: I will just
have to find another way.

workweek

Monday

I spend an hour searching my apartment for the manuscript and the rest of the day in ALT.COFFEE, checking my email and calling voice mail every ten minutes for a message from Evie. Nothing.

Weird.

Tuesday

I decide to go into the office at five A.M. so I can search for the manuscript without anyone around. Joey P. Romano almost faints when I enter the building and flash him the ID.

"The hell you doing here so early?" he says.

I'm about to complete our usual ritual but suddenly "Getting fired" seems all too appropriate. "Just some stuff," I say.

I search through Paula's piles. It's possible I gave her the manuscript to copy, but it's not there. I check subrights. I check permissions. I think maybe I put it down somewhere and forgot to pick it up. I even wade through the recycling bin.

Nothing.

And still there are no messages from Evie on my email account and nothing on voice mail. At noon I write her an email. I don't want to admit any wrongdoing or any awkwardness, so I

try to compose a note that is solicitous and friendly without acknowledging that anything is out of the ordinary. This is what I
write.

TO: egoddard
FROM: hdriscoll
RE: The Loch Ness Evie

Experts have been trying for days to get a glimpse of the elusive
Loch Ness Evie. There have been sightings in and around the
area of Mott and Grand, but these claims are as yet
unsubstantiated, and their authenticity is somewhat suspect, as
all witnesses were either drunk or just plain Scottish.
Researcher and philanthropist hundredaire Harry Driscoll,
however, thinks he is on the right track and that the fabled Loch
Ness Evie does in fact exist, and that he can prove it.

"The Loch Ness Evie is a subtle, sensitive creature," Dr.
Driscoll told reporters Tuesday. "She is extremely intelligent and
resourceful. She is also very leery of contact with humans she
perceives as potentially threatening. But if we, as a species, can
convince her of our benignity, of our fundamental goodness, of
our wild desire for contact, then I think we can establish a
relationship with her that will be mutually rewarding."

Dr. Driscoll has established a hot line for any information
regarding the location of the shy hydrosaur. Please feel free to
contact Dr. Driscoll at 212 521 2652 or at hdriscoll@prestige.com.
Thank you.

By ten-thirty at night I still haven't heard from her. I call her
at home and get her machine.

"Evie," I say. "Harry. Do not adjust your phone. It is not broken, but—ta-da—I bought some new lotion. That's right. *I* bought some new lotion. Me. Gold Bond Medicated stuff. Good for rashes, they say. And I hereby afford you the opportunity to apply it to my back. All you have to do is call."

Ha, I say to myself. *That* ought to do it.

Wednesday

"And still no contact?" Keeno says. "She must know about Date."

"No way. There's no way. How could she?"

"What about that phone call?"

"Maybe I misdialed."

"Maybe it was Madeleine getting work to bring home for Evie. Maybe she knew it was you. Maybe she star-sixty-nined you."

"You think?"

"I hate to repeat myself—no I don't; I love it—but I'm telling you, Harry, call up Evie and say, 'Evie, I'm sorry. Evie, I love you.' "

"I can't fucking believe Madeleine would snoop around like that. That is so unprincipled."

"Unprincipled? Who's the one getting his cake eaten by two?"

"Would you just pick a side and stay on it, please?"

"What are you going to do?"

"I'm going to fucking wait her out, that's what."

Thursday

"This is all wrong," I say to Horst. "She should have called by now. Where is she? Maybe she got fired?"

"I don't think she got fired."

"I knew she shouldn't have showed that awful Drakkar manuscript around. The editors may have laughed her right out of her job."

"I don't think she got fired."

"Oh man, I bet she got fired. And she's mad at me and too proud to tell me. Shit. Poor Evie. Maybe we should call her. You want to call her?"

My phone rings and I snatch up the receiver. "Harry Driscoll!" I almost yell.

It's Nadler. I say, "Yes, sir. Doing paperwork now. All edits finalized, all forms filled out. Just making copies for design and copyediting. They'll have it in the next twenty minutes. O.K. Right, sir. See you Monday. Bye."

Horst looks at me with that indurate Teutonic disapproval.

"Shut up, Horst. It's around here somewhere."

I make a cursory last-minute search of my desk and environs but of course the manuscript is nowhere to be found. I need to come to terms with the fact that it might be lost for good. I haven't talked to Judith since the weekend, but now seems like a good time. I dial her number and leave a message on her machine.

"Judith, Harry. Hi. Sorry have been so absent this week. Lots of work, you know. Look, I was hoping we could have that talk about my . . . um . . . advancement . . . soon. Things have gotten a little . . . tight . . . for me around here. I don't want to rush you or anything, but it would probably be best if we could talk this over sooner rather than later. I'll be here."

Patrick McThomas, a financial VP and one of the guys I should have been buddying up to all this time, walks by my cube and I, in an unprecedented move, stop him and ask him if he knows where the hell Evie has been all week.

"If she's not in I trust she's at work on some worthwhile project," he says. "And what are you working on there, Harry?" he asks.

"Oh. Some very big projects," I say cavalierly. "You know, very hush-hush."

The VP looks over my shoulder at my computer, on which I see typed out over and over until it fills the whole screen, *I will not I will not I will not.*

Friday, or Found: One Needle

I'm sitting at my desk silently willing the phone to ring when Horst walks in, wearing a cockeyed party hat on his head and doing a Locomotiony dance.

"What are you doing being so happy?" I say.

"Didn't you hear? Evie just signed up a big book."

My intestines feel for a second like they're in free fall.

"What was that?"

"Evie signed up this book. *Love Is a Ladder.*"

"Say *what*?"

"*Love Is a Ladder.*"

"The fucking Drakkar book?"

"It's a *Men Are from Mars* kind of thing."

"I KNOW WHAT IT'S ABOUT! I FUCKING REJECTED IT TWO MONTHS AGO!"

"Well, it's going to be published now."

"This is a joke, right?"

"No. Huge galley mailing, national advertising, twenty-six city author tour—the whole thing."

"This isn't happening."

I guess this explains where she's been all week: editing. And what she was working on so diligently that night we got in the do-you-love-me fight. And when I was pleading with her to play Madame Bovary. Jesus. How long has this been going on?

"There's a party for the author on thirty-three."

"The executive floor?"

"He's a really great guy. The women are all over him."

I say nothing to this, trying to pull off a look of amused indifference.

"Hey!" he says, jubilant. "You want to come meet him?"

my big chance

I call up Judith and tell her that my mother's plans are canceled and I can go after all. Delighted, she tells me to meet her at her apartment the following night. Then I call Evie's place and leave a message telling her that I won't be able to come over for the cannonball this weekend as my mother got into a car accident—she's banged up but fine; don't worry; I just need to be there—and I have to go home to Connecticut. (That's one busy mother.) I buy myself the whole weekend because Judith wants it and because I am now dedicated to making this push.

Time for me to look out for me.

Morton Chenowith lives in a 1950s Las Vegas–movie mogul–cum-mafioso apartment on the Upper East Side, on Fifth Avenue. The place feels like it was designed to make you feel small, and it works. It has huge vaulted ceilings, massive triptych paintings on the walls, a panoramic window overlooking Central Park—everything is bigger than you are, including all the guests. I feel the way a native from some remote tribe must feel the first time he sees color TV: all these people are so vibrant, so bright that they are alien and almost frightening. I want to reach out and poke them to make sure they're real. There are photographers milling around. They're used to events like these and their senses are honed. They know that I am a tourist, they can smell it on me, and none of them snap my picture even though I stand around being very smiley. The caterers sense it, too, and not many trays come my way.

I can live with this, though, as long as no one asks me to get them a drink.

Judith is dressed in what looks like an Elizabeth Taylor–Cleopatra reproduction dress and is so engulfed in jewelry—she looks like a Christmas tree drowning in tinsel—that she makes wind-chime noises when she moves. But she does squire me around the party with emceeish grandeur. She bills me as an up-and-coming editor at Prestige who has done some work for her on the side that impressed her so much she'd been thinking about hiring me away from Hector until she realized that my tastes were more literary, etc. etc. She introduces me to people from Scribner, FSG, and Little, Brown. She does her best but I end up feeling like an ersatz prize on a game show and I don't do much to benefit myself. I'm too nervous. Whenever Judith sets me up for a witticism or an insightful remark, I can't provide it. It's frustrating because the room is vibrating hotly with what I want—this is it, I have been enduring Judith for months and lying to Evie nonstop for this very night—but I can't bring myself to participate. Instead of hauling out the sound bites I have spent days scripting to all possible topics—the Hemingway story that changed my life; what the real job of an editor is; what to do about electronic rights; whither the novel—I either offer a deflective laugh or mumble something unintelligible.

One of the only things of note I accomplish is to spill my drink on Princess Someone's shoes. Another—as I start getting more nervous and ergo more drunk—is to start doing my T-Rex impersonation. This is something I used to do at parties as an undergrad and it manifests itself nowadays as a nervous tic that crops up with unfortunate regularity. So while talking to this stylish literary editor at *Esquire* I retract my arms and make pincers out of my hands and say, "Hey, know what I am? I'm a T-Rex," while roaring and hopping around and bending down face-first over the hors d'oeuvres table to eat crab cakes without using my hands. The last thing of note I accomplish is a conversation I have with a poetry editor from Knopf, another place I've dreamed about working. She is sort of quiet and I so want to make a good impression that I end up panicking and saying:

ME: Boy. Boy oh boy. Do I ever love poetry.

POETRY EDITOR: Yes?

ME: Yeah. It rocks the casbah.

POETRY EDITOR: I see.

ME: It's so . . . *poetic.*

POETRY EDITOR: It can be, I imagine.

ME: Hey. You know Emily Dickinson?

POETRY EDITOR: The name sounds familiar.

ME: Oh, right. Of course. I mean, you know that poem of hers? I forget the title. I think it's "Because I Could Not Stop for Death."

POETRY EDITOR: Number 712, I think you're referring to.

ME: Right. You know the great thing about that poem?

POETRY EDITOR: I can't imagine.

ME: You can sing it to the tune of *Gilligan's Island.* Watch:
    Because I could not stop for Death—
    He kindly stopped for me—
    The Carriage held but just Ourselves—
    And Immortality.
See? Cool, huh? I can't reemember where I learned that. But that's the genius of Dickinson.

POETRY EDITOR: Um . . .

ME: And you can do the same thing with *Green Eggs and Ham* and Black Sabbath's "Paranoid."

Yes, I am making quite an impression on the dangerous, sophisticated gorillas. And I haven't even been introduced to the silverback—Chenowith—yet.

How many drinks have I had anyway? I wonder. I am nervous and knew I would therefore drink more than usual so I decided I'd save the toothpicks from every martini to keep a record of how many I've had. But where did I put them? I search my coat but can't find them.

"Would you excuse me for a moment?" I say to Judith. "I think I am in need of the little editors' room."

"That way," says my clinquant Date, pointing and offering me a covert wink.

I need to get away from Judith. This isn't working. All I can think of is *Love Is a Ladder* and the purple penis—I imagine a guy running around in a costume like a baseball team's mascot, only instead of a friendly Mr. Met it's in the shape of a hideous livid clavate meat club—and the way Evie has been so out of touch. A whole week and no emails? No phone calls? This is ridiculous. Before I left for the party tonight I wrote her an email but it ended up sounding reproachful or pathetic and so I deleted it.

I pass by the hors d'oeuvres table and resist the urge to pocket everything on it. I purposefully left my Ziplocs at home but now I am beginning to regret it. As I am considering how to get these puff pastries into my pocket without anyone seeing I overhear this young editor from *The New Yorker* (*bzzzz bzzzz*) make some crack about Harold Bloom's *The Western Canon* and immediately I think of Evie suffering through the endo by herself, alone and without the cannonball, and it makes me sick to my stomach. I grab another martini and go out to the balcony to be by myself.

"This balcony taken?"

The voice belongs to a woman. In the weak light of the street-lamps her skin looks white and otherworldly—larval—but when she steps closer I can see that she is an attractive, elegant woman in her early thirties. She has long, spiderish fingers and an atti-tude of understated confidence that I've seen only on successful and happy people. Jordie Wesselesh has the same look.

"Help yourself," I say, gesturing with my martini. The woman takes out a cigarette but when I reach in my pocket for a light all I pull out is a thicket of cocktail toothpicks, which she regards with cool menthol amusement. How could I have not found them when I patted myself down for them earlier? That can't say anything good about my senses of perception. Holding up the starburst of toothpicks, I say, "I could rub them together."

The woman produces her own lighter and fires one up, blowing fragrant plumes of smoke out into the night air.

"Mind if I bum one?" I say.

"Smoker?" she asks, sounding surprised as she hands me one.

"No, but I'm always on the lookout for a new vice."

"Really?"

"I find that it's refreshing to have something new to feel sorry about when the old things start to wear you down. Don't you?" After two or three puffs my asthma starts acting up and I don't have my lungs with me. Even at home the only canister of spray I've got is almost out. You can test to see how full it is by putting it in a sinkful of water and seeing how well it floats. Mine floats almost dead even with the surface of the water, which means I have maybe ten or fifteen more inhalations left, and I don't have enough money for a replacement.

I cannot afford to breathe: there is definitely a metaphor in there somewhere.

"That's an interesting attitude," she says.

"I've had a lot of time to refine it."

"You don't look like you have too much to feel sorry for. I saw you talking with Judith Krugman. She must be a good friend to have."

"Yeah. She's tops." I am not sure if I mean this literally, as in she is a good contact, or sarcastically, as in she compromises my soul, and it comes out sounding very weird. This woman doesn't appear to know what to make of it either.

"Do you work for her?"

I belong to her. I am her chattel.

"No. I work at Prestige." The galvanic charge this used to give me, this invocation of the big-name employer, is absent. In the old days I would have added, "In the editorial department," or if I was really trying to impress, I fibbed and said, "As an editor." But tonight I don't care enough to exaggerate.

"Really? Wow. What do you do there?"

I am the cliché eliminator. I am the guardian of literary originality. I am Gilgamesh, king of Uruk, builder of walls and slayer of Humbaba whose name means Hugeness.

"I'm an assistant."

"What department?"

The Lubyanka.

"Editorial."

I wish she would stop this line of inquiry. The bushido of the shitbag dictates that at moments such as this you do not think, much less verbalize, about yourself.

"Who do you work for?"

I work for a sick little plantman.

"Andrew Nadler," I say. "The dazzling Andrew Nadler."

The woman suppresses a decorous little snicker. It is entirely possible that she gets it about "dazzling." Among the lowly it is a fairly well-known joke, even at other publishing houses.

"Is he still kicking?" she asks.

"Only when you're down."

"So you know Judith Krugman how, exactly?"

The old urge to aggrandize kicks in and I say, "I did some work for her once. Back in the day," I say, intimating that I might really have some impressive experience behind me, that Judith is in fact just one contact I have out of many important people, and that oh it really is nothing, dearie, all in a day's work. "And now we're buds."

"*Only* buds?" the woman asks. She has something intimidating about her voice. Every syllable is full of assurance, and every syllable gets the same pressure from her throat. It makes the things she says almost ineluctable, like they are coming from the mouth of something automated yet divine—a goddess inside an ATM. It makes me want to agree with her about everything. It makes me want to brag to her. But it also makes me want to tell her my story, to get it all out. Suddenly that voice of hers seems to me the voice of a savior. She has come out onto this balcony to listen to my story, to absolve me. My brother has this theory about grief: you have to put it somewhere. Put it in a bottle, put it in a novel, put it in the ear of your good friend, it doesn't matter. Well, it might matter a little. He clearly chose to put his grief into a bottle and then into a needle, and that didn't get him too far, but the point is you have to put it somewhere. If you don't you'll explode like an unforked baked potato.

"Not exactly just buds," I say, feeling less starchy already.

"Really? How so?"

I spill it. The whole story. How I met Judith, how I didn't know who she was at first, how I was trying to change, how I love Evie. I tell her about Evie's finding the bruises of another night's work with Judith, the cannonball, the Rapunzel treats, how tonight represents the culmination of all these months of betrayal, how it is my big chance, the empty office that possibly awaits me, the lost manuscript, Nadler's assholery—the whole thing.

When I'm done I realize I do feel better. I feel like I've made an atonement of sorts. True, I have told Keeno about all this, but there is something different about telling it to this stranger. She has some power of absolution that Keeno does not have. If I can explain this story to a stranger, one so clearly together as this one, and she can see how I have made the decisions I have made, and understand them, then maybe I am not as bad as I think I am.

"So how is it going with Morton anyway?" she asks when I get done talking.

"It's not, exactly. I haven't even spoken to him yet. Judith has been shopping me around and I have barely been able to make conversation with those other people, let alone Morton Chenowith. Do you know him?" I keep waiting for the benediction. I feel as if she should make some obscure yet simple gesture of religious significance over me—dipping her fingers in her drink and spraying my head with the alcohol, making the sign of the cross with an olive over my chest while reciting certain Latin phrases in a sonorous and grave voice—but no benediction is forthcoming.

"Yes, I know Morty."

"Really? That's neat. How do you know Morty?" I say, deliberately using the diminutive also, as if to indicate that despite the story of lowliness I've just related I in fact have some people keeping their eye on me.

"I work in publishing, too."

"Who do you work for?"

"Holt."

"Wow. I love Holt! What do you do there?"

"I work in editorial."

"Man, this is getting weirder by the second. Evie, the woman I told you about—"

"The one you should be with tonight instead of trying to further your career via deception and treachery?"

"Yeah. She has a friend at Holt. She's sort of a"—I take a moment to try to determine how vulgar I can be with this refined woman, who suddenly seems she might be able to help me professionally too, then after a moment I conclude that I can take the chance—"bitch. She really hates me. Always trying to get Evie to break up with me. Real manipulative angry you-go-girl type of person. Anyway, this person aside, I think Holt's really cool. What's it like working there?"

"It can be great. They give you a lot of freedom. They have a nice list. You know how it can be."

"Right," I say, thinking: I have no idea how it can be.

"Boy. Those are some troubles," she says.

"I know. What do you think I should do?"

"Let's find out. What sign are you?"

I tell her.

"Oh. Hmm. Strange. I would have thought you were a Cancer. What year were you born?"

I tell her.

"Interesting."

"Are you an astrology person?"

"A little bit. What's your mother's name?"

"How is that going to help anything?"

"Trust me. It will help a lot."

I tell her my mother's name.

"And your father's?"

I tell her that too.

"Have any pets?"

"Used to have a cat. He died recently."

"What was his name?"

"Mosby," I say. "Is all this really going to help with . . . whatever it is you're doing?"

"Oh yes. It will be very helpful. Trust me on this. I can't do the necessary interpretations out here with you but if you sit tight I will be right back. O.K.?"

"Sure. O.K. Thanks. But do you really think this sort of thing works? I mean, what kind of results can you really get with this sort of thing?"

She gives me a complicated smile and says, "I expect immediate results."

Forty-five minutes later it starts to rain. Leaning on the railing, looking down over the city, everything is numinous and webby—like slugsilver—in the new rain. It is a city of luminous decay. It is like the beautiful work of death.

The woman has still not returned with her pronouncements. I pace around the balcony, wishing I had another drink and some crab cakes. I'm not willing to risk it, however. The last person I want to see right now is Judith. Out here on the balcony I feel better about things because I feel alone.

Minutes leak by. Before I know it almost half an hour has passed. I don't mean to but I can't help it—I start to think about myself, and what I think of is this: I never used to be this way.

When I was younger I did all sorts of harmless things. Good things, even. When I was a kid and living in Connecticut I was the savior of innocent baby squirrels, for God's sake. Every spring some baby squirrels—their eyes not even open yet—would fall out of their nests. They'd be injured and their mothers would just abandon them, so I'd rescue them. I'd collect them in a basket that I lined with warm soft towels straight from the dryer and feed them warm milk from an eyedropper—I tested it on my wrist and everything—until they were big enough to eat wet cat food. I was Florence fucking Nightingale to the entire neighborhood population of unlucky rodents.

What happened?

When did I change? I used to be so considerate. I used to be this big softie. Want to know what my first CD was? Wilson Phillips. I'm not kidding. I played it so much that the RA on my hall freshman year at college said that if he ever heard the sound of Wilson Phillips coming through my door again he would get security to let him into my room and he would destroy the CD himself.

My favorite movie—when no one is looking—is *Mannequin*. I must have seen it ninety-five times. I own my own copy. When I'm down or lonely because Evie isn't over I'll put it in and watch the whole thing (last month's total: 16). I like to rewind to the moment when Kim Cattrall comes to life and Andrew McCarthy goes sprawling to the ground in shock. I can't get enough of that. No one has done anything wrong. They still have everything ahead of them.

I never buy porn. The only thing I ever jerk off to are the Noxzema girls.

When I was eight I tried to make a citizen's arrest when I saw someone run over a possum.

In college I paid other people's late fees at the library.

My first year at Prestige I gave remaindered books to hospitals and prisons.

I cry at DeBeers commericals for God's sake.

How did I change? How did I go from this person to the one who loses the only extant copy of an important manuscript, who has become embroiled in a despicable affair with a woman he cares nothing about while the woman he loves is sitting at home, alone and in agony, waiting for him to come cannonball her?

Where did I go?

What happened?

Consider what my mother says about what I have become since I moved to New York: furtive, shady, unlawful.

The woman is still not back with her pronouncement but in a way she has helped me come to one already. Being alone out here has forced me to consider all this, and it seems clear to me now: I don't have to be this way. I can be like the old Harry.

QUESTION: What would the Harry who saves squirrels and re-maindered books and cries at DeBeers commercials do right about now?

ANSWER: Scrap this scene and go administer a cannonball to the woman he loves.

This I resolve to do.

I push through the party. The crowd is thick and moving though it is like moving through seaweed: struggling only makes it worse. As I ease past a crowd of slick young glamorniks one of them mocks me with a pincer gesture and some T-Rex noises that makes the whole group chortle but I do not stop to redress the wrong. I will not be altered from my course. Not even the bar or the hors d'ouevres table distract me. I am at last within sight of the door when Judith intercepts me with Morton Chen-owith on her arm.

Shit.

"Harry," she says, twitching her head in agitation so that her bijouterie clatters in alarm. "There you are. I have somebody here who has been waiting to meet you. Morton Chenowith, this is Harry Driscoll. Harry, Morty."

"Ah, Mr. Driscoll," says Morton Chenowith, slapping me chummily on the shoulder. "I hope you weren't leaving. There was something rather particular I wanted to talk to you about."

This is the moment I have been waiting for. This is why I have been enduring double-crossing, two-timing, lying, worshiping the high priestess, sexual humiliation, bruises, drunken stupors, self-disgust, self-hatred, and guilt. It is a moment crystalline with everything I have been planning for—telesis made flesh.

"Well?" Judith says.

"Well?" Chenowith says.

Yes, this is my big chance all right. It is my big chance to make things right with Evie.

I bolt.

sprayed and neutered

Evie does not answer her window. She will not pick up the phone. She does not respond to screaming from the street. To get into the building I have to wait until an old lady with a pair of rachitic, stilting terriers emerges from the doorway, eyeballing me suspiciously as I dash past her and up the stairs. By the time I get to the sixth floor I can barely breathe. My lungs aren't getting any air and my legs are burning. Leaning against Evie's door for support, I use what strength I've got left to rap on her door. Finally the door creaks open, but it's not Evie standing there.

It's the woman from the party.

"Don't just stand there wheezing at me," the woman says. "Verbalize. Is there something you want?"

"You," I wheeze out, incredulous.

"Yes?"

"But I—"

"Yes?"

"We just—"

Suddenly it makes sense. She's from Holt. She is an important young editor. How did I not see it before?

"Is this a pronoun game? I'm not sure it's shaping up to be much fun. I *am* glad you came by, though."

Madeleine starts to close the door but I shove my foot in the jamb.

"Wait. What have you done?"

"That is really the sort of question you should be asking yourself, Harry."

"What?"

"You fucked up, Harry."

"I need to talk to Evie. Let me in."

"She's not here."

"Let me in. I want to see. She's having the endo tonight."

"I know."

"She needs me."

"I am sure you don't have anything she needs but you are welcome to look around."

Madeleine lets me in and she's right: Evie is not here.

"Where is she?"

Madeleine has the fully asserted, compressed look of someone who has rehearsed her denunciations. Her refractory smugness fills the room.

"She is staying with me, Harry. I imagine she will be staying with me for quite some time, actually. Once I explained everything to her she seemed to have an urgent need to get out of the apartment. Oh, thank you for all that personal information, incidentally. It made it a lot easier for me to convince her that you weren't really in Connecticut. For some silly reason she has this habit of believing you instead of me. I think we have just about broken of her that, though, don't you?"

"Where are you going?" I say as Madeleine starts for the door.

"I just came over to pick up something or other for Evie. Some kind of tea. Something for cramps."

"*Dong quai*," I say, feeling blood pumping through my heart. "It's called *dong quai*."

"Whatever. I'm going now. I don't think I can leave you to root about in her apartment like the piggy little frog you are so you had better hop along." I follow her out and down the stairs, and on the sidewalk she turns to me and says, "Whatever do you think you're doing?"

"I need to see Evie."

"You're *following* me?"

"I need to see Evie."

"I'm not sure how I feel about stalking, Harry. Wait a minute. Yes I do." Madeleine reaches into her purse and produces a silver and red canister, which she holds up to my face. "I think you'd better turn around and go home, or to Judith's or wherever it is you go. I have been looking for an excuse to use this for too long, Harry."

"I'm coming with you, Madeleine."

She brandishes the canister a foot in front on my face.

"You wouldn't," I say.

Madeleine cocks her head to the side thoughtfully. We stare

at each other. A Chinese kid dressed in strap-on mirrors streaks by with both fists full of exploding gold sparklers. A couple hunch urgently into each other in the recession of a nearby doorway. The smell of fish and gasoline hangs heavy in the air. Madeleine's eyes look dead, like balls of lifeless matter floating in egg white.

Finally she says, "You're right. I may be German but I'm not a savage." Then she unzips her purse and puts the canister away, pauses, looks up at the windows of the building as if remembering something important, pulls the canister back out, and sprays it directly into my face. There is a blinding spray of light in my eyes and my lungs explode in searing pain. I fall to the ground, scratching at my eyes and jerking my legs around violently. It looks like I am trying to kick-start myself.

"But boy are Germans ever fickle," I hear her say happily above me. "*Gosh* that was fun, though."

sis's place

The next day I need to be around people worse off than me so I go to Sis's Place.

Sis's Place is an illegal bar on Avenue B that is in the basement of this old woman's apartment. She doesn't have a liquor license or the right zoning or anything like that. In fact, Sis doesn't even have a cooler. She has a fat old fridge in which she keeps all the cans of Pabst Blue Ribbon—the only beer she offers. I think she just buys them at the grocery, retail, and walks them home and throws them in the fridge. And she has the place furnished in the way she thinks young men like. There are those 1980s-style posters of bikinied women spread out on the hoods of Ferraris, mirrors with Pabst stencils, and an untouched speed bag in the corner, shiny and flaccid from disuse. In back is a pay phone covered with scars from the six times I allegedly tried to use a screwdriver to break it open for quarters.

But the place isn't the sort of raucous East Village joint you might expect. No one is trying to pick anyone up. There isn't a jukebox. In fact, there's almost no noise at all. The crowd consists mostly of regulars and they rarely talk to each other. Kriedel is a welfare drinker who is obsessed with figuring out the schedule of traffic lights in the entire city. Sometimes he disappears into the bathroom and hits his head so hard against the paper towel dispenser that you can hear it on the street. Twenty minutes later he'll reappear, eyes red and swollen with tears, and sit back down like nothing happened. Amtrak spends his days at Penn Station at the head of the ticket line, saying "No, no, please, I insist, after you" to everyone and then letting them cut in front of him. No one knows Tug's story. All he ever does is stare at the TV, which is always tuned in to PBS, and puff out his scrotal cheeks in disapproval or disbelief. Today he's watching some show with Carl Sagan pointing to a staticky smear of stars. Tug's eyes, vitelline and cankered, do not move.

The veiny, mothlike women are a mystery, too. There's Lulu, Freddie, Zosia, and Pink, whose purse is full of nails. ("You never know," she says sagely.) The women have been waiting in this bar for years for something to happen to them, and every night at closing time, when they reluctantly shuffle out into the gas-ripe night air, they look stunned and broken.

I know how they feel.

Tonight it's the same as ever: the women are lined up on bar stools like carnival ducks waiting to be knocked down and the men are hunched protectively over their beers, plotting to win the lottery. In the blighted, interstellar quietude of Sis's Place, no one minds anyone else. You can ease into your personal oblivion unmolested.

After a few quick shots I call Evie's number. Finally the phone picks up and a man's voice on the other end of the line says, "Hello?"

"Sorry," I say. "Wrong number." I hang up and dial again. The same voice picks up.

"Is this 423-3773?" I say.

"Yes it is," the voice says. "Who are you trying to reach?"

"This isn't the Carl Sagan infoline?"

"No, I'm sorry. This is a residence."

"Carl Sagan's residence?"

"No. The Goddard residence."

My heart spasms like an electified lab rat.

"Ah. So sorry. I've made a mistake."

"No problemo."

No problemo? Evie has a guy at her apartment who says No problemo? I can't fucking believe it. The kind of people who say no problemo also say Don't go there and use "antique" as a verb.

FUCKWAD A: Honey, want to go antiquing this weekend?
FUCKWAD B: No problemo.

I could kill her.

messages

When I get home I have two messages on my machine. The first is from Meredith Crosswhite.

"Harry, this is Meredith Crosswhite, your mother's friend. I understand that you're thinking of leaving publishing for the world of private secondary school teaching. My husband and I were very gratified to hear this. We've always thought you'd make a wonderful teacher, and that Bancroft-Ash and Harry Driscoll would make a good match. At the moment it happens we are hiring in the English department. Why don't you call us or stop by the campus when you're next in Connecticut. Oh, and in the meantime, good luck with that big novel you've signed up."

This is the way it is with my mother and me. She tells her friends that I want to leave New York and teach prep school; I tell her I'm an important young editor working on a big-deal novel.

Symbiotic dishonesty: the only way to get by in the Driscoll family.

The next message is from Nadler. He wants to know why copyediting and design have not received the calendar manuscript. He called Friday afternoon to check up on it and is "mystified" about this "communication gap" and wants me to call him "a-sap" in the country. He also says he is coming back from the country Tuesday and expects to have a "chat" about my "imminent performance review."

I delete the message and call his office number. I'm experiencing some motor difficulties and it takes two tries to dial the number correctly. When I speak into the receiver I can smell the toxic fumes of my mouth. "Nadler, Harry. I got message. Your. Must be assistants didn't paperwork forward bosses. To. Know how assistants can be, ha ha ha. Pass to press A-OK, though. Went through fine. No problemo. Look forward to synod. Our."

Then I call Judith. It takes three times to get the numbers right. When her answering machine picks up I tell her how grateful I am for being invited to the party and how great it was to meet Morton Chenowith and that I am sorry I had to run but that I was having an asthma emergency. (I can hear Keeno: Don't you find it worrisome at all that lying is becoming such a reflex to you?)

"Anyway," I conclude on her message machine, "thanks again for me up with Chenowith. Setting. Let's hope I get some action soon."

out of the cubicle

I do get some action soon. The pronouncement is on my voice mail when I get to work Monday.

"Harry," Judith's voice says, "I've been in touch with Hector and Morty. You should hear something from upstairs today. You should get what you so richly deserve, at long last."

That morning when I get to my desk—chair without jacket, computer off—Horst is on his second bottle of Nutella. That's his worry food but it doesn't seem to be doing much good. His face is showing some brown smears that he doesn't bother to wipe off. That's not like Horst. Brandishing a spoonful, he tells me Nadler knows that the manuscript hasn't been passed to press. Possibly he knows that it's lost. He's due in at noon and— Nutella falling to the desk—he sounded pretty mad.

"I think you're in big trouble, Harry," he says.

"Don't worry, Horst. It's going to be a good day. Just watch."

I keep hoping Nadler will show up, but all morning long he is nowhere to be seen. This is disappointing because I have envisioned how things would be different, how this time I wouldn't feel like a kid in the principal's office, how this time walking through his door wouldn't make me feel like I was walking the plank, how this time I would deliver my sentences in a cool, cavalier, manner:

NADLER (*with menace*): So.

ME (*cheerfully*): So!

NADLER: No one in copyediting has any record of the calendar.

ME: Egad.

NADLER: Nor anyone in design.

ME: Lordy.

NADLER: Would you care to explain this mystery to me?

ME: It's no mystery.

NADLER: It's not?

ME: No. It's quite simple. The manuscript disappeared.

NADLER: "Disappeared"? What do you mean by "disappeared"?

ME: I mean *poof.*

NADLER: Am I to understand that you still haven't edited it?

ME: You are to understand that it has poofed and gone. Sayonara.

NADLER: What have you done with the manuscript, Harold?

ME: It was too small. I had to throw it back.

NADLER: I am going to do us both the courtesy of disregarding the foregoing and I'm going to start over.

ME: Do what you like but the answers are going to be the same, Andy. *(Phone rings from my cubicle.)* Oh, excuse me a moment. This has really been a *dazzling* conversation but I'm expecting a call. *(Exit Nadler's office, the last five years of hurt and humiliation churning behind me in a wake of triumphant excitement. Nadler doesn't move or say anything. He just sits there in amazement.)*

It would be the most perfect moment I've ever had at Prestige. Needless to say I am feeling disappointed he is not around, when suddenly my phone finally rings.

"The human resources department on thirty-three?" I say into the receiver. "Of course. I'll be right up."

"Who was that?" Horst says.

"Watch and learn," I say, hanging up. "You don't get promoted in this business by publishing fortune cookies like *Love Is a Ladder*. You get promoted for having a zero tolerance policy for clichés. You get promoted for knowing how to network. Stick with me, Horst, and one day you may even get a permanent job as an editorial assistant. Who knows?" With that I gesture extravagantly to the blank name plaque on the door of the empty office.

"Harry Driscoll," I say grandly. "Editor."

It doesn't take long. Thirty minutes later I am back at my cubicle—attended by a security guard I've never seen before—and boxing up my personal items. Paula passes by and asks me what I think I am doing. I don't tell her that the people on thirty-three urged me to quit "for everyone's sake." I don't tell her that I overheard some subrights people snickering about how "pure" I am.

Instead I say, "I'm moving to *Time Out New York*. They liked my egg-breaking story and want me to write a column on book publishing." When Paula considers the security guard I say, "This is Reggie. He's helping me move. Give me a hand with this, will you, Reg?" I say, handing him a box.

"My name's Donald," he says, and drops the box.

"Purist," says Paula.

After fifteen minutes I'm almost done. I pack up the smelling salts, the toothpicks, the coffee cups, the Pilot V-Balls, the SEVEN STEPS TO PRESERVING HARRY'S BACHELORHOOD list. Then I stop and think, *Fuck it*. I'm going to throw everything away. Clean break. I don't leave my password to my computer. I don't leave my code to voice mail. I throw away the stamp with Nadler's editorial code number on it so my replacement will have to write out all thirteen digits every time he needs to mail something or fill out a review order or requisition all the supplies he'll have to replace. Small victories, I think.

Then I think, Why small victories? Why not big victories? Why not fucking Hiroshima?

When the guard isn't looking I trash the file containing all the contracts waiting for signatures and the one containing contracts for books pending publication. References schmeferences. In this business, the only thing that matters is visibility and gossip value. If you're going to be fired, you may as well go out in a fireball of passive aggression.

Right?

Then I get this strange feeling. Suddenly this last sight of my cubicle overwhelms me with nostalgia for all the Treehouse Talks I had with Evie and for the future I might have had but won't. A wad of sadness swells up in my throat. Evie's emails, I realize, were one of the things that sustained me in this cubicle. I try to print out my EVIE email folder but the guard won't let me.

"Sorry, pal," he says. "Personal items only. You have to leave the computer alone."

"Really? O.K."

I make for the keyboard and he physically restrains me. "Just get your belongings," he says.

"Just let me print out a few personal emails, O.K.?"

"No can do."

"Come on, man. They're not The Colonel's secret recipe. They're just emails from my . . . girlfriend. Yeah, that's it. My girlfriend."

"Sorry."

"O.K. All right. You're the boss," I say. Then I make a desperate lunge at the keyboard, but the guard is too fast. He does something painful and embarrassing with my arm behind my back. When Horst walks in I am dancing on my tiptoes and making gurgling noises.

"Hey, Horst," I say when the guard finally releases me. "I'm glad I caught you. Maybe you could help me with something. I overheard someone use the term 'pure' the other day. Do you happen to know what that means, by chance?"

"It's an acronym. It means 'Previously Unrecognized Recruiting Error.' "

messages

From Sis's Place I check my messages. My mother says she hasn't heard from me for a while and wants to know how it went with Meredith Crosswhite and how the book is progressing and shouldn't it be ready for publication soon? It's very exciting, she says, having a son editing the Great American Novel. And just think how important those references will be when it comes time to apply to prep schools like Bancroft-Ash. I've really paid my dues, she says. Soon I can put all those contacts to good use.

I seventy-six the message.

Then I dial up Evie and leave her a message.

"Sixty-five thousand!" I blurt drunkenly into the receiver. "Sixty-five thousand books are published every year, and most of them are a waste of trees. Let's say you get a thousand books a tree. That's a hundred trees you're going to kill to publish your putative book. You're going to kill Tompkins Square Park. Just to publish *Love Is a Ladder*, which, I have to say, sucks so bad you can hear it all the way down here." I make a tremendously loud sucking noise into the receiver. "*THHHHUUUUURRRRRPP.* Hear that? *That* is the sound of your book sucking. So congratulations. Congratufuckinglations on your big break. Oh, and one more thing, *mon editrix,* here's a bit of editorial tid you might find useful: You might want to actually edit the manuscript. I flipped through it on your desk and there are six misspelled words in the first fifteen pages. I don't know how they got past your shrewd editor's eye, but I thought you ought to know before the book goes to press. Good luck finding them."

For a moment I taste the complicated acetic pleasure of revenge—I know the message will hurt Evie, and that she will spend a lot of time searching for typos that don't exist—but then it subsides into grief. I feed in another quarter and dial her number again to apologize but when the machine picks up it says in a robotic monotone, "I'm sorry but I am unable to take your call right now. Please call back later."

Evie's ancient machine: maxed out with messages. Perfect timing.

Back at the bar, next to Tug, I order another drink. I knock it down and order another. And another. And one after that. My plan is to drink until I can't feel anything. But it doesn't work. I just keep on feeling.

special delivery

When I get home I discover a sagging trash bag on my doorstep. It's full of wet, milky, and moldy Grape-Nuts. I almost laugh. Grape-Nuts were a running joke with me and Evie. They are her absolute favorite snack and she always said that I unerringly called or stopped by when she had just sat down to eat some. I have apparently ruined countless bowls of bliss, for which she always threatened a severe and obscure revenge: another point I should have taken seriously.

I chuck it in the trash chute and spend the next three hours giving the Geronimo treatment to all her stuff: her hatboxes, her Bumble & Bumble, her wire brush, her Cajun CDs that I never understood a word of, her boxed sets of *Shark Week* and *Croc Rock,* bras both black and white, two smart little Bebe outfits, the signed copy of *Sophie's Choice* she joyfully bought me, the first-edition copy of *Love Story* I begrudgingly bought her, her happy-daisy mug and the container of coffee and chicory she likes so much, her Tony Chachere's cooking spice, her makeup towel and period panties, all her Tampax and Always, the Curel vitamin E lotion she brought over for my back, the special slipper-socks I bought her, two containers of Percocet, her various endo teas (white peony for toning the blood and relaxing tissues, *dong quai* to decrease the severity of cramps, raspberry to relax muscles and dilate the cervix), her constipation chewing gum, her Surfak, her vitamin C and E pills—everything.

The last thing I throw out is the VIVA LA EVIE lamp. I clutch it in my hand like the idol of a supposedly dead god, look at it for one last time, and drop it down the chute. I watch it fall away into blackness and instantly I feel like I've made the biggest mistake of my life. I don't want to trash the lamp, I think.

I love that lamp.

That lamp loves me.

In my underwear I run down to the basement, but the trash compartment is locked up and kicking isn't getting me anywhere. There's only one thing for it: the super.

The super is highly off-limits to me. Darrell won't let me talk to the old-lady neighbors, but he doesn't even want me to be *seen* by the super. "If you ever go near him," Darrell said once, lips everted and glistening like chicken fat while meaningfully skinning an apple with one of his paring knives, "I can't be held accountable. That's all I've got to say."

But there's nothing for it tonight. This requires emergency action. In my underwear I pound on the super's door for what seems like a very long time. Finally he answers. After half an hour of badgering he lets me down into the trash room and I rummage through the pile in my bare feet. At last I find it, covered in what looks like a baby's meal that has been returned to sender: something banana-smelling and something purple in a liquefied state of semidigestion.

"Ees found?" the super says as I sit there atop a throne of reeking garbage. "You hahh-ppy now?"

incommunicado

I spend much of the next week at Sis's Place. From my stool I watch Tug crocodiling in his beer, his face submerged up to his nose, eyes ominous and dead but missing nothing, waiting to see what he wants. Only what he wants never comes into view and so he just idles there for a long time.

I resolve to call Evie again. I have called every day this week but her machine is always full. Still, I have to try. I don't want to turn into Tug. I don't want to be Eviscerated. Finally her machine picks up, but when it beeps something happens: I lose my voice. I want to tell her that I'm sorry for the awful phone call I made about *Love Is a Ladder*, that I'm proud she signed up a real book, that I know she has doubtlessly heard some outlandish things from Madeleine and that we need to talk about them. I squeeze the phone hard against my ear but it doesn't accomplish anything. I just freeze.

I hang up and dial Judith's number. She has also been incommunicado since my firing. When her machine picks up the same thing happens and I have to hang up on her, too.

The only person I manage to speak to is Keeno. She doesn't immediately want to talk as she is in the middle of a new Relocart project, putting Peeps—those marshmallowy Easter chickies—into the microwave and blowing them up. Apparently when you subject Peeps to such treatment they expand to the size of a melon. She plans to plant these swollen confections all around the paths of Central Park so people have to jog or Rollerblade out of their way lest they trample a Peep. She plans to videotape their efforts. Problem is, she tells me, that once you take Peeps out of the microwave they tend to deflate fairly quickly, and she is at the moment trying to figure out a way to make them stay puffed up. Do I think painter's fixative would work?

So she says she can't talk right now. When I tell her I need some help, when I explain the situation, she isn't especially helpful. In fact, when she hears all the details she implies that maybe I am getting what I deserve. She implies that had I not been such an inveterate slider shitbag, Evie might be accepting my calls. She further implies that had I done a fraction of what my job called for at Prestige, I might still be employed. She additionally implies that it would make good moral sense if I've caught something unpleasant from Judith.

When I imply that maybe life isn't as easy for everybody as it is for Keeno, that not everybody can have a happy, healthy love life and buy a stylish East Village loft on money made from blowing up fucking cupcakes, she says, "You know, Harry, I think it would be best if you didn't call me for a while," and hangs up on me.

Then, for some reason, I look up Jordie Wesselesh's number and call it. His wife picks up. In the background I can hear sounds of laughter and of silverware scraping on plates. I can imagine the scene: Jordie's having a dinner party. Maybe he has his lexicographer friends over. I imagine it being like *Where the Wild Things Are*: lexicographers turning into adventurers by night, taking their private boats to Jordie's apartment, crying out, "Let the wild rumpus start!" One of his dogs yelps happily in the background.

QUESTION: Why oh why can't I be Jordie Wesselesh?

ANSWER *(pronounced in Keeno's accent)*: Because you do not treat Evie with dignity and respect. Because you treat your job like recess. Because you do not have any friends to invite over to dinner parties. In fact, if Evie isn't returning your calls and you've offended me so much that I am not talking to you either, who do you have left?

"Hello?" his wife says again.

"Sorry," I say, near tears. "Wrong number. My mistake."

house call

The next night when I still haven't heard from her I scale the fire escape outside Evie's apartment. I try the window but it's locked. That's new. It's O.K. though; this is my chance to be the mod, fast-lane Buddha. I will sit and wait and clear my mind of desire and anxiety and the world will come to me. I try to sit in a lotuslike position but it hurts my knees so I end up leaning back against the wall. Urban Buddhas don't have to sit funny, I decide. Nor do they have to renounce alcohol, which is fortunate as I have brought a bottle of Darrell's Gilbey's with me.

I have done this a million times. I have waited out here for her to get back from work, to get back from going somewhere out of town, to get back from nights out with Madeleine, but tonight it feels different. I feel creepy sitting up here. I'm worried that someone might see me. And through the glass Evie's apartment looks funny. Her bed is always immaculate but tonight it seems immaculate in a new way. It is so well made, the sheets so tight, that it looks desolate, like no one has slept in it for a long time. And her desk, normally cluttered with slush, poor thing, is also clean. And there are no dishes rising from the sink.

I'm just being fanciful, I'm sure. At any rate, when she comes home I'll ask her why so clean.

Midnight, no Evie.

One, no Evie.

Two, no Evie.

Watched pots, I think. So I climb down, planning to run to the corner deli for some PBR. But climbing down the fire escape gives me vertigo so I sit down on the stoop to regain my equilibrium. I sit down for a second and for some reason the concrete under me feels so good—so certain—that I fall asleep.

I wake up the next day when a street sweeper blows past me in a cloud of flying grit. Squinting, I realize that either 1) Evie came home last night and walked over me on her stoop; or 2) Evie didn't come home, hasn't been coming home. I'm not sure which option I like less.

Then there is a broom in my gut. It is Elmo, sweeping madly at me trying to brush me off the stoop with great zeal while thrusting something at me and yelling unintelligibly. For a moment I recoil, then I realize what's going on. I can't understand what he's saying but the sign he is wildly pushing at my face makes his meaning clear. And he's right: NO DODO HERE, PLEASE.

the cronkite

The only person who seems to be interested in talking to me is
Madeleine. I beg her to meet with me and she agrees, setting a
date for a latte before work at a bright coffee shop in Chelsea
with oversized velvet furniture in Fauvist colors and a clientele
so stylish it makes me nervous. Madeleine arrives forty minutes
late but I am still there. What choice do I have? I need to get
Evie to talk to me and the antagonistic girlfriend is my only hope.

"Well," she says when she sits down. "This is fun."

"Madeleine, I know you hate me. I know you have a lot of
reasons for hating me. I would probably hate me too if I were
Evie's friend. But I need your help. I need to talk to Evie. Her
phone machine is never on and I haven't been able to find her
at her place. It's like she disappeared. You're my only way of
getting in touch with her. You know it's hard for me to ask you
this, but please: would you help me get in touch with her?"

"I'm not her agent, Harry. If she wants to talk to you I imagine
she'll call you. Otherwise you're out of luck, I'm afraid."

"Please," I say. "Please."

"Sorry, Harry. I do hate you, of course, but at the same time
I sort of don't care much about you anymore, if you see what I
mean. So I might help you out if I could, but I just can't. Evie's
awfully busy and I can't make her do anything she doesn't want
to do."

"Can you at least tell me if she's all right?" Talking to Madeleine like this, sitting at the coffee shop with my cold cup of coffee in day-old clothes, makes me feel like a kid sitting at the adult table. "Can you tell me if the endo is O.K.? She had sort of a bad endo night right before . . . you know. . . . and I'm worried about her." Madeleine looks for a moment like a teacher trying to decide if a student really has to go to the bathroom or not. "Can you at least give me that?"

"The endo is fine, Harry. No thanks to you. After I left you at the party I went to her apartment and she was drinking some tea—"

"Raspberry probably. She always drinks that first."

"And reading an old issue of *Metropolitan Home*." Oh God: one of my old Rapunzel treats. "Later that night the cramps got a little worse but not much worse than usual."

"So the endo's O.K.?" I say.

"The endo's O.K."

That's a relief. It makes my betrayal less total.

"And otherwise she's O.K.?"

"O.K.? Harry, I hate to say it—well, no, actually I don't mind saying it at all, as a matter of fact—but since Evie left you everything has been going great for her. The book is getting terrific in-house buzz. Publicity is going to town. Subrights has sold it to five foreign publishers already. They're making it a lead title. I don't even want to tell you what the first print run is going to be."

"Hector really likes it that much?" I say, incredulous.

"Enough to skip right over assistant editor to associate."

"They promoted her to associate editor?"

"There have been a bunch of promotions. Some German floater replaced you and apparently is doing very well."

"Horst?" I say. "Horst Schrodt?"

"Yes. I think that's it. He found that missing manuscript. It was mixed in with a pile of old slush or something. Nadler was so grateful he gave him the job."

No wonder I never found it. The one place I was least likely to look: a slush pile. I should be jealous of Evie and angry about Horst but I'm not. Evie deserves it. And as for Horst, it just proves the sorry colligative truth of assistants in publishing: who cares who you are? Who cares that you're a goner? There are plenty more where you came from. Plus Horst will have to deal with Nadler. Let him have it.

"Yes, it seems like a lot of your blunders have been coming to fruition lately," Madeleine says.

"What do you mean?"

"Well, your double-dealing with Judith, for one. Let me give you a little hint you might find useful in future: when engaging in an illicit affair, try not to use the name of your girlfriend when you are in bed with the Other Woman."

"Huh?"

"After meeting her at Morty's, I took the liberty of asking Judith to lunch. She's a complete doll, by the way. Anyway, she was very interested to know about your other friends. As soon as I mentioned Evie's name Judith got this funny look on her face, like she was remembering something. She put two and two together and realized that you called out Evie's name in the sack at, shall we say, a moment of intimate *agitation*. Endearing, in a way. Sort of a shame it had to be your downfall."

"You've really outdone yourself." Even as I say this I am relieved. It feels good to be free of Judith. Never again will I have to hear the words "Are you available?"

"It was hardly necessary. You did most of the work yourself. As you did with Evie. Calling from Judith's apartment."

"So that was you on the phone?"

"But of course. And that package with your underwear you left at your desk." This I had forgotten about, but now I realize that when I was packing up my personal items the day I got fired my ANIMAL WANT WOMAN boxers and the note didn't show up. "And the bruises. None too swift, Hairball, I have to say. You really gave her a push in the right direction. I couldn't have done better myself."

"What does that mean?" I say as the corners of the coffee shop start fluorescing with purple light. "Push in the right direction?"

"I just mean that Evie's moved on, Harry."

"What do you mean, moved on?"

Madeleine takes out a cigarette and lights up. She holds the cigarette with a practiced furtive gesture, a trick of legerdemain that conceals the cherry. I heard once that snipers do the same thing so that their mark doesn't see them coming.

"Evie is dating someone new, Harry. That's what moving on means."

"That's ridiculous."

"What's ridiculous is how long it took her to"—Madeleine cannot suppress a satisfied smile—"upgrade."

"Who is this alleged new paramour?"

"There's nothing alleged or para- about him."

"What's his name?"

"J.J."

"J.J.? What kind of name is that? It isn't even a real name. It's a disc jockey name. What does it stand for? Johnnie Joe? Jimmie Jon?"

"It stands for Jason Jonathan," she says cleanly. "Jason Jonathan Drakkar."

In high school a teacher once put a can over a Bunsen burner and created a vacuum that made the can crush in on itself. I feel like that can. Or maybe a collapsing universe.

"Say *what*?" I manage.

"Jason Drakkar. You know, the author of *Love Is a Ladder*."

QUESTION: What's worse than the woman you love more than anything on earth leaving you?

ANSWER: The woman you love more than anything on earth leaving you for the man who is the instantiation of everything in the world you hate most.

"Are you fucking kidding me or what?"

"What."

"I can't believe it. I don't believe it. She couldn't possibly date that guy."

"Why ever not?"

"Because she loves me, for starters."

"She was confused about you, Harry. That's all. And I can see being confused by you for a little while. You could be some fun. Limited fun. But that's it."

"What do you mean?"

"Look at yourself, Harry. You're unemployed. Your clothes are filthy. You've got some kind of skin condition. You're an alcoholic."

"I'm not an alcoholic."

"You've been drinking this morning already. I can smell it." It's true. I've been drinking this morning but only a little bit, and only after I decided it was permissible as I am under extenuating circumstances. "Evie deserves more than you. Forgive my saying so, but she deserves a lot more than you. And J.J., well, he's got it all. He's kind, he's fair, he's generous, he's adult. He takes her out to dinner, and I don't mean stealing olives and cherries for her when bartenders aren't looking. He takes her shopping, and I don't mean just going out and trying on clothes in some kind of game *as if* she were shopping. He's introduced her around to all his friends. He's introduced her to his mother. He doesn't live in a hovel. He doesn't break into her apartment. He manages to control himself when strange women walk by. He is gainfully employed. And now he is a successful writer."

"He's an idiot!"

"Take head out of ass and thumb out of mouth, Harry. Put on your big-boy pants and deal with it. She's left you. She's with J.J. And yes, he's a good writer."

"He's not a writer! He's a Hallmark card maker. And it's not even a book, it's wisdom stolen from bumper stickers."

"Well, he's got a contract with Prestige and they're putting it on a crash schedule to bring it out for Christmas. They're printing fifty thousand copies. Somebody there believes it's a book, apparently. Which reminds me: how is *your* writing going? Any contracts we should know about?"

"Fifty thousand copies?"

"That's the word."

"This is bullshit. You're just making this shit up. I'm going to talk to Evie. I'll just wait outside Prestige for her."

"You are welcome to loiter around Prestige if you like, Harry, but you won't find much profit in it. Evie is going over the final edits with J.J. at his place in the country. She won't be available for at least a week."

I feel it: I am about to start redlining. But I need to maintain. If this is true, Madeleine is my one hope at getting Evie to listen to me. What finally comes out is "But they can't be printing fifty thousand copies. I've read the manuscript. The guy doesn't know the first thing about love."

Madeleine extinguishes what's left of her cigarette and lights another one. Her thin, red mouth—a bloody paper cut on her face, straight and severe—looks too small for the long cigarette. She takes a thoughtful drag and exhales with luxuriant slowness, then cocks her head, considering. I can almost see the options flicking over her retinas.

"Look who's got the girl."

message

A few days later I come home to find all my books torn out of the bookcases, their pages shredded, lying open on the floor and flapping madly in the breeze from the open window like the wings of injured birds. In my room the carnage continues. My bed has been slashed and the stuffing is littering the floor; notches have been cut into my desk; my clothes are in tatters. Run through and stuck to the wall with Darrell's prized commemorative Civil War bayonet replica is a note:

> Count yourself lucky if you're reading this note. I know about
> you and the super. He came by today. Which means he might
> be on to me. Which means you now have two choices: 1) get the
> hell out of here before I get back tonight or 2) get severely
> fucked the hell right up.

I throw the things I will need into a bag—my laptop, my unshredded clothes, any surviving books, toiletries, condiments, everything. The only thing I can't find is the VIVA LA EVIE lamp. I look and look and look for it. Then I get this sinking feeling. I go back to the note. It is written on a canvasy material. Upon closer inspection this material has what appears to be Elmer's glue on it. On the floor by my feet is what's left of my last artifact of Evie. The lamp has been crushed into a pile of ceramic shards and the shade has been cut into long jagged strips, its metal bracings tied into knots. There is a note attached to the pile that has a smiley face on it and the words DEADA LA EVIE YOU LITTLE FUCK.

I scoop together the remains of my prized possession and whisper reassuring things, holding them tight to my chest like children.

a home where the cockroaches roam

The only place I can find on such short notice is on the Upper East Side. Not in Judith's Upper East Side, either, but on First Avenue in the Eighties—Fratville. There are no Cajun restaurants, no shops like Keeno's, no Lithuanian restaurants whose waitresses mother you. The building itself is structurally sound but infested with roaches and rats, which I can see nightly rappelling down the string of my bedside blinds to the floor, where, on the calzones and half-filled beer bottles I can't bring myself to throw away, they have a sabbat of unrestrained gluttony and copulation.

At least someone's enjoying life, I think.

The two new roommates are salesmen. What they sell I don't know, but they have a redoubtable collection of porno movies and are like parodies of salesmen: they have a limitless store of mindlessly effusive positive energy that manifests itself primarily in punching me in the shoulder and calling me Chief and Buddy and Slugger. And, like high school gym teachers, they only call themselves by their last names. Stabnick. Berko.

Stabnick is a self-proclaimed master of the subway grope and Berko's big goal in life is to get a handicapped permit for his car.

Do I feel a sense of grateful relief that Berko and Stabnick do not disturb the peace with inane jingle-recording? No. Do I thank my lucky stars that they are buffoonish instead of violent? I do not. Am I begrudgingly moved to explore my new neighborhood and discover its hidden charms and benefits? Please.

I despise my new place.

I hate my new roommates zealously.

I miss the East Village and its simple rhythms of sin and penance. I miss the dog run in Tompkins Square Park. I miss Sis's Place and the Blue & Gold and Two Boots and the TVs in Vendetta Laundretta that are always tuned in to infomercials. I want to order the Kiev breakfast sampler and join in the kaleidoscopically milling crowd on St. Mark's and watch skate rats flailing in the gutters by the Astor Place cube. I want to stretch out on top of one of the cement undulations in Washington Square Park and stare up at the clouds while inhaling the sweet smell of pot. I want to step out of my door and walk a hundred feet to Bouche and Limbo. I want to watch the Rollerbladers on the courts slalom through orange cones, their legs crossing and uncrossing in a tentacular series of Xs and Os until they blow past you at the end and you're enveloped for a moment in their cloud of speed and sweat. I want to scale Evie's fire escape and sneak in her window and surprise her at the sink. I want to wake up in the orange light of my room while cannonballing her and rubbing the wax-papery skin of her feet.

I know I haven't moved to a different city, but it feels like I have. I can't figure anything out. I trip off curbs and get yelled at by cabbies. The buses are confusing. None of the bartenders let me stay past closing. One day I step off a curb and into the path of an oncoming bike messenger, who goes sprawling onto the pavement in front of one of the ubiquitous sports bars, brown packages flying.

Back when I lived in the Village this never happened. I knew where all the parking meters were, where the shade was going to be at any given time in Tompkins Square Park, where the rats would appear on the tracks on all the subway stops. I knew instinctively what cabs would stop for you even when they had their OFF DUTY sign on. I could time the lights right so I never had to stop while walking down Avenue A. I was in-step, on-rhythm— geosynchronous.

I miss it. I miss all of it. I even miss that crazy Birdie materializing out of nowhere, for fuck's sake.

When will I have a home?

One morning over a bagel at some diner I force myself to look at the Help Wanteds in the paper. DRIVER NEEDED, an ad says. GET OUT OF NEW YORK NOW! LEAVE YOUR TROUBLES BEHIND! ANSWER THE CALL OF THE OPEN ROAD! FLEXIBLE SCHEDULE AND BEN-

EFITS. INQUIRE AT LONG HAUL ENTERPRISES. STARTING PAY $10–$15/HR. More than what I made at Prestige, I think. And it has the added advantage of putting distance between you and your troubles. There are other ads, too: EXPERIENCED PAN OPERATOR WANTED FOR GROWING CONSTRUCTION COMPANY. That sounds like fun. I could operate a pan, right? The same company is also looking for a BUCKET OPERATOR. Buckets and pans, I can see doing that. LEARN THE ANCIENT TRADE OF BAGPIPE REPAIR, another one reads. BECOME A GUARDIAN OF ANCIENT HISTORY! NO EXPERIENCE NECESSARY!

Publishing wasn't what I always wanted to do, anyway. I had these other ideas. When I was a kid I wanted to be a skin diver. I would be chaste and tan and enigmatic and I'd wear linen and eat raw oysters. I'd live on the outskirts of a small fishing village and talk to no one except dolphins and seaweed. The townspeople would regard me with a respectful sense of mystery and admiration.

It's stupid, but I'd give anything to have another life right now. Any life. It doesn't have to be Jordie's life. I'll take anyone's life. Even though I despise him, I'd even take Lowengrab's life. Why didn't I learn to hold my breath? Or operate pans or buckets? Why didn't I learn the musical properties of sheep bladders or train to drive the big rigs? Why isn't it me who published a big-deal book?

Fuck, why isn't it me who has *written* the big-deal book?

The waitress comes by and tosses down my credit card in the manner of a tourist throwing peanuts to an animal at the zoo.

"Problem?" I say.

"Wouldn't take your card."

"Do you take watches?"

"Not that one."

I fish around in my wallet but the only thing I have in there are the dollars I have won off of Jordie Wesselesh in our logomachy, with the winning words written on them in red pencil. I squeeze them out of my wallet and push them toward the waitress.

The last one I hand over has PROTEMPLORATE on it. I am so reluctant to give it up that the waitress has to pry it from my fingers.

No Evie. No job. No East Village apartment. No VIVA LA EVIE lamp. No Jordie dollars. I am sheer.

the very famous it

Evie doesn't understand the principle of saturation. She will fill up her coffee, her lemonade, her iced tea with so much sugar that it collects at the bottom in a murky white sediment that she will stir off and on for the life of the drink, thinking that perhaps just one more good stir will help it get absorbed. We have had conversations about this, but Evie never yields. Why should I bother her about the way she drinks her drinks? Why don't I mind my own drinks? What does the sugar content of drinks have to do with me anyway?

She is right, of course. It shouldn't matter to me one way or another. So she likes a lot of sugar. So what. But I do love watching her so diligently trying to coax the overdose of sugar to dissolve in her glass with gestures of increasing concentration and frustration. And it is precisely this love of watching her mad stirring that almost gives me away.

Since she is not returning my calls and Madeleine has been harboring her, I have taken matters into my own hands. For the last four hours I have been waiting outside Prestige for her to leave for the day. Sitting around on the bench across the street in sunglasses with a newspaper in front of my face—waiting, waiting—makes me feel like some bit actor out of a spy movie.

QUESTION: What do you think you will accomplish with this stalking?

ANSWER: Stalking? No no no. How can it be stalking to be waiting to talk to the woman you love? How can it be loitering to be standing around the place you used to work? And besides, what choice do I have? I need to see her.

QUESTION: What do you hope to accomplish by this?

ANSWER: To get her back, of course.

QUESTION: How do you intend to do that?

ANSWER: I am going to tell her I am sorry. I will try to explain why. And then I will tell her I love her.

QUESTION: Want to make a bet?

Finally, around eight o'clock, the revolving doors disgorge Evie and I trot across the street to meet her. But something won't let me touch her. The plan was to take off the sunglasses, ditch the paper, and affect a look of happy surprise—wow, what a coincidence!—but the closer I get to her on the sidewalk the more wrong it feels and I end up watching her turn into Ess-A-Bagel. I follow her in and watch her with her lemonade, pouring in way too much sugar and spending a couple of minutes stirring in futile hope of making it dissolve. It is so overwhelming seeing her do that again, so heartwarming, that I nearly let out a burst of joyous laughter.

Now that she's done stirring she exits Ess-A-Bagel and heads back to Prestige. I grab a few extra sugar packets and follow her around the corner until I spot Paula clicking by and have to retreat.

If I didn't feel like a stalker before I sure do now.

I have to take the long way around the block. Finally inside Prestige, I flash the night security guy my newly discovered ID. This is a bit of good luck. When I had my exit interview the human resources people repossessed my ID. ("Why is there a picture of Tennessee Williams on this?" they wanted to know.) Last night, though, I realized I had another ID tucked away, the one that I was originally issued when I started work at Prestige, one that I thought I had lost and so had replaced. It has existed only as a memento for so long I had forgotten all about it. This morning when I peeled off the picture of Tom Waits I barely recognized the twenty-two-year-old version of myself. I looked healthy and alert. My skin was clear and my eyes were bright with hope. I can almost remember the feeling.

For a moment the security guy balks at the photo. He holds it up to the light and squints dubiously at it, then nods and says, "Guess that's you after all."

"Guess so," I say.

I sign the logbook and cruise to the elevators. The doors wheeze open and I step out onto eleven and all the old smells wash over me: stale carpet, old paper, copier ink, frustration, failure, and the warming plastic scent of outdated computers.

In the assistants' area everything looks the same except my ignoble cube. It has been transformed. No more the crumbling piles of slush manuscripts, no more the smelling salts, no more the list of psychological ailments for which Western science has no name. Instead there is only a triumphant order and cleanliness. All the trays are labeled and all the piles are neat. The WHILE YOU WERE OUT message booklet is cleverly next to the phone and the datebook is in clear view. I don't know what I expected—some kind of spiritual residue, an emotional afterimage?—but I can hardly believe that I ever sat here.

There is no trace of me left.

I suppose there is one other difference too: Evie's cubicle. Nothing of hers is there. Everything of hers is in her new office—the once-vacant office on whose door I had aspired to have my nameplate. But now it says

EVIE GODDARD
ASSOCIATE EDITOR

and when I finally work up the courage to peek into the office it makes sense. She is bent over a manuscript, her hair tumbling down her forehead and over the stack of pages. It looks right. Like Uncle Booloo said, she is giving all those books the Goddard help they deserve.

"Care for some sugar in that sugar?" I say finally.

Evie looks up. "Harry," she gasps, but it's hard to tell if the gasp and the expression in her eyes are happiness or just surprise. "What are you doing here?"

"I thought you might need some extra sugar," I say, tossing the packets on the table.

She doesn't say anything. A long, granitic silence passes between us.

"Evie," I say at last. "Look. I don't know what to say. I know you don't want to talk to me. I know you've been avoiding me for the last couple of weeks, and probably with good reason. But I needed to see you."

"Now is not a good time for me, Harry."

"Why not?"

"This manuscript needs my attention."

No, I think. *I* need your attention. *Me.*

"Well, do you think we could talk after you're done?"

"Sure. When is convenient for you?"

"When is con*ven*ient for me?"

"Just trying to figure out what will work."

"No. That is what you say when you're making a lunch date with someone you've never met. That's not what you say to me, Eves. Not *me.*"

"Harry, I don't know what you're thinking but I don't especially owe you anything. I certainly don't relish the idea of talking to you right now, but I'm willing to do it later. I think that's plenty generous of me," she says. "Considering."

I almost say, " 'Considering'?" but don't because it occurs to me what the response would be: considering that you've been lying and cheating on me for months, considering that you stood me up on a dire endo night, considering that you've generally been a bastard about my first book and my promotion, and, well, considering pretty much everything else.

"I just want to tell you I'm sorry and maybe we could—"

"You're not sorry."

"Yes I am too sorry. I'm stark-raving sorry. I'm so sorry my eyeballs are popping out of their sockets over here. I have spent the last few weeks—"

"What you have spent the last few weeks feeling is disappointed."

"It sure feels like sorry."

"You're disappointed because your plans with Judith didn't work out, because you can't string me along anymore, because the book you hate is becoming a success. You're just sore because you didn't get your way, Harry. Your *ego* is sorry, and that's a lot different from real sorry."

"I just want to explain—"

"You know, I'm sure this would be a fascinating story but I really have to go meet someone. I'm late already, so maybe we could get a coffee next week?"

"Who do you have to go meet? The buzzworthy J.J.? Is that who you have to go see so urgently?"

"He is my author, after all." When she says this she looks different, like someone else. She is radiant with superior knowledge. She knows things about advances and agents and production costs that I will never know. And there is something powerfully unapproachable about her now. There is a pruritic rush in my ears. It's the same feeling I get when looking at paintings I don't understand.

"*Only* your author?"

"That's not your business, I'm afraid."

"So it's true? You're dating him?"

Her eyes stare at me in a sibylline poker face and then, finally, she gives up an airtight smile and says, "Yes. Yes I am seeing J.J."

"That miserable little New Age/Kenny G/Greenpeace/tinted-sunglasses / decaf-soy-latte-cappuccino / Raygun-reading / Yanni / from Mars and Venus motherfucker! How could you? You should be with me! Me me me me me!"

"Calm down, Harry. If you think you are going to ambush me here in my own office and start yelling nastiness at me, you are mistaken. In fact, your assholery right now has an inverse relationship with my reluctance to call security on you. So unless you want to have another scene here in the office I suggest you calm down."

"Look at me. Have you ever seen someone more perfect for you than me? I have been custom-ordered from God just for you. Drakkar can't know you like I know you. I am an expert on you. I am the scholar of you. I am the professor fucking emeritus of you. Ask me anything. Really. He doesn't know you're afraid of grasshoppers because one got stuck to your lip when you were living in Mississippi, does he? I bet he doesn't know you love playing car-racing video games while drunk. Am I right? And he doesn't know you hate chocolate because Sadie Thibedoux tricked you into drinking motor oil by saying it was chocolate sauce when you were eight years old, does he? And I bet he gives a shit cannonball. No one knows how to cannonball like me, do they?"

"Love isn't expertise, Harry."

"What's so great about Drakkar? What does he do that I don't do?"

"He's mature. He's considerate. He's serious—not sarcastic—about his work."

"That sounds pretty dull."

"Is 'passionate' a better adjective? O.K. then. He's passionate about his work." It seems to me that Evie is pronouncing the better adjective with just a little too much relish for my liking. "And he's passionate about love. He's so passionate he has written an entire book on it."

Somehow I manage to resist derogating the book. The effort makes my toes curl inside my shoes.

"You don't even have to say it, Harry. I see what you're thinking. What was the put-down you were considering? That it's a fortune cookie? That it's bumper-sticker wisdom? It won't matter to me. You're wrong about *Love Is a Ladder*. It's good. It's not James Joyce but it isn't trying to be. That was one of the most maddening and juvenile things about you, you know."

"What was? My discrimination?"

"Your lamebrained knee-jerk trigger-happy dismissals of things you don't know anything about. When you rejected *Love Is a Ladder* from the slush pile you didn't even read it, did you?"

"Who reads anything in slush? It has a sickening title and I could see right off he has the writing style of a twelve-year-old."

"Harry. You're wrong. This is your defining characteristic, in fact. You are wrong about everything. All the time. And you don't even know it."

"What am I wrong about?"

"God. Where to start? *The Gingerbread Man*. Nature adoring a vacuum. *Love Story*."

"I'm not wrong about *Love Story*. Anyone who titles a movie *Love Story* ought to be killed by lethal injection of potpourri."

"You haven't even seen it, Harry."

"I don't have to. I know."

"See?" she says, the scars at her forehead flashing white. "This is exactly what I mean. You are just so . . . wrong. And you always, always think you're right."

"All right. Let's call these things a draw. What else do you think I am wrong about?"

"Me for one. You think that you can go around doing whatever you like behind my back. You think that because I love you it means I will forgive you anything. God knows I forgave you enough, that's true. But it's like you think forgiveness equals love. Like if you keep doing these atrocious things and I keep forgiving you for them that demonstrates my love for you. I know you detest yourself, Harry, and that you have always detested yourself. I know that your shitty family life has contributed to this. But there comes a time when you have to take responsibility for yourself. You know? Taking it out on me isn't fair. And eventually I just got sick of it. Contrary to what you might think, I am not willing to take your shit forever. I'm sorry I haven't been returning your calls and that I am not willing to sit down and talk you through this, but I think I have really spent enough time just sitting around."

"What do you mean, sitting around? When did you just sit around for me?"

"When did I sit around for you? I was like Whistler's fucking Mother for you. All I did was sit around and think about you like an ass while you were off doing despicable things with women I tried not to think about." Something hardens in her face. "I don't think I especially owe you much in the way of indulgence right now, do you?"

What can I say to that? What I finally say is "And things are so much better with Drakkar?"

"Yes, things are much better with J.J."

"Do you love him?"

"You know, with you it always felt like you were the immovable object and I was the utterly resistible force. And with J.J. it's just so . . . easy. Uncomplicated. After a few weeks with him I began to see you and me in a different way. I saw how exhausted I was, how sick and tired I was of everything. Of your lying all the time. Of your always smelling like a shot glass. Of your Charlie Browning around the office. Of your humiliating me. And most stupid of all, I saw how tired I was of waiting for you to change."

"I can change."

"No," she says, resolute. "This, I'm afraid, is the very famous it."

A tear slides down her cheek like a single silver bead of mercury.

"But he's your *author*," I say, desperate. "How could you?"

"You're hardly in a position to be sanctimonious about anyone else's behavior, but, if you must know, he took me out! To a restaurant. He said kind things to me. He looked at me when I was talking instead of tracking the ass of whatever waitress was going by. We had a conversation and before I knew what was happening—POW!—the Jiffy Lube was open for business. You know the really stupid thing? The stupid thing is that I kept thinking you'd get over it—over *yourself*—and that it would work out for us. We're not star-crossed lovers, after all. We're not even sparkler-crossed lovers. Our houses aren't feuding. No one's killed anyone in a duel. There was nothing working against us. There was no reason for us to be unhappy. It's just all so stupid. And tragic. And I'm at a point in my life when tragi-stupid is no longer funny.

"And do you want to know the really funny thing? Honestly, you're going to hemorrhage when you hear this, I think it will appeal to your refined sense of irony. The real cliché, Harry, is being so afraid of love that you lose it."

"So I'm the cliché? Is that what you're telling me? I'm the cliché?" Never in all my memory has anyone ever accused me of being a cliché. I can taste the anger in my mouth.

"That's not even the be*ginning* of your clichés. 'Oh I'm so sad. Oh the world is so cruel. Oh I don't know what to do. Therefore I drink a lot while brooding and gnashing my teeth and shaking my fist ruefully at Fate, the source of all my misfortune. I am a young man devoured by angst and uncertainty—so stylish, isn't it? So *poetic*—and I must drown my agonies in liquor and the saliva of women. Woe is me. *Wooooooooooooeeeeee* is me.' " For a long punitive moment Evie stares at me wordlessly. Then, "Yeah. Real original, Harry. A real groundbreaker."

"I'm the fucking cliché?"

"Good night, Harry."

Evie gets up from the desk and starts packing her bag with efficent, soldierly movements. Behind us the lights in the hallway click off, motion sensors detecting no one moving. The gluey smell of carpet cleaner is thick in my nose. I try to force myself to think about what I say next because I know it will matter for the rest of my life.

Never the master of myself, I haul out all manner of profanity and insults about Drakkar's manuscript. When I am done the only sound is the humming of the fluorescent lights overhead. Evie shoulders her bag gracefully, heads toward me, and says, "I hate you, Harry. But it's O.K., because I hate you for all the right reasons."

When she's gone—striding balletically out of the office and down the hall, into her unfolding new world without me—it occurs to me that during the entire discussion I didn't really apologize. Nor did I explain why. And I didn't even tell her I loved her.

consider this

The next day, in the scarifying light of morning, I confront the awful, stupid truth of my life. I line my failures up in my mind and pick them off like clay pigeons: one career, ruined (six years); one home, lost (three years); one love, *poofed* (the rest of my life?). I realize my life sounds like a slush manuscript I rejected last spring. I can still hear the author's desperate voice on the phone:

"But clichés aren't clichés when they happen to you!"

work ethic

I know it is the thinking of a superstitious paranoiac, but the world seems to be going out of its way to punish me. I spend my days searching for a job I can tolerate and nights staring at my ceiling, giving my pillow the cannonball and whispering Viva la Evie to it reassuringly. When I finally fall asleep I have this recurring dream in which a magpie pecks out my heart and says, "Sorry for the inconvenience, but it's a lovely piece and I have just the right place for it."

One day a brochure from the Bancroft-Ash School arrives in the mail from my mother. I had never seen the campus before. It's bigger than my undergrad campus and more beautiful. There are pictures of ivied Gothic buildings and playing fields enshrouded in morning mist with deer in the woods that do not look airbrushed in. There are shiny, robust children, K through 12, in dress code, hunched studiously over books (I can make out Laurence Sterne, Goethe, and Paul Verlaine, which is embarrassing because I have never read those guys) and hoisting Bancroft-Ash banners at some tradition-laden sporting event against a rival prep school that they doubtless regard with amicable antagonism. Their endowment is larger than that of most colleges; many of their faculty have Ph.Ds. They have an art museum, a theater, an ice-skating rink, and an observatory. They have a writer-in-residence program and I recognize three of the people they've had there in the last five years. Their mascot is the great blue heron. "Gooooooooooo Herons!" is their fearsome cry.

It is a place refulgent with success and achievement and bright, beautiful children.

Inside the brochure is a note from my mother. It says that Meredith Crosswhite wants me to come in for an interview; she thinks there might be something available in the English department. I agree. I set up an interview for a Wednesday morning and arrive an hour early to look around the campus. It is as beautiful as the brochure and the kids are all perfect. They have flawless dentition, precise elocution, daunting intellects. You know the way everything in advertisements is too perfect? Tomatoes too red, sky too blue? It finally occurs to me that this is what has happened to Bancroft-Ash. I keep expecting it to betray something invidious about itself—this is the breeding ground of dangerous, sophisticated gorillas, isn't it?—but it does not happen. Bancroft-Ash is a fantasy world of beauty and privilege.

During the interview I don't have the heart to lie to Vernon Crosswhite. When he asks me about the Great American Novel I've been editing I tell him there is no such novel. When he wants to know about my accomplishments and responsibilities at Prestige I tell him the most recent thing I did was to lose the only extant copy of a manuscript under contract. When he shows curiosity about my decision to leave behind the cutthroat world of adult trade publishing for the cloistered life of private school teaching I tell him that it wasn't really my decision, that in fact I was recently fired and replaced by the German guy whom I was supposed to be training and whose grasp of English could best be described as "Hooked on Phonics." I also tell him that this is not too surprising as a reasonably well-trained circus monkey could perform my job and that if I don't find some source of income soon I will be out on the streets breaking eggs on my head.

Then something weird happens. Vernon Crosswhite suggests we take a walk around the campus. He gets this sort of paternal look and tells me he admires my candor and is relieved he can shoot straight with me. He was once a lot like me, he tells me. He worked in magazines and became disillusioned fairly quickly. He cast about for something he could believe in, something with meaning. He too had an ignominious exit from the publishing trade, but he found his calling a short drive away, here in the woods of Connecticut, at Bancroft-Ash, working with gifted and diligent children. As the years passed and he became less a teacher and more an administrator, he lost touch with the student body, until recently, when he realized that the school was too remote, too elite, rarefied. He decided he needed to start an "urban outreach program" to bring some of the real world into it, something of the hardness, the unfairness, the ugliness.

"And that's where I come in?" I ask, unoffended.

"That's where you come in," he says, extending his hand. "What do you say?"

I spend a few days thinking about it. My mother calls to ask me how it went and I tell her the shocking truth: that I have been offered the job. Included in the offer—a three-year contract—is free room and board and a light teaching load to allow for me to take kids on excursions into the city. I tell her I pretty much can't believe it and she says well, that's the least they could do, considering.

"What does that mean?" I ask her, although I fear I already know the answer. And I do. Begrudgingly the story comes out: she and my father have made certain contributions to the school, which they were really going to make anyway for tax purposes, honey, and which she's sure didn't really have any real impact on their decision to hire me because what with my resume and that Great Novel I edited that is due out any day and my glowing recommendation from Nadler who could be a better candidate?

QUESTION: You've spent much time and effort trying to get a job illicitly handed to you via Judith's influence and failed. Now that you finally have a job offer that's been bought for you, do you take it, considering that you have rent due in five days and your credit card bills are compounding at a rate of 18.5 percent a month and you have no gainful employment in sight?

ANSWER: No I do not. I will not fill quarter rolls with kitty litter. I will not sell my plasma to stab labs until I pass out or endure humiliating mistreatment from women while tripping the light fantastic or spend my nights breaking eggs on my head. I will not become Laura Dingle. I will not do it.

I tell my mother that she is sweet, then I hang up and call Vernon Crosswhite and tell him that I regret to say I cannot accept his kind offer. Probably I will be out on the street by next week, but at least I will know I did it all on my own.

Finally I find a job through a temp agency. I make enough to cover rent and I get medical insurance for a new inhaler but the work is hard on the old ego.

After a harrowing interview ("You don't know Excel? You don't know PowerPoint? You've never done data entry? What *have* you done?") I'm assigned to WD, Worldwide Drama, a channel devoted to the soap operas and daytime TV of all nations. On their channel all day and night it's *Neighbors* and *Home and Away* and *East Enders* and some Spanish and Chinese shows I've never heard of.

I am to man the phones.

"Welcome to the dubba-dubba-dubba-dubba-dubba-dubba-dubba-you D," I'm supposed to say. "How may I direct your call?"

My supervisor—a large, vibrissaed woman who looks like a cosmeticized mole—explains this to me my first day.

"And then you transfer them to the appropriate extension and say, 'Have a nice day and thank you for calling the dubba-dubba-dubba-dubba-dubba-dubba-dubba-you D.' Any questions?"

"Just one," I say. "How many dubbas is that? In toto?"

"Fourteen," she says very seriously. "Think you can handle that?"

It's not long before I get reprimanded for omitting dubbas. I don't like the dubbas. They enrage me, in fact. I want to tell these people that it's absurd. I'm an editor. I know bad use of language when I see it. They should listen to me on this.

QUESTION: Don't they know who I am?

ANSWER: No they do not.

"It's not difficult," the mole says after I've been reprimanded a few times. "Just answer the goddamn phone. Five-year-olds can do this, for God's sake. You can do the work of a five-year-old, can't you?"

1-800-pls-help

Having no one else in the world to turn to—no Evie, no Keeno, no one—I call the 800 number of an airline and beg the woman who answers to talk to me.

"Please," I say. "This is not a crank call. I just need some help."

I tell her the whole story. I tell her I hate myself. I tell her it was all my fault. I tell her the grief is breaking my bones.

But she doesn't want to talk about philosophical issues. She wants to know about my post-Evie sex life. So I tell her.

The background clattering of her keyboard stops and she says,

"Sitting around the house talking dirty to an MTV chick does not constitute a sex life."

I tell her I'm not as bad as my roommates, right? How come they are such unconscionable Miocene men and how come they live in such bliss? Where is their honor? Where is their respect for women? For themselves? How can the girls they date put up with that treatment?

"Let me just get this straight," she says. "You lose your job because you didn't work. You lose your apartment because you took advantage of your landlord. You've lost all your savings because you didn't deign to take a job for a month after you got fired. Am I on track so far?"

"Yes," I say, choking on the word.

"And the girl—the girl you lose because shortly after she has this big operation so she can have sex with you, and after having sex for the first time in the last ten years or so, she finds out you've been cheating on her? To save a job you wouldn't have had to save if you hadn't been quote unquote Charlie Browning around in the first place?"

"Yes," I say. "God."

"And all this time, even when you return to confront her at the office and apologize for everything and try to get her back, you still cannot manage to tell her you love her? Because you got mad when she said you were a cliché? A part of speech stopped you from telling her you love her?"

"All that's true," I say miserably. "Yes. Yes yes yes."

"Well," she says, "as far as I can tell the only difference between you and your roommates is that they do shitty things to women they don't really know and you do shitty things to the woman you love."

eviscerated

Berko is in the living room having sex on the futon with a kindergarten teacher he thinks is named Sarah so I am trapped in
my bedroom.

"Who's your favorite student?" he says over the slapping, mu-
cilaginous sound of sex. "O.K. then. Call me Charlie. Charlie's
taking over."

Finally I hear her leave and I'm able to come out of my bedroom. Two rats, fat as burritos, are dead in a glue trap in the
kitchen, the cheese a millimeter from their dissolving faces. I get
some Triscuits and sit down in front of the TV. There's a show
on the Discovery Channel about Egypt and when the guy in khaki
says, "The dead are always *evi*scerated before mummification," I
start crying uncontrollably.

Berko asks what the problem is, dude, and I—desperate and
lonely—pour out the story to him. Naked and couchant on the
futon with the postcoital extravagance of a dissipated monarch,
he offers his advice: get another girl. Simple as that. Come the
fuck out with me pussy to another bar tonight and get another
girl. You're not a bad-looking guy. With your looks and my
brains, hell yes, you can get all the vitamin P you need. Fuck yes,
my fellow pussynaut. Clear the runway for snatch.

I want to tell him he never saw Evie's mouth quiver when she
was mad, that he doesn't know the infinite smallness of Evie

sleeping, that he could never understand the joy I felt by giving her Rapunzel treats or the cannonball or what it was like when she appeared at my cubicle: like I had received a pardon from the death row of boredom and pointlessness. What it felt like to be in the Treehouse.

I want to tell him that he's a presapien yahoo who wouldn't know love if it were a Hootersian bartender giving away free tequila shooters at his favorite sports bar. Instead I say, "How do you know so much?"

"Hey," he says, immune as ever to sarcasm. "I'm a man."

I wake up under the desecrated toilets at Sis's Place. This is not entirely new. This time, though, when I come to on the wet tiles I have a crusty stream of vomit leading from my mouth to the floor. It is very thin and seems to be composed mainly of cherries and olives. My brain feels decorticated and my hands are shaking. It's so bad I don't even feel like a man with a hangover. I feel exsanguinated, reconstituted, a packet of freeze-dried protoplasm brought to life by adding water—part human, part sea monkey.

I splash cold water on my face, wipe my mouth with a paper towel that reeks of Russian cigarettes, and roll back out into the bar. I don't want Sis to know how drunk I am so I concentrate on my walking, which makes my movements retarded and florid, like an astronaut spacewalking. I squeeze out some crushed bills from my pocket and push them across the bar like the cards of a losing poker hand.

They all watch me—Tug, Amtrak, Kriedel, Pink, Zosia, the rest—as I spacewalk toward the door.

"Love," Tug says sagely, looking up from his Carl Sagan and appraising me with his undreaming, juiceless eyes. His head— a clayey bulb of hair, scar tissue, and gelatin—bobs knowingly at me. "Love is both particle *and* wave."

Sadness pushes me out of the bar.

On the street I get mugged by two Lithuanian kids I've seen around playing basketball very poorly. I do not resist. One of them holds me while the other one punches me in the nose. It makes a crunching sound—like a beanbag being squeezed— when the cartilage gives way. I can taste the metallic flavor of blood in my mouth. The force knocks me down and I fall quite easily to the ground. They rifle through my pockets while I sit there and feel the warm coppery sensation of blood dripping down my throat. For a long time after they are gone I try to concentrate on the pain, try to make it last—it gives me some-thing to think about besides Evie—but it doesn't work. All I can think about is her.

Later a fluty voice says to me, "Hey, Mr. Please, you don't look so hot. Let me give you a hand with that. I got some napkins here." Small hands are all over my face, wiping up the blood and snot and tears. I do not resist. "How did this happen? You got a lot of blood for such a scrawny guy." With surgical daintiness, Birdie dabs at my nose with textured napkins.

Last winter Evie was bothering me about going on vacation together. We had never really done anything like that, not to-gether. In fact, in my whole adult life I had never been on any vacation that was not with my parents. But Evie insisted. Trouble was, we didn't have any cash. None. So I told her I would come up with something. I waited until Darrell went to Chicago for the weekend and then invited Evie over. Before she arrived I turned on the oven, opened the oven door, and placed fans in the hallway to blow the heat down to my room. I'd borrowed some reggae discs from Keeno. I'd bought some coconut-scented suntan lotion to rub on her feet. I had been stealing flowers from the office for days in preparation and had scattered the petals around the apartment and on my bed. As for sand, well, the linoleum was already plenty gritty, so that took care of itself.

That was that. Our first and only vacation together.

"I'm going to have to make some bullets," Birdie says, shaking her head. "Sit still. This is going to feel . . . funny. Don't worry, though, I'm rocco at this. Do it all the time." She squints in concentration, making her eyes look pinched and stellate. I barely feel the napkin suppository enter my nostril. "There. How's that?"

After a while she says, "Hello?"

Then she knocks on my skull. "Anyone home?"

Before Evie and I started dating, before our moment outside the Blue & Gold, before our first kiss in the cab, back when she was still dating Luther, the ex of cigarette-lighter fame, she and I had this conversation on the phone. I had called her from the pay phone at Sis's Place. I was in danger of passing out and she kept me awake enough to find my way back to my apartment, where I called her up again on the phone. "What do you wear to bed?" I asked.

"Pardon?"

"What do you wear to bed? Pajamas? T-shirt? Special girlie night things? Nothing? I'm just curious."

"I'm not so sure that's any of your business, Hairball."

"Why? Can't you talk? Is *Luther* over? Is that it?"

"No. I'm alone. I just can't talk."

"Alone? That can't be good. Is it awfully dark and scary? You know, I'm not at all afraid of the dark, and if you needed—"

"Thanks but no thanks. I'm O.K. for tonight, I think."

"And you won't tell me what you're wearing? Or not wearing?"

"Mmm," she said. I could tell she was really considering it. "No. I think no."

"But you're in bed, right?"

"Yes."

"O.K. At least tell me what position you're in."

"Why?"

"Just please."

"You're the strangest thing, but all right. I am on my side."

"Which side? Left or right?"

"What is this about?"

"Left or right?"

"Left, left, sheesh. Why do you want to know so bad?"

"Give me a second." My proprioceptive deficiency was such that it took me a moment to change my position. "There," I said happily. "Now I'm on my left side, too, and I've got my arm around a pillow."

"So?"

"It's like I'm spooning you over the phone."

Birdie examines her handiwork. "No wonder those guys rolled you. You're really tanked, aren't you?" She leans down and sniffs me. "Whoa. Guess so. You got a powerful thirst, Mr. Please. That's for sure." Birdie cocks her head to the side inquisitively. "Hey. Why you looking so Ezra Pound? You going to talk to me or what? Speak. Hey. Earth to Harry."

Then she says, "No shit. This is weirding me out. Snap out of it already."

Six months after Evie and I started dating I went back to my college to appear on this panel about publishing. Evie was supposed to come with me—for kicks I had wangled her an invitation, too, and besides: she knew the business better than I did—but she got sick at the last minute. Not the endo, just sick. So I went alone.

Things were fine during the day but at night it was intolerable. The college was way out in the country with no towns nearby. So every night it was just me and the stars. I would wander by myself out past the woods onto the far playing fields and spread out on the earth, staring up at the sky and wishing Evie were there with me. Then one night something strange happened. I was driving back from a bookstore in a neighboring town and as I came around a corner on the desolate road toward campus I almost got into an accident. Suddenly there were so many lights in front of me I thought I was about to collide with a bunch of cars and I had to slam on the brakes. But it wasn't a bunch of cars. It was a bunch of fireflies.

"I didn't mean it when I called you a dumb fucking Stimpson," Birdie says. "I take it back. I take it back twice. I take it back infinity. Just talk to me!"

It was like a plague of locusts, only it was a plague of fireflies. They were everywhere. The windshield of my rental car was covered in dusty explosions of glowing luciferin from the ones I had already crushed, and all around me, bobbing up and down and filling the pristine country night air with a subaudible phosphorescent electricity, were thousands of fireflies. I caught some in my hand and held them but I couldn't feel anything. They gave off no heat at all. Yellow light leaked out between the cracks of my fingers, but all I could feel was their wings beating against my skin.

"How about we get out of here? How about that? Want to go? Here, let me give you a hand up." She's silent for a second, then she fumbles for my hand and says, "What? No hand? Still no hand? Not even any hand to help you get up with? God you're squidy. Guess I'll just have to pull you up by your hair." After a pause I hear her say, "You really don't care, do you? God damn you are one squidy individual. I mean you have gone one hundred and ten percent pure squid."

Then she grabs me by the belt and says, "All right, Mr. Hands Off. We'll do it this way."

I let the trapped fireflies go and they dipped and pulled in the air of the playing fields. The insects filled the wide open space. I remembered hearing that when fireflies light up they are trying to attract mates, and standing there in that field I knew that was right. I could feel it. If you watched carefully you could see that what looked like one glowing orb of light was really two fireflies moving together. You could feel the energy of their search for love. It made my cells boil and lift up out of my body. I spread out on the ground and let them cover me while the earth spun wildly on its axis. They were tiny yellow deities. They were stars floating in an aquarium of black water. They were a hallucination of pure love.

It was one of the most beautiful things I had ever seen. I should have been elated but I wasn't. It meant nothing to me except heartbreak because Evie was not there. Even today it is my loneliest memory.

And now every day feels like that night with the fireflies: every moment is ruined because Evie is not here to share it with me. It is as if things aren't happening.

"Easy, easy," Birdie says. "We're here. Finally. Take a load off. Go on. Kick back."

I am sitting down on a sheet of cardboard. It is part of Birdie's box, her home. My head is on a pillow made out of a shirt stuffed with newspaper and human hair. Birdie has told me about this before: she goes to barbershops and they give her their clippings at the end of the day.

"You get hit in the skull, too? Got some kind of damage? Why don't you talk to me?"

Later she says, "I swear to God." And after that, "You're still bleeding. How about some ice? Guys at St. Mark's Pizza always let me have ice. You want some ice?"

She paces back and forth by the curb, twanging the antennas of parked cars. Then she comes back and hunches over me, staring into my eyes. She holds a magazine up in front of my face and says, "I got a good idea. Maybe you'd feel better if you read to me. You like *Discovery*? Me too. This one's a little old. 1987. What you going to do? See here? Look at this one with all the planets. That one looks good, huh? Check out how all of them spread out look like a game of marbles. That's nice, right? How about that? How about you read me that?"

A minute later she says, "Well, I guess that's a good sign. No hand-holding, no reading. Your reflexes are still good. All systems normal I guess, huh?"

A thready rain starts to come down, revitalizing the street odors of stale car exhaust and stale human discharge.

After a long silence she says, "Fuck it. I don't know what to do. Why don't you tell me anything? What do I have to do? What do you want?"

I want to go back in time. I want to go back to that night with Judith when I found out who she was, when she asked me what I thought was sexy, when the stars were doing their worn-out trick in the sky, when we ended up under the awning in front of her building. I want to go back to that night and tell her that I find fidelity sexy, that I am already in love with another woman, that she's a very wonderful dancer and lovely woman but that I really have to be going now and to have a nice evening. I want to spread out with Evie in a field of grass ablaze with fireflies. I want to be there every night she ever has the endo again.

The light turns and taxis speed by the city of boxes, filling the air with the flashing of their headlights in rain, and I keep thinking: all these lights and still no Evie.

time

Time flips past in a blur of meaningless color and motion. Who knows how many weeks pass? My days are all dispirited, indistinguishable, inspissated—sleep-thick. My sense of taste disappears. I pour Tabasco on everything I eat but I can't taste it. And I don't notice anything happening. Hair grows, trash collects, the temperature drops, things contract.

It is fall.

My life is peeling away. I can feel it. The rashes start cracking in the cold and I have to start wearing Band-Aids over my nipples to keep them from bleeding on the walk to work. Berko and Stabnick sit around watching *SportsCenter* while putting back beers and picking off rats with a BB gun. And me, I become confused. I chronically take elevators to wrong floors. I find myself suddenly in a shop, baffled and unable to remember what I was planning to buy there. Once I put liquid detergent in the dryer at some Upper East Side Laundromat and have to run out the door trailing dirty socks and underwear, fleeing the manager's violent gesticulations and whitewater stream of vitriol.

What does it mean? I don't know.

The world seems immensely complicated.

instant karma gets me

Drakkar's book hits big. Ads for it occupy bus stops and subway cars and buildings all around the city. Radio shows talk about it. I overhear a woman on the E train one day talking about how great Jason Drakkar was on *Charlie Rose* last night.

"He is so wise," she says. "He knows so much about love. I wonder if he's single."

Four days later it hits number eight on the *New York Times* nonfiction list.

In the acknowledgments Drakkar thanks his intrepid agent and, "most of all, Evie Goddard, editress extraordinaire, the wonderwoman with the courage and talent and vision to make this book happen."

Print, radio, TV: the media all adore *Love Is a Ladder*. What a story. What a writer. What insight into the human heart.

Even my roommates hear about the book. "Hey. Prestige, you

pussy. That's your old place, right? Wow. Congratufuckingla-tions. Must be pumped."

I can hear Madeleine say it: Drakkar gets on *Charlie Rose? Love Is a Ladder* hits the list? I guess he knows how to write after all. I guess he knows something about love, too. And you, Harry? What have you written lately? What do you know about love?

scenarios

I develop a rare and lethal disease of unknown origin. No, scratch that. I get run over by a truck while heroically saving a crowd of schoolchildren in cute little Catholic school uniforms crossing the street with puppies on leashes. In the hospital Evie comes to see me. As I sit there, surrounded by the flowers of grateful children whose lives I have saved, Evie has an epiphany: I *am* a good person. I am the beloved of children and puppies. I reflex-ively endanger my own life to save the lives of young innocents.

But oh no: I am unconscious. It may be that this is the last time Evie will ever see me alive. It may be that she will never again have a chance to tell me how wrong she was about me, about Drakkar, how she would gladly trade her own life for the chance of having one last night with me alive. She will lean down over me, her hair brushing my face, and kiss me, and I will wake up and all will be forgiven.

In a related scenario Evie develops a rare and lethal disease. I get the word from Madeleine. From deep within a coma Evie had started whispering a word. It was so faint it took a while to figure out what she was saying: Hairball, Hairball, Hairball. Despite Madeleine's misgivings about me she bravely calls me and I come rushing to the hospital.

Drakkar is there at Evie's bedside, holding her hand and speaking soft words into her ear. Idiot, I think. He looks up and sees me, shrinking because he senses it: it is I, Harry Driscoll, the rightful person to be at her bedside. It is I who has the best chance of bringing her around. Sheepishly, he gets up and offers me the chair.

"Leave us," I say, very grave and regal.

When everyone is gone I sit down and start rubbing her feet. I have brought lotion. I put the video I have brought with me, *Endangered Species Bite Back*, on the TV. Then I rub her feet again and arrange her limbs into a cannonball. We fall asleep this way. When she wakes up Drakkar, Judith, and the endo have disappeared. It is only Evie and me.

A second scenario: when a serial killer is apprehended the cops discover a copy of *Love Is a Ladder* in his pocket. During the interrogation it comes out that he was inspired to commit the crimes by Drakkar's book. ("Insanity by cliché" is the astute diagnosis.) Overwhelmed by bad press, the book's sales drop precipitously. By the time Sunday's *New York Times* comes out it has fallen off the list, never to reappear. The week after that, the big chains take *Love Is a Ladder* off their shelves. Tens of thousands of copies get returned and pulped. Drakkar, his name forever linked with the murders, never gets another book contract and moves to Bhutan.

Nine months later my novel appears in print. Like Cary Grant in *Affair to Remember*, the work I finally produce is beautiful because it's inspired by love and loss, and Evie, like Deborah Kerr, is moved by it. On the page she sees the love I could never verbalize and is overcome with emotion. One day when I am giving a reading at the Astor Place supermegadeluxe bookstore I look out into the crowd and see her. We have coffee after the reading. We have dinner at Two Boots. I walk her home and there, on her stoop where I have kissed her so many times before, I kiss her again. Then we go upstairs and make love. And there is none of this Operation or crying-wolf business. It is good. It's great. It's so great it's superhuman. It is almost paranormal. You know, the whole deal. The big O. Dams breaking, angels singing, Valkyries flying.

Third scenario: I get spiritual. I start taking yoga and Pilates, burning incense, hanging tie-dye tapestries. Channeling all the force of my self-loathing into newfound spiritualism, I become an underground sensation. No one can sit cross-legged like me. No one can make humming noises like I can. I am *it*. I am the Great White Hope for Buddhistic equanimity and poise. People come from all across the country trying to get a piece of my vibe. Eventually Evie hears about the radical new Stimpsonism everyone is talking about and comes to see me. When she does she is overcome with my emanations and realizes that no amount of Drakkar's infantile scribbling about love can compete with this.

We spend the rest of our lives together.

Fourth scenario: I give Drakkar a lethal flying spinning flipping kick to the head. But it's a very special flying spinning flipping kick to the head. It doesn't kill him so much as make him disappear. Instead of leaving a corpse he just sort of vanishes, all memory of him evaporating as well. All the copies of his book mysteriously disappear from the shelves. Critics forget about him. When I ask Evie if she misses him she gives me this confused look and says, "Who?"

Fifth: I confront Drakkar at one of his readings. I stand in line like a fan waiting for him to autograph *Love Is a Ladder* and then I spring on him, scattering copies of the book everywhere and knocking over the table. I will take Drakkar hostage and start making demands: the warehouse must burn all the copies of the book. The clerks at the bookstore must tear the pages of every copy in the store so that they are unsellable. Hell, I will demand that every clerk in every store in America tear the pages of the book. They won't do it, though. They will think I'm bluffing, so I will have to shoot off one of Drakkar's toes. That'll get some pages torn, all right.

Then it occurs to me that Drakkar can't write if he has no fingers so I start shooting off digits, starting with the thumbs. And while I'm on appendages, if he does not have any genitals, he can't represent much of a sexual threat so—

No. Stop. This isn't funny. This is sick. This isn't me. I'm not like this. Not always. I know I'm not a great person, but I'm not this bad. I'm not the kind of person to fantasize about torturing someone. I used to be different. I used to be good. I can be that way again. Right?

Right?

happy birthday to me

Finally my birthday rolls around. I had forgotten about it until a card arrives from my mother with a picture of a mama jungle cat (long eyelashes, lipstick) on it hugging a baby jungle cat (diapers, hat with propeller) with a caption that reads IT'S BEEN GREAT BRINGING UP BABY. On the inside both jungle cats have aged appreciably and the caption reads BUT NOW THAT YOU'RE ALL GROWN UP I STILL LOVE YOU AN OCELOT. Inside is a check and a note inside saying

> Harry honey, I'm sorry about the job at Bancroft-Ash. Your father and I just want what's best for you, and we thought we could help you out a little bit at the beginning. (And we really think you would make a wonderful teacher . . .) Vernon Crosswhite was impressed with you, though, honey, and wanted me to tell you that if you ever need anything from him or from Bancroft-Ash you just need ask him.
>
> > Happy birthday and big kiss,
> > Mother
>
> P.S. Why don't you come home for a visit. Your brother would like to see you. He wanted to send you a card, too, but wasn't sure what to say. Why don't you give him a chance. He has his life together. Why don't you come home and see him. He would like that.

P.P.S. I'm enclosing another brochure of Bancroft-Ash in case
you needed their phone number for anything. (I know you lost
the first one.) It is so pretty there! But don't take it the wrong
way. I compeletely respect your decision, honey. I just thought
the brochure might be nice . . .

I don't know what my father has on old Vernon Crosswhite
but it must be big. I can't imagine why anyone would go out of
their way to offer me favors like this. When I was a kid I was
baffled to find out that the owners of the Polo Grill never charged
our family for dinner even when we all ordered steaks. Kurt told
me it was because as a tax lawyer our father was often in a
position to do sensitive and important work of a morally and
legally ambiguous nature and that often such work accrued mys-
terious favors. I started paying closer attention and it seemed that
our father never paid for anything no matter where he went:
meals, baseball tickets, drinks, you name it. The older I got the
more I realized that he was treated like some minor mobster and
that most of the town owed him something.

I can only imagine what he has done for Bancroft-Ash to make
them feel so beholden that they are willing to create a sinecure
for a twenty-eight-year-old publishing rejectnik. Even more interesting is that if the trend is true to history, they will not feel
comfortable until they fulfill the obligation—a very reassuring
thought. Maybe I could at least make use of their cafeteria when
I run out of food money. I slip the brochure into my wallet in
case I have a nutritional emergency.

As for my brother: I wonder. My mother has lied about this
before and when we did get together in the same room one
Christmas long ago it ended in our drunkenly chucking mince-

meat pies at each other around the tree and being pulled apart by appalled houseguests.

I also get a card from Ida Duffendack, slushie from Dubuque:

Dear Harold Driscoll,

Well, here we are again: your birthday. Who knew that five years ago when I wrote that letter to Prestige about my children's stories we'd still be in touch all this time later? Well well well. My best birthday present for you this year is good news: I finally sold one of my children's books!!!!! It's called HARRY THE HAPPY GNOME. Get it???? I named the gnome after you!!! Because of all your kindness to me!!! The letter your friend wrote me from Prestige Juvenile so impressed an editor at Knotty Pine Books that she signed me up!!

Can you believe it??? Isn't it the greatest?? The title is a "mis-gnomer" (get it?) of course. Harry is a very unhappy gnome and does all the wrong things in Gnometown because he's misunderstood by all the other gnomes and he mopes around all the time. Then he finds the magic potion Never-Be-Sad and is made happy and never mopes again and spends his time doing good deeds for his gnome "gneighbors." Isn't it sweet? Anyway, I hope you like it and happy birthday and thanks again for all your kindness. I know you didn't have to be so nice to me back then (out of all the publishers I sent my manuscripts to, you were the only one to write back at all, let alone be so personal and nice and all), and I know I owe everything to you.

> Happy happy!
> Ida

What would I give for some Never-Be-Sad.
The last piece of birthday mail I get is from Keeno. It is a

squarish package wrapped in brown paper with a note scrawled on it:

H—

My latest piece of Reloc-art, and, if it works, no doubt it is also my greatest. Happy birthday, I guess. —K

Inside the brown wrapping is a Magic 8 Ball. It takes me a second to realize what's different about it, then I see that the shell has been opened and resealed, that in fact Keeno has customized the little icosahedron that floats inside the dark fluid. She has changed out the usual "You May Rely on It" and "Cannot Predict Now" and "My Sources Say No" etc. for her own prophesies.

When I ask it if I will get Evie back and shake it the replies I get are "If You Weren't Such a Selfish Prick" and "If You Didn't Lie and Cheat All the Time." When I ask it if I will get a real job ever again it says, "If You Weren't Such a Lazy Asshole." When I ask it how long it will be before I can move back to the Village and get a real apartment and start a real life it says, "Think About Someone Else for a Change, Fuckwad." This one comes up such an inordinate number of times that I wonder if she's written it on several sides of the icosahedron.

I steal some of Stabnick's beers and spend the rest of the night sitting in my room shaking the Magic 8 Ball.

The next morning I am awakened to the sound of Stabnick pounding on my door.

"Dude, you asshole," he yells. "You drank all my Blue. I had a whole twelve in there." My whole body feels like it's been laminated in warm puddingscum and my lungs feel like they've been sprayed with defoliative—I am hungover again and apparently I've been smoking. Not good when you have asthma and are almost out of spray. I realize I am cannonballing a plastic bucket impregnated with thin watery vomit.

"The fuck is that?" he yells, shocked. My stomach spasms and I hunch up and puke chaotically into the bucket.

"Could you keep it down please? I can barely hear myself puke."

"Dude, what the fuck is with your bricks?"

"What do you mean?"

"*That's* what I mean," he says, pointing to the gray bricks that make up my wall. Each one of them has been meticulously numbered in pencil, from zero up into the hundreds. If I could focus better I might be able to find where they end. "What the fuck have you been doing in here?"

Once I read an excerpt of a CIA handbook on psychological torture and one of the symptoms of isolation torture was "an intense love of any living thing," including the rats and roaches that might occupy the prisoner's cell. If all the rats have been disintegrated in glue traps or shot by BB guns and the roaches are away, I suppose the best a prisoner can do is bricks.

Looking up from my bucket I say to Stabnick, "Keeping myself company?"

misoneism schmisoneism

When I was in college I went through a brief humiliating Tony Robbins period. I became very positive and started observing all these personal-power gimmicks. Chief among these strategies was leaving myself a bunch of you-can-do-it notes in places where I knew I would see them every day. Inside my Latin book I wrote PLUTARCH SCHMUTARCH; YOU ARE THE BOSS OF LATIN. On my sheet music (during the half-semester when I made a stab at playing the piano, before Toby ridiculed me out of it for playing "When the Saints Go Marching In") I wrote YOU OWN THIS PI-ANO; MOZART IS YOUR BITCH. Another note, taped to my mini-fridge, said, YOU DON'T HAVE TO DRINK UNTIL PUKE.

But the most important note I had was under my mirror, inside my closet door. This one said MAKE YOURSELF WORTH SOMEONE. I wrote this because even back then I knew that I would not fall in love with anyone at my college so I decided that the best thing I could do was spend these years making myself the best Harry I could be so that when I *did* meet someone I could love I would be ready; I would be worthwhile. Ergo my plans to play concert piano, to know about philosophy and religion and the human body, to play a sport skillfully and with passion. Of course, none of this would come to pass. Instead of doing these things I became the person my friends started calling Letter Man when I joined the MADC, TADC, WADC, ThADC, and FADC—the Monday, Tuesday, Wednesday, Thursday, and Friday Afternoon Drinking Clubs.

Instead of devoting hours to making myself worth someone I spent days and days in the drink. I thought it was amusing. I thought I was being Falstaffian. Har har, I thought, look at me amid the cakes and ale! Isn't it a riot? Aren't I wild? *Carpe drinkum*, people!

I wish I could figure out at what point it stopped being good fun and started ruining my life and coprofying my soul. When I cheated on Evie with the first meaningless Date? When I stood outside Judith's apartment, with the rain hammering out typewriter clatter on the awning and the stars boiling out of the Milky Way, and made the decision to follow her inside? Or now, when my sins have caught up with me and I have finally lost Evie and am left, alone and miserable at last, to get through this annihilating stupor of days?

I don't know. Maybe it's always been this way. Maybe it's not even the drinking. No, drinking is just a symptom. Every time, all these mistakes, always only one thing has been responsible for them: me.

Harold *Stimpson* Driscoll.

Evie's right. And Drakkar's right in his own detestable way. And Keeno and the airline woman and Madeleine too.

I am the cliché.

I don't know anything about love.

I deserve this.

I am as bad as—worse than—my roommates.

I am the Frog King.

Suddenly, lying on the floor of my bedroom, fiercely cannon-balling a bucket warming with new vomit, I make a decision: enough is enough.

I am going to implement some changes.

The first thing I do is make a sumptuary drinking calendar. I buy a copy of the *Marathoner's Calendar and Logbook* (it's the least I can do for the author) and hang it next to my bed so I see it when I go to sleep and when I get up in the morning. For every day I drink anything at all I put a red X in that day's square; for every day I do not drink I put a blue one. I put a number in the corner if I can remember how many drinks I have had; if I can't remember I put a question mark. If I drink to the point of puking I make a bucket icon. If I am drunk at WD I draw a little phone. On any given day if I cannot remember how much I had to drink, I drink to the point of puking, and I drink at work too then I make a red skull and crossbones.

For the first couple of weeks there are nothing but red skulls and crossbones, but it's O.K. I now have a record of it and for the first time in my life I see what kind of role drinking is playing in my life. I wonder if it is the same role it used to play in my brother's life before he started with heroin. Eventually some blue Xs start surfacing. On these days I allow myself a treat. I go to the fancy lighting store on Third Avenue and buy myself a finial. It isn't too long before I have a nice little collection burgeoning in my bedroom.

I resolve to start flossing. I heard somewhere that when your gums start to recede there is nothing you can do about it, and I don't intend to let it get any worse. At first it's like Bosnia in the sink, but after a few days the bleeding stops and it doesn't hurt too much.

Figuring I could get better temp jobs if I were good at computers, I get a bunch of back copies of *Wired* and read them cover to cover even though I don't understand them.

I buy a body pillow and cannonball it at night.

I start running. I figure: I edited the fucking *book* on running, right? Why not put that knowledge to use? In the beginning it is very hard on the asthma and I do not produce any sweat. I run and run but secrete nothing. What happened to my sweat glands? Has anyone ever heard of sweat disappearing before? I don't know where it's gone but it's not there. It's a disconcerting feeling. Finally, after the red skulls and crossbones start diminishing, translucent droplets start forming on my arms and face. The running actually feels like it is making my lungs stronger and eventually I do not even have to spray before running.

Of course, I am not fast or anything. There is this old Korean lady who must be in her seventies who runs the same route I do along Carl Schurz Park and she passes by every day while eyeballing me. Probably just my imagination, I think, but no: she is staring me down. One day when she blows past me in a blur of pink and silver reflective materials she makes the cutthroat gesture and I think, Oh no you don't, lady. By this point I have been running for a couple of weeks—it seems to me that I have lost some pudge, too—and I am well enough conditioned to sprint after her. We end up in a race, neck and neck, to Gracie Mansion, the spot where we both end our routes. My legs burn and my chest hurts and I have a cramp that feels like someone is kicking me in the spleen, but it looks like I will beat her: I have her by a stride and a half. It looks like I will beat her, in fact, until the inglorious moment when my legs give out and I go tumbling to the asphalt.

"Dude, you slammed so hard," some kid in brakeless Roller-blades says to me. From the fence around Gracie Mansion where she is stretching languidly the old Korean lady gloats at me. "You got your ass *smoked* by that old lady, ha ha ha," the kid says, snickering with his friends.

They can laugh and gloat all they like. I'll get her soon. I will. You wait and see. I am going to *own* that seventysomething Korean lady in her stylish pink and silver running outfit.

I start washing my clothes more regularly and my rashes diminish.

I work at saying the correct number of dubbas at work.

I begin sending in checks for more than the minimum payment due on all my credit card bills and my accounts get reactivated.

I rent *Love Story* and cry so much that I have to rehydrate afterward.

One day I send Cassie a replacement Alanis Morissette CD with a note saying sorry I toasted the old one. When she calls to thank me I ask her if I was such a bad boyfriend and she says, "Don't take this the wrong way or anything, but you were always kind of a snob."

After that I make a special trip down to the roach coach guy outside of Prestige to pay him back the money I have owed him for over six months. As I approach he starts yelling at me unmentionable things in a language I do not understand but when I push the neatly folded dollar bills through the window he stops and stands there, mute and blinking.

One of the books that survived Darrell's knifing is the cookbook I worked on. I crack it for the first time ever and make a stab at cooking. Not just making cold foodstuffs warm, but actual cooking, with ingredients and measuring and mixing and whatnot. Every time I make a new dish I feel like it is bettering my soul one molecule at a time, that it is proof of some new burgeoning goodness. It makes me want to prove it to people, like Evie might take me back if I could get a signed letter of recommendation from my spatula.

Unable to avoid *Love Is a Ladder,* I buy it. It seems a lot less insipid in print than it did when I first saw it in the slush pile. Of course, it probably helps that I actually read it this time.

CORRECTION: It still seems plenty insipid but it doesn't seem *wrong,* if you see what I mean. He sort of makes some sense. For example:

The first "step" on the "love ladder"—I know, I have to grit my teeth too—is "to love yourself." Drakkar says that it is impossible to love another if you do not feel good about yourself. One of the things he recommends in order to maintain a good opinion of yourself is to keep a GOOD THOUGHTS notebook in which you find a way to rethink the troubling events of your life, to retrain your brain to think positive. This I do. I even label the notebook GOOD THOUGHTS, as per Drakkar's recommendation. (One day:

BERKO: GOOD THOUGHTS? What kind of pussy talk is that?

ME: Fuck off, Berko. Why don't you go park in a handicapped space somewhere.)

When I have to buy potatoes and Ramen because I only get three days of answering phones at WD one week, I write down, "Hunger reminds you that it is necessary to provide for yourself. No one else—Judith, parents, etc.—can do it for you." When *Love Is a Ladder* reaches number three on the list and I see Drakkar on *The View*—not as short or nerdy or wimpy as I had hoped he would be; he doesn't have a receding hairline; he isn't fat or ill-proportioned; he doesn't look flagrantly stupid—I force myself to write down, "It is good that Drakkar's book is selling well because that means it is good for Evie's career and that he is helping a lot of people feel better about their lives."

QUESTION: Isn't this disgusting to you? Are you not overwhelmed with nausea and self-reproach for considering—let alone embracing—the strategies of Jason Drakkar, pseudo-shrink?

ANSWER: Yes, it is sickening in some ways. Most ways. But in some other, confusing ways, it is not so sickening. Besides, I am desperate. I'll do anything.

One day I even work up the courage to write my brother a letter. It is the first contact we have had in eight years. Five days later I receive a reply. Both our letters are stiff and awkward. Back in the day when we were friends we never used each other's real names; we always used our nicknames for each other. I don't think I have called him Kurt since I was five years old. But now, in both letters, we use each other's real names. "Dear Kurt," I write. "Dear Harry," he writes back. It's a little disappointing but a little heartwarming too: it means we are being careful with each other. We are both acknowledging that we are different people than we used to be, and that maybe we might find a way to be new friends.

I call Keeno too. I tell her how sorry I am about our last conversation and how much her birthday present means to me.

"Did it work?" she wants to know. "Have you moved at all?"

I tell her about everything I have been doing.

"So do you feel better or what?"

"Evie is still gone. She still doesn't return my phone calls or emails. She is still what I think of first at morning and last at night. And I still wake up from dreams about her in tears, but I think the self-hatred is a little less."

"Wow. It sounds like you are turning into a real human being. Welcome."

I want to tell her that she is right, that everyone besides me was right, that it feels good to be good—it's a brand-new bushido. It's the bushido of the real human being. A tiny aspirated soblike noise comes out of my mouth when I say, "I guess so."

"So what are you going to do?" Keeno asks.

"Do?"

"You know, with your life? You can't answer phones forever. You can't live with those fuckwads on the godforsaken Upper East Side forever. You will develop chromosomal damage if you stay up there too long."

"Tell me about it."

"All this shit you're doing has got to go toward *something*, right? If Evie is really and truly gone, what is your something?"

This is a very good

QUESTION: What do you do when you expend all this energy making yourself worth somebody and the only somebody you will ever want is loving somebody else?

ANSWER: What do you think? Scribble GOOD THOUGHTS in notebook after notebook all the livelong day? Buy up all the finials in Manhattan? Spend the rest of your life cannonballing your body pillow and crying when you hear the word "eviscerated"?

dates redivivus?

After a while I succumb to the pressure of Berko and Stabnick and go on a few dates—that's a lowercase d—but they are all awful. They can be beautiful, funny, smart, wealthy, interesting, you name it, but ultimately they are all interchangeable, penumbral, Müllerian women.

In other words: not Evie.

Also I discover the cruelty of New York geography: everything is everywhere. The city is a collage of warring histories and hurtful memories. My favorite places have become places to avoid at all costs. One night when a date wants to go to the Blue & Gold it feels like a plagiarism. A novel impulse for honesty makes me want to say to this woman that this whole drinks scene is unethical, that I am trying to pass this off as fresh material.

"This work has already been done by another girl," I want to tell her. "It's not fair."

During a game of pool my date—a carefully selected Donna, Donna Mohr; nary an E to be found anywhere in that name—starts talking about the deforestation of South America and it makes me think of the time I called Evie and left that horrible message on her machine about all the trees killed for Drakkar's book and of all the awful words that flew out of my mouth like wickedly disobedient birds. It makes me sick. It makes me feel even more biospherically lonely and desperate.

I cut the date short and hit Krispy Kreme because the sugar and grease smell like forgiveness.

The employees there have gotten to know and hate me in recent months because it always takes me forever to decide what to get—even though every time I end up getting the same thing—and the girl behind the counter, a girl I've seen many times, looks pissed just seeing me waiting in line. When my turn comes, before I've had a chance to speak or even delay, she says, "Not this fucking guy. You think you maybe might know what you want this time? Other people want doughnuts, too, freakshow. Make up your mind or you're out of here."

Behind the girl fresh doughnuts are faithfully coming out on the conveyor belt, soft, steaming, and glazed with wet sugar. I realize the girl truly despises me. I realize for the first time how beautiful she is. In the old days this would have fulgurated my libido. It would have set off a reflexive stream of pixilated flirtation. But now my heart—that fugitive grasshopper—doesn't even twitch.

There is a vast electrical silence in my nerves deadening all the messages between my heart and brain and genitals.

I am totally unsexed.

protemploration pt. ii

One day I start writing.

Maybe the GOOD THOUGHTS journal is responsbile. Or maybe

it's because I have something to do besides drink these days. I don't know. But I begin keeping a journal in which I talk candidly to myself about my history with Evie. Then I start writing these re-creations of our fights in dialogue form to see if I can understand them—and why I can never say what I mean—and before I know it these re-creations become little fictional sketches. But these sketches keep expanding like a marauding supervirus and before I know what is happening they start coalescing into a novel. I have to wake up at five A.M. to write as I have to be at the WD answering phones by eight, so it's not ideal. I have to beg Stabnick to let me put his coffeemaker right by my alarm clock on my bedside table—otherwise I don't have a prayer of getting up that early—but it works. Every day without exception I get up early and write. Soon I start accumulating pages.

And I don't hate what I write. It seems sort of O.K. At least it feels true. It also proves Evie's point about books: they are all love letters. I now understand that that is what was wrong with my other stories. They were all about meaningless events I made up. But this story, the story of Evie and me, is pure, unalloyed, devoted love.

This, I realize one day in a flash, is why I have spent two years trying to read the dictionary. I have been looking for the right words to say "I love you." I was closing in on love, one word at a time.

"Wow," says Stabnick one day while I am hunched over my laptop. "That must be such a good psychological purgative."

I think: Purgative? You moron, I am spending every hour of the day thinking about the woman I love, what she is like, what she is doing now, and with whom, and what I did to bring this on myself. It is not a purgative.

It is punishment.

"Sure is," I say.

"I mean, to get all that shit down on paper. Get it out of your system. It's a great way to get over her, huh? Retire her number and shit."

"Bull's-eye, Stabnick. Retired. Absolutely."

But what I am thinking is: You've got it all wrong. Do you want to know what I am really doing? Have you ever seen those movies when a ghost comes back to visit a loved one and the loved one cannot believe it and starts weeping for joy and then there's a noise offscreen and the weepy loved one looks away for a moment but when he looks back the ghost is gone and he is heartbroken and thinks if only he hadn't looked away, if only he had five more seconds with the ghost, but he doesn't—he *has* looked away—and he breaks down because he has nothing left but the irrelevant, loveless, ghostless world? You know that moment?

Well, that's what I am doing here. Evie is the ghost and I am the loved one, only I am not taking my eyes off her. You know how? By writing this book. That is what this book is—a way to keep my eyes on Evie forever.

This way she will never disappear.

we meet again, at long last

Evie was right: it is a glamorama. If I hadn't been wearing the frog outfit I never would have gotten past security. Everyone—

ICM, Doubleday, Condé Nast, movie people—is here, and the party is uproarious. It is only ten o'clock and already there are people in costumes passed out in corners, their limbs jutting out at wild angles from the mess of their bodies like roadkill. When a hobgoblin hunched over by the table takes off his mask to gobble hors d'oeuvres I am pretty sure the face I see is Norman Mailer's. Not far away, under one of the spangled HAPPY NEW YEAR banners, a pair of women snicker decorously as the hobgoblin spills pastry crumbs down his front. The first woman is dressed as a pig (written on her back is "Yes I am a PIG: a Pretty Intelligent Girl") and the other as Rosie the Riveter.

The room is vivid with chandeliers and alive with celebrity. The air is sweet and thick with the exhalations of hundreds of voluptuous flowers and the music feels like it is being played just for you. But the bioacoustics are all wrong. The room is full of discarnate humanoid noises I care nothing about. I only care about the sounds produced by one person.

And I can't find her.

When I got dressed in my Frog King outfit my skin was so dry that when I bent over to attach my prosthetic frog-flipper galoshes over my shoes the skin on my back cracked open. But now I am so nervous, my skin so slicked with sweat, that my prosthetic hand-flippers keep falling off my hands. I do not even know what I am going to say to Evie when I see her. I want to show her how much I have changed. (If only I had that letter of recommendation from my spatula, I think.) I want to say that I have learned from my mistakes. But even after all this time and all the pages I have written I still don't know how to say it.

I thought at first I would say it with a hat. Yesterday I went back to Bendel's to buy Evie the flappery hat she has coveted for so long. Though Rhonda did not recognize me she graciously showed me where they had put their remaining off-season merchandise. The hat was nowhere to be found. When I described the hat and the matching dress she said, "Oh yes. I remember that outfit. It was lovely. I am sorry to say that I sold it to a gentleman just a few days ago. I *am* sorry. But we do have some other lovely hats over here."

I managed to say "Thank you" before limping out of the store.

I have been saving up for this hat for over six months and when I finally get enough money for the purchase, it is gone. Someone else got it first. There's a metaphor in here somewhere if I were brave enough to look for it.

So instead of saying it with a hat I decided to say it with fiction. I had not planned on showing the fraction of a manuscript to anyone, let alone Evie. But in some way it seems like the right thing to do. Probably she will hate the first couple of chapters I have printed out for her—they are not as good as they could be; they are not as good as Evie herself—but what choice do I have?

She can love me or not, but I need to show her. I owe that to the new Harry.

A caterer passes by carrying a tray glittering with gold effervescent liquid in slender glasses. "Champagne, sir?" he says.

"No thanks," I say, clutching my manuscript fiercely in my flipper like a cheap apotropaic talisman, a crucifix made of tongue depressors.

"White wine?"

"Um . . . no thanks."

"Cocktail?"

"No!" I almost shriek. "Sorry. Alcohol is lethal to frogs, ha ha. Only algae and fly juice pass these lips."

"Of course, sir," he says, supremely unamused.

"Actually, I wouldn't say no to some water if you have any," I say.

"Sparkling or still, sir?"

I cannot remember ever ordering water before.

"Which one tastes more like vodka?" When I get no response I say, "Still is fine. Thank you."

When he returns with the water I take my mask off to drink. Someone dressed in what looks like a giant T square approaches me.

"Harry?" the T square says. "Harry Driscoll?"

"Ribbit ribbit," I say. "Who wants to know?"

"Jordie Wesselesh."

"Jordie?" I say, feeling a surge of relief. He is probably the only person besides Evie I would like to see here. "What are you supposed to be? The letter L?"

"I'm a bookend."

He is wearing black face paint to match the costume, but even under all that paint I can see his face twitch for a second in embarrassment. "My wife thought of it. She's around here somewhere. She, ah, she's the other bookend."

There was a time when I might have chortled at it but now it seems so sweet, so intolerably lovely, that I want to tell him what a beautiful expression of love and togetherness it is. O to be a bookend with the woman you love!

"That's good," I say.

"What about you?" he says. "You look a little . . . amphibian."

"Salient?"

"Batrachian, even."

"Ranidian, in fact." I let Jordie think for a few gratifying seconds before I say, "You're not going to get me on this one, Jordie. I know all there is to know about frogs."

"I give up."

"Ranid—Ranidae—is a family of frog. They have dilated transverse sacral processes. Good jumpers."

"Of course," he says. "*Rana* is frog. Interesting."

"Ranalamadingdong."

It is the first time I have ever legitimately beaten Jordie at logomachy, the first time I did not have to resort to Don Kinging. I suppress the urge to moonwalk triumphantly.

"Just like old times," he says. "You know, it wasn't the same around Prestige when you left."

"Really?" I say. I would hug him if the leg of his L weren't in the way.

"No."

"Well . . . thanks."

"No nepenthe for you tonight?" he asks, seeing my water.

"I'm Method-masquerading, and frogs can't drink."

"Ah."

"Yeah. So . . ."

Again I become awkward with Jordie. For a few moments neither of us say anything. The awkwardness stretches between us in a thin, tympanic silence.

QUESTION: How do adult men become friends without aid of dirty jokes or alcohol or racing to brush their teeth or seeing who knows more cool words?

ANSWER: By standing around without making eye contact, apparently.

"So . . . what are you doing these days, Jordie? Still at Prestige?"

"No. I moved on myself. It was time for a change."

"Oh. What are you doing now?"

Please don't say Internet shit. Please don't say Internet shit. Please don't say Internet shit.

"Remember that Internet opportunity I told you about? Well, I took the plunge. Word.com. We are doing some very cool things. We've been getting a lot of hits. William F. Buckley contributed to our debut issue. Ice-T is doing something for us now and we've got Nikki Giovanni and Edward Albee and this cuneiform guy lined up. It's been a gas. And you? Now that you've done the sensible thing and left publishing behind?"

"Me? I . . . um . . . I work in a specialized subfield of the telecom industry. Very high-tech, sort of hard to explain. Fiber optics. Irradiation. String theory. Variables, all sorts of variables, variables up the kazoo, really. That kind of thing."

"Ah," he says.

"It's pretty complicated stuff."

"Right," he says. "Sounds like it."

"So . . ."

"So . . ."

"Hey, Jordie. Have you seen Evie around? I haven't seen her yet."

"I think I saw her upstairs. Have you been upstairs? Half the party is up there."

"Um . . . is she . . . *accompanied* tonight?"

"What do you mean?"

"Did she have some kind of an . . . escort?"

"Oh. You mean an . . . authorly escort? An escort who commits acts of cliché upon innocent bystanders? That kind of escort?"

For a second I almost come to Drakkar's defense—clichés aren't clichés when they happen to you, Jordie—before I catch myself.

"Exactly."

"I don't think so, Harry. She came with a crowd, but I didn't see Drakkar anywhere."

"Thanks, Jordie."

"Sure," he says. "Oh! I almost forgot." Jordie produces a dollar from somewhere inside his costume and scribbles something on it. Then he cuts a curt and gentlemanly bow, handing it over. "Ranidian," he says. " 'Of or relating to a family of frog distinguished by dilated transverse sacral processes.' You got me."

"Thanks," I say, feeling myself expand with pride.

"Sure," he says. "And Harry?"

"Yeah?"

"It's good to see you."

"Same here, Jordie."

As he teeters away through the crowd—toward a matching bookend, I see—I get this warm feeling in my stomach: Jordie is my friend. We might not know how to deal with each other, but I am pretty sure that what just passed between us was a transaction of friendship. If it's true, then I now have two friends, Keeno and Jordie. My friendship quotient has just doubled. I need to remember to write this down in my GOOD THOUGHTS notebook.

Something lurches violently inside me, like a bridge breaking a cable: there she is.

Evie is standing in a crowd of people I don't recognize—they all look confident and outgoing; they are either drunk or agents—with her back to me. Even at this distance, from way across the ballroom, I can see all the little muscles in her back, the convexities of her spine. Her dress scintillates. All the pristine white light of the chandeliers sucks down out of the air and sprays off her shoulders like the bright halogenated breath of angels.

No sign of Drakkar.

As I approach she breaks away from the crowd and heads for the bar. I ease into position behind her in line. I am standing so close I can feel the heat signature of her body. For a moment it is as if I am cannonballing her again in my bed. Then I realize something. She is wearing the hat from Bendel's. Not only that, she is wearing the dress. And the shoes. The whole outfit. Rhonda said that some man bought it. That must mean: Drakkar. Something hot and gastric pinches in my chest but I will it away. Now is not the time for jealousy.

Now is the time to act like an adult.

"Tanq and tonic," Evie says to the bartender.

"Sorry, miss. Out of Tanq."

"Oh *merde*."

"Would you care for Boodles?"

"Oh yes. Great. C'est bon."

"Hey," I say to her back. "Watch the language. There are English speakers present."

Evie's head tilts to the side. The muscles in her back twitch. Her shoulders contract. Then, without turning around, I hear her say, "Oh my God."

"Hi there," I say when she turns around.

"Hi yourself."

I have probably written five dozen reunion scenes in various drafts of the novel. I have put Evie on the top of the Empire State Building, under the Christmas tree at Rockefeller Center, on the sidewalk in front of the Blue & Gold, by Wollman Rink in Central Park, and at this very masquerade party too. I have probably written a hundred pages of we-meet-again-at-long-last dialogue, but suddenly I cannot think of a single thing to say. What I finally manage is:

"So . . . kind of cold lately, don't you think? But it's a *dry* cold."

"I guess so. Cold, sure. And dry," she says.

"Right."

"So."

"So."

If the awkwardness was bad with Jordie it is excruciating now. Every position I assume feels false, arranged by others. My joints are all at uncommon angles and my body is overly formalized, like figures from the wall of an Egyptian temple. Sweat oozes out of my pores and one of my prosthetic flippers slides off and falls to the marble floor. I feel a bone-deep urge to have a drink but I resist it.

"I like your crown," she says. "Where did you get it?"

"Burger King. I like your dress too. And the hat. Maybe you won't believe it but I just went to Bendel's the other day. I was going to get it for you. It was already gone. Obviously."

"Obviously."

"You look beautiful in it, though."

"Thanks. You look very . . . handsome . . . as a frog."

"Thanks."

"So . . . how have you been?"

"Good. Fine. I haven't had a drink in seventeen days."

"That's great."

"It's my New Year's resolution but I figured I would get a jump on it."

"Good for you."

"Even tonight—nothing. Check this out. Water."

"That's great."

"Go on. Smell it. See?" I put the drink up for her to smell but she recoils a little, not letting me into her capsule of space.

"That's really not necessary. I think I'll just believe it from afar, if that's O.K."

"No joke, Eves. Seventeen days. And counting. It's all liquor under the bridge."

"I *said* congratulations. What do you want me to do? Interpretive dance?" she says. Then, "Sorry. I'm sorry, Harry. I just didn't expect you to crash the party tonight. It's kind of a shock."

I don't know what I wanted her to do. Leap up into my arms and declare all forgiven because I've managed to go two weeks without poisoning my liver?

"It's O.K. I understand. Can we rewind? Take it from the top? All right? Let's start over. Hello, Evie. Nice evening."

"Hi," she says cleanly.

There is a dead space between us. Evie is not participating. She has a look I have never seen before: inertia. Boredom. The overeducated auctioneer on speed I know so well is nowhere to be seen. She is treating me the way she would treat any other common biped.

"Thanks. Um, I never said congratulations really for the Drakkar book. So: congratulations. It isn't as wrong about everything as I thought it was. In fact it is a little bit right here and there."

"Thanks. It's been selling pretty well."

"Number three on the list is better than pretty well."

"We're pleased."

"So . . . did Drakkar buy you that outfit?"

"Harry . . ."

"Just asking. No reproaches. Just idle curiosity."

"No. He didn't."

"Really?"

"No. J.J. and I aren't seeing each other anymore."

My heart leaps. It trampolines.

"Really? I'm sorry. I know he was, er, good to you."

"He was great. In many, many important ways. But the spark wasn't there. You know?"

QUESTION: DO I KNOW?

ANSWER: HOLY SHIT, EVES, DO I KNOW!!

"Not like us, then?" I say, and then laugh quickly, as if I were half-joking.

"Not at all like us, Harry."

These are the words I have been waiting—how long? it seems like my whole life—to hear from Evie. Yes, there is only Evie and me in the Treehouse. No, there are no common bipeds allowed. Yes, she loves only me. Me me me. There is a rush of blood in my brain and the room dilates around me. Then a surge of people making for the balcony—it's almost midnight; the ball is about to drop—push us together. For a moment my nose is in Evie's hair again. It makes my heart break. Evie smells of juniper berries and clean skin and fresh sweat and metal and flowers.

I detect my own emanations too. They are fear and public transportation.

"Oh Eves," I whisper into her ear. "Viva la Evie. Viva la viva la viva."

As people start preparing for the big countdown the room suddenly comes alive with hundreds of floating, oily bubbles—a party favor: bubble-blow—each one a glistening sphere of possibility, a shiny little globe of hope. The innocent, soapy scent of the bubbles mixes with the smoke of imported cigarettes and the fumes of innumerable cocktails and the air becomes charged and endorphinated—full of promise—but as I am again pushed into Evie and take her cheek in my hand and turn my face into hers, my mouth finding her mouth, it is all ruined. Her face jerks and turns away from mine—the same motion you use to shake water out of your hair—and I see the change in her.

There is suddenly something hard and treated—anodized—in her expression. Her scars are not glowing. The little ballet in her eyes is dead. In its place is something unmoving and remote—stratospheric. She is somewhere else, someplace where the air is cold and the oxygen thin and I am somewhere way below, terrestrial, a blur of color and motion, if anything at all.

"Harry, I . . ."

"I don't understand, Evie. I thought Drakkar was—"

"He is," she says. "But . . ."

"But what?"

"I loved you, Harry. Real love, and not in some disgusting Hallmark way that you're always so afraid of. It was wonderful, Harry. It was something else." I would give her everything I own right now if she would just call me Hairball. "But you know what? It was also awful. You did some really atrocious things to me on a fairly regular basis, and—I don't know, maybe I'm old-fashioned—but I just . . . it's just . . ."

"What?"

"It just hit the saturation point, Harry. That's all there is to it. No postmortem is going to turn up anything new. It's just finished."

I want to tell her that I know, that she's right that I was atrocious in all the ways she isn't enumerating. But I also want to tell her that things are different with me now, that I have changed 180 degrees. No longer is every meal comprised of stolen condiments and liquor; now I cook, Eves. (I can make sesame salmon, vegetable soup, chilaquile casserole, and some mean Rice Krispie Treats.) Employee number 13667—that's me; I finally have a number at WD—consistently has the fastest pickup time and the lowest number of hang-ups and misconnections. (The new me is able to take even a silly job seriously.) I bought a copy of the *Marathoner's Calendar and Logbook* and now run three times a week. (Do you not notice an alluring reduction in pudge?) The rashes are not gone but they are substantially reduced. (A result of better hygiene habits and an attitude of self-care. In other words: responsibility, Eves.) Hell, six days ago I had Christmas with my brother. (It was the first time we had seen each other in eight years. We went through the same Burger King drive-thru backward and played Frisbee golf in the snow. Each one of us kept trying to let the other one win and kept missing our shots on purpose. It took us two hours to finish one single match because we would stand ten feet in front of a tree and throw our Frisbees wide over and over. That's big of me, right? That indicates an ability to think about other people, does it not?)

And I am so aware of my mistakes now, Eves, that I am writing an entire book about them.

One hundred eighty degrees, Evie. I mean volte-face.

All these things I want to say, but I can't produce any words. My larynx just bobs uselessly in my throat.

"I'm sorry, Harry. I *will* always love you"—when she says this there is something wrong with her voice; it has the overly pneumatic tone of someone making a lunch date she has no intention of keeping—"but just because I am not with Drakkar doesn't mean that we are going to get back together."

Evie smiles at me in a way that is supposed to be wistful but

I can tell it is simulated and wan—juiceless. She is trying to make me feel better, being magnanimous. Even worse: she is being polite. Her whole being is too animated, too deliberate. She is like an actor struggling with a foreign accent. I want to grab her by the shoulders, shake her, and say, "It's me! Hairball! The man who cannonballs you! The man you said you would love for the rest of your life! You wanted to have children with me!"

Suddenly I realize something unpleasant: she is being this way not to be punitive, but because she is genuinely untroubled by seeing me. She has—as Madeleine would affirm—really and truly moved on. I am officially out of the Treehouse. How did she do it so fast? I used to be able to do this before Evie. I was world-famous for making seamless, adiabatic transitions from Date X to Date Y. There would be a postdehiscence break of nary a day before I was dialing up the next Date and making chitchat with her on the phone while watching Discovery Channel on mute, but that was because I didn't care. I moved on because it just didn't matter. But Evie, I now understand, has moved on so quickly because whereas almost all of my memories of her are sweet, almost all of her memories of me must be awful.

It's O.K. for her because she hates me for all the right reasons.

In my mind I can see Keeno's Magic 8 Ball explanation for why Evie would prefer another man over me: He Doesn't Treat Her Like Dirt, Dumbass.

The manuscript weighs heavily in my prosthetic flipper. I had forgotten it. Maybe if I can show her what I have done, that I am composing my own love letter to her—even if it's awful— she will see how much I have changed. It is my last chance to convince her. It is my last possible proof.

Wordlessly I hold up the box in front of her, which gives me a dreadful, door-to-door-salesman feeling of foisting something on innocent people who don't want it in the first place.

"Eves," I say, crepitant and meek. The syllables dribble out of my mouth and fall lemminglike directly on the floor at my feet. "I want to show you something important. It's the first few chapters of a manuscript. My manusript. It's a new novel, a real one this time—" But as I say this the crowd begins to chant "Ten, nine, eight, seven" and starts mothing around the windows.

"Oh God," she says, looking down at her hands. I now see she is holding two drinks—no hands free. She shrugs. "Crap crap crap. Sorry, Harry. Messenger it if you want," she says, looking around the room with the focused urgency of a pilot searching for a place to make an emergency landing. Finally her gaze locks onto a handsome man in a Roman Legionnaire outfit by the windows who waves frantically to her from atop a pair of chairs. "I've got to run. It was good to see you. Good luck with"—she gestures with her chin toward the manuscript—"everything."

Without making eye contact she gives me a crabbed, socialite hug with the fruit of her wrists and the side of her cheek. Then she's off. She leaps onto the chair the handsome Legionnaire was saving and he gathers her into his arms. They kiss as the crowd roars "zero" and bubbles explode all over the room and dance in the air around Evie, making her look insubstantial, vaporescent, like a wraith, like maybe she was never there at all.

resolution

QUESTION: What good is making yourself worth someone if the only person you were changing for is out of your life forever?

ANSWER: No good at all.

Everything I have done in the last few months—especially that risible GOOD THOUGHTS notebook; I can't believe I stooped to Drakkarism—is humiliating to me now. Without Evie there is nothing good about being good.

QUESTION: If a heart breaks in a forest with no one around to hear it, does it really count?

ANSWER: No it does not.

So here is my revised New Year's resolution: fuck it. I am going to get some nepenthe and drink without remit.

These are the things I think about when I go back to the scene of the crime, Seventh and A, where the cab hit me so long ago. The outline of my body still has a bottle in its hand and now, tonight, for the first time in over two weeks, so do I. Sitting on the curb, I clutch my manuscript in one hand and a bottle of Gem Clear 190 in the other.

(REGISTER GUY: Hey, don't you want a mixer?

ME: What do you mean?

REGISTER GUY: You can't drink grain alcohol without a mixer. It can kill you.

ME: I have one.

REGISTER GUY: You do, huh? What do you have?

ME: Saliva.)

It hurts the first time I bring it to my lips but after that I am numbed and can't feel anything—the ideal nepenthe.

I sit there on the curb with my hands full until the revelers call it quits and Avenue A is again flattened by quiet. The only sounds are the wind and the cars and the wrong church bells ringing out in the cold night air. A brittle, wafery moon idles unimpressed over the tops of the buildings and some homeless guys are leaning up against the wall, eyeballing my bottle. Every time someone walks by they outstretch their hands in the savage cold, moving slowly but with exquisite attention—like carnivorous flowers—toward what they want.

Sadness shoots through the street like punishing angels.

Then something happens. Two pigeons—one with mutilated feet and one with a huge Benjamin Franklin goiter—flap noisily down to the pavement and land in the middle of the outline of my body. They bob and coo stupidly at each other and rub their heads together. One of them beats a greasy iridescent wing at the other. At first it looks like antagonism, but it is not. It is a gesture of affection. It is protective and loving. The other bird accepts it with a happy spasm of the neck. If they weren't so ruined it would be sweet.

Suddenly this gives me an idea.

Tossing my bottle to the homeless guys, I pull myself up from the curb and start running west. I tear through the streets and vault over the sidewalk wreckage of New Year's revelers, skidding around corners on a thin skin of new snow. The cold air makes hot tears stream down my face and freeze into my neck. All the diners and bars and liquor stores turn into a blur of cheap light as I sprint past, finally sliding to a stop at my destination:

Astor Place.

All the boxes are quiet and closed up. They look like a city of ravaged presents. Breathing plumes of white steam, I ease up to Birdie's box and tap on the cardboard. "Hey," I whisper. "Birdie, it's Harry. Hey, you in?" I wait a moment, then try again. "Birdie. It's me. Mr. Please, asking you please to wake up. Please please please. Pretty please with Omar Sharif on top." Again I knock on the cardboard and get nothing. Pushing open the flap, I peer inside. There are old magazines scattered around and a small hammock for clothes made out of plastic six-pack rings tied together and the pillow stuffed with human hair. But there is no Birdie.

"Not in," a nearby voice says. The owner of the voice is a pouchy woman with sad, exhausted eyes and newspaper fanning out of the neck of her sweater. "Visiting friends in the penthouse apartment."

"What?" I say.

"Unit 69," she says, leering at me and gesturing with her thumb. "Jammers' condo."

No, I think. Not tonight. Not now. Not if I can help it. No no no.

I sprint down the sidewalk under the scaffolding, banging on all the boxes and calling out for Birdie. At the very end of the line I see it: a refrigerator box twitching with the sounds of grunting and tussling. Wrapped over the closed flaps of the box is a tie-dyed sheet and a motel's DO NOT DISTURB sign hanging on it. The whole arrangement is held in place by two weights atop the box: a pair of bright red elf boots. The bitter taste of acid and bile washes up into my mouth. I feel like I might pass out. I am scared and furious and don't know how to behave. Never in my whole life have I perpetrated any real violence on anyone. I don't know how to do it.

But now is certainly the right time to find out. I tear the box open. A powerful burst of hot air thick with the smell of human secretions and burnt hair hits me, making me blink. Then I see them: both naked, entwined, legs wrapped around each other's hips, hands on each other's skin, eyes shining with shock and anger.

It is Jammers and one of the Lithuanian kids who mugged me.

"Sorry," I manage. "Wrong . . . place. Sorry. My mistake."

I drape the sheet back over the opening and stagger away down the sidewalk. My Band-Aids have peeled off and a burst of wind tears through my frog costume like razor blades. All my muscles, I realize, have been shivering for hours and are now undergoing some kind of failure. It feels like I barely have the strength to stand up. I collapse onto the scaffolding, clinging to a crossbar and resting my head in a joint, exhausted by defeat and heartbreak. The metal on my skin feels good—cold, hard, unmysterious, unrequiting.

Finally I am bereft of everything.

A memory of Birdie comes to me. It was when I first started doing the volunteer story hour routine at Beth Israel. She was trying to convince Night Staff to let her stay with Max. She wanted to sleep in his bed with him. Or at least in a chair. Anywhere, really. She just didn't want to go back to the shelter with her mother. She hated going anywhere with her mother.

"I'm sorry," Night Staff said. "Only people who are sick or hurt can stay overnight in the hospital."

"But I am sick," Birdie begged. "I do hurt."

What did I think I could do for her anyway? I can't bring back her brother. Or her father. Or make her mother less crazy or get her off the street or save her from Jammers the next time he feels like some action. I can't take away her sickness or her hurt. It was a stupid idea coming here. Put it down to holiday-inspired delusions of altruism.

Still, when I squeeze shut my eyes against the wind hot tears leak down my throat.

"Move over, bacon," a fluty little voice suddenly says to me. "You can't hog the whole scaffolding, you know."

It is Birdie, glorious Birdie. She is wrapped in an overstuffed white padded coat that is so big it comes down to her knees. Her hands are invisible inside the sleeves that dangle alongside. On her head is what appears to be several layers of panty hose, with the legs thrown debonairly over her shoulder in the manner of a WWI flying ace. She is wearing a beaten-up pair of brown military-looking boots.

"Birdie!" I exclaim, almost scooping her up in my arms before I catch myself. "It's you!"

"Sure enough."

"Where have you been? I went looking for you. I went to your box. I thought you were with Jammers and then I . . . You haven't been with Jammers, have you?"

"Nah. I told Jammers he can stick it up the old Nebuchadnezzar."

"Thank God," I say, wiping at my eyes.

"Where you been all this time?" Birdie says. She tries to cross her arms but can't quite do it because of the trailing sleeves so she ends up putting her hands on her hips. She is trying to look disapproving, but it just turns out ridiculous. "Haven't seen you in ages."

"I've been busy. Working on some things."

"What things?"

"Just things."

"Get them done?"

"I think so," I say over the pounding of my heart.

"You don't know if you got them done? Damn you are one squidy individual."

"I know. One hundred ten percent pure squid. You read anything good lately?"

"Nothing better than this," she says, pushing back a sleeve so she can dip her hand into her pocket, then producing some wads of paper that say ROOMMATE WANTED and FOR SALE.

"You want to read a menu, maybe?" I ask her.

"What?"

"You know, a menu? A listing of foodstuffs offered at an eatery?" When she continues to look at me funny I say, "Do you want to go get something to eat? The first food of the New Year?"

"Slapshot!"

Inside Odessa Birdie takes off her coat. She is wearing about five layers of clothing but on top of all of them is the same HELLO KITTY T-shirt. When she takes the panty hose off her head a chain of dilapidated braids falls down around her shoulders. Then she sniffs herself, wrinkles her nose, and reaches into a pocket for a handful of perfume sample strips and rubs them on her face and under her arms.

"Had that not-so-fresh feeling," she explains.

We select a banquette by the window. When I sit down she stares at me crossly.

"What are you doing?" she says.

"Just sitting."

"I have to sit facing out. I can't sit with my back to the door. It makes me crazy," she says.

"That's funny. Me too."

"Well," she says.

"Well," I say.

"I guess we're going to have to share."

"Share?"

"Don't worry. I won't touch you."

"No, no. It's fine. Go ahead. Sit right down."

"Do you like my new boots?" she says. "I outgrew the red ones."

"I saw that. Very nice."

"Yep," she says happily.

Birdie orders hot chocolate and potato pancakes with sour cream and applesauce galore, and I have coffee and a broiled steak. While we sit there eating I am overwhelmed by the smells and sounds of the kitchen—the grease, the heat, the spices, the bleach, the starch of the waitresses' uniforms, the sound of cooking and people talking to each other in excited voices. It feels like home. But not any home I have ever had. It feels like a home that I haven't had yet, but maybe could have.

When she's done eating Birdie asks me to rebraid her hair,

which I do. With her hair pulled tight into these two braids I can see the pristine skin of her scalp. It is white and porous and fleshy, like the spongy inner lining of an orange. "You're so rocco at that," she says, even though I know she is lying. I know I am not good. But I am willing to try.

After I finish one braid she turns around to thank me but stops mid-sentence, squinting at me. Then she hands me a napkin. "Here," she says.

"What's this for?" I say.

"You're crying."

"It's very cold out," I say, taking the napkin.

"Right. Right. Cold."

"I'd better make good on this bill," I say to change the subject. When I dig in my wallet Birdie sees my old Prestige ID in its plastic window and makes a grab for it. A brief tug-of-war ensues, ending when the wallet rips in two, the contents spilling onto the table.

"Whoops," she says. "Call me egg-breaker. Sorry."

"It's O.K. It was hurting anyway. You just put it out of its misery."

"What's this?" she says, picking up the brochure of Bancroft-Ash.

"Just this school in Connecticut."

"Connecticut?"

"That's where I grew up."

"With your brother?"

"Yes, with my brother."

"What's he like?"

I tell her. I tell her about how we used to be best friends and about the crazy times we would have, the drive-thru, the Frisbee golf, the Food Language. As I explain to her all about Food Language—she is fascinated by this—she jots down notes on a napkin.

"Your brother sounds fun."

"Yeah," I say. "My brother is fun."

"I'd like to meet him someday." Then, piecing it together from her notes, she says, "I mean, 'Pizza fresh green pepper to meet your steak someday.' Right?"

" 'Father' is steak," I correct. " 'Brother' is fried steak."

"Damn."

Then I notice one of the dollars on the table. It's Jordie's dollar. But instead of "ranidian" and the definition on it I see he has instead written

INTUSSUSCEPTION: the drawing in of something from without, the assimilation of new material. We could use a neologist like you at Word.com. What do you say?

—JW

Outside the yellowed window of Odessa the new wet snow is melting and making everything glisten like reptilian eggs, as if whole new streets and buildings were being born—a new city, drawing breath around me—and something small and new and beleaguered opens up in my heart.

I don't know what I am thinking exactly. It all comes in a rush. Maybe I will take Jordie up on the job. Maybe I will leave the city entirely and go someplace quiet where I can finish the novel—not for Evie but for myself. Maybe I will take Birdie to visit my brother and mother in Connecticut. Maybe I will call up Vernon Crosswhite and tell him that I want him to enroll Birdie in Bancroft-Ash as a boarding student. Hell, maybe I won't even have to invoke my father's favor—if I take Jordie up on the job, I might be able to pay the tuition myself. Birdie could tell the Bancroft-Ash kids a lot more about the hard life in the city than I could, that's for sure.

I'm not sure exactly what I will do. But there is one thing I am sure of: I will not make the same mistakes. I will not be selfish and deceitful and corrupt. I will not be lazy. I will not drink like a madman all the time. I will not be furtive, shady, and unlawful.

I will be brave and full of love.

"Hey," I say to Birdie. "I've got an idea. How about I read you something? I just happen to have a little something with me right here. I can't vouch for how good it is—probably you'll hate it—but I thought maybe it would be fun."

Birdie stares at me, mute and unmoving. It is the longest I have ever known her to be silent.

"If you want me to, that is. I don't have to. We can just have some more hot chocolate."

"No!" she cries. "I mean yes. 'Do you want me to read to you?' Did you really just ask me that question? Do I want you to read to me? Does a ping pong? Does a jack hammer? Holy shit do I want you to read to me!"

"Easy on the language," I say.

"Sorry. Go on go on go on."

"I'm not sure you'll like it. It's got some unsavory characters and well, come to think of it, some of it is sort of adult, you know, and—"

"GO ON!"

"O.K. O.K. O.K. already. You don't have to go all ballistic squirrel about it."

"Read already!"

I crack open the manuscript box. I have never really told Birdie about Evie. In fact, I have never even told my parents or Kurt about Evie. Almost no one knows about us. About her.

Never disappear, I think.

"Come on!"

I have a moment when I realize that Birdie is a lot like me. She has this life she hates and she wants to get out of it. So do I. Maybe we can help each other. Birdie burrows into me, putting her head on my shoulder. She smells of garbage and melting snow and old nylon and a suffocating chaos of cheap perfume samples. Her eyes are alive with something vivid and luciferine and full of hope. She tries to hold my hand and I let her. Her hand in mine is so small and warm it doesn't even feel like a hand. It feels like an agglutinated wad of marshmallows.

I think to myself: I can do this. I can do anything.

"Well begin already before I get all Cotton Mather on your ass!"

And I begin.

ACKNOWLEDGMENTS

First thanks must go to my family. My mother, father, and brother, Chris, have stuck up for me—and put up with me—all these years.

My other family, Liz Smith and Cynthia McFadden and Spencer McFadden Hoge, have kept me on the good foot.

The people at Syracuse University's M.F.A. program who have helped me immeasurably are Mary Caponegro, George Saunders, Junot Díaz, Arthur Flowers, Jason Ockert, Adam Desnoyers, Matthew Schellenberg, Jeff Parker, Maile Chapman, Jon Fink, Chris Kennedy, and Terri Zollo, bless her. And where would I be without the redoubtable Geri Clark? Nowheresville.

Marci S. Breedlove is an inspiration.

I thank my lucky stars for The Glorious Kinklosity, Abigail V.L.C. Leafe, E. Beth Thomas, and R. Todd Giardinelli.

Roberta Skripol, Bill Klein, Ron Sharp, Deborah Laycock, Royal Rhodes, Daniel Menaker, and Sensei Dan Webster all taught me things I needed to know. Meg Cramer and Jan Tibbett generously talked to me at length about endometriosis, for which I am deeply grateful. Stewart O'Nan, Patrick McCord, Jesse Sheidlower, Bill Kretzschmar, Josh Campbell, Tad Reynes, Matthew Meyer, Erik Michaels, Matthew Bennett, Julie Checkoway, Michael Hendrick, Rebecca Rego, Vivian Alexander, Bob Moss, Caryl Yanow, Harry Evans, Monica Fitzgerald, my students and

colleagues at Syracuse and the University of Georgia—you all
know what you've done.

At Riverhead there are many superstars, the brightest of whom
are Liz Perl, Craig Burke, and Rick Pascocello. Thanks also to
Lindsay Sagnette—poet, pugilist, page-cutter—for her expert
contributions and constant, infallible care.

Julie Grau, my editor, worked miraculous, Ovidian changes
on this book. Thank you, Julie.

And viva la Esther Newberg, my agent. She gave me the most
important phone call of my life. I wish I could pay her back better
than this.

Adam Davies went to Kenyon College and received his M.F.A. from Syracuse University. He has worked as an assistant at Random House, a teacher of English literature and creative writing at the University of Georgia, and is currently at work on his second novel. He lives in San Francisco.